FOREVER THEN

RACHAE STEVENS

Copy editing and proofreading by Gabby D'Aloia - GCD Editorial

Cover design by Melissa Doughty - Mel D. Designs

Blurb by Jessie Cunniffe - Book Blurb Magic

Self-published by Rachae Stevens

Author's Note

Dear Reader,

Forever Then is an emotional romance with a guaranteed happily ever after. However, it deals with some subjects that may be a sensitive spot for some of you.

In addition, while this is an open-door romance, I've made every attempt to make all on-page spicy content tasteful and rooted in deep emotional connection and intimacy with minimal use of foul language. However, I understand some of you may prefer a more fade-to-black reading experience.

That said, I've provided a page with a list of content warnings as well as a spice reading guide. I'm aware some readers consider such warnings and outlines to be spoilers. As such, I've placed this page at the back of the book if you wish to seek it out before you begin reading.

Thank you for giving Gretchen and Connor's story a try. I hope you love them as much as I do!

Playlist

"Don't You (Forget About Me)"—James Morrison version

"Lost My Mind"—Finneas

"All These Years"—Camilla Cabello

"Sugar Sweet"—Larkins

"About You"—The 1975

"Exile"—Taylor Swift (feat. Bon Iver)

"Somewhere Only We Know"—Keane

"I Wanna Be Yours"—Arctic Monkeys

"Nights Like These"—Benson Boone

"Sexual Vibe"—Stephen Puth

"Nobody Gets Me"—SZA

"Cardigan"—Taylor Swift

"I Like Me Better"—Lauv

"The View Between Villages"—Noah Kahan

"Stargazing"—Myles Smith

"Favorite T-Shirt"—Jake Scott

For my big brother.
You're the bravest person I know.
Also, please don't read this.

Prologue

YOU HAVE A MATCH

GRETCHEN

six months ago

DNA IS A FASCINATING THING. A little spit run through some fancy machines overseen by a team of scientists and, *voila*, a comprehensive ancestry report, complete with a list of any genetic matches in their system, lands in your inbox.

Spit, seal, send, and all my burning questions would be answered in one little email.

Last summer, I returned to my hometown in Illinois before starting my senior year of college. I worked my usual summer job at the coffee shop to save for the upcoming semester. My scholarship paid for tuition and some of my housing expenses while my parents managed to cover the remainder, which, as they have pointed out to me ad nauseam over the years, is the equivalent of the tuition costs for nearly four full years at a state school where I had earned a full-ride scholarship.

Yes, the cost of living in Manhattan is astronomical, but I was content to work my way through school, earning the money necessary to fill the gaps. And I have…and then some. Hell, I had to budget months in advance to even afford that DNA kit because every penny counts in my life.

I had my reasons for picking New York.

Studying fashion design and merchandising was my dream and what better place to do that than Manhattan. But it wasn't only about the degree. The melting pot drew me in, too. A city where more people looked like me.

I love my family and small hometown, but my olive skin and black-as-night hair alongside my fair-skinned, light-haired family has always left me feeling like a fish out of water. My mom does have a fraction of Native American blood in her heritage, but it's been watered down by generations of cross-cultural and cross-country marriages. Next to me, she doesn't look native at all.

The older I've gotten, the more I've yearned to know where I came from.

It took me twenty-one years to muster the courage to take this one small step. Despite the unconditional love of my well-intentioned parents and brother, I knew this was something I had to do on my own.

So, on a sizzling summer day last June, when I walked out of the coffee shop after my shift and heard that *ping* in my pocket, my heart lurched.

As I settled in the driver's seat of my dad's old Honda Civic, I opened the email on my phone. There it was, plain as day: *Your results are in!*

I quickly navigated from the email via the link and read through all the information with bated breath.

My ancestry results were not necessarily news to me; my parents had told me as much. I'm predominantly of Hispanic/Latino, specifically Mexican, and Indigenous Peoples, specifically Native American, heritage. What I was most interested in were my DNA matches. Those would be my ticket.

After endless scrolling, I finally found what I was looking for. I clicked the link, lungs seizing as the results appeared on my tiny screen.

No matches.

I wept—ugly tears there in the parking lot. I had put all my hope in that vial of saliva.

Instinct had me reaching for my phone to dial a familiar number, but reality crashed in—I hadn't told anyone. Not even *him*.

There's only ever been one person in my life I imagined sharing this with, but it'd been two years since we'd last spoken. After everything that had happened, Connor Vining still came to the forefront of my mind. Because, come hell or high water apparently, he's always the first person I think of when I need a *real* friend, and real friends have never come easy for me.

I pasted a smile on my face for the rest of the summer, checking my account every day hoping that my DNA match page would reveal something helpful.

All I needed was a starting point, but it never came.

When my senior year of college officially began, I re-prioritized. Between my studies, working part-time, and the fast pace of New York life, I barely had time to think about it. My daily check-ins on my genetic report became less frequent until it was out of my mind completely.

Almost.

Resigning myself to Plan B—whatever that was—I decided to wait until after graduation to pursue anything further.

It's now finals week in my next to last semester of college. The last few weeks have been chocked full of late-night study groups, coffee and waning willpower.

I find my seat in the lecture hall, settling in for my last exam of the semester. My phone pings with an incoming email. I pull it from my bag, silence it and then tap to my inbox to delete what is sure to be another promotional email from Crate and Barrel. You buy one throw blanket two years ago and suddenly you're in a digital marketing relationship with a stage five spammer.

The screen transitions and I suck in a breath at the subject line: *You have a DNA match!*

My chest constricts, stomach twirling. Before I can open it, my professor begins to distribute the test packets. I quickly stash my phone away, willing my thoughts into focus for the next hour.

It's the longest hour of my life.

As soon as I hand in my completed exam, I bolt out the door. Juggling my bag in one hand, I clumsily maneuver myself into my winter coat, one arm and then the other. To anyone passing by, I probably look like a frenzied mess, bag flinging, arms pushing and pulling, while I maniacally traverse three flights of stairs.

When I'm finally outside, I stop to retrieve my phone. My thumb hovers over the email icon, like tapping it might activate the next nuclear bomb.

It's been six months since my initial, lackluster results came in. I'm twenty-one years old and I've never met another person with my DNA. This mysterious match is my family. To what degree, I don't know. But it's a start.

A beautiful start.

At some point within the last thirty seconds, I've started to cry—this happens to me a lot. I can't do this here, not amongst the throng of students pressing in around me. No, I'll use the scenic route home to calm myself down, lower my expectations, so I can approach this with more logic than I'm capable of right now.

Can you call it a scenic route when you run the whole way and don't take in any scenery?

Twenty minutes later, I'm at my apartment, relieved to discover that my roommate is still out. I discard my winter gear in the entryway and book it to my room where I grab my laptop and settle on the bed. Navigating to my email, I refresh the screen and find the unread message sitting at the top of my inbox.

One last deep breath and I open it.

Gabriella Ruiz, 3rd Cousin—once removed, New Mexico—no photo attached.

I imagine that whole "Six Degrees of Kevin Bacon" thing. The complex sequence of connection points between myself and a third cousin might as well be rocket science. I can't make sense of it.

There's an option to message her directly, but I hesitate. What would I even say?

A quick search on social media reveals countless options. A few accounts list their home as New Mexico, but only a handful of those are public accounts wherein lie hundreds of pictures—more faces than I could even begin to weed through in my hunt for answers.

I don't know where to begin, so I busy myself with packing for my flight home tomorrow, whipping up my fourth packet of ramen this week and watching the next episode of *Emily in Paris*.

A text from my brother is a welcome distraction.

> **DREW**
>
> Hey! Reagan and I can't wait to see you at Christmas. It's been too long. Miss you!

> **ME**
>
> Me too! I fly home tomorrow. What day do you guys get there?

> **DREW**
>
> We only have a few days off. We'll be there middle of next week.
>
> Promise me you'll take an Uber to the airport.

> **ME**
>
> *insert eye roll emoji* I've told you. The subways are not that bad.

> **DREW**
>
> 1: Use the emoji
>
> 2: Promise me, Gretch.

> **ME**
>
> 1: Never
>
> 2: Fine. I promise. Later, loser.

As his little sister, it's my duty to never grant him the satisfaction of being right. Also, I already scheduled my Uber.

It's midnight when I climb into bed. I grab my phone to stare at that name again: *Gabriella Ruiz*. If I read it enough times, maybe some groundbreaking detail will appear that I missed before.

"Screw it," I mutter as I open a new browser tab.

I type out the words I've never allowed myself to put into a search engine since I first heard them on a *Dateline* special back in high school.

It's probably expensive. I probably can't afford it. But what else are emergency credit cards for? I deserve to know where I came from.

I search: *adoption detectives.*

Chapter One

SO, I WAS WONDERING...

GRETCHEN

"You guys aren't invited next time," I say.

"Wait. There's gonna be a next time?" My brother quirks a brow.

Of course there won't be. I've finished college and I don't plan on doing it again, but the point stands. My family is officially uninvited to any future events where I'm being recognized for... anything.

"What's a college graduation, honey, without some hollering misfits in the audience?" The wicked half smile from my mom screams *you know you loved it.*

Fine. She's not wrong. I love my family. I may not share their genetic code, but I'll claim them as mine any day, just as they claimed me twenty-two years ago.

"Sure, but a foghorn? Seriously?" I look to Dad—the one with the guilty face.

"I don't know what you're talking about." He pulls me in for a hug, planting a kiss on my temple. "Proud of you, kiddo."

I step back as my sister-in-law, Reagan, leans in. "I tried to confiscate the foghorn, I swear."

"She actually bought it," my brother whispers from my other side.

Reagan slaps Drew on the chest, but he catches her hand and hauls her to his side.

Our family may be small but we're really close. Something that I hope bodes well for me when I ask Drew for a big favor later.

Over the next hour we pose for family photos, while I'm pulled away every few minutes to say goodbye to my classmates. We pose for pictures in our caps and gowns before waving each other off into our mostly unknown futures.

When pictures are done, my family and I trek back to my campus apartment where I've *voluntold* them to help me finish packing. My roommate opted not to walk at her graduation ceremony, so she drove off with her car packed to the brim earlier this week. Honestly, I wish I were her right now. Gridlock traffic, moving trucks bogarting entire blocks and stairwells clogged with people on move-out day is not for the faint of heart.

"Honey!" Mom hollers from the kitchen while Reagan and I pack up my bedroom closet. "Do I need to take you to see a specialist about your ramen hoarding problem?"

"Don't speak ill of my boyfriends, Mom!" I call back. "They may be unhealthy but at least they're cheap and easy."

"Gross, Gretch!" Drew yells from the living room. Reagan chuckles as she zips up the first of many suitcases.

Dad pokes his head around the doorframe, announcing he and Mom are headed out to grab dinner for us. I could remind him that he's in New York City, the food delivery capital of the world. Anything we want could be here in twenty minutes or less. But what he's not saying is that Mom wants to explore.

When my family has visited in the past, we'd spend hours exploring the city. Bookstores, coffee shops, Central Park, Times Square, Broadway—you name it. We did it all. Mom has always had wanderlust in her veins, while Dad is the homebody. She moved to rural Illinois to live the quiet life he craved, and he makes sure to sweep her off for an adventure as often as he can. Two years ago, he surprised her with a ten-day Alaskan Cruise. The year before that it was two weeks in the United Kingdom and Ireland. And next month they're off for a four-week tour of Italy. Today, it's the one hour they can spare to stroll the streets of Manhattan in search of food.

My parents offer quick goodbyes to Drew and Reagan since they'll be heading to the airport soon, and hurried plans are made for us all to meet in Chicago next weekend for a belated graduation celebratory dinner.

After they leave, Reagan returns to my bedroom to continue her assigned task. Meanwhile, I find my brother in the living room where he's transferring everything from my bookshelves into boxes.

I take in a deep breath. "Thanks for coming, Drew."

"Of course. We wouldn't miss it."

Drew and I weren't always this close. With our six-year age difference, the years we spent under the same roof consisted of him being my brother in the traditional sense. He was protective—and a nuisance—the way you would expect a big brother to be, but it wasn't until we were grown that we developed the bond we have now.

I take a seat on the couch, fingers fussing with the hem of my shirt. Drew transfers my *Little Women* collection to the box at his feet, his features looking more and more like Dad every day.

It's not jealousy, but it's something akin to it that I can't quite identify. I swallow past it, same as I've always done.

"Everything okay?" he asks.

His question tugs my attention back to the moment. "Huh? Oh yeah, fine."

He stares at me, unconvinced, before turning back to the shelf. My gaze shifts to the window and I settle my thumbnail between my teeth.

The couch shifts beside me. Drew gently lowers my hand from my face as he says, "What's up, Gretch?" At my bewildered look, he adds, "You chew your nails when you're nervous."

I glance down at my thumb, evidence on full display where my nail has been bitten to the quick. "Right," I breathe. I tuck a leg underneath me and turn to face him. "I wanted to ask you something."

"Okay."

Now or never. "My friend and I planned a trip for the end of next month out to Sedona. Kind of a graduation slash birthday thing."

There is no friend. Also, the trip has nothing to do with my birthday or graduation, but I'm looking for the path of least resistance here.

I soldier on. "Anyway, something's come up and now she can't go." *Lie.* "The resort and my plane ticket are non-refundable." *Truth.* "And I don't wanna go by myself." *Also truth.* "So, I was wondering if you'd like to go with me?"

He doesn't seem appalled by the idea, but he does hesitate.

"The resort's already paid for," I rush to add. "It's a one-bedroom suite but there's a sofa bed. My friend felt really bad about cancelling so she's not asking for her money back or anything." *Another lie.* Fictitious friends can't ask for their fictitious money back. "You'd only have to buy a plane ticket."

A *yes* is all I need for now. I'll explain everything else when we get there.

"It sounds fun, but I don't know if I can swing—"

"You should go," Reagan interrupts as she plops down next to Drew. I forget how small this apartment is.

He narrows his eyes at her. "I should?"

"Yeah! You've got all that unused vacation time and you can use our credit card miles for the flight."

Damn. It didn't even cross my mind, but maybe I need to invite Reagan too.

The truth is, the person I always imagined doing this with hasn't spoken to me in almost three years. Drew is my next best option. I adore my sister-in-law, but I'm anxious enough as it is without becoming the third wheel.

Reagan ignores her husband's reservations and asks, "What are the dates?"

This is why she graduated from Law School at the top of her

class—yes, even ahead of her husband. She's got the badass woman energy of Joan from *Mad Men*. Quiet confidence when the situation warrants it, but calls the shots and gets stuff done when nobody else will. The curvy figure, fair skin and strawberry blonde bob easily land her in the category of doppelgänger.

Basically, Reagan is the antithesis of me. Nothing about my appearance seems to make guys' heads turn the way Reagan's does. I mean, sure, I want guys to see beyond what I look like, *blah blah blah.* He should be interested in my personality above my appearance, *yada yada yada.* But somehow, *"Your personality is so hot! Can I ravish you inside this maintenance closet?"* doesn't have the same ring to it.

"Last week of June. Wednesday through Monday," I answer.

She turns to Drew and I sit witness to a wordless conversation whereby thoughts are communicated through some sort of marital eyeball trickery.

Drew: *I don't think this is a great idea.*

Reagan: *Stop being a dick and take your sister to Sedona for her birthday.*

Drew: *What are you gonna do while I'm gone?*

Reagan: *That's for me to know and you to never find out.*

Drew: *You're gonna eat ice cream straight from the container and binge-watch romcoms, aren't you?*

My eyes sling back and forth between theirs as this silent exchange unfolds. A few seconds later, Drew says. "I guess I'm in."

I squeal in delight, throwing my arms around his neck. Over his shoulder, I look at Reagan and mouth a sincere, *"Thank you."*

It's 2AM. My alarm goes off in four hours, but my mind is reeling. Drew and Reagan left hours ago and my parents are dead to the world in my roommate's old room.

When I got word from the adoption detective several weeks ago that he had tracked down the name and current address of my biological mother, I considered hopping on a plane and showing up at her doorstep the next day. If only I was the kind of person that could be that confidently spontaneous.

The reality is, my nerves humbled me. Up to this point, I've tackled this process by myself, which I know was the right decision. But I'm not too proud to admit that I don't want to do the next part —the hardest part—alone.

Unknowns and what-ifs make me nervous. I actively avoid being the center of attention as often as possible. Bottom line, I don't know this woman. She may not care to know me. She could shut her door in my face.

If for no other reason than to talk me off a ledge of paralysis by analysis, I know that I need somebody there with me.

I should have asked Drew sooner, but with finishing up my Saks Fifth Avenue internship, final exams and the general chaos of grad-uation, I found ample excuses to put it off. There's also the fact that I've been on the brink of calling the whole thing off, every other second of every single day. And maybe a not so small part of me was holding out hope, wishing on stars, and sending up prayers that the person I always imagined doing this with would find his way back to me.

What a fool's hope that was.

Then, there's my parents—the inevitable conversation I've decided to save for after I get back. Even still, the thought of telling them what I've done sends waves of nausea coursing through me.

For now, I have to remain focused on the most important of all the plates I'm balancing. I'm going to meet my birth mom.

I don't know if she's married or if she has other kids. I wonder if she's still in contact with my biological father. The detective was successful in tracking down a photocopy of my original birth certifi-cate form where he got my mom's name, but my father's name wasn't included. He offered to continue searching, but I had already charged so much to my credit card for his services, I decided that, for now, my birth mom's name and address was enough.

The last six months have been a whirlwind of emotions— anxiety over what may or may not happen, fear of this all possibly being for nothing, excitement that I'm finally on this precipice, and now, relief that I won't be doing it alone.

But, as it always does, the familiar ache creeps in. Because *he* always comes to mind. It doesn't matter what I'm feeling or how badly I wish I could forget. It's always *him*.

There was a time when he was my first *and* last call. My best friend. My everything. Mine. At least, I thought he was. I thought I was *his*, too. But I wasn't.

Pain reverberates in my chest like a relentless wave beating against a stone wall over and over. A feeling I've become all too acquainted with over the past three years.

I wish I could call Connor.

Chapter Two

CHUG, CHUG, CHUG

GRETCHEN

I'VE AVOIDED the city since Drew and Reagan's wedding. Chicago's not small, but even the microscopic chance of running into a certain someone has been enough to keep me away.

While I was in college, it was easy to keep my distance. I'd fly into O'Hare, head straight to Bloomington, and stay there until my parents drove me back to the airport. But I've graduated now. No matter how much I want to, I can't avoid the city forever.

Alas, I'm here with a smile on my face, trying not to let the paranoia of barreling into his chest around the next corner consume me whole.

Skyscrapers tower over the city streets below. The familiar hum of the hustle and bustle along the sidewalks, commerce everywhere, lives under my skin. I've always loved Chicago. But now it only reminds me of Manhattan. A place I'm ready to return to as soon as possible.

After a brief walk from the parking garage, we make it to the upscale steakhouse on the Magnificent Mile where Drew and Reagan are already seated. Hugs are exchanged all around before we sit. As I take the seat next to Mom, I notice two empty seats across the table, leather-bound menus resting atop their pristine place settings.

To nobody in particular, I ask, "Is somebody else coming?"

The answer I expect is something along the lines of *they're extra menus* or *the hostess only had a 7-top available.*

"I invited Connor and Lauren," Drew replies, tone casual.

My stomach sinks. Anxiety settles at the back of my throat and my chest pulls tight. I have so many questions.

After three years of silence, he's gonna show up just like that? Tonight? Who's Lauren? His girlfriend, obviously. There's no way he's still single at twenty-eight.

Masking my shock with indifference, I say, "I didn't realize you guys still talked."

Instantly, I know it's the dumbest thing I've ever said because my lack of knowledge as to the status of Connor and Drew's friendship is in direct proportion to the number of times I've inquired about Connor over the past three years. *Zero.*

"What?" Drew asks incredulously. "We've been best friends since we were fifteen and he was the Best Man in my wedding. Of course we still *talk.*"

There's no time to form a reply because that's when I see them —two figures approaching the table in my peripheral vision. While the rest of the table moves to welcome the new arrivals, I grab my water glass and chug it down, praying for the liquid cascading down my throat to sweep me out to Lake Michigan. The water might be a little cold, but it's better than here.

"Paul, Kelly, this is Lauren," Connor says of the woman at his side. I don't hear Lauren—I don't even see her—because…*his* voice. The depth with its smooth, yet rough, timbre that has only improved with age, has now taken up rent-free residence in my head. Again.

Chug, chug, chug.

I take him in over the rim of my water glass. He looks exactly the same as the day he left me alone on that balcony. It's infuriating. *Devastating.*

At just over six feet, he's not too tall. Still built like the teenage quarterback he was for so many years, he's long, toned and lean with enough muscle underneath his navy dress shirt to pull the fabric taut across his pecs and shoulders. That hair that's dirty and blonde in all the right ways—he's grown it out some, but the longer on top, shorter on the sides look works. The scruff along his jaw is that sexy in-between kind that I want to drag my fingers through.

His arctic blue eyes are as hypnotizing as they were looking back at me through a phone screen my freshman year of college. The same eyes that were pure warmth and friendship the day I met him on my back porch thirteen years ago.

I'm locked in the swirl of them before I realize he's staring at me, too. His expression is strained, like the mountain of words unspoken, the memory of how things ended—all of it hangs on a clothesline tethered between our chests. I slap that thought away because it can't be true. He's with Lauren now. If he's tense, it's because this is awkward.

So awkward.

He rounds the table as his girlfriend is swept up in conversation with my parents. The thirty-seven seconds I was given to prepare for this was not enough. He claps Drew on the back and drops a peck on Reagan's cheek. Before I know it, I'm on my feet, standing toe to toe with Connor Vining.

The hesitation lasts a fraction of a second—or maybe I imagined it—before he pulls me in to his chest, arms wrapped around my waist. With nowhere else for my arms to go, they lock around his neck. He squeezes me close and for a brief, beautiful, fleeting moment, the past is forgotten and I melt into him.

The exhale of relief I hear could be mine...or maybe it's his.

"Congratulations, Gretch," he breathes. The weight of his head against mine, the sincerity of his whispered words only meant for my ears, leaves me discombobulated. When we step back, I can't bear to look at him. With the loss of contact comes the remembrance of everything that happened and I'm uneasy all over again.

The cumbersome silence between us is interrupted when Lauren positions herself back at Connor's side. She extends her hand to me and I offer mine. I see her lips move, but I'm not listening. How can I when I'm still off-kilter from the feeling of Connor's arms wrapped around me? Images of his hands frantically moving down my chest and up my thigh flood my mind.

I muster up a genuine-*ish* smile and enough composure to spit out, "It's nice to meet you, too."

The conversation up until the appetizers arrive sounds like one big *whir* in my ears. However, I manage to catch a few key points that are particularly painful: Connor and Lauren met at work, her dad is their boss and the two of them double date with Drew and Reagan…a lot.

Every effort I've made over the last three years to avoid the subject of Connor—to *never* ask Drew about him for fear of the truth of what happened between us being written plain as day across my face—was a mistake. A big, huge mistake. I should have asked all the questions. If I had, maybe I wouldn't feel two inches tall right now.

Between the three happy couples at the table, the conversation moves along fine without me. I try to pretend he's not here, but it's a wasted effort.

Chancing glances in his direction between the five pieces of bread and three glasses of water I've consumed wouldn't be so embarrassing if his eyes weren't *right there* every single time. Our gazes catch for two beats too long and there is nary a smile, smirk, scowl or furrowed brow—not even a wink.

As though she senses the need to send my heart into a complete and utter tailspin, Mom asks, "How long have you two been together?"

Lauren smiles as she reaches her hand across Connor's lap. "Almost two and a half years."

Mom coos in adoration and I'm…frozen.

Pause. Rewind. Two and a half years?

I had reasoned a long time ago that Connor moved on. After all,

I've tried to move on myself. But I clearly spent a lot more time than he did grieving what we almost had. What was lost.

My breaths come shaky and unpredictable. Pressure builds behind my eyelids and in my chest. If I sit here another second, I may burst. "I need to use the restroom," I announce, shoving back from the table with a loud screech of my chair.

When I make it to the ladies' room, I find the stall in the back corner. My vision clouds over from the tears that have already begun to fall as I fiddle with the latch on the door. I finally secure the lock, close the toilet lid and slump on to the seat.

In the wake of him cutting me out of his life without warning, I spent month after month scraping by. While I was crying myself to sleep, he was here, moving on with someone else. The only explanation is that it must have never meant to him what it meant to me. *I never meant to him what he meant to me.*

But…that can't be it. I was there. I saw the way he looked at me. I felt his touch. I tasted his desperate lips on mine.

Knowing I can't sit here and cry for the entire night, I compose myself. I push back the rest of my tears and let righteous indignation overtake the sadness.

I hate this feeling—betrayal. I *know* this feeling. *Connor* knows I know this feeling because I told him about it. Even though the hurt magnified with every day that he didn't call, I never imagined Connor capable of treating me the way *she* did. Maybe it isn't exactly the same as what happened in high school, but the bones are: I let somebody in and they didn't turn out to be who I thought they were, leaving me looking like a fool.

I have the uncharacteristic urge to punch Connor in the throat. But that would be undignified, not to mention the questions it would raise.

If he had ever told my brother about what happened between us, I'm certain Drew would have asked me about it.

As if on cue, my familiar friend, *doubt*, creeps back in: *Why didn't he tell anyone? Was he ashamed of himself? Of me? Was it so forgettable he never cared to mention it? Was he drunk and doesn't remember?*

I'm spiraling. And, I remind myself, I never told anyone either.

After using the restroom, I wash my hands and check that my makeup is in order and all remnants of tears are gone. Squaring my shoulders, I return to the table where our entrees have arrived.

As I sit down, Reagan leans into my ear to ask if I'm okay. I panic internally for a moment, worried that I've been too transparent, but she seems to accept my excuse that I simply had too much water.

Nervous energy buzzes through my veins. Thankfully, I have an enormous steak knife and a medium rare filet mignon sitting in front of me. I dig in, perhaps too aggressively, but everything bubbling under the surface of my barely contained emotions has to go somewhere.

Easy conversation continues between the three couples surrounding me. The story of Connor and Lauren's recent visit to the Outer Banks to see his family over Christmas was especially torturous. Mom and Dad recite their entire Italy travel schedule, never mind I've heard it at least twice already. Drew regales the table of the Double Date Twins' plans to attend a Cubs game in a few weeks. Connor gives a Cliffs Notes version update on his two older brothers and their families. And so it goes and goes.

I should be offended that we're all at a dinner to celebrate me and I haven't been included in but ten seconds of conversation. Yet, given the turn of tonight's events, I'm not complaining.

Let's be honest, I prefer to fly under the radar in most situations.

Just when I think I might get through dinner without uttering a single word, Lauren is the one who turns the spotlight on me. "So, Gretchen, what was your major?"

Forced to look up from my plate that I've been meticulously admiring for the past half hour, it's only now that I fully see her. It hits me like a wrecking ball: she's stunning. Her blond locks are beach-wave-curled to perfection and her blue eyes give Connor's a run for their money. If he's the quarterback, then she's the head cheerleader.

I swallow down a bite of my steak and a gallon of envy. "Fashion merchandising."

"That's so cool! I can totally see that. Your dress with those earrings is incredible. I can tell you've got an eye for fashion."

I've paired a warm yellow spring dress donning a soft peplum embellishment around the waist with a pair of turquoise drop earrings. The floor length dress is light and airy but still fancy enough for a restaurant like this. My earrings, though, are the best part. I've styled my hair into a heavy fishtail braid pulled around one side so the turquoise gems can shine. The fact that she notices and offers the compliment so sincerely makes me like her. Which, incidentally, pisses me off.

"Thank you," I say.

"What's your plan now? You have a job lined up?" This must be what Connor loves about her—she's the social butterfly who never meets a stranger. My polar opposite.

"Well, we certainly hope she finds a job closer to home," Mom interjects. "We miss having her here."

I smile at Mom and turn back to Lauren. "I would love to be closer to home but the fashion industry is really centralized in Manhattan so...don't be upset, Mom and Dad"—I throw them a wink and another smile—"but I plan to go back to New York."

Mom sighs, more wistful than upset. "Kids. They never listen to their parents."

The grin on my face lingers but falls the moment Connor's stare finds me. I'm bound, shackled in place. Elbows on the table, one hand over the fist of the other pressed against his mouth, his eyes pierce directly into mine.

Disarmed, I look to the left and right to make sure nobody takes notice. With everybody's attention drawn elsewhere, I find him again. This time, his gaze is soft and searching, shoulders slumped and stiff, hand white knuckling his own fist.

I know what I'm looking at—it's indisputable. *Regret.*

I can't think past the lump in my throat, but I force myself to look away.

Chapter Three

DAMN KARMA

CONNOR

DINNER with the Fisher family was a mistake.

Damn Drew for the invitation. Damn me for not finding a good enough excuse to get out of it. Dammit to hell that I really, really wanted to see her.

And damn karma—the evil bitch.

"Gretchen isn't what I expected." Lauren's voice snaps me back to the present.

"Why do you say that?" I ask cautiously as we walk back to my apartment.

"None of you told me that she was a freaking goddess!"

Stunned, I come to a halt on the sidewalk and Lauren turns to me. "What are you talking about?" While I agree that *goddess* is a fitting description of my best friend's sister, my girlfriend saying it feels like a trap.

She hits me with a look of exasperation. "Connor, come on. She's this dark-haired, tan, exotic beauty and I can't believe nobody ever mentioned it."

I've intentionally minimized mentions of Gretchen in our conversations over the years. There's a zone of comfort I've created that I've kept limited to the most surface level facts: she's Drew's little sister who was around some when we were kids. That's it. The deeper truth beyond that, my best friend doesn't even know.

Lauren, for all her good qualities, is pretty insecure. She's beautiful, yet constantly puts herself down. She's great at her job, yet constantly chases the accolades of her coworkers. I've never judged her harshly for any of it because everyone has insecurities and she's a great person in so many other ways.

My prolonged silence threatens to raise her suspicions, so I say, "Well, her brother doesn't think of her that way and I mean…I guess she's pretty, but I've known her since she was nine so…I don't know, I've never really looked at her that way." That last part is a bold-faced lie because Gretchen most certainly did not stay a kid forever. Neither did I. When she grew up—when we *both* did—I took notice.

Lauren hums thoughtfully, then spins on her heel and starts to walk again. Our strides find their rhythm, heels clicking on concrete, car horns blaring in the distance, when she adds, "I guess I expected her to be more like Drew. You know, playful, full of life, never stops smiling. She just seemed like she didn't want to be there."

Something sharp and heavy settles over me. Karma doing her thing.

Gretchen's always been quiet; an introvert. But the girl I remember would come alive around her family…and me. Tonight, though, she looked like she wished she could be anywhere else except at that table. I'm the one to blame for the apprehensive girl with the forced smile who avoided eye contact like the plague, who barely looked up from her dinner plate. Except when she did, those magnetic brown eyes found mine, making my heart seize in my chest.

As we enter the lobby of my building, the knots taking shape in my stomach have me feeling sick. I suggest to Lauren that she sleep at her own place tonight. I may not be legitimately ill, but her comments have left me unsettled.

When her Uber arrives, I give her a kiss on the cheek and tell her I'll call her tomorrow. As the car drives away, I've never been more thankful that we have separate apartments. Though we've discussed the possibility of moving in together plenty over the course of our relationship.

The first time the subject came up, we were a couple weeks shy of our one-year anniversary and I had taken her home to meet my family over Thanksgiving. While they would never speak badly about her to me outright, it was obvious she didn't fit in with our family.

To be fair, Lauren wasn't herself that weekend and I don't entirely blame her. She was so nervous. Meeting your boyfriend's family is a big deal, but I didn't anticipate how uncomfortable she would be.

My mom, the warmest person on the planet, invited her to help her, my sister-in-law and brother's girlfriend with meal prep. Lauren politely declined. Instead, she retreated to the dining room to fuss with napkin folds that nobody cared about. Meanwhile, my dad, top-tier conversationalist, couldn't connect with her at all. Once she started on about her privileged childhood—the Chicago penthouse apartment, full-service housekeeper and family chef—Dad checked out. He stopped talking so she talked more thinking it would get him to talk, but he kept not talking so she kept talking and…well, the loop became insufferable.

Lauren's upbringing has always stirred up my own feelings of inadequacy. She's not a snob or entitled, but she's open about wanting the life she had growing up. She wants the penthouse apartment and the husband who takes over her father's company when he retires, but I love my cozy one-bedroom and owning a business has never been a life goal for me.

Our priorities are very different; an issue that sends red flags flying at full mast in my brain any time she brings up the idea of living together. I'm ashamed to say, I've continuously kicked the cohabitation can down the road with empty promises like *maybe after the holidays* or *let's talk when my lease ends in six months.*

If we move in together, the next step is marriage. After two and half years together, I should want to marry her. But I don't. I've been in such denial about the state of our relationship that I'm constantly reminding myself of all the reasons she's great.

She's gorgeous. She's fun. She makes me laugh and loves to be the life of the party. She makes a really big deal out of birthdays and milestones. The people in her orbit always feel appreciated and seen. She's great with kids and will make a kick-ass PTA president one day.

The truth is, the right guy—*her* right guy—would be lucky to have her.

Two hours later, I'm lying in bed, locked in a staring contest with my ceiling. My mind races with thoughts of nothing and everything.

Lauren. Gretchen. Drew. The Cubs game. Work. My lips on Gretchen's neck. Lauren. Gretchen's hands fisting the lapels of my jacket. Lauren. Work. Lauren. Gretchen.

Gretchen.

The rush of affection I felt when I saw her, the warmth that coursed through me when I hugged her, the ache that echoed in my chest with every second of eye contact, only reminds me of the self-inflicted wound I've spent three years trying to bury.

A wound that's never healed.

I thought enough time had passed, but I was wrong. Terribly, horribly, unequivocally wrong.

Before I can talk myself out of it, I grab my phone from the nightstand. I open up my texts, prepared to do what I should have done three years ago. My fingers hover over the screen as memories of that night invade my senses.

I remember everything. The black dress with the thigh-high slit that made my mouth go dry. Long onyx hair draped in waves down the bare skin of her back. The fire in her eyes right before I kissed her. And the hurt that replaced it when I made the worst decision of my life and walked away.

I need to make things right, but not like this. She deserves more than an apology text. Instead, I start small.

ME

It was good seeing you tonight, Gretch.

My pulse soars as I hit *send*. It's only then that I look up and see our last text exchange from the day before Drew's wedding. Shame clouds my vision. Glutton for punishment, I scroll up. Guilt shreds my heart on-site with each downward swipe of my thumb. A year's worth of texts. A year that felt like the start of what I hoped would be *everything*. Until it became the end neither of us wanted.

I wait several minutes for three little dots that never come.

An hour and a half later, my phone pings. Rubbing the sleep from my eyes, I swipe the screen to life.

GRETCHEN

You too.

It's fewer words than I had hoped for, but it's a start.

TWO WEEKS HAVE PASSED since I texted Gretchen. I haven't reached out again. I respect Lauren too much to be texting Gretchen while I try to figure out what to do about our relationship.

Lauren and I have continued on like normal. We've gone out to dinner a few times, including a double date with Drew and Reagan. She's been at my place in the evenings, where we've ordered takeout and binged Netflix like we always do. We've slept over at each other's places several times, but neither of us has initiated sex. I was too tired some nights, we were both exhausted others.

Through every moment spent together and apart, I've tried to remember all that's great between us, to look past my reservations over marrying her. I've told myself that our issues are all in my head. I've imagined what a life with Lauren would look like and, honestly, it's a great life. There's a nice home, a few kids, and a woman who's an amazing mom and a supportive, faithful partner.

But, in all the visions of our possible future, I don't see a woman that I'm madly in love with.

I love Lauren. But I'm not *in* love with her. It's a reality I should have faced a long time ago. Instead, I've tried to will the puzzle pieces to fit, hoping that someday things would click and we'd make sense.

Except, the *click* never came.

I can't ignore it anymore. The denial I've been living in, the issues I've made excuses for in the name of *but she's such a good person*, have only served to give her a false hope of a forever together. That's not fair to her.

Approaching the restaurant where we're meeting for lunch, I spot Lauren through the glass windows. I bypass the hostess and head straight to the table. When her smile rises to greet me, the paralyzing guilt rushes in and it almost—*almost*—convinces me to scrap this whole plan.

I don't want to hurt her. But if I don't end things now, I think I'll live to regret it.

Chapter Four

HOT. MESS.

GRETCHEN

IF AVOIDING MY PARENTS' inquiries into my life plans was a competition, I'd be the reigning champion. Deflection and avoidance is the name of the game.

When the subject of Sedona comes up, I play along for a bit, but as the questions pile up and the risk of me losing track of my half-truths and straight-up lies becomes too much, I change the subject.

Then there's the matter of my relocation back to New York. They're my parents, so of course they have questions. *What jobs am I applying for? Where will I live?*

My former boss from my spring internship at Saks, Monica, promised to let me know if a position opens up that I could apply for, but that's about as much effort as I've put into my post-college career plans. Instead, I've poured all my focus—and funds—into this trip.

If Mom and Dad have noticed I've been avoiding them, they've had the decency not to let on. Lucky for me, they leave for Italy in a few hours.

The truth is, ever since our dinner in the city over a month ago, I've been distracted.

Connor showing up at all was a punch to the gut I wasn't prepared for, but showing up with a serious girlfriend on his arm felt like a knife straight to the heart. To wrap up the whole mess of a day, he texted me for the first time in years. I saw the text the second it came through. After a quick inner struggle over how to respond, I decided not to because I owe him nothing. Any tension between us is on him. It can't be my job to fix it.

Then, my good senses gave way to delirium as I did nothing but think about his message for the next ninety-seven minutes—yes, I counted. One message, I thought. One blunt reply so I could close the open tab in my brain and finally get some sleep.

Spoiler: I didn't sleep.

Connor hasn't messaged me since. But it's fine. I'm fine. Everything's fine.

Spoiler: I'm not fine.

Many sleepless nights later, I'm here working on the final plans for my trip which is now only three weeks away. I distract myself on Reddit and Yelp, browsing reviews for hiking trails and restaurants, and cross-referencing them with Mom's recommendations. I do a deep dive into the resort's amenities, considering if and when we'll be able to take advantage of them.

Five nights at a nice resort might have been overkill, but a cheap motel didn't really scream *birthday celebration*. Between the resort, airfare and the detective, my emergency credit card has taken a beating, which is why I've vowed not to use it again until it's paid off.

I click over to the resort's photo gallery to get a lay of the land at the same time my phone pings from the bedside table. Laptop pushed aside, I grab my phone and roll onto my back, holding it above me to read the text.

DREW

The only flight I could get with my miles
lands me in Phoenix three hours after you.
You cool to hang out in the airport to wait
for me?

ME

No problem.

DREW

How are we getting to Sedona?

Crap. New York living has become so second nature to me with ride shares and public transit that I didn't even consider how we'd be getting around.

ME

Umm...Uber?

DREW

Seriously? It's like a two hour drive.

ME

Right...I'd rent a car but I'm not 25,
soooooo...

DREW

HA! Ok. I'll get a car.

ME

Let me know what I owe you.

There goes my plan to stop spending money.

DREW

I got it.

ME

You don't have to do that, but thank you!
Text me your flight details.

Love you.

DREW

Love you more.

Grabbing my laptop, I sit up against the headboard and map the distance between the resort and my birth mom's address.

A rush of anxious energy courses through me. The longer I keep the truth from my brother, the deeper I dig this proverbial hole. I need to tell him.

As much as I'd like to think this news wouldn't come as a shock since it's natural for adopted kids to want to find their biological parents, Drew and I have never spoken about my birth family. Lack of resemblance aside, our bond has never felt a drop shy of full-blooded. It's possible this has never crossed his mind.

I shouldn't wait another three weeks to tell him. This isn't a conversation to have over the phone either. With my social calendar full of nothing and no one for the next three weeks, I have no excuse for not making it up to Chicago to see him.

Taking a deep breath, I grab my phone and hit the call button before I talk myself out of it. He answers on the second ring.

"Hey, Gretch."

"Hey!"

"Okay, I'm looking up rental cars. Do we need an SUV or will a compact do?"

"Whatever's cheapest. I'm sorry I didn't think about that sooner."

"It's fine. I don't mind."

There's a prolonged silence as I clamp a fingernail between my teeth. Drew cuts the silence. "Stop chewing your nails, Gretch."

I yank my hand to my lap and scoff. "How did you know?" He releases a teasing sigh. "Never mind. Don't answer that. I was calling to see what you're up to over the next few weeks. Mom and Dad are leaving soon and I'm gonna be here alone with nothing to do."

"Well," he begins, "Reagan and I have grownup jobs so we'd probably be boring as balls to hang out with."

"Ew! Stop being such an adult, you loser."

"Right? Zero out of ten, do not recommend. Oh wait! We have an extra ticket to the Cubs game next weekend if you wanna come."

"The game you and Connor were talking about?"

"Yeah. Reagan will be there. Lauren was supposed to come but Connor said she had something come up."

"Oh…um…" My spine straightens and I have the immediate urge to bite my nails again. "I don't know—"

"Come on, it'll be fun!" Drew's voice is way too cheery for my current reality, which, I remind myself, he knows nothing about.

I rack my brain for an excuse not to go. Except, I literally just told him I have nothing to do. No plans. None. I fall back to my pillow, palm plastered to my forehead. "Ok. Sure."

I disconnect the call when Mom and Dad announce their departure from downstairs. A quick farewell at the car turns into a ten-minute run-down of the household checklist I'm responsible for in their absence, as if I didn't live here for eighteen years.

Set the alarm every night.

Don't forget to turn on the vent hood if I cook bacon. *Good grief, you forget* one *time and your family never lets you forget about it.*

Water the plants every other day.

Clean Franny's litter box every day.

No house parties. *They must be confusing me for my extroverted, frat boy brother.*

And, finally, they give me the name and phone number of the neighbor down the street who they've already lined up to check on Franny while I'm in Arizona.

I nod along and give them both a hug before waving them off down our long gravel driveway. Back inside, I shut the front door behind me and lean against it. A half-sigh, half-groan sputters out of me as I think back to my conversation with Drew.

All I had to do was make plans to see him. Instead, I've somehow agreed to a non-date-double-date with my brother, sister-in-law and my brother's best friend who happens to have ravished me on a balcony—and subsequently ghosted me—three years ago. Oh, and he has a girlfriend.

My stomach grumbles, snapping me out of my thoughts. I head to the kitchen and stare into the fridge. A baking dish of Mom's homemade tuna casserole lies in wait with a sticky note attached that reads, *"There's another in the freezer."* I smile—she knows it's my favorite thing that she makes. I reach for it, but pause. I think I'm craving something else. Changing course, I retrieve the ingredients for my ultimate comfort food instead.

I'm scooping the toasted mozzarella and pesto grilled cheese sandwich onto a plate when my phone buzzes in my back pocket. Once I'm seated at the kitchen island, I pull out my phone.

CONNOR

Drew says you're coming to the game next weekend.

I guess he's texting me again. I can't tell if it's excitement or apprehension that churns in my belly.

ME

Yeah, maybe.

The three dots appear and disappear three times before he finally replies.

CONNOR

Oh. Well, I hope you can make it.

I drop my phone to the counter. *Apprehension. It's definitely apprehension.*

If I go, I'll be using Lauren's ticket. If the roles were reversed, I'm not sure how I'd feel about my boyfriend going to the game with another woman. That's ridiculous, though, right? It's not like I'm a threat. Connor and I wouldn't be there *together.* He'd just be one person sitting next to another person—adjacent humans, as it were.

Clearly, my thoughts are an incoherent mess. So, naturally, I send a panicked reply that I hope reads *cool as a cucumber* and not *hot mess express.*

ME

Is Lauren okay with me using her ticket?

Three dots appear, but I reread my message and feel the need to clarify.

ME

I don't want to make her uncomfortable.

Wait, that sounds like I think Lauren should be uncomfortable.

ME

Scratch that. I'm just trying to be respectful of her...non-single woman to single-woman, I guess.

Hot mess, Gretchen. Hot. Mess. Also, sliding in your current relationship status? Seriously?

ME

You know what, forget it. I think it's best I bury my head in the proverbial sand from the safety of my childhood bedroom where the walls are padded, the parents are gone and the alcohol cabinet is stocked. Cheers. *insert clinking glass emoji*

I slam my phone down and groan into my hands. There was not a syllable of cucumber calm anywhere in that tapestry of word vomit.

My phone buzzes.

CONNOR

Gretchen...

An ellipsis. An ellipsis that might as well be his voice telling me to breathe. My lungs fill with air as the three dots pop up again.

CONNOR

Lauren and I broke up.

33

The synapses in my brain fire and misfire in every direction, breath faltering.

> **CONNOR**
>
> I haven't told Drew yet. I'd appreciate it if you didn't say anything.

My heart tumbles like it might fall out of my chest. Why did he tell me, then? *It's because you were a rambling basket case, Gretchen. He probably wanted to shut you up.*

> **ME**
>
> Of course, I won't say anything.
>
> I'm sorry, by the way

I can't discern if it's relief or fear that has my head collapsing onto my forearms. I'm so confused. Confused about Connor, about the timing of all this. And, most of all, confused about how I'm supposed to feel.

Maybe I shouldn't go to the game. Things will be awkward and if *things* are awkward, then I'll definitely be the most awkward. Awkward does not sound like fun.

> **CONNOR**
>
> I really hope to see you there, Gretch.

Well, it looks like I'm going to a baseball game next weekend.

Chapter Five

I'VE MISSED THAT SMILE

CONNOR

AFTER TEXTING GRETCHEN LAST WEEK, I knew I'd put off telling Drew about my break-up with Lauren long enough.

That same night, I invited him out for a drink.

I shouldn't have been surprised to find out that he already knew. The guy had known since the day it happened because Lauren had called Reagan in tears and he'd been waiting for me to come clean about it.

I apologized for not telling him sooner, but that didn't stop the cross-examination. He ranted about Lauren being the best thing to ever happen to me, that I was making a mistake, how she was this saving grace that swooped in and turned my life around.

There's so much he doesn't know about those few months before Lauren and I began dating.

The tongue lashing lasted for an hour before the tension in my bones reached critical mass. If I didn't get out of there, every secret about my harbored affections for his little sister was going to pour out of me or I was going to punch him.

35

Rising from my seat, I interrupted his interrogation with the parting words: *"I know you think I'm a dick and you're not wrong. But breaking up with her is not the worst thing I've done. What's worse is that I didn't do it sooner because she deserves someone who loves her the way you love Reagan."*

I didn't give Drew a chance to respond as I slapped a twenty on the bar and walked out the door.

Despite my dramatic exit—or, maybe, thanks to it—Drew hasn't pushed the subject since, so I'll take that as a win. I need every win I can get with my best friend because all other areas of my life seem to be in limbo, at best, and pure hellfire, at worst.

It's now Friday afternoon. Ten business days that I've spent trying to schedule a meeting with my boss. There's no big work emergency or design project to discuss, but now that the dust has settled a bit, I figured a meeting—man to man—to apologize and affirm my commitment to my job is in order.

I broke up with his daughter a month ago. The same daughter who sits in a cubicle a mere twenty feet beyond my office door.

"Mr. Driskill is booked solid through the end of the month," his assistant, Bethany, regretfully informs me.

"Bethany, it's me. Is that the truth or is he avoiding me?"

The pause on the other end of the line is confirmation enough. My head sinks to my chest.

"I'm sorry, Connor."

"Let me know if anything opens up in his schedule."

"Will do, dear," she says kindly before disconnecting the call.

I hang up my desk phone and run a hand down my face. For the first time, genuine concern over the security of my job drops anchor in my mind. Lauren is his only child and I broke her heart. If he doesn't want to keep me around then who am I to blame him?

Over the past month, Lauren has reached out several times, but I haven't responded. She could easily storm into my office and corner me into a conversation, but she hasn't. Maybe she's at a loss for words the same way I am. I don't know what else I can do other than hope, sooner rather than later, she understands for herself that ending things was the right thing to do. For both of us.

~

I DIDN'T SLEEP last night. Whether it's panic, excitement or sheer adrenaline that propels my steps from my building to Drew's, I'm unable to harness the nerves coursing through my veins into anything other than something akin to a teenager who drank four too many Red Bulls.

I still haven't heard whether or not Gretchen is coming to the game today. Every time I thought to text her, I couldn't follow through.

As much as I want to be her person again, I can't text her like nothing has changed, like it wasn't me who ghosted her for three years. Apologies and explanations have to come first. If she can forgive me, maybe we can forge a new friendship. And this time, *God willing*, maybe that friendship can exist out in the open. I won't hold my breath for more because, frankly, I don't even deserve that much.

By the time I turn down the hallway to Drew and Reagan's apartment, I've accepted that I'll probably be third wheeling it today. When she sat across the table from me at that dinner nearly six weeks ago, it was painfully obvious how uncomfortable I made her. Why would I expect her to want to spend all afternoon at a baseball game with me?

I rap my knuckles on Drew's door.

A few seconds later the door swings open and my face splits into a stupid big grin. She came.

"Hi," Gretchen says, beaming a smile that's as beautiful as it is haunting. *God, I've missed that smile.* I don't deserve that smile. Maybe it's only there because it's disorienting to come face to face with a person you haven't seen in so long, but hell if it doesn't ignite a flicker of hope in my chest that wasn't there before.

I step inside. "Hi."

Drew and Reagan move about their bedroom around the corner and I steal these few beats of privacy to take her in.

Gretchen has an effortlessness about her. It's something I recognized from our first FaceTime. The call connected and a radiant smile and big, beautiful eyes filled my screen. A simple NYU hoodie and hair pulled into a knot on top of her head and the breath caught in my lungs.

Even now, in her cut-off denim shorts, vintage Cubs t-shirt and her dark hair swept up in a ponytail that she's threaded through her baseball hat, she's perfect. She's all any guy would see when they enter a room—*a goddess*, you might say.

"You came," I say.

"I came. I don't know if you remember, but our hometown is boring as hell."

A husky laugh tumbles out of me. She smiles again and...*damn*. I want to be more than just her friend.

COME TO FIND OUT, the four tickets we have aren't together. It's two seats on one row and then two more seats directly behind them. Before anybody can suggest otherwise, Reagan announces she and Gretchen will sit together while Drew and I take the upper row.

If the Uber ride was any indication, it's best I'm not seated next to her. In a dramatic display of chivalry, Drew declared that the front seat was Reagan's, which left the three of us to squeeze into the back of the small sedan. Gretchen slid into the middle seat while Drew and I took the window seats. Her entire right side, from shoulder to knee, aligned with mine—*pressed* into mine—and it was the most alive I've felt in years. Definitely a feeling I should avoid with her brother right there.

By the top of the third, I couldn't tell you what teams are playing because I'm too busy scowling at the two drunk guys seated next to the girls. Reagan has the aisle seat, but Gretchen is stuck right next to an obnoxious asshole who doesn't even attempt discretion every time he checks her out.

The girls seem unfazed, if not unaware, but every time he checks out Gretchen's legs and then leans into his buddy's ear to whisper some off-color joke, my hands squeeze into fists.

Drew leans in, voice quiet. "Can you believe these guys?"

"Dude, I know!" I whisper back. "I wanna punch that one in the throat."

Gretchen and Reagan share a laugh over...something—I don't know what because all I see is red—and then she's on her feet, squeezing past Reagan to go to the restroom. She makes it three steps up the path before Tweedle Dumb Drunk is out of his seat, trailing after her.

"Oh, hell no," I mutter. Drew jerks his head for me to follow after his sister as if I wasn't already on the move to do so. I step over him into the aisle. He hikes a leg over the empty seats below and drops into the seat next to his wife while I rush up the stairs to the concourse area.

It only takes a second to spot him up ahead, hot on Gretchen's heels. I break into a jog and breeze past him, but I don't slow down until I reach Gretchen. As I come up beside her, I take her by the hand, matching her stride.

Gretchen's head whirls to me. Shock morphs into confusion as she takes in my face. Her gaze lowers to where I've intertwined our fingers. "What are you doing?" she asks.

"That drunk guy followed you up here," I answer, tone flat as I push down thoughts of how simply holding her hand sends an exhilarating rush of energy on a one-way course straight to my heart. Does she feel that too?

Gretchen draws us to a stop. Together, we look over our shoulders to find Tweedle Dumb Drunk has reversed course and is headed in the opposite direction.

"So, what?" She turns back on me. "You thought I was gonna be assaulted? Here? There's hundreds of people around!"

My jaw slackens before I clamp it shut a second later. I survey the busy concourse area bustling all around us. She's absolutely right; there are people everywhere. Only an idiot would try something with this many witnesses around. Then again, I wouldn't put it past the guy; he seems like idiot material.

"Or you thought he'd stand in that line with me"—she points to the mass of women forming a line outside the entrance to the bathroom—"and then feel me up in one of the stalls?"

The onslaught of mental images of my own hands on her, my palm gliding over smooth skin, her body pressed against that balcony wall, invade my mind. I blink them away.

Anger flashes in her eyes as she waits for me to respond, but I've forgotten how to speak. "I don't need you to rescue me, Connor. You can't just show up and act like things are norm——" She stops herself, the words stuck in her throat.

"I know. I'm sorry. I just..." The anger in her gaze a moment ago is gone. In its place is something even worse: indifference. I swallow thickly. "I wanted to make sure you were okay. But you're right. I'm sorry." Her mouth twitches. "I'm sorry," I say again, quieter this time, pleading. *For everything.*

One...two...three breaths. The thoughts moving through that beautiful, perfect, overanalyzing brain of hers paint themselves over her features. The dart of her eyes across my face, the crease pushing and pulling between her brows, the lips that can't decide if they want to scowl or frown.

Unbidden, our eyes simultaneously drift down to where our fingers remain woven together. My thumb moves in slow circles over her knuckles. Her hand squeezes mine so tight I can feel the pulse thundering through her palm.

Her grip loosens, throat bobbing before she whispers, "You can let go of my hand now."

Chapter Six

IT FEELS LIKE THEN AGAIN

GRETCHEN

CONFESSION: I went into today expecting a few awkward interactions with Connor, but mostly I'd planned to avoid him. Then, I swung open Drew's door and he smiled at me.

In an instant, I relived every FaceTime call. Every late night conversation where we talked about everything and nothing. All the times he made me laugh so hard I cried.

That flicker of *then* had me smiling back, the *now* forgotten.

Being seated next to Reagan was the distance I needed to regain a level head. I did *not* need to be in proximity to Connor with all his chivalry and backwards ball cap.

I knew the drunk guy followed me up the stairs. My fist was primed for a punch to his face when I felt a strange hand in mine. But it was Connor. He was there, our fingers intertwined, and a rush of emotions careened through me. A million feelings at once: I was annoyed, shocked, confused, angry, disappointed...safe.

By the time I exit the bathroom, something new clamps around my chest, its claws digging in: guilt. Regardless of all that's unresolved between us, I overreacted to what was simply a sincere attempt to protect me.

Drew has taken my seat next to Reagan, arm thrown around her shoulders, which leaves me next to Connor. He doesn't look up as I settle down into the seat beside him. The empty chairs next to Drew are a sure indicator that the drunk guys must have left.

We watch in silence as a few pitches are thrown and a batter strikes out, sending the game into the fourth inning.

Hands between my knees, I playfully lean into Connor's shoulder, bouncing myself off him. He turns and a reluctant, regret-laced smile unfolds across his face before he nudges me back. I angle myself away from Drew and Reagan, pressing close so only Connor can hear me when I say, "I'm sorry."

"No, I'm sorry. You were right," he whispers.

"No...I mean, yes. I was right." I give him a sly smile. "But you were only trying to help and I shouldn't have reacted like that." I pause for a beat, throat tight. "I guess I'm confused—"

Connor lurches to an upright position, eyes swinging to the row in front of us—to Drew. It's not the time or place for this conversation.

The moment sobers and I shake the cobweb of thoughts away. "Whatever, just...I'm sorry," I sputter out before I turn away and pretend to care about a baseball game.

DURING THE SEVENTH INNING STRETCH, Connor announces he's headed to the concession stand. After collecting Drew and Reagan's orders, he turns to me.

"You?" he asks.

"No thanks, I'm good."

He narrows his eyes. "You sure?"

I narrow my eyes right back. "I'm sure."

"Yeah, okay."

He returns ten minutes later with a lap box full of snacks.

"Hungry?" I tease.

He holds out a fresh Diet Coke, seemingly unaware of the still half-full soda resting in the cup holder between us. "You stopped drinking it in the fourth inning because the ice melted."

Warmth flitters inside my chest. I place the watered-down cup on the ground behind my feet and take the fresh drink from him. "Thank you," I say through a grin, my teeth clenched around the straw.

He bites back a smile, swigging his beer as he passes a bag of popcorn over Reagan's shoulder.

A few minutes of comfortable silence pass as batter after batter step up to the plate. I absently sip my soda every few seconds and Connor tips back his beer in tandem. Without a word or even a look, he reaches into his pocket, whips out a bag of peanut butter M&Ms, and sets it on my knee, proud smirk in place. Looking down at my favorite candy, I can't help but smile at the gesture.

I waste no time before I rip into the bag. "This may say 'share size' but don't get any ideas."

Connor guffaws. "Please! Nobody wants to share that trash."

"He's not wrong," Drew pipes in without so much as a backwards glance.

I clutch the candy to my chest. "Blasphemers!"

Connor chuckles as I pop a handful of the candies into my mouth. I answer his throaty laugh with a pestering look as he pulls another swig from his beer. I track the swallow that moves down his throat. Our eyes catch. Heat and memories creep in before his gaze drops to my mouth. The visible pulse point on his neck matches the rhythm of my own heart pounding wildly behind my sternum.

I clear my throat and avert my eyes, cutting the tension, as I reach for more candy. Connor shifts in his seat until all points of bodily contact between us are lost. The change in his mood is palpable. Jaw clenched, he removes his hat and pushes a hand through his hair before he takes another drink, his other hand flexing a few times on his knee.

I'm halfway through my M&Ms when Drew turns around to face us. "Let's all go out after this," he says.

"I can't," I answer. "I need to get back home to check on Mom's cat."

"I still can't believe she got a cat. Dad hates cats."

"Yeah, but he loves Mom, so…" I shrug.

"Your dad is such a lovesick little puppy. It's adorable," Reagan interjects.

"If you say so," Drew and I say in unison, like the annoying siblings we are, and it makes the lot of us laugh.

My brother turns to Connor. "Vining? You wanna come to IHOP with us? Breakfast for dinner sounds hella good."

"Nah, I'm gonna head home. Not really up for being a third wheel tonight."

"You know, that wouldn't be the case if you'd get your head out of your ass and work things out with Lauren," Drew says, tone clipped.

Connor stares sharply at his best friend, unflinching. Drew ignores the warning with a shrug. "Well?"

Nobody is more curious than I am to know what happened between Connor and his long-term girlfriend, but he's made it clear the subject is not up for discussion right now.

Reagan diverts the conversation, digging her forefinger and thumb into Drew's bicep. "Drew! Leave him alone!"

"Ahhh! Shit, babe! Your nails penetrated my skin," Drew cries as he grasps his injured arm.

I take a sip of soda to stifle my laugh.

"Yeah, not a good enough reason to use the word penetrate, man," Connor offers, tone dry, posture stoic.

The snort shoots up my throat before I can contain it and I inhale soda into my nose. My laughter breaks loose at the same time I gasp for air. Choking, howling, who knows what's happening, as I alternate between coughing up a lung and cackling like a hyena. Reagan's shoulders bounce and I turn to Connor whose expression is nothing short of proud amusement. He knew exactly what that would do to me. I clutch a hand to my chest, head thrown back in hysterical laughter.

Drew is far less amused. "Ok, I get the joke, Gretch. I didn't realize it was that funny." He looks to Connor for an explanation whose only response is two hands raised in surrender as if to say *"don't look at me."*

I press the heels of my hands over my eyes as laughing tears stream down my face. After a few seconds, I rally. Kind of. "I'm sorry. It's not—" Another burst of laughter escapes. "It's fine. I'm fine."

At that, Drew turns and sits back down.

I spin back to Connor who meets me with the goofiest grin— smug and silly. He and I both got his *Pitch Perfect* reference that was absolutely…pitch perfect. Within moments, my laughter's back and, this time, Connor's laughing, too.

And just like it did when I opened Drew's door, it feels like *then* again.

~

WHEN I MAKE it back to Bloomington, it's after dark.

Franny is fine. I'm pretty sure she could survive the apocalypse without me if her feline eyerolls are any indication. Her lack of interest in my company is astounding.

While I dish up the cat's food, my mind wanders back to the events of the day. Despite our interactions toggling between awkward and easy, being around Connor was…nice. I still don't know how to feel about everything and it's obvious there's still a physical attraction there, but maybe that's all it is.

Maybe that's all it ever was.

I don't have the mental capacity to fall down the Connor rabbit hole right now, so I focus my thoughts on the trip.

I had an opportunity after the game to come clean to Drew. The Uber dropped us all back at his building and Connor was gone a minute later, headed for his place a few blocks away. Reagan bid me a quick goodbye before she went inside, leaving Drew and me on the sidewalk. I couldn't bring myself to say it.

Guilt coursed through me but was replaced by love just as quickly when he pulled me in for my all-time favorite brother hug—

my arms around his waist, cheek resting against his chest and his chin on top of my head. Even if I can't get the words out until the last possible second, I know he'll be there for me.

After I change into my pajamas and wash my face, I swap my contacts for glasses and return to the kitchen for some of Mom's tuna casserole. Standing over the sink, I've eaten my way through a third of the baking dish when my phone buzzes on the counter.

> **CONNOR**
> I had fun today.

I set the dish aside and hover my fingers above the keyboard. Another message comes through before I can reply.

> **CONNOR**
> Do you think we could meet for coffee or something soon? To talk?

Now he wants to talk?

I felt something today. Something warm and familiar and secure. But it was a farce, because whatever his reasons are for dropping me three years ago, I can't forget the heartbreak. The devastation.

He walked away. I cried.

He never called. I cried.

He moved on with someone else while I was still crying.

He's had three years to *talk*. Yet, he hasn't.

Just like that, I'm right back where I started the night he left me alone on that balcony: devastated and confused.

If I don't keep my hands busy, I'll send a panicked reply that I know I'll regret. I bypass the dishwasher, flip the faucet to fill the sink with water, and squeeze in some dish soap. When the suds have risen above the layer of dishes, I sink my hands into the warm water —plunge, scrub, rinse, repeat. My hands move mindlessly, but as my thoughts spiral, frustration turns to indignation and my blood begins to boil.

He wants to do this now?

Before I realize it, my efforts turn aggressive and sloppy. A puddle of water has formed at my feet and soapy water coats the countertop. Suds drip in rivulets down the face of the cabinet doors below.

Moving to clean up my mess, I pull the drain and wipe down the counter, cabinets and floor. By the time I finish, I'm crying. I don't know how or when it started but the tears escalate into choking sobs as I lower myself to the kitchen floor. Knees tucked to my chest, I bury my head between them and wait for this wave of emotion to pass.

Even as the tears subside and my breaths find their steady rhythm again, I still can't move.

My resolve is shaky, because my heart wants to run toward him —every part of me wants to run toward him. But it doesn't matter because now's not the time.

I can't go into these next few weeks—this trip, meeting the woman who gave birth to me, telling my family—with Connor consuming my every thought. It's not that I'll never have this conversation with him, I just can't have it on my plate right now.

I get to my feet and grab my phone. The screen comes to life, my text thread with Connor still open in front of me. I release a blast of air from my lungs as I reply.

ME

I'm not ready to talk.

Before he can respond, I block his number.

Chapter Seven

TELL ME WHAT YOU NEED ME TO DO

CONNOR

"Mr. Driskill will see you now, Mr. Vining."

"Bethany, I thought we were on a first name basis," I say with a wink as I rise from my seat. Outside his door, I take in a deep breath and straighten my spine before stepping into my boss' office.

Six weeks post break-up, Lauren's dad finally had an opening in his schedule and I swooped in to grab it.

Lauren has continued to reach out to me every couple of days and I still haven't responded. She could barricade herself in my office at any time and demand that I talk to her and I wouldn't blame her one bit if she did.

"Connor, have a seat," Mr. Driskill's imposing voice commands my attention. "*Have a seat, son*" was the norm for the better part of the past two years, but I've lost the right to that title.

"Good morning, sir." I drop into the chair across from him.

He spends a few moments wrapping something up on his computer before he turns to me. "Sorry about that," he says as he clasps his hands on his desk. "You wanted to meet with me?"

"Uh, yes. Well…" I fidget in my seat. "I know things around the office have changed recently and um…" I pause to gauge his expression, but he remains unreadable. "Anyway, I felt it right to touch base and assure you that it won't interfere with my work."

He rubs a hand along his jaw. A moment later, he opens his mouth to speak at the same time my cell phone vibrates in my pocket. With my thigh pressed up against the wooden arm of the chair, the incessant buzz sounds more like a rapidly pulsing freight train.

Quickly, I reach blindly into my pocket and send the call to voicemail.

Mr. Driskill flashes his eyes briefly to the hand in my pocket, ensuring the interruption has been dealt with before he says, "Yes, we do find ourselves in an interesting situation here, don't we? I appreciate your efforts to try and minimize the fallout, but I'm not—"

My pocket buzzes again.

"I'm so sorry!" I send the call to voicemail once more and shift my body so that my phone is no longer wedged against the arm of the chair.

"As I was saying," he continues, "I'm not sure coming to me was the answer."

"Sir?"

"Connor, you're a damn good graphic designer. Probably the best one I've got. As your boss, I like you. So much, in fact, that when you started dating my daughter, I didn't have the slightest bit of concern."

My gut churns, uneasiness settling in, but I don't let myself look away. I have to face this head on.

"It's none of my business what happened between the two of you. I'll tell you the same thing I told her. As it relates to this company, frankly, it's best I don't know the details. You're both grown adults and relationships get messy and complicated sometimes. As the CEO of this company, I cannot let personal matters affect business operations."

The slightest wave of relief hits me until he goes on.

"That said, I'll shoot straight with you."

I shift in my seat. "Okay."

"As your boss, I like you. As my little girl's father, I'm not your biggest fan right now." The words sting on impact, but I can't fault his candor.

"I respect that, sir."

"Alright then. So, things might be weird around here for a little while, but people go through stuff, they hurt, they grieve and, with time, they move on."

Thankfully, I don't sense any blame or ridicule in his voice, but that doesn't relieve the guilt I feel for hurting Lauren.

"That's fair," I say before rising to my feet. "I won't take up any more of your time. Thank you for meeting with me."

We exchange a quick handshake on my way out the door.

Passing Bethany's desk, I pull out my phone and see two missed calls from Drew. There's no voicemail, but he sent a text message.

DREW

Emergency. Call me!

My heart labors. Drew and Gretchen leave for their trip today, but the word *emergency* has panic flipping my stomach on its head as I jog back to my office. I press the call button the second I cross the threshold and the phone's already to my ear when I shut the door behind me.

Less than half a ring later, Drew picks up. "Connor! Thanks for calling me back, man."

"What's going on?"

"Dude. It's a lot. Um..." His voice breaks as he takes in a stilted breath, the unmistakable sound of tears coming through the line. I haven't heard him cry since he recited his wedding vows.

"Fisher! What's going on? Is everybody okay?"

Gretchen's face pops forefront in my mind, every memory sweeping in like a deluge.

A week and a half ago, she told me she wasn't ready to talk. It was a tough pill to swallow, but I'll give her whatever she needs. If that's time, so be it. I'll wait. I texted her a couple times over those first few days with friendly chatter—just trying to keep the line of communication open—but she never replied. I know a Gretchen hint when I see one, so I backed off.

But if something has happened to her—

Drew's voice cuts in, "Yeah…I mean, no, not really…um…" He inhales sharply and there's nothing for me to do except wait. Wait as my best friend fights tooth and nail to say his next words. "It's Reagan. She's okay," he quickly adds. I let out a sigh of relief as I sink into my chair.

"Listen," he continues, "I can't get into the details right now. I promise I'll tell you everything soon, but I just need to be here with her these next couple of weeks."

"Okay. Is there anything I can do for you guys?"

He says nothing at first. Only the rough sound of Drew's hand running down his face cuts the heavy silence.

"I need a favor, Vining."

"Of course. What is it?"

He sighs. "It's Gretchen."

"Gretchen?" I question and then awareness sinks in. "Oh, damn! Your trip."

"Yeah." The defeat in his voice sounds like he's got the weight of the world on his shoulders.

"You can reschedule, right?"

"I can't. She was on an earlier flight and I wasn't able to reach her before her plane took off."

Now I'm the one scraping a palm down my face.

At the baseball game, Gretchen told me how excited she was about this trip. When she lands in Arizona and finally talks to Drew, she'll be crushed…and alone. I can't stomach the thought of it.

"What can I do to help?"

"How much vacation time do you have?" Drew asks.

My brows furrow. "What?"

"Vacation days? I know you and Lauren took that trip out to Colorado in February but that was only three or four days, right?"

"Yeeaaahh."

"But you get at least two weeks paid vacation every year? Or paid time off or whatever? Maybe you have some personal days accrued? I mean, I don't think I've ever known you to—"

"Fisher!" I pipe in. "Take a breath, man."

He takes one heavy breath and then another. Frankly, I do the same because I've already figured out what's coming, but I need to hear him say it.

"I have plenty of vacation days, sick days, personal days, you name it," I say calmly. "Tell me what you need me to do."

One beat of silence. Two. Three.

"I need you to be on a plane to Arizona in four hours. Gretchen needs you."

Chapter Eight

I DON'T WANT YOU TO BE ALONE

GRETCHEN

"I PROMISED I'd come through for you, didn't I?"

As my plane descends into Phoenix, I replay the phone call I received right before I boarded in Chicago.

"Ahhh! I can't wait to have you back here," Monica had squealed in delight. She's ten years older than me, but we clicked from the first day I started my internship back in January—boss on paper, but kindred spirits in every other way. "I'll send over the job description for you to review and you send me your resume. I'll pass it along to the hiring committee. Interviews will be the week after the July fourth holiday."

I thanked her profusely for the referral and promised to get my resume emailed over by tonight. The job isn't a guarantee, but the interview *plus* Monica's letter of recommendation increases my chances. It's the bit of distracting good news I needed to start this trip.

Out the window across the aisle, orange hued mesas and buttes line the horizon. The sky the brightest shade of blue I've ever seen, the desert palm trees and cacti gleam green and bright under the blazing sun, resting against a backdrop of city buildings and residential areas.

As the landing gear touches down on the runway, a new wave of butterflies swoops low in my gut. If all goes according to plan, I'll tell Drew everything over dinner tonight and, in three days, I'll meet my birth mother.

The hustle of the other passengers has me on my feet in the aisle when the seat belt sign goes off, reaching for my carry-on in the overhead compartment. As I emerge off the jet bridge a few minutes later, I pull my phone from my pocket and switch off airplane mode. I make my way over to the large monitor display that lists upcoming arrivals. Before I can spot his flight number on the screen, my phone begins a symphony of buzzes and pings in my hand.

Dozens of notifications. Missed calls, voicemails, texts...all of them from my brother.

I fight an eye roll. His plane should be in line for takeoff by now, but I suspect I'm about to find out his flight is delayed. I open the texts first and my irritation turns to panic as I read the messages. The first one was sent a few minutes after I switched to airplane mode back in Chicago.

> DREW
>
> Gretch! You're not answering your phone. Please call me.

Two minutes later.

> DREW
>
> Dammit. You're probably already on the plane. Call me as soon as you land!

Ten minutes ago.

> DREW
>
> Have you landed yet? Have you listened to my voicemail? I'm so sorry. Please call me!

Two minutes ago.

DREW

Forget about the voicemail. Just call me.

I ignore the red voicemail icon and call him immediately.

"Gretch! Thank God!" His panicked voice leaves no space for pleasantries. Heartache from an unknown source consumes me—if he's answering his phone, he's not on a plane.

Travelers whizz past me and the intercom overhead blasts announcements every few seconds, a cacophony of noise from every direction. I plug one ear as I try to speak above it. "Drew, what's going on?"

"I'm so sorry. Something came up and I can't come."

My breath catches. I must have misheard him. "What do you mean you can't come?"

"I swear to God, Gretch. I wouldn't be bailing if it wasn't serious."

"What happened?" I ask as I move through the terminal in search of a corner, hallway, restaurant, any goddamn place where I can hear better.

The anguished exhale on the other end sends shockwaves of fear to my heart. "I can't...I can't tell you right now and I know that sounds so shady, but I need you to trust me."

"Oh...okay. You promise everybody's alright?"

"Everyone's going to be fine. I promise." They're *going* to be fine, but they're not fine right now. I nod, concern and disappointment catching any response in my throat. "Gretch, you there?"

"I'm nodding," I say, voice trembling.

"I know this trip was really important to you and," he lets out a tired sigh, "am I right that maybe it's about more than just graduation or your birthday?" I nod again as I swipe the first tear away. "Gretch?"

"Still nodding," I reply. "How did you know?"

"Brother's intuition maybe." A light chuckle breaks past my defenses. Tears cascade down my cheeks and I clear them with the back of my hand. "I don't want you to be alone, so I—"

"No! It's fine. I mean, it's not, I guess. But I'll be alright and I hope whatever is going on with you ends up being okay and, um… you don't have to worry about me." I ramble the words on unsteady breaths, parsed with sniffles.

"Connor's coming."

My heart stops, feet screeching to a halt in the middle of terminal C. People push past me on all sides as I attempt to catch some sort of mental foothold to process what I *think* my brother just said.

I scan my surroundings and spot an alcove that leads to a hallway of airport personnel offices and equipment closets. Luggage in tow, I wait for a clearing and dart across the path of travelers. Once I'm around the corner, I lean against the wall and slide to the floor.

"Did you hear me?" Drew asks.

"I'm gonna need you to say that again." My tone lands somewhere between despondent and white-hot rage.

"Connor's coming." Yeah, that's what I thought he said.

I bring my knees to my chest. "Why would you do that? Call him right now and tell him not to come." His heavy silence settles over the line. I hang my head, foot nervously tapping in agitation on the speckled tile. "Drew!"

"He's already on his way. I panicked and then it all happened so fast. I thought someone should be there that you know and that I trust to look out for you."

A sob sputters out of me before I can stop it.

"Gretch, please don't cry. *God!* I'm sorry. I didn't know who else to ask. Mom and Dad are in Italy and I don't know any of your friends."

That's because there aren't any.

I had casual friendships in college, people I hung out with regularly, like my roommate and a few others who shared my major. We had a good enough time together, but they never *really* knew me. In my entire life, I've only ever had two friends that I've truly let in: my high school best friend and Connor. Given how those relationships ended, I haven't opened myself up to anyone since.

"You could have sent Reagan!" I accuse.

He lets out a shaky breath. "No. I couldn't."

Something sharp yanks my heart into its grip. "Drew, is Reagan okay?"

"She's gonna be. Look, I promise to tell you everything as soon as I can, but you don't need to be worried about us. I swear."

"Okay. I'm just…I'm sorry."

"It's okay. But…" He pauses, his frustration riding a tired sigh. "Is having Connor there really so bad? You guys seem to get along fine."

"We do. I don't have a problem with Connor." *I mean, unless you're referring to the relentless self-loathing I've been drowning in since he face-mauled me at your wedding and how things are so weird between us except for when they're damn near perfect, but mostly they're weird because we've never talked about it. Oh, and I blocked his number.*

Drew's voice comes sincere, if not pained. "Do you wanna just tell me what all of this was about to begin with?"

I consider it. As excited as I've been about this trip, the loneliness of carrying this big, scary truth by myself has eaten at me. I'm exhausted. But my brother's going through something, too. Drew would never bail on me if it weren't something serious. The distress in his voice, the panic in his texts…no. No, whatever he's carrying is heavy enough as it is.

"It's nothing," I say.

"Gretch."

"Okay, it's something, but"—I wipe my nose with the back of my hand—"it can wait."

"You know you can tell me."

I drag a hand under one eye and then the other and whisper, "I know."

"Can you at least tell me that you're safe? You're not in trouble, are you? In case you've forgotten, I'm a lawyer. If you need help escaping the country, I can make that happen."

A laugh erupts from my chest and I'm thankful for the levity. "One: I'm safe. Two: I'm not in trouble. And three: you're a patent lawyer. If I needed to escape the country, pretty sure Mom would be my first call."

"Fair," he says. "You promise to tell me eventually, right?"

"Yeah. You?"

"I promise."

"I love you," I say.

"I love you more."

After we hang up, I clock the time on my home screen. I usher myself through a few deep breaths to ward off another wave of tears.

Connor and I will spend the next five days together. Him and me. Car rides. Meals. Hikes. Hotel suites.

God, there's no way we'll get through this unscathed.

I have to remain focused on what I came here to do. I didn't come this far, spend all this money, to get distracted by my brother's best friend. Damn him and his perfect face, kissable lips and penchant for showing up when I least expect him to.

And damn him for breaking my heart.

Picking myself up by my bootstraps, proverbially speaking, I collect my things—along with my sanity—and make my way toward Connor's gate. I find a pub style restaurant and settle into a booth near the back to wait out the next couple of hours.

Once I've placed my order, I retrieve my phone and open Connor's contact. Ten days ago, I blocked his number. I never intended for it to be a conclusive message as to the status of our relationship. I was only trying to minimize distractions.

Except, thoughts of Connor haven't minimized at all. They're fully maximized. Every browser tab in my brain is open, my heart clicking the refresh button every few seconds.

There was a time when his comfort was my favorite kind. It's hard to imagine ever getting there again, but I want to believe it's possible. Not all that long ago, I was still wishing, hoping and praying I would wind up here with him.

And he's on his way here. To me.

My mind shifts back into focus as the waitress sets my turkey club in front of me.

I've already begun to overthink everything and, overthinking, I remind myself, will only make it worse. With that, I straighten my spine on a resolute breath and unceremoniously unblock Connor's contact.

"It is what it is," I mumble, words for only me, myself and I to hear.

Chapter Nine

THE KISS

GRETCHEN

three years ago

MY CHEST RISES and falls in long breaths, my lungs heavy like hundred-pound weights behind my sternum. Music pulses a steady thrum from the ballroom on the other side of the wall. There's a predatory look in his gaze that's half hunger, half tortured.

I know what I want and it feels like he might want the same thing.

The summer heat has subsided from a blistering sizzle to a balmy haze since the sun has dipped below the horizon. A breeze sweeps across the balcony sending wisps of hair fluttering around my face and the loose bow tie tucked under the open collar of his dress shirt jostles with each gentle wind. The slit of my gown billows open on a mild gust, exposing my leg to my upper thigh.

I swallow the lump in my throat. "What now?"

His eyes dip to my mouth. Then he wraps one arm firmly around my waist, his open palm on the bare skin of my back as he guides us around the dark corner. He pins me against the stone wall with the weight of his body and my breath catches with the exquisite pressure.

I fist the open collar of his shirt. He lowers his face toward mine while he brushes a lock of hair behind my ear. His thumb moves over my bottom lip and they part for him.

Mouth in a hover above mine, he asks, "Why didn't you bring a date tonight, Gretch?"

His wanton eyes reverently glide across my features before finally meeting my gaze. "Because you weren't supposed to have a date either."

Our lips collide. Tongues clash and plunge. Heads swivel in a passionate frenzy. We devour each other, grabbing and tugging in every way we can.

He presses into me, hips meeting hips, chests plastered together and still, he's not close enough. My body says *closer, more.*

I jerk back to catch my breath and his mouth moves over my jaw and down my neck. My nipples pebble beneath the fabric under his touch. Palms cupping my breasts, he pushes them up and the flesh swells over the top of my neckline right before he lowers his hot tongue to my equally feverish skin and drags it from one side, down the valley of my cleavage and up the other side in one fluid motion.

He groans against my collarbone, the sound reckless and feral. The next second, his mouth surrounds mine again, hand buried in my hair.

I touch him everywhere, my hands all over every inch I can reach.

His hands, his lips, the intensity is too much. Every brush of his tongue fans the flame igniting my core. I need him. Every intentional touch—the gentle, yet firm, motions of his mouth and his rough, ardent grip on my waist—says he wants me. That he *needs* me, too.

Has he wanted this as long as I have? If today had started off differently, would we have gotten here sooner? I don't know and, honestly, I don't care, because this moment, with him, is the only place I want to be.

Both of us gasping for air, he rests his forehead against mine as we suck in a breath…and then another.

A soft hand settles on my cheek then glides down my neck. I tilt my head to grant more access. His eyes trace every movement of his hand over my body, a dealer studying a priceless piece of art. The deliberately torturous journey of his touch travels down to my hip and then around to palm my backside.

Lips against my ear, he rasps, "Your ass in this dress, Gretch. It's been driving me crazy all night."

He squeezes my ass, his gentle touch turning rough as he snatches me closer. The area between my legs throbs and I moan at the slightest contact of him hard beneath me.

A hand slides through the slit of my gown, warm palm grazing my bare leg. He doesn't need to ask for permission; I hike my leg up to his waist and the satin falls open. I'm exposed up to the hinge of my hip bone and it only fuels my need for more—I need his hands, his mouth everywhere. He knows what I need, he always does. His palm glides all the way up to find the bare skin of my ass.

"God, you're sexy as hell," he groans.

I writhe into him and his body shifts to meet me, both of us chasing that friction. When we find it, he smothers my moan as our mouths meet again. Our lips and tongues tease and chase as our bodies rock in tandem.

The frantic passion that started this turns wild, daring. My lips swell from the intensity of our kissing, but I don't want to stop. I never want this to end. Because, right now, it feels like he's mine and I'm his. *Finally*.

My hand moves down his chest and over his belt. I palm him through his pants, applying a bit of pressure, and he groans. His breath catches in his throat and I smile against his lips.

Then, something shifts. Time stops.

No. *He* stops.

Labored breaths land heavy on my neck. His hands come to the wall on either side of my head and the leg I had wrapped around his waist drops to the ground. Every point of contact suddenly gone. He pushes off the wall like a warm blanket being peeled off me in the dead of winter. I'm left motionless before him, breathless and waiting.

A raw current of vulnerability spears through me when he averts his gaze. The man that just kissed me into oblivion, touched me in ways nobody else ever has, can't even look at me.

He rakes a hand down his face before he sputters, "I'm...I'm sorry." My heart sinks. "That was a mistake."

"What?" I breathe.

"I can't do this. I'm sorry."

Before I can stop it, he walks away and he doesn't look back.

Chapter Ten

DO YOU WANT ME TO LEAVE?

CONNOR

Gretchen needs you.

Talk about my personal kryptonite. Even if I'm three years too late to play the I'll-always-show-up-for-her card, a week and a half of Gretchen's radio silence still wasn't enough to stop me from getting on this plane.

"I don't want her to be alone," had been Drew's words to me earlier. While I rushed to wrap things up at the office, I asked my best friend to explain the situation to me. He didn't have much to offer other than that he suspects Gretchen is hiding something.

The guilt nearly destroyed me on the spot.

If Drew knew half the truth I've kept from him, he wouldn't have asked me to come, that's for damn sure.

I made him a promise. A promise that I broke three years ago in colossal fashion.

But she had kissed me back. Like, *really* kissed me. For long minutes that felt like an eternity and the blink of an eye all at once, that balcony was heaven on earth. Until it wasn't. Until my guilty conscience grabbed me by the balls and I stopped it.

I told myself that it was the right thing to do as Drew's threats and warnings from years past echoed furiously in my ears.

What Drew's cautionary voice didn't account for at the time—and that I learned too late—is that, while Drew is my best friend, Gretchen was an unexpected bright spot that had been slowly, innocently burrowing into the deepest corners of my heart since we were kids. We both grew up and suddenly, my heart wasn't just a heart anymore. It was a Gretchen shaped ball of hope. And that hope fell dead in my wake with each step I took in the opposite direction.

The jolt of the plane hitting the tarmac startles me awake. The haunting melody of James Morrison's "Don't You Forget About Me" drifts through my headphones. The higher powers-that-be must have my name on their bingo card today. I press the *skip* button.

My gaze turns toward the window. In the distance, beyond Phoenix proper, a sea of orange-red hued mesas pierce the blue sky above. The late-June heat practically rises off the rock formations in every direction.

I toggle off airplane mode on my phone and wait for it to recalibrate to the new time zone. Gretchen landed a few hours ago. Surely she's been in touch with Drew by now, but I still don't have any messages from her.

The fasten seat belt sign goes off and everyone rushes to stand. I'll never understand the whole *let's stand up so we can wait* plane debarkment philosophy. As the sound of passengers collecting their luggage from the overhead bins fills the cabin, I remain in my seat and navigate to my texts to let Gretchen know I've landed.

I'm mid-text when a message pops up on my screen.

GRETCHEN

I'm at your gate.

Ten minutes later, I step off the jet-bridge into the crowded gate area. Headphones looped around my neck, I eagerly scan from left to right. It's her long black hair I spot first. Her face comes into view as she bounces on her toes to look over and around the other passengers.

Her shoulders dip in relief when I step into her line of vision. Just like when she answered that door eleven days ago, the stupid grin on my face can't be stopped. The return smile that curls the corner of her lips is less gleeful-delight like mine and more irritated-amusement. Beautiful, all the same.

"Are you always the last person to get off the plane?"

"Yes," I deadpan.

She pins me with those dark eyes, beguile gleaming at their centers. The urge to scoop her into a hug is so natural, so intense that I almost miss her next words.

"Hmmm. So, is that, like, your superiority complex or something?"

I blink. "My…superiority complex? Wasn't aware I had one."

She scoffs. "All men have a superiority complex, Connor."

A laugh bursts out of me and her almost-smile goes rogue, face bright with joy.

"Do tell how letting everyone ahead of me off the plane equates to a superiority complex," I say.

"Easy," she shrugs. "That plane and all the other lowly passengers are mere peasants at your feet. Everyone else files off the plane row by row, you know, as normal people do, while *you* sit in your ivory tower of judgment thinking to yourself, 'these poor people have it all wrong.' I bet at least half a dozen people offered to let you go in front of them and you just kept your headphones on and pretended not to hear them."

I purse my lips.

Her brows lift. "I'm right," she adds.

"I didn't say that."

She leans in conspiratorially. "You didn't have to."

"Maybe I prefer the comfort of my seat instead of standing shoulder to shoulder with a bunch of sweaty strangers."

"Airplane seats are not comfortable," she retorts as she crosses her arms over her chest. I order my gaze to avoid the hint of cleavage that peeks over the neckline of her white tank top.

I lift my hat to run a hand through my hair, stifling another smile. "When you're six-two sitting in the window seat and the options are"—I hold out one flat palm—"mediocre chair and"—I hold out another palm—"hunchback of Notre Dame, the answer is pretty straightforward."

Gretchen's lips fold inward, her own wry smile barely in check. "You see, maybe the window seat was your first mistake."

"Beggars can't be choosers when you buy the ticket three hours before take-off." I lower my head. "My options were limited."

She takes in a deep breath, releasing it on a heavy sigh. "Right." She clears her throat and fiddles with the handle of her carry-on. "Well, I'm sorry you got dragged into—"

"Don't be sorry," I say pointedly. "I'm not sorry."

Her expression sobers as luggage wielding strangers whizz by, streaks of color zigging and zagging in a blur all around us. Our gazes lock. Memories of conversations and touches and kisses materialize in the two feet of space between us. I wonder if her heart pounds as hard as mine does when she looks at me in that way that makes time stand still?

"Excuse me," a stranger says from my left, breaking our stare.

I move aside to let him pass. A breath later, when I step back into my previous position, the moment's over.

Gretchen opts for a subject change. "Did Drew tell you anything about what's going on?"

"Nothing. You?"

Shaking her head, she worries her bottom lip. Nervous fingers fidget with her luggage handle again as she avoids my stare.

"I'm sure everything's fine, Fish."

Her startled eyes jump to mine like I've just slapped her.

"Are you alri—" I begin as someone slams into me from behind and I'm pushed forward. Instinctively, I grab Gretchen by the arm to keep us both from toppling over. The offending stranger hollers a quick apology over his shoulder as he sprints off and I steady myself on my feet.

Reluctantly, I remove my hand from her arm as I pretend not to notice the electricity that pulses through my fingertips where my skin touched hers.

"I'm sorry," I say, desperate to get a read on her thoughts.

"For what?" Her throat bobs. "For calling me that or for bumping into me?" Her shoulders may be square and her spine straight, but I recognize the ruse. All the signs are there—no eye contact, the luggage handle she can't decide if she wants up or down, unsteady feet shifting beneath her. She's uncomfortable.

I said the wrong thing.

With a restrained release of breath, I squeeze the back of my neck. "Both, I guess."

She nods imperceptibly before she finally meets my gaze, her face and tone both schooled into the same forfeiting expression. "Look, I know I said I wasn't ready to talk, but I'm not under any ridiculous assumptions that we're gonna be able to spend the next five days together and *not* talk about it, so I—"

"Why have you been ignoring my texts?"

"What?"

"You weren't ready to talk and that's fine. I'll wait. But what about my other messages?" Her eyes bounce around so fast I can't catch them.

"I didn't see your other messages." She swallows, voice sinking to a whisper. "I blocked your number."

I blink. Sorrow and disbelief stab at that three-year-old wound until it's ripped clean open. "You blocked me?"

"It wasn't gonna be forever, okay? I just…needed…I have a lot on my mind and I needed to not think about"—she waves a hand between us—"this right now."

My chin drops to my chest. I take in a hard sniff to squelch the emotion I already feel at the back of my throat.

She blocked me.

When I lift my head, I find her glassy-eyed gaze and I force myself not to look away. My resolve does nothing to steady the quiver in my voice. "Gretch, if you don't want me here, I'll go buy my return ticket right now. No hard feelings, I promise. I don't wanna be here if you don't want—"

"That's not what I'm—"

"Do you want me to leave?" My voice rises above the fray, landing decisively on the woman in front of me who looks like she's carrying the burdens of a thousand men.

With every silent beat, her shoulders soften, but the tears are right there, ready to fall at any moment. Finally, she whispers, "No."

That's all I need to know. "Let me see your phone." I hold out my hand.

"Why?"

"Because I'm not letting you block me." I curl my fingers toward my palm. "I'll wait until you're ready to talk, you have my word. But you don't cut me out in the meantime." When she makes no move to reach for her phone, I add, "Give it."

She pulls her phone from her pocket and drops it in my hand. "You're already unblocked, dumbass. I texted you fifteen minutes ago, remember?"

"Yeah, yeah," I quip, my smirk a reflection of hers. "Tell it to the judge. Passcode?" I ask.

"0630," she says.

I tsk. "Your birthday? Seriously?"

"Seriously. What's yours?"

I input her password. "0817," I say as I navigate to the contacts icon on her home screen.

"Your jersey numbers? Seriously?" She clutches her chest in mock outrage.

Chin still to my chest, my fingers freeze. I grin devilishly as I eye her from beneath lifted lashes. Gretchen Fisher remembers my jersey numbers.

She holds my stare for only a second before she rolls her eyes to the rafters and says, "Oh, shut up!"

I bite back my proud retort, confirm that she's left me unblocked, and hand over her phone. Once she stuffs it back in her pocket, Gretchen yanks the handle of her rolling bag to the highest locked position. I take the carry-on she has draped over her shoulder and throw it over mine.

I nudge my head toward the exit, signaling for us to go.

"Thank you." Her words come quiet, reminiscent of the shy nine-year-old girl I met thirteen years ago. I look over at her and she says it again. "Thank you for coming."

"You're welcome."

Chapter Eleven

THE NICKNAME

GRETCHEN

thirteen years ago, summer

I'M ONLY a few chapters into *Anne of Green Gables* when my brother and his new friend rush onto the back porch in a mad dash. Mom's stern voice telling them to close the door is cut off with the sound of the sliding door clicking shut.

The boy I don't know runs past me with a football in his hand as Drew rushes past even faster on my other side. It happens so quickly, I pull my knees to my chest for a second, afraid they might crash into me.

"Vining! I'm open," my brother yells as he hops over the corner of the pool with a hand in the air on his way to the yard beyond.

For the next several minutes, I read while they toss the ball around. My attention is mostly on my book but is occasionally pulled the boys' direction when their voices are loud enough to distract me.

"Fisher! Go long!" I look up to see Drew's friend jogging backward while my brother runs the other way to the far corner of our large backyard. The ball flies through the air, but when Drew reaches out to catch it, it bounces off his fingers, hits the top of the fence and flies into the greenbelt.

Drew curses—as he always does when Mom and Dad aren't around to hear it. Ha! Now he has to venture into the brush behind our fence that hasn't been mowed in months. Serves him right.

"What are you reading?" I turn toward the voice. Drew's friend now stands at the edge of the patio.

"*Anne of Green Gables*." I hold up the book to show him the cover.

Drew yelps something about snakes and critters as he wades into the waist-high brush.

"I'm Connor."

I hold a hand above my eyes to shield the sun when I look up at him. "My name's Gretchen."

"Do you read a lot?" he asks.

I shrug. "Yeah. I read about two books a week." Mom tells me to say that proudly, but I'm usually nervous to tell people.

"Wow! That's really cool."

"Some of the kids at school think it's weird."

"Nah, those kids are weird. I think it's awesome." Connor winks at me and it makes me feel a little better.

We're quiet for a few seconds as we watch Drew behind the fence, *still* on the hunt for the football.

"Your brother gonna be okay back there?"

I laugh. "If not, he deserves it."

Connor laughs too and the sound makes me smile.

A thought comes to mind. I close the book and look back to Connor. "Why do you guys call each other by your last names?"

He squints for a moment. "I guess it's because that's what Coach calls us."

"Why does your coach do it?"

"The last names on the back of our jerseys are the only way he can tell us apart when we're on the field."

I guess that makes sense.

"Found it!" Drew yells, football held high above his head.

"It was nice to meet you, Gretchen," Connor says over his shoulder as he heads back to the yard to join Drew.

A little while later, I'm still reading. Drew and Connor are still tossing the football, but they're not running plays anymore. Instead, they're lobbing the wildest passes they can come up with. Most of the time they end up laid out in the grass, either from diving to make a catch or laughing so hard they can't stay on their feet.

I have my nose deep in chapter ten when the football bounces on to the porch beside me. I lean over the armrest of my chair to pick it up.

"Little fish, right here," Connor says. He smiles at me, hands up ready for me to throw it back to him.

Little fish. The nickname makes me grin. Nobody outside of my family has ever given me one. I like it, except for one thing. "I'm not little."

He twists his lips like he's thinking. "Okay, how about just Fish then?"

CONNOR STAYED FOR DINNER TONIGHT. Mom and Dad spent most of the time talking football with the boys and asking Connor about his family.

I didn't say much but I listened a lot.

His family recently moved here from a nearby smaller school district to give him a better chance at a football scholarship. He and my brother met at the first day of football camp earlier this week. He has two older brothers: one who's three years older and begins college this fall and the other who's five years older and is about to start his senior year of college. He said since it's only him and his parents now, it was easier to make the move. Something about downsizing, although I'm not sure what that means.

But my favorite part of dinner was Connor calling me *Fish* when he asked me to pass the parmesan cheese.

Chapter Twelve

IT'S THE MOST PAIN I'VE EVER FELT

CONNOR

"I ALREADY HAVE dinner reservations for tonight." Forty-five minutes into the two-hour drive from Phoenix to Sedona, Gretchen finally speaks. "It's some place my mom found online. I thought it'd be nice."

"I'm sure it will be," I say, checking my blind spot to change lanes. "What kind of restaurant is it?"

"A steakhouse, I think. They have a dress code, but I know you probably packed in a rush so we don't have to go if you—"

"Drew told me. I'm all set." I chance a quick glance her way and only manage to catch her gaze briefly before she looks away.

"Oh. Well, okay. Good."

Silence consumes the car again, the hum of tires over pavement grating like nails on a chalkboard. Gretchen's intent gaze is locked to her passenger window, fingers knotted in her lap. It takes everything in me to not reach across the console and grab her hand to reassure her that, despite everything, I'm still her friend.

At least, I want to be.

It's too early to force an unwanted conversation, so I roll my neck to relieve some of the tension and turn up the volume on the radio. Not five minutes later, Gretchen's asleep—head on her hand, elbow propped on the window.

My phone buzzes in my pocket. I pull it free and see Lauren's name flashing on my screen. On a quiet sigh, I silence it and drop it in the cupholder.

Another conversation with Lauren feels inevitable now, but hell if I know what I'm supposed to say. I'm certainly not going to try and figure it out with Gretchen two feet away.

When we're about fifteen minutes from the resort, Gretchen stirs, groggily stretching her arms out in front of her. "How long was I out?"

"Maybe thirty minutes."

She stifles a yawn. "Sorry. I was up at four this morning."

"No worries. We're almost there."

She offers no response, only turns back to the view outside her window.

When silence threatens to take over the car again, I can't help myself. I want her to talk to me, *dammit.*

I turn the music down. "When are you planning to go back to New York?" She turns to me with a bewildered expression, like she forgot I was here. Like her mind was a million miles away. Not gonna lie, level ten hurt right there.

She gives her head a quick shake and says, "I'm sorry, what?"

"I asked when you're planning to go back to New York."

"Oh, um…I'm not sure." She twists her hands in her lap. "The company I interned at has a position available that I'm applying for. Interviews are in a couple of weeks. I suppose if that goes well, I could move back before the end of summer."

"That's awesome. I'm sure you'll do great." She shrugs. "You don't think you'll get it?"

"I don't know. My boss really liked me and she's the one who recommended me for it, but I'm trying not to get my hopes up."

"What company is it?" I've missed so much of her life. Her ups and downs. Her accomplishments. *Her.* The Connor of Gretchen's past wouldn't need to ask. I'd have known all there is to know. She'd have texted to tell me all about it and then we would have Face-Timed for an hour to talk about it some more.

There's that ache again.

"Saks Fifth Avenue."

An incredulous huff tumbles out of me. "Are you for real? Gretch, that's amazing!"

One corner of her mouth curves up before she rakes her lower lip between her teeth. "Have you ever even been inside a Saks?"

"Um, excuse me," I say, feigning outrage. "I may be a dude, but I don't live under a rock. Yes, I've been inside a Saks, Gretchen."

A broad smile spreads across her face as a genuine laugh pulls from her chest. *Thank God.* The way my heart constricts and softens at the same time leaves no room for misunderstanding—it still belongs to her.

"Buying a gift for a woman, I'm sure," she teases.

My phone buzzes.

I sneak a quick look—Lauren's name lights up my screen again. I decline the call, flip the phone around and pretend Gretchen didn't see me send my ex's call to voicemail.

"What makes you so sure of that?" I ask in hopes of breezing past the interruption.

"I've studied fashion for four years, worked alongside the buyer for menswear at Saks for an entire semester, and I've seen what you wear, Connor."

"I can't decide if I should be impressed or offended." I eye her sidelong before I force my gaze back to the road.

She snickers. "Your wardrobe is fine, but I can tell you don't shop at Saks."

The joggers and t-shirt I have on are nothing special and I'm sure my baseball cap isn't doing my unruly hair any favors, but I changed clothes in a panic earlier. Between packing my suitcase, absorbing all the travel details that Drew was relaying and booking my flight via speakerphone, I didn't pay much attention to how I looked.

"Come on," she goads. "It'll feel so much better to admit it."

I rub a hand along my jaw. My smirk wants to run full tilt when I glance over and find shrewd glee written all over her face, but I tame it into submission. "Lauren ordered a pair of shoes and I picked them up for her," I finally concede.

"There it is," she says with a satisfied expression before her grin settles into a thin line. "You don't have to ignore her calls just because I'm around."

I take in a steadying breath before I answer, "It's not that." I blink slowly once as though it'll erase the shame. It doesn't. "We haven't spoken since the break-up."

The voice of the GPS guide mercifully interrupts the moment, directing me to the next exit. I roll the car to a stop at a red light at the end of our exit ramp and a weighty silence settles in as we take in the scenery.

The sun is still a few hours from setting and we're far from the urban landscape of Phoenix now. The view outside is no longer bustling highways, office buildings and sprawling neighborhoods. Now, it's nothing but the orange-pink glow of the sun cast down upon the red-toned desert mesas in the distance.

Gretchen's the first one to speak, voice cautious and soft. "Drew seemed really upset with you about the breakup."

I let out an exhausted breath. "Yeah."

"I'm sorry. We don't have to talk about it if you don't want to."

"It's fine." I remove my hat and rake a hand through my hair, tugging at the ends as the light turns green. "Drew was kind of blindsided by the whole thing. I get why he's upset."

Warily, I meet her gaze. There's no malice or judgment to be found in the soft lines of her face, only a sort of watchful concern as she waits for me to go on.

I slide my hat back on, my other hand wound tight on the steering wheel. "Things with Lauren were more complicated than he ever knew."

Gretchen looks at me like I'm a puzzle she can't figure out. "How so?"

Sighing, I bolster myself for my confession. The resort looms as we draw closer. "I, um…I thought I loved her, but…" My voice trails off. There's no good way to end that sentence.

"But you were together for two and a half years," she says.

Guilt clamps around my vocal cords as I whisper, "I know."

We scan the property as I turn into the parking area. Several burnt sienna colored stucco structures are laid out in front of us. Blending perfectly into the red-hued natural horizon of rock mesas beyond, the separate buildings designate the lobby from the spa and guest rooms and private villas. Cacti and desert ground cover make up the patches of landscape around and between each of the buildings. If one could ever consider a sweltering desert a paradise, this would be it.

Once I find a parking spot, I turn off the engine and shift to face Gretchen. The curious look in her eyes tells me we're not done with this conversation.

"Why would you date somebody for that long if you didn't love them?"

I roll the car keys over in my hand. A queasy feeling rises in my throat, but I swallow it down. "I really thought I did." I shake my head. "I don't know, it's like I tried so hard to convince myself it was true that I eventually started to believe it."

Like a hostage, Gretchen holds my stare. "So, you loved her once and fell out of love, or you never loved her at all?"

"It didn't…it…it never felt the way it was supposed to feel." *It never felt like it did with you.* "I know it was some form of love, but I wasn't *in* love with her."

The moment I realized Lauren wasn't it for me is a memory I've tried countless times to forget.

It had been six months since we had exchanged *I love yous.* Lauren and I were at Drew and Reagan's place playing Cards Against Humanity. Everything was great—bellies full, tons of laughter. Lauren's hand was on my thigh and mine was on her nape, massaging her neck. Our friends darted off to the kitchen for another round of beers. Lauren leaned in to whisper something in my ear, but I didn't hear a word because my gaze was caught on my best friend and his wife across the apartment.

Drew came up behind Reagan and she turned to meet him. He smiled down at her and she melted into him. The two beer bottles she'd been holding were set aside as my best friend wrapped the love of his life in a hug and swayed back and forth four, five, six times.

For those twenty seconds, it was like nothing else existed. Lauren and I weren't there. The stresses of work, family and finances were forgotten. It was just the two of them, dancing to no music at all, barefoot in their kitchen. And there I was, sitting next to the woman I supposedly loved and I couldn't picture anything like that with her. I should have ended it then. Instead, I spent the next year trying to force a square peg into a round hole.

Gretchen inhales deeply, rolls her lips and brings one leg up on the seat as she turns to face me.

"Are you gonna say anything?" I finally ask.

"I'm not sure you wanna hear what I have to say." Her voice is gentle, but the words hit like a sledgehammer.

"I never should have let it go on as long as I did but I don't know…I…" Thoughts fade in and out of focus as Gretchen glares at me, arms crossed. "I didn't want to hurt her and I know how dumb that sounds because the longer I waited, the more it hurt her in the end. I know I messed up."

"So, what? You're gonna ignore her calls forever?" Her edged words slice through me, hitting their mark.

"No," I sigh.

"No?"

"No, Gretchen. I'm not!" My growing frustration is unwarranted because I know I'm in the wrong, but I can't help but feel a little defensive.

As if she's read my mind, she responds in kind, accusations launched like arrows landing bullseye every time. "That woman gave you two and a half years of her life. I was at that dinner. I saw it. She loves you. She was probably expecting a proposal from you. Then you dump her out of nowhere and you can't even answer her calls?"

That flicker of hope I'd been clinging to, that we could maybe restore our friendship and, perhaps with time, it might turn into more, dies in an instant. She looks at me like I'm a stranger and it sucks the air from my lungs, suffocating that ember to ash.

Why would she give me another chance? A man who, for all intents and purposes, led someone on for over two years. The same man who had the only woman he's ever truly wanted in his arms three years ago—the only woman whose lips have ever felt like home—and walked away.

I left Gretchen there. I never called. I never texted.

Regret strangles any defense I have left. When I don't respond, she continues. "She needs closure, Connor. You owe her that."

I absorb the cruel truth of her reprimand. "You're right."

This isn't how I expected things to start off between us. I was so hung up on mending things with Gretchen, I couldn't see the forest for the trees. But I see it now. The big picture beyond the details. I can't make things right with Gretchen without giving my relationship with Lauren the proper closure it—*she*—deserves.

"You're awfully wise for all of your twenty-two years," I say, hoping to break the tension.

"You mean *almost* twenty-two years. I've still got a few days left." She preens with a dainty hand under her chin. The face scrunch and the constellation of freckles across the bridge of her nose highlight the hint of mischief glimmering in her eyes.

Damn, she's so pretty.

"My mistake. *Almost* twenty-two. Still, though, you're not supposed to be better at relationships than me. I'm *almost* twenty-nine." I mirror her playful expression.

She lets out a mirthless laugh that punches me straight in the gut. Her body turns away and it takes every bit of humor with it. She grabs the purse at her feet and says, "I actually don't know much about relationships. But I know how much it hurts to not get closure." Door open, she moves to get out of the car but stops with one leg still inside. She turns her profile on me, but doesn't meet my eyes. "I think it's the most pain I've ever felt."

Gretchen climbs out of the car and doesn't look back, leaving me alone with nothing but karma and regret to keep me company.

Chapter Thirteen

DON'T BE WEIRD

GRETCHEN

I DIDN'T STICK to the plan.

How was I supposed to avoid *the conversation* when he shows up in black joggers, a faded University of Michigan t-shirt and a backwards ball cap? The attack felt personal, if I'm being honest. *Thanks, universe.*

Before he landed, I told myself not to bring it up yet. That it was best to wait until things between us felt more comfortable. A fresh start, of sorts. We could take a day—or five—and find that natural rhythm that we always seem to find and then...*then* we could talk about what the hell happened three years ago.

But he stepped off that jet bridge looking all *him* and that damn tug was there again. Like your favorite throw blanket or that one coffee mug you reach for every morning even though you have three dozen others on the shelf.

Or your favorite nickname spoken by your favorite person. For all the familiar feelings of comfort and safety it brings, it also blurs the edges of your well-advised boundaries.

Fish. That's all it took.

I managed to deflect the conversation to later, but not before I'd already said too much. Not before I'd confessed to blocking his number. Not before implying he should give Lauren the closure he never gave me.

Heart on sleeve plus hot guy in joggers divided by *Fish* equals Gretchen spiral.

As we approach the door to our suite, I construct a mental checklist of all the things I need to do going forward.

1. Stop being weird.

That's it. That's the list.

Being aloof and all *woman-scorned* will get me nowhere. Tonight, I have to tell him why I'm really here. Connor, I remind myself, dropped everything to be here and that has to count for something. Friendship, at least. Right now I could use a friend.

Connor swipes the key card and shoves the door open, holding it in place for me to squeeze past him.

I quickly take stock of the complete space I've become all too familiar with by viewing the resort's accommodations pictures online. A modest kitchenette is tucked in the back left corner, a small dining table surrounded by four chairs setting on the far wall on the same side. The wall straight ahead, beyond the living area, isn't a wall at all. It's one enormous sliding glass door with unob-structed views of the desert landscape in the distance. To my right is a set of double doors, propped open to reveal the bedroom complete with its own patio access door, a king-sized bed and an ensuite bathroom—the only bathroom.

Connor empties his pockets on the entry table and I turn to face him. "The sofa has a pull-out bed. I'll sleep there and you can have the bedroom."

Connor chuckles and the knots in my chest instantly unravel at the sound. Dropping the car keys to the table, he doesn't even look up when he says, "No."

"No?"

"That's not happening, Gretch. I'll take the sofa bed, you take the bedroom."

"Are you sure? I mean, we could alternate nights."

He halts what he's doing, his gaze a question as creases form between his brows. Slowly, a self-assured grin ticks up the corner of his mouth.

"Seriously, Connor. You're like…tall. There's no way that sofa bed is big enough for you."

"Was Drew gonna get the 'you're like, tall' speech when he insisted you take the bedroom?" A playful twinkle flickers in his eyes.

Without missing a beat, I quip back, "Of course not. He still owes me for all those times I 'didn't notice' he was sneaking out after curfew." The air quotes emphasizing *didn't notice* really drive the point home.

The room warms with Connor's deep, boisterous laugh and my face splits into a smile. "Is that right?"

"Damn straight. He's indebted to me for at least another ten years."

He closes the distance between us. "Well, that may be so, but"—he stops in front of me—"I'm still taking the sofa." He bops his index finger on the tip of my nose and says, "Bedroom's yours," before sweeping past me to prop his bag against the wall.

Resigned, I head into the bedroom and toss my suitcase on the bed. When I open the closet door, I'm pleasantly surprised at the space available. "The closet's huge," I holler toward the living room. "You can at least unpack your stuff in here."

This olive branch, thankfully, he accepts without protest. Twenty minutes later we've split the bedroom dresser drawers between us and the closet is full of our hanging items.

I offer Connor the bathroom and bedroom first to get ready for dinner. Settling in at the dining table, I wait for my laptop to boot up as I send off a text to my brother.

ME

Made it to Sedona. I hope you and Reagan are doing okay. Please update me when you can.

Love you.

When the three dots don't immediately appear, I set the phone aside and open my email on my computer.

As promised, Monica sent me the job description for the Executive Assistant position. She included the details of my first-round interview in a couple weeks. After I add the interview to my calendar and input the appropriate reminders, I send her a quick reply with my resume attached.

I spend a few minutes reviewing the job description. It's nearly the exact job I was doing in my internship, just in a different department. With Monica's referral and my experience with the company, I really am perfect for this position.

My former boss and I email back and forth for the next fifteen minutes. By the end, we've scheduled a video chat for next week where she's offered to prep me for my interview as well as penciled in tentative plans to grab dinner together while I'm in town.

I close my laptop as the bedroom doors swing open and Connor steps out. His attention is on buttoning the cuffs of his shirt, and I unashamedly drink him in. Gray dress pants over his long, thick legs. Solid black dress shirt that's fitted perfectly so across his chest. The top two buttons he's left undone seems like another personal attack from the universe, but...*whatever.*

Don't. Be. Weird.

"Your turn," he says absently, finishing up with his right cuff. Before he can catch me gawking, I jump from my seat and duck past him into the bedroom.

The weight of Connor's stare as I dash back and forth across the room disorients me. I pretend not to notice as I collect my blush pink pencil dress from the closet and drape it across the bed. After laying out my makeup palettes on the vanity and plugging in my curling iron, I turn toward him, praying my face doesn't betray me.

There he is: one shoulder leaned against the doorframe, right ankle crossed over the left, hands tucked in his pockets, all easy and unbothered.

"Why are you looking at me like that?"

"It's just dinner, Gretch."

Except, it's not—it's a confessional. Can it ever be *just dinner* between Connor and me? I'm not convinced it can. I'm suddenly at a loss for why I ever decided to make this dinner reveal such a big deal.

A rush of air escapes my lips as I stumble over a reply, "Of course. I know that."

"Okay," he says, unconvinced, as he pushes off the wall. "You just kind of seem like a hamster spinning in a wheel right now." In other words, *you're being weird* and of course he sees right through me.

I can't bring myself to admit he's right. "I'm fine." I'm not fine.

I swipe my toiletry bag from the vanity table and head to the bathroom, but Connor's voice stops me. "Hey, I saw a pharmacy up the road. I need to grab a few things I forgot. You need anything?"

"I'm good. What'd you forget?"

"Toothpaste."

"You can borrow mine if you—"

"And a toothbrush."

I grimace. "Okay, gross. I can't help you with that. Sorry, not sorry."

He grins. "I'll be back in twenty. Text me if you think of anything."

I wave him off and close myself in the bathroom. I don't need to shower. All of my makeup and hair products are in the bedroom. I have no reason to be in here other than the six-foot-two man hoarding all of the oxygen on the other side of the door.

The sound of the front door closing vibrates the wall at my back and I let out a long breath.

Connor's cool, calm, collected nature has always been contrary to my perpetual state of a little worried and a lot trying-to-act-like-I'm-not.

Has he forgotten the events of the past several weeks? To start off, we see each other for the first time in three years, then he dumps his girlfriend *and then* he drops everything to jump on a plane to be here with me and, despite the lack of closure, he still manages to look and feel completely effortless even though us being here together is totally bizarre…and weird.

This whole situation is *freaking* weird and I hate how it doesn't seem to faze him.

I'm probably overthinking everything, so I throw my hair in a messy bun and decide to hop in the shower after all, to clear my head. To regroup.

I came here to meet the woman who gave birth to me. Everything—every*one*—else is secondary.

Wrapped in one of the plush resort robes, I emerge from the steamy bathroom half an hour later.

It's not the muffled sounds of the television coming from the living room or the fact that the bedroom doors that were open before are now closed that gives his presence away. It's the tension in my shoulders easing, the warm smile that spreads across my face at the sight of the fountain Diet Coke and bag of peanut butter M&Ms on the vanity that tells me he's here.

And my hamster wheel slows to a crawl.

Chapter Fourteen

EARN BACK HER TRUST

CONNOR

LAUREN

> We broke up and now you don't want to talk to me. I don't get it but I guess I have to learn to be alright with it. But will you please tell me if you're okay? You ran out of the office this morning in a panic. I've called Drew and Reagan but they're not responding either. I'm worried, Connor.

ME

> I'm sorry. I promise I'm okay.

> Can I call you later tonight so we can talk?

LAUREN

> Of course. I'll be up. I want to talk to you.

THE PRESSURE in my chest releases. Do I know what I'm going to say to her? Not entirely, but I can't run from it anymore.

I slide my phone into my pocket as Gretchen serpentines through the restaurant on her way back from the restroom.

She stepped out of the bedroom earlier and I almost kissed her. No warning, no context, just damn near swept her into my arms and kissed her. The light pink dress atop her olive-toned skin that hugs every curve from her chest down over her narrow hips and around to her backside had me weak in the knees. The slit that opens over her right lower thigh is far from scandalous, but visions of another dress with a slit that sent my hands sweeping up the bare skin of her leg came to mind and I had to force those thoughts away.

Gretchen strides toward me from across the restaurant, the image of a goddess in perfect form. Her high heels give her legs for days on her five-seven frame.

A simple pair of diamond stud earrings are her only adornment. Even her makeup is simple, the beauty of her natural skin shining through the faint layer of color she's swept across her cheeks and eyelids. She never tries to hide the light freckles dotting her nose. No fake lashes. No bold lip color.

She's stunning with so little effort it utterly captivates me.

Gretchen lowers to her seat as she loops her loosely waved hair around to one shoulder, leaving her neck and collarbone on the other side exposed, less the narrow strap of her dress.

A noticeable breath pulls from deep in her chest before she releases it. Dropping the white cloth napkin to her lap, her gaze settles over her place setting before she nervously fidgets with the silverware.

I think she's hiding something. Drew's words from earlier slam into me. He's trusting me to be here for her.

It's not lost on me that the one person who probably shouldn't trust me around his sister is the one who's put all of his trust in me. Meanwhile, the one person I want to trust me the most in the world feels like she's slipping through my fingers, scared to give me these pieces of herself again because I didn't tend to them the way I should've the last time.

Make her comfortable. Earn back her trust.

"Tell me more about this job," I say.

Her shoulders relax a bit as she replies, "It's an Executive Assistant position for one of the Buyers in the shoe department."

"What exactly does a Buyer do?"

She takes a sip of water as I spin my own glass in my hand. "Buyers decide what items the store is going to carry. It's a lot of shopping different designer merchandise, testing products and consumer research."

"And you'd be involved in all that stuff?"

"Mmm," she says with a shrug. "Yes and no. It'll be a lot of paperwork and managing orders mostly. But assistants get to test out potential inventory sometimes, so I guess there could be a lot of beautiful shoes in my future." She smiles and it's the first moment I sense her guard dropping.

"Did you get to take a lot of inventory home when you worked there last semester?"

She chuckles. "No. I worked for the Buyer in the Men's Sportswear department. Not much for me to test out. Plus, I was only an intern, so it was mostly grunt work for me."

The waiter returns to the table and pours us each a glass of white wine. Gretchen eyes the bottle nervously as he leaves it on the table and walks away.

Leaning forward, she whispers, "Did you order this?"

"I did. Do you not like white wine? We can order something different if you want."

"No, I do. It's fine. Thank you." She takes a tentative sip as the tension returns to her body, walls resurrecting, brick by brick.

"Gretchen, just so we're clear, this meal is on me."

"No, Connor. *I* am paying for dinner. You didn't ask for any of this and I already planned to pay for it anyway."

She means that I didn't ask to be thrown onto a plane with only a few hours' notice. She assumes that, if I had a choice, I wouldn't be here. She's wrong. But even if she wasn't, I'd still want to pay for her dinner.

"There's no way I'm letting you buy me dinner," I say through a humorless laugh as I peruse the menu.

"What is that?" she says, distaste lacing her words.

"What is what?"

"That," she says so pointedly I can almost feel an invisible finger pressed into the center of my chest. "That condescending, male ego thing. You did it earlier about the sofa bed. I can pay for my meal as well as yours. Shocker, I know."

Our gazes lock until the server returns to take our order.

"Look," I say, watching the waiter's back for a moment before fixing my attention back on her. "I'm sorry if I came off arrogant or…domineering. I know you're capable and self-sufficient and you don't *need* me."

Her chin lowers, brows pinched as she swallows hard.

"And, for the record," I continue, "I know I didn't ask to be here." Her eyes lift to mine. "But of all the people who could be here with you, I'm glad it's me."

I see it then—that flicker of hurt that still remains. She wants to cry, but I know Gretchen. She's strong and stoic, almost to a fault. For a girl who cries easily, she doesn't give her tears over to just anybody. If you're not in her inner circle, she'll hold on to those tears. She'll blink them away all while pretending that everything is okay.

My heart splinters right down the middle, when she does exactly that.

"Gretch, if you'll let me, I'd like to buy you dinner."

The fact that it sounds like I'm asking her out on a date doesn't stop me. A flurry of thoughts cross her expression in waves like the light bouncing off a disco ball.

If I say yes, does that make this a date? Does he want it to be a date? Why now? Why not then?

It's time for a subject change. I can't let my regrets or her spiraling thoughts dampen this night before the entrees even arrive.

Make her comfortable. Earn back her trust.

"We don't have to decide right now. Tell me about your friend that was supposed to come with you. Drew said she was your roommate?"

Gretchen's face twitches as she reaches for her wine glass. She empties it in three gulps before placing the glass back on the table and bringing a fist to her mouth as she forces the last bit down her throat.

God, I must be batting a negative thousand at this point. I cock my head, concern mounting. "Gretch, what's going on?"

Cheeks flushed and hands trembling, she swipes the wine bottle and pours another glass. I reach out and lay a hand over her arm before she can toss it back.

"I'm not going to watch you get yourself drunk just so you can avoid talking to me. Tell me what's going on. Please."

I follow her gaze to where my fingers have circled around her wrist.

She pulls her arm away, whispering, "I lied to Drew. My room-mate was never coming."

"Okay," I exhale as I lean back in my seat. "So, the resort, the room…" My voice trails off, thoughts searching. After several drawn out seconds, I lean forward, forearms on the table. "Drew said you split the cost with your roommate and then she had to bail. But *you're* saying that you paid for it all from the beginning?"

She nods. "And before you jump in and demand to pay for half, just save your breath. It's already done."

I drag a hand down my face. Five nights at that resort must have cost her a fortune. She's fresh out of college and not even working yet.

"Why plan a trip, fake your friend bailing and *then* ask Drew to come? Why not plan the whole thing together and split the cost?"

"Because…" Her voice fades, eyes glassy. "*I* needed to plan this trip. I didn't want his input or his questions. I needed to do this for me, on my terms." She shakes her head. "And it wasn't about the money. I'd been planning this for a long time and I always imagined being here with…someone else. I love my brother, but he wasn't my first choice," she confesses, the last part coming on a hushed breath.

Jealousy that I have no right to feel burns inside me. "Who was your first choice?"

She reaches for her wine glass, her answer hidden behind lowered lashes. "It doesn't matter," she says.

"Gretch." I duck my head, begging for her to look at me. "What is this all about?"

I think she's hiding something. The apprehension that stirs in my stomach morphs to dread the longer she doesn't respond.

"It's not a vacation," she finally says to the napkin in her lap.

"Gretch, look at me. Please." Her head lifts, her features displaying a confidence that I know is all for show. "Whatever it is, you can trust me."

Over a taut silence, her wistful eyes search mine for any hint of malice or dishonesty. She won't find any. No matter what it is—however crazy or scary or illegal, even—it doesn't matter because I'll take it to my grave if she asks me to.

I'll do anything for her.

"I found my birth mom."

Chapter Fifteen

I MISSED THIS

GRETCHEN

THE WORDS LAND like poison on my tongue. I've held them in for too many months. Connor's invasive stare doesn't help either.

Unease hangs in the air between us, only interrupted by the waiter returning with our salads. The few beats of broken eye contact allow me to distract myself with my napkin, placing it just so, grabbing my fork and offering our thanks as the waiter exits.

Connor's vacant gaze ricochets all over me, taking inventory. Eyes, *check.* Hair, *check.* Fingers, *check.* Lips, *check.* Collarbone, *check.*

"Will you please say something?" I finally ask.

"I'm sorry, I…Your birth mom? You *found* her?"

"Yeah. Well, *I* didn't find her but I hired a professional who did."

His face slackens. "And you didn't tell anybody?"

I shake my head timidly as I shift the salad around with my fork. "I was planning to tell Drew tonight."

"But why'd you keep it a secret? Did you think he wouldn't support you?"

"Of course not. I know he would, but it's like I said: *I* needed to do this. If I told him everything beforehand, he would have started that big brother meddling thing and then he'd guilt me into telling Mom and Dad and I...I'm not ready for that yet. I wanted to plan everything, get him here and then tell him so he didn't have a chance to go all *Drew* on me."

Connor snickers and it eases some of the tension in my shoulders. "He is a meddler, isn't he?"

"The worst," I say through a mouth full of salad.

Connor studies his plate, fork in hand. "So, nobody else knows?"

"No," I admit. He takes in a big breath and gathers his first bite on his fork. Subject dismissed, it seems. "You're not gonna tell him, right?"

A set of disbelieving eyes land on me. Jaw clenched, he says, "Gretch. Surely, you know you don't have to ask me that."

"Don't I, though? It's been a while since we were—" I stop myself before I say too much. "I mean, isn't there some sort of best friend, bro code oath or something?"

He laughs to himself, although I don't sense any real humor in it. Crestfallen, his features turn solemn, brows knit tight as he takes a sip of his wine. "Yeah, something like that."

If Connor's fork were a criminal out for blood, it finds its next defenseless victim in his garden salad. It's subtle, all the stabbing and slicing, but I recognize it as an obvious marker of Connor's strained composure.

"I won't tell him. I promise," he finally replies.

I whisper my thanks and we finish our salads in silence.

By the time our plates have been cleared, the dead air is killing me. After the initial shock of my news wore off, I thought there would be smiles and celebration as we excitedly discussed plans for the days ahead.

Instead, I mostly just feel...heavy. And I know he feels it, too.

Connor clears his throat. "Listen, Gretch. I know that um...I know that I screwed up and I don't deserve your trust—"

"Connor, I don't want—"

He holds up a hand to stop me. "I know this isn't the time or place and I respect that. I'm not trying to rush you or force the conversation, I swear. Honestly, I'm terrified that you'll never want to talk about it and I will have ruined what we had forever. But can I at least say one thing?"

I blink slowly and nod.

"If I could go back in time and have a redo of that night, that weekend, I would do a million things differently, but I can't. All I can do now is say that I'm sorry for…all of it. You deserved so much better."

Heart, meet Break.

Except, we've already met. Abandoned on a balcony three years ago, we became best buds. And here we find ourselves again.

He regrets *all of it.*

"Gretch, I need you to hear me," he continues and I push down the emotion thundering behind my sternum. "I understand if you hate me, because I deserve that. But no matter what, you *can* still trust me. That'll never change. With all of it. With everything. You can trust me with it."

That's the crux of it all, I realize. That, in the face of everything, I've never been able to let him go.

Despite the hurt, he's always been the person I've wanted to run to when I'm hurting. Even though he ghosted me for three years, I still held out hope until the last possible second that it would be him here in Arizona with me. Regardless of the fact he was able to move on so quickly, I still can't find it in me to stay mad at him because, before it all, he was my best friend.

That's the funny thing about best friends—the wounds of mistakes and regret bleed red like any other, but it can also be the most natural to forgive. Unlike another best friend in my past that I forgave and left in my rearview, my friendship with Connor is one I can't bear the thought of losing for good.

"You're one of the most important people in the world to me, Gretch. I know that may be hard to believe given the past few years, but…" Our eyes lock, everything we've missed about each other floating in the current between us. "I would never do anything to intentionally hurt you. If you ask me to never tell Drew or your parents about this. I solemnly swear to God"—he raises a scout's honor hand—"Fish, it's done. It goes with me to my grave."

I reach for my water and huff out a breath. Thank God he can't see my insides that turn all warm and fuzzy.

"Yeah, I called you Fish. I think, deep down, you still love it."

I peer at him over the rim of my glass, unable to hide the smirk on my face.

Connor questions my ability to trust him when the reality is, I do trust him. No matter how hard I may try for the contrary, my hopes and dreams, stories and secrets, always manage to find safe harbor in this man.

"And if this trip goes off the handle?" he continues, lightheartedly. "Say, we meet this woman and she's some sort of crazed lunatic and you need to hide a body? I got you."

His smile beams and my shoulders drop, meeting my somersaulting heart in my chest.

"We go on this hike tomorrow—you said that's tomorrow, right?"

I roll my lips between my teeth to contain the smile that threatens to split my face in half and he takes it for the confirmation that it is.

"Yeah, we're hiking and you bite it. Your bone breaks through your skin, we're miles from civilization, cell phones aren't working. I'll Usain Bolt it outta there to find help."

Contained amusement rattles my chest. "You'd leave me there?"

"Exactly. Hear me out. I'd leave you there, but then I'd come back on a white horse with an EMT, Diet Coke and peanut butter M&Ms in tow," he finishes, face alight with heroic pride.

My head falls back on a full laugh. When I look back to Connor, I can't get a read on his expression.

"What?" I ask.

"Nothing. It's just...I missed this." He runs his gaze over every inch of my face like he's committing me to memory—or getting lost in a memory—and I don't miss when he pauses on my lips for a moment too long. "I missed *you*."

The column of Connor's throat bobs slowly, his face transforming from soft to pained. His brows furrowed just enough for me to take notice, but I'm not sure he realizes he's doing it.

"I know I may not have been your first choice, Gretch." He fights a scowl before leveling his features. "But I'm really glad I'm here."

You've always been my first choice. My throat locks up at the confession—it gives away too much of how I feel.

Friends, I remind myself. "I'm glad you're here, too."

The waiter interrupts with our entrees and Connor and I launch into an easy flow of dinner conversation from there.

He asks about my last three years of college and I tell him about some of my classes and professors. He asks more questions about my internship and I don't hold back. He doesn't ask about any of my romantic relationships and I don't tell. Not like there's much to tell anyway.

The most genuine gleam of pride flashes in his eyes when he asks me what I read these days and I confirm I lean mostly into romance and historical fiction, but that I do still like to reread *Little Women* every couple of years.

He asks about the journey to finding my birth mom and I tell him about the lackluster DNA kit results and the detective I hired.

He updates me on his family. His parents, Andrea and Patrick, have fully embraced retirement out on the Outer Banks of North Carolina since Connor graduated high school. Everett, his oldest brother, has two daughters with his wife and his next oldest brother, Owen, got married last year and they're expecting their first child, a son, in January.

And so the conversation goes, back and forth, without any forced subject changes or awkward silences. We smile, we laugh and it all feels so easy. It feels like...*us.* The us we were *then.*

When the check arrives, he insists again on paying for dinner and, this time, I don't fight it.

On our way out of the restaurant, Connor places a hand on my lower back as he ushers me out the door. The warm summer air envelops us like a cozy blanket freshly pulled from the dryer. The sun has set and only the faintest hint of color remains in the sky, broad strokes of soft amber glowing along the horizon.

A lot can happen in a day.

Today hasn't gone how I expected. But now that I'm here, I'm content to be here with Connor.

I could have kept his number blocked, cut him out of my life, moved back to New York and never looked back all in the name of retribution. But he's here and it's forcing me to acknowledge the truth of the matter, which is that no amount of hurt I feel over what happened discounts how much I've missed him.

I know that inevitable conversation is looming, but I'm not scared of it anymore.

When we reach the car, he holds the passenger door open for me. Instead of getting in, I drop my clutch on the seat and spin to face him.

Connor stands with one hand on the door, the other hanging loosely at his side. I close the small gap between us and wrap my arms around his neck while his loop around my waist.

We linger. Stalling, waiting, I'm not sure. He surrenders to my lead, his hold on me only as tight as mine on his. I know he'll let go as soon as I'm ready.

But I don't want to let go.

With a tortured breath against his ear, I whisper, "I missed you, too."

The heavy sigh that flutters my hair feels like relief and *finally*. I squeeze him tighter and his arms do the same, drawing me to my toes. His head nestled against my neck, we begin to rock gently from side to side, one foot to the other and back.

We stay right here. Swaying. My forehead on his shoulder, his breaths coasting my collarbone, as though a single hug can make up for a thousand missed ones.

Chapter Sixteen

THE BOOK

CONNOR

twelve years ago, summer

"Dɪᴅ a garbage truck hit you on your way over?" I arch an eyebrow at my friend's disheveled hair and gnarly t-shirt that I'm pretty sure is the same one he was wearing when we went out last night. Willing to bet he slept in it, too.

"Something like that." He tosses his gym bag into one of the storage cubbies, stifling a yawn. "Sorry I'm late."

"It's cool, man. I'm almost finished."

Drew lowers on to the weight bench next to me, sticks in his earbuds as I replace my own and we settle into our respective workout circuits.

Ten minutes later, I finish all my reps and plop down on the empty bench beside Drew with my post-workout drink. I give the shaker cup a quick jostle and gesture for him to remove his earbuds.

"What did your parents say?" My family has rented a cabin up in Door County, Wisconsin for next weekend. Both my older brothers will meet us there and, to my surprise, Mom and Dad said I could invite a friend.

"Dude, I can't. I forgot it's Gretchen's birthday next weekend. My parents won't let me skip her party." Drew drops his weights to the ground between sets.

I take a swig of my drink, snickering to myself. "Where do they have you locked down? Trampoline park? Petting zoo?"

Drew shakes his head and picks up the weights again. "Nah, it's nothing like that. Gretch doesn't really do friend parties. It's just a family thing at the house."

"Bro, my tenth birthday was killer. Me and like fifteen friends played paintball. I took a close range hit to my thigh, had a nasty bruise for two weeks. It was epic." I grin fondly at the memory. "Fish is missing out."

"I don't know, man." He pauses between bicep curls, meeting my eyes in the mirror. "My parents ask her every year if she wants to invite friends from school and she always says no."

When I met the guys at football camp last summer, we clicked right away. But it was Drew who quickly became my best friend. Whether it's the two of us hanging out or a bunch of the guys taking over their pool, the Fisher house has become my second home.

And you can't make a stop at the Fisher house without a run-in with Fish. The sweet, shy girl—who hates being called little, by the way—who almost always has her nose in a book. If it's not a book, it's an art project.

"You think it's a curse of having a summer birthday?" I ask.

"Could be. She's a total introvert, though." He returns the weights to the rack and turns to face me. "Whatever it is doesn't seem to bother her much."

The conversation ends there, but my heart stalls on the issue. I know Gretchen is quiet and reserved, but introverts have friends too. She's a gentle-hearted soul and the thought of her not having friends to invite to her birthday party doesn't sit right with me. If I wasn't going to be out of town, I'd show up to the party with bells and a party hat.

A week later, I arrive at Drew's house fifteen minutes earlier than we had planned for. He and I are going to run some drills before the rest of the team comes over later for a pick-up game in the front yard.

I also come bearing gifts.

My family and I leave tomorrow and Gretchen's party isn't for another two days, but her actual birthday is today so it worked out perfectly.

When I enter through the side door into the empty kitchen, I'm greeted by the remnants of a birthday pancake breakfast. Balloons hang from the pendant lights above the kitchen island and a hand-made *Happy Birthday, Gretchen* banner is held secure by scotch tape on the breakfast nook wall.

Upstairs, I drop my football bag in Drew's room. One ear tuned to the hall bathroom tells me he's in the shower, so I grab Gretchen's gift from my bag, head across the hall and knock on her door. When she doesn't answer, I head around the corner and find her in the open loft area at the top of the stairs.

Gretchen sits at her art desk, headphones on to block out the world around her. The late morning sunlight illuminates the tabletop where she has an array of colored pencils and sketch paper at the ready.

Quietly, I move in closer and peek over her to see what she's coloring. Another day, another princess and her ballgown.

I tuck the gift behind my back and tap her on the shoulder.

She removes her headphones and swivels her head, her toothy smile beaming across her face when she sees me. Who wouldn't adore this girl? *Kids are assholes.*

"Happy birthday, Fish."

She blinks a confused look as she spots the wrapped gift I set in front of her. "That's for me?"

"Of course it is. You know anybody else who has a birthday around here today?" When she doesn't move to open it right away, I ask, "Is it okay if I watch you open it?" She bobs her head, and I add, "Read the card first."

It's silly, really. The small three by five card doesn't have a printed message, but the goldfish on the front made me smile. Inside, she finds my handwritten note.

> To my favorite 10-year-old,
> I feel like you already have all the books, but I really hope you don't have this one.
> When I get back from my trip, I want to hear all about it.
> Happy Birthday, Fish!
> Love, Connor

The spoiler of what's inside has her rushing to rip the package open, wrapping paper tossed aside in shreds.

Book in hand, she runs her fingers across the curvy scripted title on the cover: *Little Women*. She turns the book over in her hands, excitedly inspecting every inch of the vintage hardback.

"We have a family friend who's a book collector in the city and he said this was a good classic for your age. He had this 1950s edition at his shop that I thought was pretty cool. Do you have this one already?"

She shakes her head as she gently tucks the card inside the front cover. "Thank you, Connor."

"You're welcome," I reply, ruffling her hair. "What are you working on?"

She sets the book aside while she smooths out her hair. "Just coloring."

I toss a backward glance around the corner to confirm Drew's still in the shower as I grab a colored pencil and settle into the seat beside Gretchen.

"Are you excited about your party?" I ask.

She shrugs. "I guess."

I pull at my bottom lip, gaze locked on her profile, but she stays focused on her task. I could ask about her friends at school, but Gretchen's sharp—she'll see right through that. Maybe some reverse psychology is in order. Turning back to the coloring sheet, I say, "Yeah, I don't really like parties all that much either."

I wait for her to say more, but she doesn't.

A minute later, her soft voice, barely a whisper above the sound of the pointed tips of our pencils dragging across the paper, finally says, "Do you think my parents think about me on my birthday?"

Stunned by the question, I halt my pencil. Shoulders hung low, she stares blankly out the window in front of us.

"Of course they do, Gretch. I saw the balloons and the banner in the kitchen. I know they're so excited to celebrate you."

She shakes her head and something knots inside my chest. "No. Not them," she says. "I mean my real parents. The ones who gave me away."

Gretchen being adopted isn't a secret, but it's not something I hear her family talk about, at least not while I'm around. Honestly, most days, I forget altogether that she's adopted. That's when it hits me: if it's this easy for me to forget this major detail about somebody who is a frequent presence in my life, how much easier could it be for her own family to forget? You could argue that's a good thing because it means they've fully embraced her as their own, but it must be so different from Gretchen's perspective.

Perhaps her birthday is the hardest of all days to forget. Maybe, of all days out of the year, today is the day she wants—*needs*—this part of her to be remembered.

The details of her adoption aren't something I've ever thought to inquire about. I'm the last person to wax poetic about her situation, much less know the right thing to say here.

As best I can, I muster a response that, I hope, can settle her vulnerable heart without speaking out of turn. "I think you were given to some pretty amazing people. I know your parents love you. And Drew?" I click my tongue. "That dude is freaking obsessed with you."

Finally, she smiles in a fit of giggles.

I take in her dark hair that's nothing like the light brown hair donned by her dad and brother, or the blond hair her mom has. Her deep, tanned skin that's a stark contrast to the fair complexion of the rest of her family. Then there's the dark chocolate eyes and light freckles over her nose; the two standout features on her face that hold zero resemblance to the saints who've raised her and the brother who adores her.

"If I knew your birth parents, I'd tell them how amazing and creative and smart you are. I'd also tell them about what a badass family you ended up with."

"You're not supposed to say *ass.*" She says the last word on a whisper behind a cupped hand. I lift two guilty hands in surrender.

"You've got a family here that loves you, Gretch. I know I'm just Drew's friend, but I hope you know that I love you, too."

I think she might cry, but she launches forward and wraps me in a hug instead. The awkward angle of our chairs butted up next to each other has her cheek buried in my chest with one arm thrown over my shoulder. I reach around her neck as best as I can, resting a hand on her head.

"You can be my friend too, Connor."

"I'd love that, Fish."

With one final "Happy Birthday" on my way out, I begin down the stairs. Pausing to look back, I watch as Gretchen sets her pencils aside, pulls her headphones back over her ears, grabs her new book and clutches it tight to her chest.

A second later, she opens to the first page and I smile.

Chapter Seventeen

SHE WAS NEVER MINE

CONNOR

GRETCHEN STEPS into the living room still wearing the pink dress from dinner, high heels swapped out for fuzzy slippers. Long black waves are thrown into a messy knot on top of her head, a few rogue strands framing her face. And there, on the bridge of her nose is a pair of tortoiseshell glasses I've never seen before.

"When did you get glasses?" I ask.

Gretchen grabs the ice bucket in the kitchenette and spins to me. "Um…" She pushes the glasses up a bit and there's a modesty there that I find way too charming. "Couple years ago, I think. Apparently, reading too much leads to tired eyes. These are only for when I don't have my contacts in."

"They're cute." She avoids my stare, but I don't miss her grin as she passes by me.

"You can have the bathroom first. I'm gonna go fill this up," she says as she waves the empty bucket over her shoulder and swipes a room key off the entry table. I'm left smiling like a starry-eyed fool when she walks out the door.

~

I USE the bathroom to brush my teeth and change into a pair of athletic shorts and a t-shirt, Gretchen schlepping in gobs of face and hair products as soon as I tell her I'm done.

Once I hear the shower turn on, I text Lauren.

ME

Can I call you now?

My anxiety as I wait for her to reply turns to frustration when I realize I forgot about the two-hour time difference since Arizona doesn't observe Daylight Savings.

Several minutes later, her reply finally comes through.

LAUREN

I'm up.

Stepping onto the balcony, I close the sliding door behind me and steady myself with a deep breath. She answers on the second ring.

"Hi," she says.

"Hi." I settle on one of the patio chairs. "How are you?"

"I'm okay," she exhales. "Are you okay?"

"Yeah. Sorry I scared you. I ended up having to leave town suddenly."

"Oh—"

"And I forgot about the time difference. I'm sorry it's so late."

"That's okay. Where are you?"

"I'm in Arizona." I pause, momentarily paralyzed over how much I should tell her. Lauren's insecurities got the best of her when she met Gretchen at dinner last month and I don't want to give her a reason to spiral when there's nothing to spiral over. But I don't want to lie to her either.

"That trip with Drew and Gretchen?" Her subdued tone strikes my analyzing thoughts dead.

"Yeah, so…" I pinch the skin along my forehead. "Drew called this morning in a panic. Something's going on with Reagan, but he

106

won't tell me what it is. Gretchen was already on her way here and he felt terrible for having to bail, so he asked me to come instead."

I lean forward and rest a forearm on my bouncing knee.

"Oh." The sound of defeat nearly guts me, but she goes on. "I guess that explains why Reagan hasn't returned my calls."

"Yeah. Drew promised they're gonna be okay, but that's all I know."

"Well, that's good, I guess."

Her voice quivers, breaths shallow and tight. "Lauren, please don't cry," I plead, head in my hand. *God*, I hate making her cry.

She sniffles. "It's okay. I'm fine. I promise."

"I'm really sorry. Not just for today but...everything. It was really shitty of me to not return your calls or messages. You don't deserve that."

"Thank you," she whispers.

For one, two, three beats, we sit in intimidating silence. Her sadness seeps through the line like a leaky faucet, every drip landing like burning acid on my heart. I've been a terrible friend to her over the past few weeks.

"Are you and Gretchen having fun?"

I sober immediately because there's suspicion there. Uncertainty over whether or not Gretchen and I have a future beyond friendship aside, the things she confided in me tonight, the truth behind this trip—it's not my story to tell. But Lauren deserves as much honesty as I can give her without breaking Gretchen's trust.

"It's not that kind of trip."

"Oh. I thought Drew said it was some sort of birthday trip."

"Yeah, that's what I thought too, but it's—" I stop to reorganize my thoughts. "Gretchen told me some things in confidence tonight that Drew doesn't even know yet. I'm sorry, but I have to leave it at that for now."

"Alright," she says on a dramatic sigh. "Sooooo, how's the weather out there?"

I snicker. "Is that the type of friends we are now? We don't have anything better to talk about than the weather?"

"Shut up!" she laughs. "I'm trying here."

"Okay, okay." I lean back in my chair and prop my feet on the table in front of me. "It's a beautiful night here, actually. Seventy degrees, not a cloud in sight. I'm out on the balcony staring at a sky full of stars."

For the next several minutes we volley from one random topic to another. I ask about a project at work she's been worried about. She tells me about her family's upcoming trip to the Bahamas. The more we talk, the easier it becomes.

When we reach our first lull in conversation, she says, "We never did this."

"Did what?"

"This casual, easy chat. The way friends do."

Four words. A single statement that packs a punch large enough to draw our entire relationship into focus as though we lived with blinders on for the past two and a half years.

The way friends do.

Your person should be your best friend. But I wasn't hers and she was never mine—a reality that's hard to stomach after spending so much of your life with someone.

"I know," I respond.

Silence falls again and I scrape my nails over my jaw, searching for some combination of words to fill the abject void. When I come up empty, Lauren says, "I'm not mad at you, Connor. Not anymore, at least."

"It'd be okay if you were, though."

"I'm not gonna say it doesn't still hurt, but I heard what you said. Everything about how there really was love there, but maybe not the kind I deserved. If I'm honest, I think I felt the same about you."

I tuck a hand behind my head and crane my neck back against the headrest to take in the stars above that feel like a weighted blanket settling over me—a calm sort of pressure that soothes more than it burdens. The vises of stress that have held me bound for weeks uncoil one by one in real time.

She continues, "I mean, I *do* love you, but——"

"You're not in love with me," I finish. "I still should have been honest with you sooner. I'm sorry. You deserved better."

Her words come on a hushed breath, genuine and sincere. "So did you, Connor." A fissure in my heart cracks, like a bone that has to snap in order to heal.

"I'll take the blame for this one," I say. "Do you think we could start over from here as friends?"

"I'd like that," she says. "And if we ever can't find anything to talk about, we'll always have the weather."

The sound of her laugh—of us laughing together—soothes the last bits of guilt I had been holding on to. This closure, I realize, wasn't only for her. I needed it, too.

A door opens at the other end of the balcony. "Deal," I say as Gretchen steps outside dressed in a white cotton pajama set with shorts and a button-up sleep shirt. Her hair, still wet from the shower, hangs in a single braid over one shoulder.

I clear my throat to make my presence known and she turns to face me. She pads toward me at a determined pace. "Is that Drew?"

I shake my head as Lauren says, "Is that Gretchen?"

"Yeah it is," I answer into the phone, before I point at it, look to Gretchen and say, "It's Lauren."

She slaps her hands to her cheeks, comically pushing them together in the most adorable way. The action nudges those librarian glasses farther up her nose as she mouths, *"I'm sorry."*

"Tell her I said hi," Lauren says. Whether she intended it to be an olive branch or not, my heart does something at her words.

I meet Gretchen's stunned gaze and grin. "Lauren says hi."

Gretchen straightens, hands falling to her sides like paperweights. Her expression turns quizzical. My shrug in response says *it's a surprise to me, too.*

"Hi, Lauren," Gretchen hollers toward the phone and immediately winces as though she's been rehearsing the words for hours and it still didn't come out right. It's so endearing, I have to place a hand over my mouth to keep from smiling.

Two thumbs hiked over her right shoulder, she signals she's going back inside. She makes it two steps before she pauses and grabs the top of one of the empty patio chairs. The look she gives me over her shoulder is adorably wicked. Gretchen locks our gazes together as she stalks toward the balcony door, dragging the chair behind her. The long-suffering sound of iron scraping concrete fills the air.

My chest quakes on a silent laugh. Nothing like a good *Pitch Perfect* reference to lighten the mood. The next breath I take is the easiest one I've felt in weeks.

"Gretchen says hi back," I say into the phone, eyes on the woman in question as she abandons the chair and runs inside.

"So, listen, there is something I wanted to tell you all this time that you've been ignoring me," Lauren says.

"Okay. Ouch. I thought we were friends."

"Well, admittedly, the first few weeks I mainly just wanted to scream at you, but then I…um…I met someone."

I definitely wasn't expecting that.

"It's not serious or anything," she rushes to add. "We met a couple weeks ago and we've only gone out a few times, but I didn't want you to hear it from somebody else."

Of all the thoughts perking up in my brain like little meerkats, none of them are hurt or disappointment or jealousy or judgment. As true as the day is long, my next words come from the deepest, purest part of me when I say, "I'm happy for you."

"I'm scared people will think it's too soon."

"Forget what everyone else thinks. You deserve to be happy."

She lets out a sigh that sounds a lot like mine, full of contentment and hope for the future. "Thanks, Connor."

The door to our relationship may be closed for good, but Lauren's okay. *We* are okay. And if she's able to move on, maybe it's okay that I do the same.

Chapter Eighteen

MY EYES ARE UP HERE, GRETCH

GRETCHEN

> **DREW**
>
> Glad you made it safe. Have a great time and don't worry about us. We'll talk when you get back.
>
> Love you more.

THE PING of my brother's texts wake me from a deep sleep mere seconds before the memory of me awkwardly inserting myself into Connor's conversation with Lauren plows into me like a freight train. I could crawl into a hole and die, I'm so embarrassed. Which is most definitely what I'd been thinking when I climbed into bed last night, shut off all the lights and promptly pulled the covers over my face. Mercifully, with the lengthy day of travel and the time difference, sleep came quickly so I didn't have to face Connor after he got off the phone.

The plan is to hike Devil's Bridge today; a hike I've read online is quite intense, but with a stunning panoramic photo op at the end that, supposedly, makes the climb worth it. The earlier we can get started, the better, to get ahead of the heat.

I put on my glasses and climb out of bed. Careful not to wake Connor if he's still asleep, I open the bedroom door. A sofa bed with sheets all askew greets me, but Connor's nowhere to be seen. He's probably one of those monsters who works out when he's on vacation. *Ugh. Diabolical.*

Moving toward the kitchen to brew some coffee, I round the back of the couch, and my foot catches on a set of bare feet sticking out from underneath a blanket on the floor. I barely get my hands out in front of me in time as I pitch forward and nearly face plant into the wall. "Ow! Shit!" I shriek.

Startled, Connor jolts upward, hinged at the waist. He groans, loud and long, as he slowly eases himself back into a supine position.

I lean against the wall and clutch a hand to my chest, lungs heaving. Like a beacon, my gaze pans to Connor's bare chest now fully exposed by the blanket having drifted down his frame. I've lost count of his abs when his pained sigh alerts me that I'm being a perv.

I rush to his side, kneeling by his head. "What's going on? Are you hurt?"

Another low groan pours out of him as he rolls away from me, slowly pushing himself up. The muscles in his back clench with every movement. Too many seconds for comfort later, he finally gets to a seated position and adjusts the blanket over his lap. "You could say that?"

"What happened?"

"That bed"—he gestures to the sofa at his back—"if you can even call it that, was made by a bunch of evil minion elves in the devil's workshop."

A snort tumbles out before I can stop it. "That's oddly specific."

"I had to move to the floor because it jacked up my back," he grits through a scowl.

I wince at the recollection of Connor's career-ending football injury back in college. He's told me how the pain can flare up, but I've never seen it firsthand. "I'm so sorry. Are you okay?"

"I'll be fine. My back's just stiff as a board."

Connor finally meets my gaze, all the pained lines of his face slowly softening as the corner of his mouth ticks up. "Morning, Fish. How'd you sleep?"

"Hell of a lot better than you, apparently."

After I fetch him some ibuprofen, I return to his side with the medicine and a bottle of water. Through a clenched jaw, he tosses back a few pills.

"I'm taking the couch tonight. You can't have another night like this."

"Oh, no. No way. I'll sleep on the floor before I let you spend an hour on that death trap."

"And I'll max out my credit card and reserve a second room before I let you sleep anywhere but on the bed in *there*." I point a disciplinary finger at the bedroom.

He squints at me and I smile in kind as I adjust my glasses. A slow grin unfurls across his face. "I really do like those glasses."

Before my smile gives me away, I say, "For real though, do you need to lay low today? We don't have to do the hike. We can stay in and order room service, binge some TV."

"No, no. I'm fine. I promise. I just need to get up and moving to loosen up."

His tone may sound final enough, but I'm still uncertain if he's actually well enough to go or if he's trying to appease me. "Okay," I sigh. "Well, we probably need to leave by nine if we wanna beat the heat."

He nods through another sip of his water. Putting the cap back on, he sets it aside and moves to stand.

"Wait. Let me help you." I get to my feet and extend my hand. He grabs it while I crook my other arm under his shoulder. Together, we make it a couple inches off the ground before he reverses course and lowers himself back to the floor, tugging the blanket toward his waist. "You know what? I should do this by myself." I open my mouth to protest, but he adds, "I'm not wearing any shorts, Gretch."

"Oh," I mumble as my traitorous eyeballs hastily—and not discreetly—jump to where the blanket is draped over his hips. His naked hips, I now realize. My skin prickles with heat as I force myself to look…anywhere else. Unfortunately, *anywhere else* means jack squat to my brain because now I'm staring at his chest. Yup, still shirtless.

I finally meet his gaze, his little *my eyes are up here, Gretch* smirk right there to embarrass me. I pull my thoughts, and my face, into submission, the picture of a woman unaffected by rock hard abs and nine thread count blankets atop naked lower halves. "But *can* you actually do it yourself?"

"I'll be fine. You take the bathroom to get ready and I'll get myself situated out here."

He doesn't have to tell me twice.

"DREW TEXTED ME THIS MORNING," Connor says as he settles into the seat across from me after his first pass through the breakfast buffet.

"Yeah, me too. He didn't tell me anything, though. You?"

He shakes his head. "He mainly just asked about you. I told him everything was fine here."

I'm lost in worried thoughts about my brother and his wife as I turn my gaze back to the window overlooking the lavish pool area of the resort. Other than a few early risers who have already claimed their poolside loungers for the day, the pool sits serene and peaceful against the desert backdrop. Resort employees move about with carts of fresh towels and crates of liquor for the bar as they prepare for the day ahead.

"When are you planning to go see your birth mom?"

Covering my mouth with my napkin, I swallow down my food before answering. "Um, I was thinking we could drive out there tomorrow morning. Her address is about forty-five minutes north of here, in Flagstaff."

He scoops up another bite of eggs. "Are you wanting me to just drop you off and come back or—"

I freeze, fork stuck in a hover halfway to my mouth before I set it back down. My throat dries up and I reach for my water.

"Or," Connor drawls, attuned to my reaction, "I can stay with you, if that's what you want."

My chest expands as I set the glass aside. "I don't...um..." I shift my plate and move my knife a quarter inch to the right. "She doesn't actually know I'm here."

When I dare to look up, his expression is unbothered. And when he says, "Oh," it comes out much less troubled than I feel.

"I haven't talked to her yet." Connor's eyebrows lift infinitesimally, a gentle nudge to continue. "I was gonna call her, but then I...I don't know, I got nervous. What was I supposed to say? 'Hi, remember me? I'm the kid you gave up. So, how have you been?'" I force a laugh that's more pitiful than funny. "I don't know. I just wanted to get here and then figure out the rest. It's all I could make myself do."

I snap a piece of bacon with trembling fingers and then snap it again before dropping the crumbs to my plate. Connor's countenance hasn't changed at all.

"Well, obviously, *I* am the expert on this topic," he mocks playfully, with a wink thrown in for good measure that is equal parts teasing and comforting. "There's no *one* right way to do this, Gretch. We'll figure it out together."

He's back to his breakfast, downing a sip of coffee and scooping up more eggs. The anxiety I felt a moment ago retreats and, in its place, a quiet confidence washes over me. I can have the world's weight on my shoulders, barely able to stand under the pressure, and he just saunters up and tethers my yoke to his. Doing it in a way that's so imperceptible, I barely notice what he's done before the load feels lighter. He manages it all with a simple look or a comment that makes me smile without dismissing my fears. It's relief, validation and empowerment all wrapped into one.

In a rare moment of courage, I say, "You're really good at that."

He tilts his head. "Good at what?"

"That thing where you hear everything I'm not saying and find a way to give me exactly what I need without making me feel bad for not asking for it."

Mouth tight, his jaw twitches. He sets down his fork, scratches his neck, then sips his coffee. His hat comes off so he can run a hand through his hair before quickly putting the hat back on, only to flip it around a second later. Connor Vining can fidget with the best of them.

He coughs into his hand and returns to his meal. Before he shovels more food into his mouth, he looks at me, earnest eyes holding mine in their compassion-laced grip. "It's because I know you."

My gaze searches his as everything unsaid—everything he's holding back because I told him I wasn't ready to talk—drifts in the space between us like planes circling a runway, waiting for permission to land.

How is it, after three years of no contact, he's still my favorite person? How can I look at this man who broke my heart so thoroughly and still see a best friend?

"For better or worse, Connor, I think you know me better than anyone else ever has."

Chapter Nineteen

I SAID NO FLIRTING

GRETCHEN

THE MID-MORNING AIR is warm and crisp, sun shining uninhibited as it climbs in the Eastern sky.

Navigating a pile of boulders that block the path, Connor moves with confidence from one perch to the next before jumping across a small gap to land on the trail on the other side. Then he turns and extends a hand for me.

"How's your back?" I ask as I take his hand. His other palm grazes the exposed skin at the small of my back above the waistband of my shorts to secure my landing as I make the small jump. His touch disappears as fast as it came, but the sensation lingers.

"Better. A little tight still, but not bad."

"I tossed the ibuprofen in the bag if you need some." I gesture to the small pack I loaded up this morning that Connor has slung over his shoulders.

"Thanks."

The panic I felt when I found him on the living room floor circles back in my thoughts. "I didn't realize it could get like that?"

I watched Connor get carted off the field on a stretcher through a television screen. The worry, the fear, the questions—they all rush right back in like it was yesterday. A twelve-year-old girl doesn't get blunt truth answers in real time, she gets the sugar-coated ones only looked at through rose-colored glasses.

It wasn't until my freshman year of college that Connor told me about the time in his life surrounding his injury. The copious hours spent on bedrest, multiple surgeries and missed college experiences he had to grieve. Two months into his freshman year of college and everything he'd worked for ended in the blink of an eye—he never played football again. Something he told me, in great length, he made peace with a long time ago, yet the thought still ushers in a cloud of concern when I think about it.

He pins that incorrigible smirk on me. "You worrying about me, Fish?"

I roll my eyes and he shoves my shoulder. Scoffing, I right myself on my feet and catch up to his stride. "More like worried for myself when you collapse and I have to carry you out of here"—I raise an accusatory brow—"because I don't abandon friends in their time of need." I shove *his* shoulder this time.

"Hey! I promised an EMT and snacks."

I purse my lips. "Mmmm. EMTs *are* hot. And I do love snacks." Connor snickers.

We walk in the quiet for a couple minutes, taking in the landscape around us. The red dirt path unfurls ahead, sienna hued mesas dotted with desert foliage extending beyond in every direction. The terrain on either side of the trail is a paradoxical mix of bold green shrubs amidst towering trees and oversized boulders wedged between mounds of cacti.

Into the peaceful calm, Connor murmurs, "Gretchen Fisher is worrying about me."

The sound of my full name on his lips, like he's admiring something precious, sends a blush creeping over my cheeks. "Don't let it get to your head, QB."

"Too late."

I stare at him, flat and unimpressed. The corner of his mouth hitches as he winks at me. "Don't flirt with me either," I say.

His grin widens, eyes mischievous. "I would never."

∿

WE COME to a large clearing where a backroad for vehicles converges with the path. A wooden display board pinpoints our current location on the trail and prepares us for the final, and most grueling, leg up ahead.

The sun beats harder now, both of us glistening with sweat. The shade of a patch of mature trees nearby calls our name and we step aside for a breather. As Connor sets the pack down and retrieves a bottle of water, I remove my crop top, leaving me in my mid-thigh length biker shorts and sports bra. I wipe the sweat from my face with the bundled shirt. Out of the corner of my eye, I catch Connor looking me up and down.

"Eyes up here, QB," I say as I hand him my shirt in exchange for the water bottle. The stubborn ass takes his sweet time, gaze raking over me, blazing a torturous path. A rush courses through me, a shot of scalding hot espresso direct to my bloodstream. "I said no flirting."

Our hands make the swap as he says, "And you're not playing fair."

I give a devilish shrug—two can play this game—as I tip the bottle back. His gaze burns, competing with the Arizona sun to scorch me onsite.

And, with that, we need a subject change. "So, you gonna tell me how your conversation with Lauren went?"

His face sobers in a way most wouldn't notice, but I do. The slightest twinge of anxiety creeps in. When I interrupted their conversation last night, it seemed as though they were getting along fine—notably opposite of Connor's reservations from just a few hours prior.

He takes the bottle from me and bends low to put it and my shirt in the bag. Looking up at me from under the brim of his baseball hat, a playful glint twinkles over his face as the soberness disappears. "You ready for this?"

Taken aback by the shift, I cock my head. I'm tempted to smile but I hold it back just in case. "I don't know, am I?"

He stands to his feet, settling the pack on his back. "She met someone."

My jaw drops and I rein it in just as quickly. "And how do you feel about that?" The words pour out of me like honey dripping off a comb.

"I'm happy for her," he says. "We talked through everything and, it turns out, we've ultimately ended up on the same page about...everything. I'm honestly so relieved. I'm not sure how much longer I would have put off talking to her if you hadn't said the things you said yesterday. So, thank you."

I wave off his thanks, still blindsided by the news that his ex is already with someone else. "Is that not weird for you, knowing she's already dating another guy?"

Connor struts forward. I bring my hands to my hips, pulse racing. He stops just shy of his chest brushing mine and I lift my chin to hold his gaze. "I'm here flirting with someone else, so what do you think?"

I cross my arms, defying the sinful grin on his annoyingly perfect face. His eyes bounce to my cleavage and back. "I said no flirting," I repeat, but there's no real threat behind it.

"Oh, I heard you. I just don't believe you." He squeezes the tip of my nose, gives it a wiggle, and sidesteps me to get back on the trail.

"Alright, Fish." He rubs his hands together. "Tell me what we have in store here."

Stifling my smile, I answer, "Well, according to the world wide web, this last leg is supposed to be very intense."

"Is that a challenge?"

I laugh. "For you? No. But it is a fair warning that you might have to carry me over the finish line."

"While you're wearing that? Not a problem."

~

THE LAST QUARTER mile to Devil's Bridge is nearly straight uphill. Even with frequent breaks, the high elevation and hot sun on our backs has us both wheezing to catch our breath.

"How you doin' there, QB?"

Connor's death glare lands on me for only a moment before turning to the red dirt path ahead. The trail has widened, rocks and boulders forming a series of steps and plateaus—a staircase of sorts that goes up and up (and up) as far as we can see.

"I hate you."

I flutter my lashes and quip, "Aw, do you mean it?"

He chuckles with a shake of his head as I remove my hair tie. Hair down, I flip over at the waist to collect it between my hands. With the mass of sweaty locks in my grip, I stand back up and weave the pieces through the elastic a few times, haphazardly pushing and tucking until it's secure.

Hands on his hips, breaths steadied, I hold his gaze as I fidget with the position of my messy bun until it feels just right.

He grins.

I grin.

He winks.

I flap my hand toward my face and sigh, a mocking swoon.

"Yeah," he swallows, "I definitely hate you."

The way he looks at me doesn't feel like hate.

With a burst of confidence, I stride toward him until we're toe to toe. He studies my approach, but doesn't move.

I steady myself on the rock beneath our feet with a hand on his shoulder. Reaching my arm through the crook of his, I grab the water bottle from the outside pocket of the backpack and duck my head to find his narrowed gaze on me like I'm a math equation he can't quite solve.

You and me both, Connor.

I take a sip of water then offer it to him and he does the same. Unmoving, I pin my hands on my hips and never take my eyes off his. He bops the bottle on my nose before he holds it up between us.

I look at the bottle and back to him.

He does the same—challenging, daring—before we're locked in another stare that carries enough heat to make this desert seem like child's play.

This man's had his hands all over me. He's kissed me senseless against a stone wall. When we're here, standing close enough to breathe each other's air, his phantom touch feels all too real—like we're back on that balcony—and my skin buzzes.

Slowly, I take the water bottle and reach my arm through his to secure it back in the bag. My chest barely grazes his, but he tilts his chin down when he feels it, naughty mischief glimmering in his blue eyes.

I lower my gaze to his mouth for a long moment as I step back, making certain he noticed, before I whisper, "Yeah, I hate you, too."

Flirting with Connor is, at best, ill-advised considering our little case of unfinished business. But *damn* if it isn't fun.

Chapter Twenty

I'VE GOT YOU

CONNOR

My legs feel like tissue paper and my lungs are on fire.

"'Let's go on a hike. It'll be fun', she said," I wheeze, staring ahead at an incline I find truly offensive.

"I heard that."

"Well, I said it loud, so…" I reply, tone drier than my scorched earth throat.

We approach a narrow part of the trail only wide enough for traffic to flow in one direction at a time and move aside to make room for a group of hikers descending down a tower of jagged rocks. I step in front of Gretchen to assist a few middle-aged women cautiously navigating their way down.

One by one, I offer them a hand. Each of the women take it with a death grip as they seek the right combination of hand and foot placement to make it to the bottom.

Once they've all descended safely and are on their way, I turn back to Gretchen who sports a half-smile and one hip popped out, arms crossed over her chest.

"I bet you help old ladies cross the street, too, don't you?" she says.

"Only the blind ones. Preferably with bags of groceries."

Her head falls back, smile stretching ear to ear as she erupts in laughter—loud, unashamed and beautiful.

There's plenty to admire about Gretchen's body, especially today with the dark green shorts and sports bra that shows off her lean, tight figure. Her long hair is gathered atop her head, her tanned skin glowing in the sun, silky smooth and flawless.

But her laugh, her smile—they've got my heart in a chokehold. If she'd let me, I'd spend my life chasing them.

As her laughter settles, she quirks a brow toward the tower of rocks and asks, "You ready?"

"Ladies first."

"Good call. You can break my fall that way."

LESS THAN TEN MINUTES LATER, we reach the end of the trail and the landscape opens up around us. The view is a true sight to behold.

A sharp curve in the path leads to Devil's Bridge namesake: a massive peninsular rock formation jutting out from the hillside with a large hollowed out section underneath. In the distance is a massive display of red-tinted mesas, valleys in between generously speckled with lush green trees, red dirt, and vast gaps of nothing but the horizon all setting beautifully under the clear, blue sky and high noon sun.

Several other hikers and small groups are gathered in the area, admiring the same view, taking turns walking onto the narrowest portion of the rock bridge for a photo op.

Instinctively, Gretchen and I snap pictures of the view from every angle on our phones.

When the crowd clears a bit, I gesture for her to go ahead while I hang back to take her picture from across the canyon.

"Do you guys want a picture together?" a stranger's voice calls from behind us.

Without a second thought, I hand Gretchen's phone to the kind woman and the two of us make our way around the curve of the trail together.

The bridge is plenty wide to walk on, but the sheer drop on either side, the expanse of the valleys around us, can send anyone's adrenaline into the stratosphere. Her hand brushes mine like it's searching for an anchor. I open my palm to hers and she doesn't hesitate. Our hands connect, fingers intertwining—two magnets drawn together. No sudden looks in each other's direction, no hitched breaths, no battling of inner dialogue.

She has a hand and it belongs in mine. Pure and simple.

When we reach the center of the bridge, I expect her to let go. Instead, she pulls our clasped hands up and over her head, bringing my arm to rest on her shoulder, our interlocked hands draped across the front of her chest. The motion naturally draws our bodies together and I don't allow myself a second to overthink it before I tighten my arm around her, hauling her back flush against me. Her free hand comes to rest on my forearm while mine finds her waist.

"I've got you, Fish," I say with a light pinch to the exposed skin of her midriff—teasing, but holding her secure.

We look across the gap to the woman holding the phone, fingers indicating a three second countdown. I rest my head against Gretchen's temple. When the stranger signals she's finished, Gretchen begins to move forward, but I pull her back, speaking softly into her ear. "Hold on a sec."

I keep her warm body close as I use my other hand to grab my phone from my pocket and extend it out in front of us in selfie mode. With our temples pressed together, hands held across the front of Gretchen's body, we're the image of a wholly in love couple.

Maybe it's the possibility that I'll never get the chance to be with her for real, or maybe it's seeing her tucked into me the way I spent so many years wishing she would be—all I know is that I want to capture this moment up close. I don't want the version that ends up in the picture frame with the panoramic horizon behind two tiny, indistinguishable figures at its center. I want to look at *us*—be reminded of every place her body touches mine and how, for this flicker of time, we felt perfect and right.

Gretchen and I fell into a natural rhythm of effortless banter and sparring years ago—it's what we do. This girl's been able to hold her own with me since we were kids. I shouldn't have been surprised the relationship we forged over that year—that feels like a century ago—became the most intimate connection I've ever shared with another person and we weren't even in the same state. Texts, phone calls, FaceTimes—that was all it took to turn the shy girl with the brown eyes into the only woman I've ever wanted *more* with.

Before I broke my promise. Before I touched her. Before I kissed her. I knew it even then.

I may have screwed things up beyond repair, but I'll spend the rest of my life with *this* picture as a reminder that soulmates do exist —even if I never get to call her mine.

Gretchen doesn't let go of my hand until we're safely off the bridge, away from the cliff's edge.

Opting to rest and enjoy the view before beginning the trek back, we find a patch of shade tucked up above the trail. Once we're situated on the ground, Gretchen grabs some granola bars and water from the bag while I try to work out some of the tightness in my back.

I roll my neck from side to side, rotate my shoulders forward and then back. Next thing I know, there's a pill bottle pressed against my ear being shaken like a baby rattle. "Just take 'em, old man."

Huffing, I swipe the bottle from her hand. "Geez, okay, Mom."

"Hey! Don't disrespect Mama V like that. That woman's a saint," she mumbles through a mouthful of granola.

I toss back the pills and chase them with a swig of water to hide my smile.

"You actually *are* an old man, so where's the lie?"

"Twenty-eight is old now?"

"You're almost twenty-nine, which might as well be thirty, which basically makes you forty, which, for all intents and purposes, means you're middle-aged." I snicker. "I mean, look at you. We hiked a measly three miles and you're over here poppin' pills."

I stare at her, unamused, yet entirely entertained. Gretchen eyes me sidelong, lips lifting at the corners as she tilts the water bottle to take a drink.

Faster than she can react, I reach out and give the bottle a quick squeeze. Water gushes all over her face and down her neck and she jolts forward. I casually sit back, the portrait of infantile innocence, and tear into my granola bar. When she turns to look at me, hand still wiping water from her chin, I give her my proudest grin.

"The road to hell is paved with the arrogant smiles of grown ass man-children."

"Noted."

She tuts. "Mama V would be ashamed."

"Nah. Being the favorite child has its perks."

She shakes her head in good-natured exasperation as she leans back on her palms. I mirror her position and turn my gaze to the view ahead of us. We sit in silence for a few minutes as hikers come and go on the trail below.

"You still talk to your mom every week?"

I grin. "Every Friday at five like clockwork." Same day, same time since the week I left for college. Mom doesn't let me miss our weekly phone date for anything.

"Such a good little son," Gretchen coos, pinching my cheek.

When she leans back on her hands, our shoulders brush and I turn toward her. Her gaze drops to my mouth and the air between us instantly sizzles. I hesitate even though every nerve ending in my body says to grab her by the neck and yank her lips to mine.

But it's Gretchen who leans in first. I follow her lead, my heart a jackhammer in my chest. She moves an inch, I do the same, the two of us drifting together in slow motion. Every inch gained feels like its own small finish line as an invisible string pulls us close enough that I can taste her scent on my tongue.

She pauses, eyes lowered. But mine are up, appraising her; I need confirmation that she wants this.

I sense it a moment before she says it. Her chin drops a fraction and she retreats a millimeter that might as well be a mile.

"I'm sorry. I can't," she says on a breath so close I feel it wisp over my jaw.

My lungs inflate heavily as my stomach sinks. Nearly the same words I said to her three years ago come back to haunt me. This is what I deserve. Gretchen owes me nothing. Not even her apology.

I pull back a healthy distance, determined to not make her any more uncomfortable than she already is. "No. You, uh…" I clear my throat. "You have nothing to be sorry for."

"Yes, I do," she says, voice low and weary. "I was…flirting… earlier, with you. I was flirting and I—"

"Gretch, stop."

The heels of her palms come to her temples, head shaking like it might make the last thirty seconds disappear. "I shouldn't have done that. It's just…today has been so—"

Perfect. "I know, Gretch. I swear, it's fine. I was flirting, too." She winces; the sight a shot of arsenic straight to my heart. *"I'm* sorry," I finish.

If she hears my apology, she doesn't acknowledge it as she turns away to dig through the bag—for nothing, I'm sure. Every bit of the emotion she tries to hide hits me like a ton of bricks—the quiet sniffles, the shallow breaths, the quick swipe of her fingers over her cheeks she thinks I can't see. The tears she won't show me. All parts of her that I used to have but lost.

"I'm sorry," I say once more, so quiet she doesn't hear it, yet desperate for the moment she tells me she's ready to.

Chapter Twenty-One

DON'T ASK ME WHY I STILL HAVE IT

GRETCHEN

I QUICKLY TUCK my makeshift bookmark between the pages and close the book at the sound of Connor rustling awake beside me.

"How long did I sleep?" He pulls the hat off his eyes where he'd positioned it earlier to shield the sun.

"Only about half an hour," I say, giving him my back to sneak the book in the bottom of the bag.

"Did you bring a book out here?" he asks. Not fast enough apparently.

I laugh nervously but stay focused on the task of getting the bag opened. "A true reader doesn't go anywhere without their book, Connor."

He swipes the book from my hands before I can stop him. His laughter fizzles out when realization hits. "*Little Women.*" A statement. A memory. One look at the well-loved copy of the classic, the binding that's barely hanging on, and I know he remembers everything—the day he gave it to me, the conversation we had.

Head hung low, I avoid his eyes. Gently, I take it back from him before he unwittingly opens it and finds what's inside. It's one thing to admit that I reread it regularly. It's another thing entirely for him to know I still have the same copy he gifted me on my tenth birthday. All this after I almost kissed him. I might as well have written my feelings in big bold letters on a sandwich board hanging across my body.

Once the book is buried in the bottom of the bag, I stand up and dust the red dirt off my pants. "You ready to start heading back?"

I hold the bag out for him and our gazes meet. He looks at me from his seat on the ground and I see it in the defeated look on his face—the things he's not letting himself say, the questions he wants to ask. But I know he can read me, too.

Don't ask me why I still have it or what it means.

After a few beats, he lets out a dejected breath and takes the bag from my hand. I'm five steps ahead of him on the path before he even gets to his feet.

THE HIKE BACK to the car takes half as long as the hike up, but the silence between us makes it feel like an eternity. Not even Connor blaring Bon Iver from his phone twenty minutes into the descent could fill the quiet void.

The second I learned Connor was coming on this trip, I should have hidden that book in the deepest corner of my suitcase and left it there.

Not even twenty-four hours ago I was waiting for him at the airport, the extent of my complex feelings like a good poker hand I held close to my chest. I knew my cards, and I wasn't going to reveal anything until he explained what happened after our kiss.

But things changed when we started feeling like *us* again. The flirting, the teasing, the playful banter, the way he held me on the bridge to snap that picture—all of it made a mess of my well-laid plans. My world turns on its axis when he's around and, if it wasn't obvious before, it certainly is now. Because now I look like a lovesick puppy who's been pining for him since before I started shaving my legs. And, for well over an hour, I couldn't bring myself to say anything to the contrary.

I couldn't bring myself to say anything at all.

Collapsing into the car, we fall back against our seats on exhausted sighs.

"I don't think I've ever been this tired," he says.

"Oh my God, same." Leaning into the cold air blasting from the air vents, my stomach rumbles in hunger. "I want the biggest, greasiest cheeseburger I can find."

"God, yes! And fries," he says with a groan.

"Obviously. And ice cream."

"Oh my God. All the ice cream." Connor puts the car in gear but keeps his foot on the brake. "On one condition." The softness in his words pulls my eyes to his. "You have to talk to me."

The car creeps forward as he turns his attention back to the road.

I swallow past the urge to clam up again. "Sorry, yeah. Um…I know, I've just been in my head about…stuff. Thinking, you know?"

Smooth, Gretchen.

"Must've been thinking hard. You haven't said a word in almost two hours."

Not strong enough to face the pain in his voice, I clear my throat to push away the sting.

"You wanna talk about it?"

"Talk about what?" I answer, like he's really going to buy it.

"Really, Gretch?" he asks, voice incredulous.

I half-ass a smile as I bury my thumbnail between my teeth, nerves skyrocketing. Without a word, Connor prods my hand away from my face before both of his hands land back on the steering wheel.

The simple gesture brings a faint smile to my face. I crack my knuckles so I have something to do with my hands because I don't know what to say.

"Let me guess," Connor interjects in a good-natured tone that I know is his attempt to ease the tension.

"Please, don't," I whisper. I instantly wish I could suck the words right back in. The honesty in them too raw, too vulnerable for me to handle right now.

He exhales beside me, a defeated sound. His shoulders dip and his pain feels nearly as heavy as my own. Jaw tight, he runs a hand over his scruff. He promised he'd wait until I was ready to talk, but I've read hot, cold and everything in between in a matter of hours. Yet, not even his dwindling patience is enough to make me speak. Anxiety, embarrassment, fear, and love gone too long unrequited, tie my stomach and my vocal cords in knots.

Then, a resigned sigh and his hand is on mine. I don't consider the meaning or the consequences when I open my palm to him. His hand squeezes mine and I pinch my eyes shut, commanding my traitorous tear ducts to keep it together.

Do. Not. Cry.

"Are you nervous about seeing your birth mom?" There's not an ounce of conviction in the question. It may be a valid one, but it bears no weight on this moment or the events of the past several hours.

I choke back all the things I should say, cans of worms that need to be opened. We may not recover from the mess it might make.

When my friendships crashed and burned at the end of high school, I knew none of those relationships would be salvageable, least of all with the girl I used to call my best friend. But, with Connor, there's a strength to our bond that feels solid. Impenetrable, yet fragile as silk all at once—like I'll never lose him again, he'll always be in my life, but he may never be mine either.

We come to a red light and I see it all in his crestfallen expression. He knows what I'm thinking because he reads me like that— always has. The light turns green and he stares lifelessly at the road ahead, sorrow etched into the creases of his forehead. He knows I'm not ready to talk about it, saw me floundering and, despite the risk of drowning himself, jumped in to rescue me.

I accept the question for the lifeline that it is and take the coward's way out, hoping like hell he understands.

"Yeah, I am." The words are a bittersweet omission on my tongue.

Chapter Twenty-Two

THE MOVIE

GRETCHEN

eleven years ago, fall

"Mom! All the other kids at school have already seen it."

"Gretchen, I hardly believe that's true," Mom replies without looking up from the pot of chili on the stovetop.

"It *is* true. David, Sydney, Alexis, Graham. They've all seen it and won't shut up about it," I whine.

"Who won't shut up about what?" I turn to see Drew toss a mini-cornbread muffin in his mouth, his eyes already plotting which one he'll steal next.

"What if Drew took me to see it?" I beg, hands clasped under my chin. I use my best *pretty-please* whine, knowing full well it won't work. It never works.

"What if I took you to see what?" Drew implores, but I ignore him, my attention wholly on Mom, the author and finisher of my fate.

"I'm sorry, honey, but no means no. It's PG-13 and you know

the rules." She shoves past Drew for the bowls in the cupboard above his head.

"Am I here?" Drew asks, eyes wide as he flails a dramatic hand over himself.

Mom pinches his cheek. "Hi, sweetie. How was practice?"

"No, Drew! It's my turn." I step between them, waving my hands above my head. "I'm almost eleven and a half, Mo—"

I'm not able to finish my sentence because my brother, the pest that he is, grabs my wrists and crosses them in front of my chest. He locks them there by wrapping his monster forearm around me. He laughs and I stomp on his foot, which only makes him laugh harder. "Nice try, Gretch." He uses his fist to give me a noogie and I squirm to break free. Finally releasing me, he says, "What's got you all worked up?"

I fix my hair and crane my neck to look up at him. "Mom and Dad won't let me see *Pitch Perfect* even though everybody else in my grade has already seen it."

"Gretch, you gotta let it go. The answer is no," Dad's voice booms into the kitchen from his office down the hall. I groan. Drew laughs again and I hurl a mini-muffin at his face which, of course, he catches in his mouth.

He. Is. So. Annoying.

From the front of the house, a door swings open and shut. "Seriously, you guys, what's the big deal? It's just a movie!"

"What movie?" Connor says from the kitchen doorway.

A smile spreads across Mom's face. "Connor! Drew didn't tell me you were coming. You staying for dinner? We're having chili."

"If you'll have me," he says right before Drew tosses a mini-muffin his way and he catches it, too, arms thrown up in victory. Without missing a beat, he asks again, "What movie?"

"*Pitch Perfect*," Mom, Drew and me all say in unison.

"Oh, dude, I love that movie."

I glare at him.

Drew leans into Connor's ear. "Not helping, Vining."

Connor chuckles, coughing into his fist. "Sorry, Fish," he says with a wink. How dare he wink at me at a time like this.

I bounce my attention from Connor to Mom to Drew, taking in their tickled faces. I scoff and storm out of the room.

Fifteen minutes later, we're seated at the dinner table where my parents are blathering on about their weekend plans.

"Gretch, honey," Mom says, "remember Drew is in charge. Your dad and I will only be gone one night."

Drew sports a high and mighty smirk that makes me want to kick him in the shins. "Got it," I reply unenthusiastically.

"What show are you guys going to see?" Connor asks, ever the polite house guest.

Mom lights up. "We have tickets to *Les Mis*." Turning back to my brother, she steels her expression. "I know it's a bye week for you guys, but Drew, I need you to be here with your sister. No team parties or girls are allowed in this house."

Drew rolls his eyes.

"Son, you better get your attitude in check," Dad commands.

"Andrew Fisher, I mean it," Mom warns. "You are responsible for your eleven-year-old baby sister. Don't forget that."

I roll my eyes internally because I don't want Dad to lecture me, too.

I'm *not* a baby.

∾

First, Drew banished me to my room so he and his friends can have the downstairs to themselves.

Then, I was sworn to secrecy, but I only agreed to keep quiet in exchange for two things. One, I absolutely will not help him clean up any messes. Two, he has to take me to see *Pitch Perfect* tomorrow afternoon before our parents get back.

A win-win all around if you ask me.

I locked my bedroom door an hour ago when I heard somebody come upstairs to use the bathroom I share with Drew. Not long after that, I had to put on my noise canceling headphones to drown out the music even though I can still feel the vibrations through the floor.

When I look at the clock sometime later, it's almost nine. Drew clearly forgot to bring pizza upstairs like he promised and now I'm starving.

Taking off my headphones, I muster up some courage to head downstairs to sneak some dinner, but the sound of voices outside my door stops me in my tracks.

"Dude, relax. Everything's fine." That's Drew.

"Fine? Your sister's locked herself in her room. She's probably scared." Connor's declaration startles me. One of them must have tried to come in while I had my headphones on.

"Scared of what, man? It's the guys, you know them. They wouldn't do anything. I wouldn't put her in danger."

"I know that and I know they're good guys but she's eleven and there's a house full of teenage boys downstairs. You saw McDormand bring in that flask, didn't you?"

"What? I told the guys no alcohol."

"Fisher, you're my best friend, but I'm also your team captain and I shouldn't have to explain to you the risks of the team getting caught throwing a party with underage drinking."

"You're right," Drew sighs. "I'll take care of it."

Muffled footsteps shuffle down the staircase a moment before there's a knock at my door.

"Who is it?"

"Fish, it's me."

I turn the lock and peek my head around first before opening the door completely.

"You okay?" he asks.

"I'm fine. I was gonna come downstairs for some food."

"You haven't eaten yet?"

I shake my head. "Drew was supposed to bring me some pizza, but I think he forgot."

Connor laughs but it isn't all that funny. He pinches the bridge of his nose and says, "Stay in your room, I'll bring something up for you."

He turns to leave and I start to follow after him. "You don't have to do—"

"Stay in your room, Gretch. Please." His hand comes up, stopping me. "I'll be right back."

His tone, combined with the nerves I've been trying to ignore, courses straight to my feet. I spin on my heel and go back inside my bedroom.

Twenty minutes later, Connor returns with a plate of food.

"The pizza was all gone, so I made you a grilled cheese."

Except, this doesn't look like any grilled cheese I've ever eaten.

"It's pesto and mozzarella. Trust me, it's the superior of grilled cheese sandwiches. Oh, and here." He pulls a bottle of water from his pocket.

"Thank you."

An uproar of laughter comes from downstairs and Connor pivots toward the sound, jaw clenched. Sighing, he leans against my doorframe, hands inside his pockets. "Do you like it?"

Covering my mouth, I bob my head eagerly. "It's so good. Thank you."

A scurry of footsteps come up the stairs and Connor rushes to the landing to block their path.

From my perch on the bed, I can't see the staircase, but the annoyance on Connor's face is obvious. "I thought Drew made it clear, no girlfriends invited," he scolds to his unsuspecting teammate.

The guy laughs. "It's a little late for that, Vining. Unless you wanna be the one to tell the cheerleading squad to leave. Drew's already too wrapped up in Madison Pruitt to do it himself." A girl's voice joins in on the laughter now.

Connor mumbles under his breath. "Well, this isn't a hotel, Henley. Nobody comes upstairs. Got it?"

"Whatever you say, man," Henley replies before their shadows turn and head back down the stairs.

Connor returns to his spot in my doorway. "I hate your brother."

I giggle. "You love my brother."

"Two things can be true at once."

I take another bite as the sound of screeching chairs and shattered glass rises over the pulsing music downstairs. Connor and I both go on high alert.

"You know what? Grab your shoes. Let's go." The decision is made as he pulls his keys from his pocket and instructs me to follow him.

I slide on my tennis shoes, grab a hoodie from my closet and follow my brother's best friend down the stairs, out the side door and straight to his car without anyone seeing me.

When he gets settled in the driver's seat, he keeps the car in park as he types out a series of texts on his phone. The *whoosh* sound of each one cuts the silence inside the car. After what feels like several minutes of waiting for him to finish, I finally ask him what the heck he's doing.

He sends off one final message and hands his phone to me, saying, "See for yourself," before putting the car in gear and heading down our driveway.

His thread with my brother is at the top of his screen.

CONNOR

I'm getting your sister out of the house for a while. I'll bring her back by midnight. You need to get things under control.

DREW

I know, V. I'm sorry. I'll take care of things here and make sure everyone's gone by the time you get back.

Thanks for looking out for Gretch.

The next is a message sent to the team group chat where Connor lectures them on making good choices and respecting my family's property. A few not-so-subtle reminders about the playoffs in a few weeks brought on a slew of thumbs up emojis and *aye-aye-Caps*.

Fifteen minutes later, we pull into the parking lot of the movie theater, the bright lights from the marquis illuminating the pavement outside the entrance. Before I can say a word, Connor unbuckles and climbs out of the car, forcing me to follow suit.

Inside the lobby, the screen behind the ticket counter displays all the available showtimes. Connor looks at the clock on his phone. "Would you look at that, Fish?"

"What?" I ask as I scan the screen above me.

"*Pitch Perfect* starts in ten minutes."

I jerk my head his direction and he slaps me with a goofy grin. My arrangement with my brother is all but forgotten because the only thing better than seeing *Pitch Perfect* tomorrow is seeing it tonight.

"Do you think you can keep this secret from your parents? I'd like to stay on their good side."

My smile is instant, but falters a moment later. "I don't have any money, though."

He waves his hand like he's swatting a fly. "My treat."

Connor fits his palm on the top of my head and jostles my hair as he nudges me to the ticket counter.

At the concession stand I order peanut butter M&Ms and Connor tries really hard to convince me that the peanut ones are better.

When we get back to my house a few minutes before midnight, Connor breathes a sigh of relief at the now empty driveway except for Drew's car.

Stepping inside, we find my brother asleep on the couch.

Connor moves quietly around downstairs, taking inventory of every room. Furniture is askew. Lampshades tilted at odd angles. Empty pizza boxes and soda cans litter every surface in sight, and the television screen is paused on a game of Madden, game controllers tossed haphazardly on the coffee table.

I find the culprit of the sound of broken glass from before when I see a picture frame missing off the living room wall. The shattered frame sets on a nearby end table.

I move to head upstairs, but Connor stops me. "Let me check upstairs first."

He heads to the second floor as I make a pass through the living room, straightening up what I can without making too much noise. I grab a stack of pizza boxes and carry them into the kitchen.

I'm preparing to take out the trash when Connor returns. "Upstairs doesn't look like it's been touched."

I stifle a yawn as he takes the bag from my hand. "I got this. You can go on upstairs and go to bed." I eye him for a moment. He shouldn't have to clean this up. "This isn't your responsibility, Gretch."

"It's not yours, either."

"I know, and trust me, I'm not cleaning this by myself. I'm gonna sleep on the other couch and wake your brother up before dawn to make him do the cleaning." We share a knowing laugh, before he adds, "I can at least take out this trash, though."

"Okay," I say. I turn to head upstairs but stop to face him again before I get too far. "Connor?"

"Yeah?"

"Thank you for tonight."

"You're welcome. Night, Fish."

WHEN I COME DOWNSTAIRS the next morning, I'm greeted by a spotless house and a vibrant, fully alert, innocent-looking Drew inhaling a bowl of cereal at the kitchen counter. Connor, apparently, has already gone home.

Drew notices me, drops his bowl in the sink and swipes his keys from the counter. "Alright, let's go. Movie starts at 11:30 and I need to swing by the store to buy a new picture frame."

With a pep in my step, I happily follow Drew to his car.

Pitch Perfect twice in one weekend.

Best. Weekend. Ever.

Chapter Twenty-Three

KING OF CHIVALRY

CONNOR

"You wanna talk through the plan for tomorrow?"

She's not ready to talk about us, but she can't get out of talking about this. I'll take her words any way they come as long as she doesn't keep up this silent treatment.

Gretchen smiles at the waitress as she drops off a Diet Coke refill, before turning to me. "I don't have a grand plan, really. I was kind of hoping I would know what to do once we get there."

"And if we get there and you don't?"

Her body deflates. She hasn't even met this woman yet and she's already acting like she's lost.

"What are you afraid of, Gretch?"

She meets my gaze. "What am I not afraid of? I'm afraid I've gone about this all wrong and I should have called first. I'm scared I'll get there and chicken out and this whole trip will have been a waste. Or I won't chicken out, I'll knock on that door and she won't want anything to do with me—"

"I don't think that would hap—"

"Or," she emphasizes, cutting me off, "I'll knock on that door, she'll hug me and it'll be everything I dreamed it would be and I'll have to go home and explain this all to my family—how I did it without including them." She takes a breath and lowers her voice. "Even if this goes the best it can go, I still end up hurting my family in the end."

"Why would you think that?"

"Because I asked them about her. I asked questions about who she was and where she was from. I asked them to find her for me." Her voice cracks, eyes cloudy.

"When?" I don't believe for a second that Paul and Kelly Fisher would intentionally withhold this information from Gretchen if they had it.

"I started asking questions in middle school."

"And when did you ask them to find her?"

"I was a freshman."

"In college?"

She shakes her head. "High school."

"What exactly did they say?"

Her gaze drifts over my shoulder, lips tight, before she says, "They said they didn't have any information because it was a closed adoption. That my birth mom wanted it that way."

I sigh, scratching the hair under the brim of my hat. Her parents' answer sounds entirely reasonable, but it must have sounded like a brush-off to a fourteen-year-old kid who just wanted to know where she came from.

"So, yeah," she continues, indignation in her tone, "I do have something to be worried about. She may not want to see me."

Far be it from me to know the right thing to say, but I try. "I know I don't know all the details and I can't read minds or predict the future, but..." I pause, lost in the sadness welling in her eyes, mad as hell I can't take it away. "You were *fourteen* when you asked your parents to find her." She crosses her arms and leans back in her chair. "Fourteen, Gretch. They were probably just trying to protect you. I don't know anything about closed adoptions, but maybe they weren't lying. Maybe they really didn't have any information. Your parents love you, Fish."

"I know that," she says quickly, swiping a tear from her cheek. It guts me. It's the first one she's given me, but she didn't offer it willingly.

Several beats pass with me not sure what else to say, and Gretchen's mind working overtime. If I wasn't terrified she'd reject me, I'd pull her into a hug and hold her until her pain went away.

Her sad gaze locks on mine, probing for something it can't quite find, yet I feel the inquiry peel back my heart, layer by layer— nothing to numb the pain, just bare hands and a scalpel. "Sometimes it's the people you love that hurt you the most," she says quietly.

The waitress' timing is impeccable as she interrupts the moment and sets our plates in front of us. She's gone a moment later, Gretchen's words still twisting knots inside me.

On a deep breath, I funnel all the courage I have left to the surface. I say the most honest thing I've dared say since I walked away. "Sometimes love makes you crazy. Like, you care about someone so much you can't think straight. You do things, you say things, you…walk away from them only to realize too late that you made a huge mistake."

She chews slowly, eyes never losing contact as she sets her burger back on her plate. Molars glued together, lump in my throat, I follow her every move until, finally, she whispers, "It's never too late."

AFTER DEVOURING our weight in greasy burgers and fries, we see our plan through and find an ice cream shop down the street.

It's late afternoon now. The sun hammers down on tourists crowding downtown Sedona as they peruse souvenir shops, art galleries and boutiques. We sidewalk stroll but only last a grand total of thirty minutes before deciding we're ready to head back to the hotel and get some sleep.

When we're in the car, I connect my phone and press play on my *chill vibes* playlist. We're not even out of the parking lot before Gretchen lays her head back and shuts her eyes. I move to turn the volume down.

"No. Turn it back up," she says lazily.

Several minutes later, I'm convinced she's fallen asleep when James Morrison's voice croons through the speakers singing "Don't You Forget About Me." Slower and more intimate than the original or the popularized *Pitch Perfect* cover, it's my favorite version of this song.

On more than one occasion, Drew found me drinking myself into a stupor with this track blasting on repeat. *What is it with you and this song?* he'd ask. Then he'd shut off the stereo and yank me up off the floor. I never did give him the answers he was looking for.

When I finally reached my rock bottom later that fall and Drew forced me back into the land of the living, I began to skip the track altogether—my regret too much to bear.

Old habits have my finger reaching for the skip button, but something stops me—the book she's kept for twelve years and *It's never too late*. The usual sadness I feel at the sound of the familiar mystical piano intro is absent—there's hope there now. Hope that's magnified when I chance a glance at the woman in the passenger seat silently mouthing the lyrics.

REALITY GETS its ultimate revenge when the dramatic start to our morning comes roaring to the forefront. Back at the hotel, the pull-out bed made of jagged metal and tears of orphaned children taunts us both, while the oversized bed in the primary suite that looks like heaven on earth screams *choose me, choose me*.

Two deer caught in headlights, our eyes swing from the bedroom to the couch.

"You take the bed, I'll take the sofa," Gretchen says.

"I already said that's not happening."

"Oh my God, Connor. You're chivalrous, I get it. There's no

man more chivalrous than you, oh king of chivalry. You will yourself to a life of pain before allowing a female to take poor accommodations," she deadpans.

"Are you done?"

"Depends. Did it work?" she asks, brows raised to the heavens.

"Nope."

Gretchen throws her head back on a dramatic groan. "Fine. We'll share the bed."

A boisterous cackle erupts from my chest. The confounding look on Gretchen's face has me dragging the laugh out a few seconds longer than necessary. On a dime, I straighten my expression and say, "No. You take the bed, I'll sleep on the floor. It's good for my back anyway."

"You know what's even better for your back?" She cocks her head. "A bed!"

She stomps into the bedroom like she's won, forcefully kicks off her shoes and yanks out her hair tie. *Are we fighting?* Gliding to the dresser, she grabs a change of clothes while adding, "I'll shower first."

I stop her before the bathroom door closes. "I don't think this is a good idea, Gretch."

Her eyes roll to the back of her head as she leans against the doorjamb, arms crossed, hip popped. "Don't overthink it, old man. We'll put a wall of pillows down the middle. You won't even have to look at me."

Before I can object, she slams the door in my face and cranks the shower.

I cannot share a bed with this woman.

Toeing the line of unadulterated obstinance, I strip the sofa bed and pull all the extra bedding from the closet to make a pallet on the floor in the living room. Once it's done, I collect everything I'll need for my turn in the bathroom and cradle it in my arms. Then I wait, perched on the edge of the bed like a cheetah on the hunt—ready to pounce as soon as Gretchen opens the door. She won't have a moment to protest what I've done before I lock myself inside the bathroom, drowning out her disapproving comebacks.

I'll show her.

The bathroom door at last swings open and Gretchen emerges. My feet are dead weight beneath me as I take her in. She's effortless beauty incarnate, draped in a crimson cotton sleep set that consists of shorts and a matching tank.

Are all appropriate parts of her body covered? Yes.

Does it matter? No.

Olive-toned skin made even richer after a day in the sun. The braid she's draped over one shoulder. And those damn tortoise-shell glasses that *will* be the death of me.

I repeat, I CANNOT SHARE A BED WITH THIS WOMAN.

I rush to the bathroom, close the door behind me and lock it with a forceful *click*.

Gretchen's voice calls, "What side of the bed do y—" but I cut her off with the gush of the shower jets.

When I step out of the bathroom sometime later, Gretchen sits propped against the headboard watching television, a wall of pillows, as promised, running right down the middle of the mattress. She pays me no attention as I breeze past her.

Stepping into the living room, I come to an abrupt halt. The area where I made my pallet earlier has been cleared. Every blanket, every pillow—gone.

I pad back to the bedroom and level her with a stare. Deathly calm, I ask, "Where's my stuff?"

"What stuff?"

I shift to block her view of the television, standing guard at the foot of the bed, arms crossed. "Gretchen."

"Connor."

"Where's. My. Stuff," I emphasize, finger pointed toward the living room behind me.

Her eyes follow the movement, feigning innocence. "Oh that? Yeah, I got rid of it."

"You got rid of it," I say flatly.

"Yeah. Called the front desk and told them we didn't need all this excess bedding taking up space and they came and took it away." An arrogant smirk quirks the corner of her lips. "Looks like you're sharing the bed with me after all, old man."

Craning my neck from side to side, I suck in a deep, centering breath through my nose. "Fine."

I storm over to the dresser for more clothes because my plan to strip down to my boxers as soon as I was safely tucked under the blanket in the living room is now shot to hell. She's forced my hand.

I yank a t-shirt over my bare chest, spinning toward Gretchen when I hear her restrained cackle. "You have no idea what you've done."

Her laughter whirls out of control. If I wasn't so panicked, I might stop and appreciate how beautiful she is right now. "Oh my God. You are really worked up over this."

"It's your funeral." I rip back the covers and climb into the bed, intentionally and very strategically positioning myself as close to the edge of the mattress as I can, away from the pillow barricade and away from Gretchen Fisher.

Still amused by my dramatics, her laughter subsides. "Are you planning to smother me?"

"It's possible."

"Drama queen," she singsongs.

I raise a single finger in the air, declaring, "I sleep like a starfish," and a second finger, "I'm a chronic cuddler," third finger goes up, "and my body's a fucking furnace."

"So putting on *more* clothes made complete sense." Her words drip with delighted sarcasm at my predicament.

"Need I remind you of the...state...you found me in this morning?"

Stifling another laugh, she bites her lip as she adjusts her glasses. "Oh, I remember."

I throw my head back and slap a hand over my face as I imagine all the possibilities of what this night might bring. We may not survive this.

Gretchen reaches over the mountain of down and cotton that separates us and pulls a hand away from my face before releasing it. "Take a breath. It's gonna be fine."

"Listen," I begin, worry edging my voice, "I don't know what's going to happen tonight, so I just want to say in advance that I'm sorry and I didn't mean to do it."

I can't see her face but for the flicker of light from the television illuminating the room. The glee in her voice, though? Yeah, that's unmistakable. "And what, pray tell, do you think is gonna happen?"

"I'm glad my misery is so amusing to you."

"Me too," she cackles.

"Gretchen." My hands are back on my face, then yanking at the ends of my hair. *God, is it hot in here?* I'm already sweating. "I don't know, okay? I could wake up tomorrow buck naked with my head or my hands literally anywhere."

"Don't threaten me with a good time," she says as she turns off the television, shrouding this torture chamber some might call a bedroom in darkness.

This is it. This is where I die.

Chapter Twenty-Four

HE HEARS EVERYTHING I DON'T SAY

GRETCHEN

SUNLIGHT PEEKS THROUGH CURTAINS, slowly stirring me to consciousness. I grab my glasses from the nightstand and when my eyes come into focus, so do the rest of my senses.

A solid chest pressed up against me. A bare leg hiked over my hip. Warm, lazy breaths coasting over my collarbone. A forehead wedged in the crook of my neck. A giant man hand smack dab on top of my left boob.

Wait, what?

Connor's everything draped all over me.

Shifting my leg the slightest bit, I confirm he's still wearing boxers which is at least one mercy from above. However, he's definitely shirtless.

And, *oh my God*, he was right—his body is a furnace.

I assess the situation. One, his body on mine brings all kinds of memories flooding back that I should not be focusing on right now. Two, Connor warned me this could happen. Three, I hate it when he's right.

I could wake him, be cavalier about the whole thing and move onto another subject as quickly as possible. *Or* I could sneak out of the bed and he'd never have to know.

Option two is risky, but it's the only way to spare him the humiliation *and* salvage my pride.

Connor's fingers twitch, grazing my rapidly hardening nipple and I briefly consider secret option number three: offer my body as a willing sacrifice in his unconscious grope fest.

Stop, Gretchen. Pride. Do it for your pride!

Holding in a deep breath, I shift my head toward the edge of the bed—one inch, then two—my torso following suit. With the trunk of my body separated from his chest, I use the arm trapped between our bodies to press up on my elbow.

My head is barely off the pillow when Connor squeezes my boob like his own personal stress ball, pulls me back down, and tucks me even tighter to his body than I was before. "Five more minutes," he mumbles in a sleepy haze, totally oblivious to reality.

Void of ideas and motivation to try again—*thank you, boob hand*—I close my eyes and pray for sleep to find me once more.

I've only begun to drift off when Connor stirs, head burrowing in my neck. His contented hum vibrates against my throat.

Then, he stills.

I hold my breath, braced for impact, as he slowly—*slowly*—raises his head. Cloudy with sleep, his gaze runs up and down the bed, pausing momentarily here and there—his hands, his position, his empty side of the mattress. The wheels of his brain crank and turn and I can't do anything but wait for him to catch up. I certainly can't move with him damn near on top of me.

Cavalier, Gretchen. Look alive.

Something like six days later, he finally swivels his head, meeting my calm, composed eyes. *See, everything's fine.* Connor blinks as reality hits him and he bolts from the bed in a frenzy. "Shit!"

It's not the time to notice how his boxers hug his muscular thighs or the very obvious hard-on tucked behind the cotton material. Nope, definitely don't see that. "Connor, calm down. It's fine."

"Fine?" he shrieks. "No. It's not fine, Gretch! My hand was—"

He doesn't finish that thought but the dramatic gesticulating toward my chest finishes it for him.

I pull myself to a seated position. "Yes, your hand was here, your leg was there," I gesture accordingly, "and guess what? I'm fine. *We're* fine. I'm not mad. Nobody died. The world goes on."

He hears nothing. Fingers rake through his hair, yanking on the ends until they stand at full attention. He lowers his hands to his hips and sighs at the ceiling. I try to hold it in, I really do, but a disheveled, discombobulated Connor is too funny not to laugh at.

"Are you laughing at me?"

"I am absolutely laughing at you."

"This isn't funny," he says, but I do spy with my little eye the smirk tugging at his mouth.

"For the record, I tried to climb out of bed earlier to save you this embarrassment, but you weren't having it."

"How kind of you," he says. "Wait, what do you mean I 'wasn't having it'?"

"Well, you squeezed my boob and asked for five more minutes."

I think he stops breathing. With his wide eyes and slacked jaw, I have to bite my lip to keep a straight face. "I squeezed...your boob."

That is where I lose it. Loud, from-the-belly, howling laughter roars out of me. "That you did, old man."

"I'm so sorry, Gretch," he says with a look of genuine concern that should sober me, but I'm too far gone.

"Connor," I wheeze, "would you stop already? I said it's fine."

"I just can't believe you're laughing."

I temper my amusement just enough to reply. "You're standing in front of me with unhinged electrocution hair having some sort of existential crisis in nothing but boxer briefs shielding your erection."

Instantly, awareness takes over as his chin drops and he finally sees what I've been looking at for the past thirty seconds.

Before his panic wins again, I continue, "If it's not funny, it's awkward." I pause, something shifting when he meets my gaze, humor smothered under the weight of his stare. "It *has* to be funny," I whisper.

Please, let it be funny.

Silence lingers, our eyes locked. Jaw tensing with every passing second, I can tell he's holding something back. Words. Actions. Maybe both.

He finally looks away, lungs swelling on a long breath. With a smug grin, he finally says, "I guess I should go take care of this then."

I snort. "You probably should. It looks painful." Falling back onto the bed, I drape an arm over my face and laugh some more. Connor hurls a pillow at me before closing the bathroom door. "You need some help?" I taunt.

"Don't threaten me with a good time, Fish," he hollers back as the shower jets roar to life.

⁓

"I'm sorry, I think I want to change. I'll be right back."

Connor only smiles, twirling the car keys in his hand, as I head back to the bedroom. I shut the door behind me and kick off my white Keds before tossing my denim shorts and white fitted tee on the bed.

I change into a coral and white gingham print shorts romper and grab my white sandals. I'm sliding my sandals onto my feet when my phone pings from the vanity.

> **MOM**
>
> Hope you and your brother are having a great time. Dad and I can't wait to hear all about it. Send us pics. Love you!

Guilt pricks at my fingertips as I type out my reply.

> **ME**
>
> Sedona is beautiful. Love you, too!

I haven't heard from Drew since yesterday morning and, clearly, he hasn't spoken to our parents either. Rather than dwell on everything he and I are keeping from them—I'm nervous enough as it is —I send over a few scenic pictures from yesterday's hike and tuck my phone away.

When I step back into the living room, Connor looks up from where he was fiddling with his watch.

"How's this?" I brush my hands down the front of the romper, pulling at the hem of the shorts. "I thought maybe what I had on earlier was too casual. I mean, I'm not even sure I'll meet her today, but I wanna be ready, you know? The first outfit didn't feel like the best outfit for first impressions."

I puff out my cheeks, letting out a slow breath. Connor closes the distance between us and merely the proximity of him eases my nerves. His hands come to my shoulders as he says, "You're beautiful, Gretch. In this and the other and…anything, really. It doesn't matter what you wear, she'd be a fool not to love you."

My heart soars, the thump of my pulse telling my head to believe his words.

"Big day," he says.

"Big day."

He extends a hand toward the door. "Shall we?"

ASIDE FROM THE three times I make Connor stop to accommodate my nervous bladder, the drive to Flagstaff is mostly uneventful.

We stopped for gas and he bought me a Diet Coke and peanut butter M&Ms while I ran to the restroom. "For your nerves," he'd said.

He caught me chewing my nails, stopped me, and held my hand the rest of the way like it was the most natural thing in the world. Even when I made him stop *again*, when I got back in the car, I reached for his hand like a ship finding its anchor.

As our destination draws closer, the scenery noticeably changes around us. Where Sedona is a stone and stucco town painted in fifty shades of red, the closer we get to Flagstaff, the landscape shifts from desert to mountainous. Behind us are the desert mesas and unrelenting sun. Here, the sun shines through slivers of dense forests made up of towering pines, lush with green foliage. In the distance, a mountain pierces the horizon with a single, snow-capped peak.

The GPS voice commands us to take the next exit into Flagstaff, sending my nerves into the rafters. The culmination of all that I've done to get here over the past fifteen months rushes in: the DNA test, the adoption detective, the money spent, the lies I've told and the secrets I've kept. Not to mention the countless years prior that I spent dreaming about it all.

"It's okay, Gretch. I'm right here with you." Connor squeezes my hand, matching my white-knuckle grip on his.

I blink, it seems, and we're pulling into a neighborhood on the edge of town. We pass streets chocked full of quaint, mid-sized homes. Life bustles down each avenue. A group of preteen girls, heads thrown back in laughter, ride their bikes side by side. Two young boys play catch across their yard. A woman pushes a stroller on the sidewalk.

The final turn tucked at the back of the neighborhood is ours. The abundance of mature trees creates a canopy over the street, bringing a coziness that's in direct odds to the flutters in my stomach.

"I think that's it." Connor jerks his head toward a house a few doors down.

I lean forward to investigate just as a minivan backs out of the driveway and drives off ahead of us. Red brake lights flash as it disappears around the corner at the end of the street.

We come to a stop on the curb across the street. "I think we missed her."

I hear his voice, but not his words. Everything going in my ears a muffled, hazy mess, I can't hear beyond what my eyes see.

He jiggles our held hands. "Gretch."

"Huh?" I turn, tearing the mental cobwebs away as his words finally register. "Yeah, I guess so." My gaze lands back on the house and anxiety rises like bile in my throat.

A gentle hand on my cheek turns my face until we're eye to eye. "Tell me what's going on up here, Fish," he murmurs, softly tapping my temple.

The urge to go home overtakes me. I don't know what I was thinking. I shouldn't be here. A tear breaks from the corner of my eye and Connor's thumb catches it before it hits my cheek.

"I'm not going anywhere. I promise. You can tell me."

Every self-preservation instinct I have disappears. Sobs bubble up from my chest as the words tumble out of me. "I'm thinking there's a tricycle in the yard and sidewalk chalk on the driveway and a basketball net above the garage and she has this whole life here… with kids. I want to meet them but what if they don't know about me? What if she never told them I exist and I just show up on her doorstep?" I pause to catch my breath and a sob escapes.

"Before, when I imagined her, I knew it was possible she had other kids, but they were only in my head. They didn't feel real. But now I'm here and they're real and what if me showing up messes everything up for her family? I can't do that to them."

Connor pulls my forehead to his, both hands on my cheeks, swiping tears as quickly as they fall. "Shhh," he breathes. Forehead to forehead, he waits, urging me to match my breaths to his. I grip his forearms, hands trembling, until my lungs find a steady rhythm.

"I'm sorry," I say for the hundredth time. "I thought I would get here and know what to do, but I don't."

"Stop apologizing. You are so incredibly brave. Everything you've done to get yourself here?" He huffs out a sharp breath while his thumb caresses my cheek. Tilting my head up to meet his gaze, he adds, "I am in awe of you."

I savor his words even if I find them hard to believe. I'm so thankful he's here.

"I am so absurdly proud of you."

The pressures eases in my chest. "Absurdly?"

He grins. "Yeah, like it's stupid silly how proud I am of you right now."

Our eyes catch. Pools of glacier blue delicately tether me—it's impossible to look away. Our positions haven't changed. His hands still rest softly on my cheeks while my hands clutch his forearms like they're life rafts at high tide.

"I have an idea for you to consider," he says.

"I'm listening."

"What if we left a note?"

"A note?"

"We leave a note letting her know you were here and that you'd like to meet her. We say you plan to come back at noon tomorrow and if she doesn't want that then she can leave a message with the front desk at the hotel. No exchange of phone numbers and no awkward face to face conversations until you know that she wants to see you."

"Okay," is the only word I manage, but my heart shouts so much more.

Yes! Thank you. How do you do that? This is why I never wanted to do this with anyone except you. You've always been my first choice.

Two hearts in sync, it's as though he hears everything I don't say. His thumb continues its back-and-forth path over my cheek as his eyes clamp shut, like his restraint could snap any minute.

This man.

I'm tired of overthinking it. I don't want to think at all.

Slowly, I close the small gap between us and lightly press my lips to his. His fingertips hitch along my cheekbones.

A single kiss tasting of salty tears and *then* and *now* and *best friend* and *my person*. It's not enough and I want so much more, but I pull back.

The tormented look, the anguished lines of his jaw, his brows, the pain that radiates off him in waves—it wrecks me. My heart sputters to a stop.

Terrified that I've ruined everything, I open my mouth to speak, but he beats me to it. "Don't you dare apologize to me." He drops his chin, the words landing on his chest as he presses his forehead into mine. "I'll keep waiting until you're ready. Just…don't apologize, okay? My heart won't survive it."

I nod because what else is there to say except every single thing —all the things and all the words. My words and his words, fighting to the finish. Past hurts on display like exposed nerves, a full-on assault in the form of explanations, defenses and apologies. Unspoken thoughts and feelings bubbling to the surface, finally getting the air they've craved for too many years.

No. *My* heart won't survive that.

But I'm also not sorry that I kissed him.

Chapter Twenty-Five

I FIND YOUR ABS MODERATELY REPULSIVE

CONNOR

SHE KISSED ME.

She kissed me and it took every ounce of willpower I had not to fist my hand in her hair and tug her closer, press in deeper. But I knew it didn't mean what I wanted it to mean. A sign of something good to come, maybe. Or it would become the last time I'd ever kiss her. It was hope and dread all wrapped up in the smallest, softest meeting of lips.

The apology was on the tip of her tongue and I couldn't bear to hear her say she regrets it.

Twenty minutes later, after a quick run to the nearest store for supplies, we're parked back in front of the house. The floorboard littered with a dozen crumpled pieces of paper, Gretchen's anxiety gets the best of her every time she begins again, overthinking every word, every sentence.

Over it, she shoves the notepad and pen in my chest. "Can you just write it?"

I take the supplies from her unsteady hands. "What's her name?"

"Cheyenne Ortega."

After a few silent minutes, I pass the notepad back to her. "How's this?"

> DEAR CHEYENNE,
> MY NAME IS GRETCHEN FISHER.
> WE'VE NEVER MET, BUT I'VE RECENTLY DISCOVERED THAT YOU ARE MY BIOLOGICAL MOTHER. MY PARENTS, PAUL AND KELLY FISHER, ADOPTED ME AT BIRTH 22 YEARS AGO AND I'VE GROWN UP IN BLOOMINGTON, ILLINOIS.
> MY APOLOGIES FOR SHOWING UP UNANNOUNCED. I RESPECT YOUR FAMILY'S PRIVACY, SO I DO NOT WANT TO INTRUDE.
> THAT SAID, I WOULD LOVE TO MEET YOU. IF YOU'RE INTERESTED IN MEETING ME, THAT IS.
> I PLAN TO RETURN TOMORROW AT NOON. HOWEVER, IF YOU DO NOT WISH FOR ME TO DO SO, YOU CAN LEAVE A MESSAGE FOR ME AT THE FRONT DESK OF MY HOTEL IN SEDONA (CONTACT INFO IS ENCLOSED), NO QUESTIONS ASKED.
> I HOPE TO MEET YOU SOON, BUT I WILL COMPLETELY UNDERSTAND IF YOU DECIDE YOU DON'T WANT THE SAME.
> SINCERELY,
> GRETCHEN

She reads the letter several times over before nodding her head.

"Okay. Now, here. I want you to copy that note, word for word, in your own handwriting." It may not matter who writes it, but this note has the potential to become a cherished memento for Cheyenne and she deserves to have it in her daughter's handwriting. She may not realize it yet, but Gretchen will want that too.

She swallows hard, accepting the pen and turning to a blank sheet of paper. "Yeah, okay."

When she's finished, she seals it inside an envelope and I take her hand in mine. "Do you want me to put it on the door for you?"

She closes her eyes through a steadying breath, resolutely shaking her head. "No. I can do it."

Letter in hand, she climbs out of the car, rounds the hood and crosses the street. She has no idea how strong she is. It's not only that I could never understand what it's like to grow up in a family that doesn't share your genetic code; it's more than that. It's the quiet girl who doesn't put herself out there easily, putting herself out there in the most vulnerable way. It's the quiet determination, the tenacity it took to get herself here. And I'm the lucky bastard who gets to witness it.

Once she's back in the car, I'm ready to lift some of the burden she's been carrying. "You did it, Gretch." I wrap my hand over hers. "Whatever happens now is out of your control."

"You're right." The smallest smile tilts her lips and it's the best view I've seen all morning. Gretchen sprawled across the bed, mussed with sleep, wearing those glasses, laughing hysterically at my humiliation, a very close second.

"How about we go explore that downtown area we passed on the way in before heading back?"

That tilted lip turns to a full-faced smile. "Sounds fun."

Two overpriced fancy coffees later, we're strolling through downtown Flagstaff when I spot a small indie bookstore across the road. "Let's go in there."

She lights up as she grabs me by the wrist and pulls me through the crosswalk.

A bell chimes above us when we step inside and Gretchen bolts straight to the romance and fiction sections while I peruse the rest of the shoebox-sized shop.

The center of the small space has a long row of antique wooden tables, stacks of books about crystals and astrology atop them in an ornate display alongside bowls of different colored crystals and gems. All of it very befitting for the hippie energy of this charming little town.

An array of large coffee table books showcasing the diverse landscapes of Arizona fills the shelves near the register.

I'm casually flipping through the pages of a book highlighting Arizona's most underrated tourist attractions when I notice Gretchen in the far back corner of the shop, dubbed Collector's Corner, delicately exploring a small hardback in her hands.

Gretchen notices my approach and quickly tucks the book back on the shelf before meeting me halfway.

"What 'cha looking at?" I ask.

She pops her shoulders. "Just browsing." Before I can press for more, she adds, "I'm gonna run to the bathroom and then we can go."

She dashes through the beaded curtain at the back of the shop while I go on a mission of my own. Coming to the shelf she was "just browsing", I see it right away: a single copy of *Little Women*. The aged binding and the letterpress on the cover that barely has any gold ink left tell me this must be an even earlier edition than what I bought for her all those years ago.

A few minutes later, she meets me at the exit. "Sorry that took so long. It's a lot of work to pee in a romper. Oooh, what did you get?" She eyes the brown paper bag with white tissue paper peeking from the top that I'm carrying.

"Oh, just a coffee table book about Arizona for my mom. She collects them."

She pats my cheek as she passes by me on the way out the door. "Such a cute little mama's boy."

THE FRONT DESK attendant back at the resort informs us there are no messages yet from Cheyenne.

Leaving that note, understanding it's out of her control now, has settled Gretchen. It's all over her face, her gait, her mood—she's relaxed. An afternoon by the pool is the perfect way for both of us to shake off the heaviness of the morning.

I tuck the bag from the bookstore in my suitcase and change into my swim trunks while Gretchen changes in the bathroom. Stepping out of the closet, I come face to face with the source of my latest indignity.

The king-sized bed taunts me. It thinks it's so big, of course two people can share it—I mean, look at all that space. But it's a lie. I know it, the bed knows it, and now Gretchen knows it.

My mind spins as it plots and plans how I'll handle another night sharing a bed with my best friend's sister. It spins and spins until the bathroom door opens, the woman in question emerging wearing a cherry red two-piece bathing suit. The bathing suit a frightening reminder of another two-piece I saw her in six years ago. A sight that changed how I saw her from that point forward.

An open weave cover-up falls over her shoulders, but it doesn't cover much at all. When she bends over to grab the pool bag, giving me a perfect view of her ass, I have to turn away. I grab a t-shirt and push my head through the top of the fabric in time to find Gretchen's hungry eyes aimed at my torso.

Caught red-handed, she busies herself with her sunglasses, sliding them onto her face as she asks, "You ready?"

Stifling a smile, I grab her arm as she passes by me on the way to the door. When her chin lifts, face in line with mine, I slide the pool bag off her shoulder. "I got this," I whisper, throwing in a wink to drive her crazy.

She rolls her eyes.

"Don't roll your eyes at me," I quip.

"I didn't roll my eyes."

"Oh, yes you did."

"I'm wearing sunglasses, Connor." Her tanned arms cross over her chest, a challenging grin playing on her lips.

I move in closer, her neck falling back to hold my gaze.

"Yes. You are, indeed, wearing sunglasses *inside* our hotel room." I cock my head and let my smug grin break free. "And I know you rolled your eyes, because when you do, this brow," I lightly stroke my finger across her right eyebrow, "lifts just a little higher than your other one."

She stills, the air between us a live wire cranked to eleven. Then, she uncrosses her arms and closes in. Her body, warm and all baby soft skin, presses in on mine as she brings two fingers to rest against the pulse point on my neck. "And *I* know you're turned on by this right here." She gently taps her fingers over the throbbing vein. "It's your biggest tell. Your body can't hide when your heart starts racing because this pulse point damn near thrums out of your skin."

She steps back sporting a proud grin to match mine. *Well played, Gretch. Well played.*

"I've seen it up close a time or two," she adds as she spins to leave. "That and your erection."

My panicked eyes dart to my swim trunks.

Gretchen laughs. "Made ya look." She throws a pleased smile over her shoulder as she stalks toward the door. "Let's go, old man."

"You're staring, QB."

Her red two-piece pops off her tanned skin. The strapless top with a bow detail tucked between her breasts is secured by a knot at the back. She's swept her hair up into a clip, putting the breadth of her collarbone glistening under the sun on full display. Matching retro-style red bottoms sit high on her waist and I don't even miss the skin hidden beneath the extra material covering her lower stomach. Gretchen Fisher doesn't need to show a ton of skin to be sexy.

Our eyes meet, smiles bouncing off each other.

"Oh, damn. I forgot." I lower my aviators. "There."

I swipe my t-shirt off with one pull over my shoulder and toss it into the pool bag. Gretchen props her sunglasses on her head before rubbing a layer of sunscreen over her face and down her neck.

When she hands the bottle to me, she makes a show of sliding her sunglasses back down so she can ogle me unashamedly from behind the tinted lenses. Her face breaks out in a wily smile.

"Well, look who's staring now," I say.

"For the record, I find your abs moderately repulsive." She settles into the lounger next to me. "But at least you have a pretty face."

She grabs her margarita and we clink our cups together, memories ringing through my mind like the toll of a bell.

Chapter Twenty-Six

THE PROMISE

CONNOR

six years ago, summer

It's a perfect Illinois summer night. Lightning bugs flicker and the air is balmy under the setting sun.

Thanks to Mom and Dad's relocation to North Carolina after I graduated high school, this is my first time back in Illinois since I left for college four years ago.

After a month at my parents' beach house in the Outer Banks, Drew and I have returned to Bloomington for the next four weeks. The beach was for that one last hoorah between graduation and becoming real-life grownups, while being back here is for finding a job—or, in Drew's case, starting law school—a place to live and adulting in general.

"Drew!"

The animated female voice shrieks from the direction of the house and I turn to see a head of jet black hair streak across the yard like smeared ink.

A red sports bra with a white cross on the front signifies her job as a lifeguard and it's the only thing adorning her upper half. Below, a pair of denim shorts sit atop a set of smooth bronze legs.

I can't see her face from here, but I already know the braces will be gone. There's sure to be a white-toothed smile in their place that lights up the whole night sky.

"Gretch!" Drew shouts, meeting her halfway. She jumps up, wrapping him in a hug.

"You're back!"

"Connor and I got in a few hours ago," Drew says as I grow deeply invested in Mr. & Mrs. Fisher's roofline. So many…shingles.

"Oh, is he here?"

"You ran right past him, you goof."

Our gazes meet as she turns around. For only a fraction of a second, something like surprise flashes in her eyes before they soften.

"Hey, Fish." I order my smile to read kind and platonic. *PLATONIC!*

In three strides, she wraps her arms around my neck. Platonic doesn't equal impolite, so I hug her back but only with ample space for Jesus between us.

"It's good to see you, Connor."

"You too."

Holy. Shit. Gretchen Fisher grew up real good and I definitely should *not* be noticing.

FOR THE BETTER PART OF the month, I successfully avoid her. With her work schedule at the community pool, Drew and I's social calendar, plus our weekend trips into the city to apartment hunt, our run-ins are few and far between. Awkward and generally terrible, but few and far between.

There was that early morning in the kitchen before the rest of the house was up. I was on my way out for a run when I stopped in the kitchen for a bottle of water. Only, when I found Gretchen was already there pouring a cup of coffee, I spun on a dime, stabbed my

AirPods in my ears and marched right out the front door. Water is for the weak anyway.

As far as the coffee shop run-in goes, if I'd known she was there, I would have gone somewhere else. After collecting my order from the barista, Gretchen called me over to where she was seated with a few other girls her age. My mind circled back to a time when she didn't have many friends. Softened as my heart may have been in that moment, I made quick work of saying hi to the table and got the hell out of there.

Then, there was last night.

Me along with the whole Fisher family were hunkered in the living room for family movie night. Gretchen picked *Pitch Perfect* and I should have seen that for the omen it was.

Across the room in the plush armchair, she sat wrapped in a blanket, knees tucked to her chest. Not an inch of skin was showing but she was still so beautiful.

Glass of Diet Coke over ice in hand, she was three handfuls deep on her first bag of peanut butter M&Ms when she proudly announced during the opening credits, "Hey parents, did you know Drew took me to see this when I was eleven?"

I choked on my popcorn. Drew turned on a slow-motion swivel, pure death in his eyes as Kelly and Paul erupted with laughter.

"How'd she manipulate you this time?" Paul sputtered out.

"I was not manipulated." Drew's tone promised revenge.

"No. I just bribed him. He didn't want me to tell you that he had a par—" A pillow pummeled her in the face, Drew launching three more in quick succession behind it.

Gretchen emerged from under the mountain of pillows still laughing. Minutes later, everyone's focus back on the television again, my eyes drifted. Hers were right there to meet me. She half-grinned. I half-grinned. She winked. My grin grew a little wider and I winked back.

Drew shifted on the couch, pulling my attention. My best friend's gaze was narrowed right at me, inquisition threatening.

The second the end credits began to roll, I loudly announced I needed to call my mom and barricaded myself in the guest bedroom for the rest of the night.

~

I SKIPPED breakfast for the usual reason of needing to avoid Gretchen. Only, now you can add her brother to the list.

It's lunchtime and the hangry pains are kicking in. I finally tread down the stairs, cautiously peeking around corners for signs of a half-dressed Gretchen or a nunchuck-wielding Drew. Both possibilities equally terrifying.

Finding the kitchen empty, I exhale a sigh of relief and raid the fridge.

Sounds of splashing and laughter bring me to the breakfast nook window. Gretchen and a few friends are hanging by the pool. Maybe I met the girls at the coffee shop last week. I can't be sure. But it's the two teenage boys competing for biggest cannonball that have my fists clenching at my sides. The girls laugh at their antics from their perch on the pool's edge, legs dangling in the water.

Gretchen's hair sits in a single braid pulled to one side. Instead of her red lifeguard suit, she's in an emerald green two piece. The top has a thick strap over one shoulder, leaving the other bare. Matching bottoms sit low on her hips but don't reveal too much. Sitting next to the other girls whose choice of swimwear leaves little to the imagination with the tiny straps and even tinier scraps of fabric, Gretchen shines.

One of the boys swims over and props himself up on his forearms next to Gretchen. She looks down at him and brushes his *I-don't-know-what-scissors-are* hair off his forehead. Inexplicably, I want to hurl him over the fence.

Gretchen turns. Our gazes catch and my non-existent cover is blown. She lifts her hand in a dainty wave, her smile beaming fast and wide. I wave back, but quickly turn to leave. When I make for the living room, I freeze on my feet.

Drew stands in the doorway, eyes hurling daggers at me.

"You're up," he says, expression unforgiving, as he stalks toward me.

"Yeah. I was really tired, I guess."

Standing at the window now, we face each other, but Drew's attention is cast over the pool. "Looks like Gretch has some friends over." He stares at something beyond the glass, but I keep my eyes on him.

"Yeah, looks like it."

Drew's head turns. He holds my gaze and my pulse rises. "So, I guess we need to talk about it."

"Talk about what?"

"Why you were winking at my sister last night."

"Drew, I—"

"And why you were staring at her through the window like some creeper."

"It's not what you think," I supply.

"No?"

"No. It's not."

Impatience simmers under Drew's skin as he waits for me to say more.

"I'm waiting, Vining. If it's not what I think, then tell me what it *is*. I watched the two of you give eyes at each other and then you winked at her."

"It was a joke, dude."

"A joke?" he scoffs.

"An *inside* joke," I amend.

"Why do *you* have inside jokes with *my* little sister?"

I throw out my arms. "I don't know how I'm supposed to answer that."

"It looked like flirting," he accuses.

While I can concede that the wink could be interpreted as flirtation, that's not at all how it was intended. Yes, she's gorgeous in a way that has completely blindsided me. But I'd *never* make a move on a sixteen-year-old girl.

"Are you kidding me right now?"

"Answer the question."

"No! I wasn't flirting with her. She's sixteen. What kind of guy do you think I am?"

His expression softens a bit, but he doesn't back down. "And just now?"

"I came downstairs, heard commotion in the pool and I walked over to see what was going on. She waved at me, I waved back. That's it." He releases a pointed breath through his nose, stuffing his hands in his pockets. "Look, I know she's your sister, but I've looked out for her over the years, too. Every time I came over here to hang out, she was here. So, yeah, we'd talk, we'd joke around. I care about Gretchen but you don't need to read anything into it that isn't there."

I'm walking a very fine line because I absolutely do care about Gretchen in a way that means I will always look out and want the best for her. If I tell Drew I'm attracted to her, it's over. He won't see past that one singular statement, regardless of how genuine I may be about everything else.

"Which means?"

"It means I care about her well-being. I'll look out for her. I'd step in to protect her if she needed me to."

He looks back to the window. A heavy pause fills the room to the point of torture. He coolly breaks the silence by blurting out, "Why do I wanna punch that floppy-haired kid in the face?"

"Right?"

"I do trust you," Drew says, eyes back on me.

I ignore every implication and unspoken demand that comes with that trust because what alternative response is there? "You *can* trust me."

"Yeah, I know," he mutters. He turns to leave and I follow a step behind, trying to quiet every intrusive thought that threatens to destroy the best friendship I've ever had.

Abruptly, he turns back to face me, the movement skittering me to a stop. "Promise me," he pleads.

"Promise what?"

"Promise me that I can trust you."

A little voice in my head screams *red flag, red flag*. I squash it to smithereens as I look my best friend dead in the eye. "I promise."

～

It's our last night in Bloomington before Drew and I head to Chicago for good. We'll spend the next few days moving into our shared apartment before I start my new graphic design job at Driskill Marketing Group and Drew prepares to begin law school.

Our old high school football crew swarms the high-top table as the waitress drops off another round of tequila shots. They're tossed back in a matter of seconds. Looks like I'm the designated driver tonight because we're not even an hour in and Drew's already tipsy.

"Will you be able to get me out of parking tickets?" Henley asks, eyes wide with excitement.

"Or you could just park legally," I say.

"Yes, but what's the point of having friends in high places, Vining, if not to skirt the law?"

Drew clumsily drops his pool cue to the table. He locks Henley in an intense gaze. One hand on his chest, the other aloft in a three fingered salute, he says, "Scout's honor, my man. I got your back."

"My guys!" a deep voice calls from behind. We all turn to see McDormand, former defensive lineman, saunter in.

Bro handshakes and back slaps are exchanged all around and we spend the next hour catching up over trays of hot wings and a bounty of alcohol.

Drew and I regale the group with tales of our college escapades as "campus football heroes." Their words, not mine. And it mostly applies to Drew since my injury freshman year took me out of the game for good.

I point out as much, but Drew claps me on the back and says, "Don't be fooled, yaguys," he slurs, words fused together. "Vining here got more action than allofus combined."

Stifling a smile, I roll my eyes as I tip back my glass of water… because my best friend is trashed.

"Speaking of action," McDormand interjects with a slimy look that puts my spidey senses on alert. "I saw your sister lifeguarding at the pool downtown, Fisher."

Drew's jaw tics, nostrils flaring.

Never one to read the room, McDormand presses on. "She grew up to be a sexy little thing, didn't she?"

"The fuck did you say?" Drew shouts, stumbling to his feet as Henley launches forward to hold him back.

Call it jealousy or keeping a promise, but I'm instantly chest to chest with the lineman. "I suggest you shut your mouth before it gets you in trouble."

Hands raised in surrender, he steps back.

"You keep your eyes off my sister! She's sixteen," Drew seethes, voice low and menacing.

"Whoa, whoa, guys. Everyone, calm down. I meant no harm," McDormand says, but the cocky smile that spreads across his face is the final nail in his coffin as I clench my fist. "But she's not gonna be sixteen forever, man."

Nope, I was wrong. *That* was the final nail.

Faster than I can react, Drew pushes Henley aside and lunges at him. Arms outstretched, I step between them to prevent the collision. I turn toward my best friend to plead with him to let it go just as his fist flies, meeting me square in the eye. A drunken, poorly aimed fist intended for McDormand.

My head knocks back with the impact. "Dammit, Fisher!"

Deaf to anything other than his own fury, Drew pushes past me. The rest of the guys flood in on all sides to keep them separated.

"My sister is off limits. Do you hear me? That goes for all of you. Not my sister. Not now. Not ever. Off. Fucking. Limits."

Half an hour later, we're back home. After he's puked in the lawn, I help Drew up the stairs and to his room.

"I didn't mean to punch you, I swear. McDormand's a prick," he mumbles, so close to passing out his lips barely move.

"I know. We're cool. Sleep it off."

He's unconscious before I'm out the door.

My reflection in the bathroom mirror reveals the swollen sensitive flesh around my eye already darkening with what is sure to be a nasty bruise.

I toss and turn in bed for an hour, restless, mind circling the confrontation with Drew in the kitchen to the events at the bar tonight. I know I put his mind at ease when we spoke, but his message to McDormand—to all of us—was heard loud and clear.

Thank God I'm moving to Chicago tomorrow.

Sleep continues to allude me. At 1am. I decide it's time to burn off some steam, so I throw on my swim trunks and head downstairs.

I leave the exterior lights off as I wade quietly into the water, careful not to make too much noise. After about a dozen laps, I stop at the deep end, clutching the pool ledge to catch my breath. The sound of the sliding door pierces the hum of the otherwise quiet night air.

"Midnight swims are supposed to be my thing." Gretchen stands on the porch, towel in hand, wearing denim shorts and an over-sized t-shirt.

"Couldn't sleep," I say.

"I just like the quiet."

"I get that." I quickly climb out of the pool, grab my towel and throw on my shirt, not bothering to dry off first. The cotton immediately clings to my wet chest. "I'll leave you to it then," I add as I head for the house.

"I didn't mean you had to leave. You can stay."

The plea in her voice makes me stop. Thankful for the darkness that shields the uncertainty in my face, I make myself say, "I should probably try and get some sleep."

She gnaws on her bottom lip.

I stride the final step toward the door. "Night, Fish."

Before I can get the door open, she asks, "Did I do something wrong?"

I look at her over my shoulder. "What?"

"You've been here for a month and have barely spoken two words to me." I turn to face her fully, chin dipped to my chest as I rake a hand through my hair. "It feels like you've spent the last four weeks avoiding me. And now you're leaving tomorrow."

Guilt cleaves my heart in half.

"It's been four years and I was really excited for both of you to be home this summer and then you get here and it's…weird. I get that you're seven years older and I'm just a kid, but…you never used to ignore me."

"Stop," I command, stepping out of the shadows to move in closer. "You didn't do anything wrong."

She does a once-over of my face and I realize too late what she's seeing. "Oh my God, what happened to your eye?"

"I'm fine. Just got into it with one of our old high school buddies at the bar tonight." Not a lie, per se.

"Over what?"

I shrug. "Dumb guy stuff." Before she can push for more details, I go on. "But I mean it, Gretch. You didn't do anything wrong."

The faint glow of the moonlight barely illuminates her face, making it hard to discern the thoughts barreling through that over-thinking head of hers.

"But?" she whispers.

"But…it's been a really busy time with finding a job and a place to live, going back and forth to the city. I'm exhausted, honestly."

It's a load of crap and I think she knows it.

"Well, I'll leave you alone then. I know you've got an early morning tomorrow." With that, she turns and goes to sit at the pool's edge. Still fully clothed, she leans back on her palms and dangles her legs in the water.

An onslaught of feelings rush in and I can't move. I shouldn't be out here. I need to go inside. But I don't want to leave with her thinking she's done something to deserve this.

"Did you really make Drew take you to see *Pitch Perfect* after that party?"

She swivels her head and locks me with a look of pure mischief. Sure to leave a few feet between us, I plop down next to her, mirroring her position.

"Did he know that I'd already taken you to see it?"

She eyes me sidelong. "What do you think?"

"Well played, Fish. Well played."

For several minutes, we sit in comfortable silence. The sound of our legs lazily floating up and down creates a steady rhythm of water pushing and pulling against the side of the pool. And this—sitting without the pressure to be or do—is the most natural thing I've done all month.

"I learned something new last year. You wanna see?" Gretchen asks.

I tilt my head. "Should I be scared?"

She ignores my question as she hops up and runs back inside. A few seconds later, she returns with two plastic cups. When she sits down, she turns to face me, legs crisscross apple sauce. She sets the cup upside down in front of her.

My brows lift. "You didn't."

Without any preamble she goes right into the Cups song from *Pitch Perfect*, hitting every note and movement perfectly.

I promptly turn to face her. I cross my legs like hers and set the second cup in front of me. "Okay, you have to teach me now."

For the next fifteen minutes, she walks me through the steps. At best, I do a mediocre job, but it's so much fun I don't even care. And now that the ice is broken, the conversation flows like a dam that's just been breached.

She tells me about her friends from school and my heart warms. I still want to punch the floppy-haired kid in the face, but I keep that to myself.

I ask about her plans after high school and she tells me about wanting to study fashion in New York.

She asks me about college, my new job, my family and moving to Chicago. There's no question she throws my way that I hesitate to answer. Before we know it, it's three in the morning. She never got in the pool and my shirt is now dry to the bone.

Back inside, we stop at the top of the stairs, our bedrooms flanking us in opposite directions. There's not an awkward beat between us when I haul her in for a hug and say good night before we part ways.

Gretchen's already left for work before Drew and I head for Chicago the next morning. Thoughts of her creep in and out all day. I wrestle with the juxtaposition of feeling grateful for both her friendship *and* the distance between us so I don't have to see her all the time.

Because there's one thing I can't shake no matter how hard I try, McDormand's words that echo ominously in my brain. What the hell am I supposed to do when she's not sixteen anymore?

Chapter Twenty-Seven

I NEED NAMES

GRETCHEN

"What's it like being this pool's hottest bachelor?"

The bachelor in question arches a brow from behind his sunglasses, adjusting his grip on the pool ledge. "I don't know what you're talking about."

I float in the water opposite him, my hand on the edge of the pool keeping me afloat along with my legs treading water beneath me.

"See, what *I* heard you say is that you're so accustomed to women checking you out that you don't even notice it anymore."

Connor Vining in nothing but swim trunks and aviator glasses should be illegal. The wandering eyes of every woman within fifty yards confirms this. In fact, I'd say we have a class-action lawsuit on our hands.

"I don't need you stroking my ego, Gretchen."

I fight back a grin. "It's taking everything in me to not make a dirty joke about stroking right now."

He mutters a string of profanity under his breath, fingers pinching the bridge of his nose. I stifle a laugh.

To these women's credit, his body is a sight to behold. Golden skin makes his sun-kissed dirty blonde hair sparkle and he's got the kind of muscle composition that looks like good genetics as opposed to hours spent in the gym. His abs are far from repulsive and his face is light years beyond pretty.

"Katie McBigBoobs over your shoulder hasn't stopped staring at you. She thinks those bug-eyed sunglasses are hiding it, but we both know what's going on behind those lenses."

He chuckles through tight lips.

"Then there's Jessica VonSunlessTanner laid out on her stomach with her head oh-so-conveniently turned toward you and she thinks I don't notice every time she opens one eye to make sure you're still there."

Face charmed, he shakes his head. "You're crazy."

I lean in close and whisper, "And they both look like they want to murder me."

Connor's jaw tics before his hand plunges under the water and he yanks me toward him. I gasp as he turns us so my back is pressed against the side of the pool. His arms on either side of my head cage me in and I reach for his waist to stay afloat.

My gaze traces the column of his throat all the way up to his eyes. Even with sunglasses, his attention lances straight through me like a laser beam.

"Wrap your legs around my waist so you don't sink," he says, voice husky.

Because touching him is my new favorite pastime and my body is absolute putty in his hands, I do exactly as he says. I link my ankles around the solid pillar of him. His body presses in closer until only inches separate the space between my legs and his lower torso.

"Now wrap your arms around my neck," he commands, widening his arms to give me space to obey. Once my arms are in place, my body quite literally propped up on his, he narrows his grip on the pool's edge and that infamous Connor smirk comes out to play.

"Good girl," he murmurs. "Do you think they're staring now?"

My breaths come shallow, small bursts of air parching my lips until I skim my tongue over them. "I would assume they're fashioning some sort of shiv to stab me with in the bathroom later."

He drifts closer—or maybe I've pulled him in—my breasts now pressed into him.

"What are you doing?" I whisper, the ache between my legs building, demanding friction.

He rests his forehead against mine. "I need to make sure Katie and Jessica know I'm not interested."

Skin to skin, my soft flesh wrapped around the hard planes of his, his proximity sets my body ablaze, yet quiets the noise inside me all at once. If all I had for the rest of my life was the nearness of him, I wouldn't want for anything.

Heads fused together, we stay locked in our embrace, breathing each other in. Everyone and everything else fades into obscurity; it's just us. Him. Me. And the *us* we almost were back then.

Connor's cell phone rings, severing the moment in two.

He checks his watch. "I have to answer that. It's my mom."

We untangle our bodies and he climbs out of the pool. I prop myself on the pool deck, forearms crossed under my chin, as Connor scampers around our lounge chairs, righting himself. He shakes the excess water out of his hair, runs a towel through it and across his bare chest, before accepting the FaceTime call.

"Hi, Mom," he says as he slides his aviators to the top of his head and settles into his seat. A few moments pass and then, "I'm in Arizona until Monday."

I unilaterally decide it's time for another round of margaritas.

As covertly as I can manage, I collect my cover-up from my chair, successfully dodging the camera's lens.

In one fell swoop, Connor blindsides me, tilting the camera my direction as he says, "It's a long story, but I'm here with Gretchen."

I drape the material over my shoulders and give Connor's mom a quick wave. Before I can turn toward the bar to give them their privacy, Andrea Vining squeals in delight. "Ahhhhh, is that little Gretchen Fisher?"

Now that I've been spotted, I take a seat. "Hi, Mama V."

"Connor, honey, move the phone closer so I can see her."

He rolls his eyes as he lugs my chair flush to his. "There, Mom, you see her."

"Oh Gretchen, sweetheart," she coos, "I haven't seen you since you were a little girl. How's your brother doing? What about your parents?"

"Drew's good. Mom and Dad are good, too. They're actually touring Italy right now."

"Patrick, did you hear that?" she hollers off camera. "Gretchen says Paul and Kelly are in Italy."

"Gretchen?" The camera jostles and then Connor's dad squeezes himself into the frame.

"Well, I'll be damned. That can't be Gretchen Fisher I see." They're as charming and adorable as I remember.

Connor runs a palm down his face. "You guys are unbelievable."

Patrick adjusts the glasses on his nose. "Where are you guys at?" He squints, trying to parse out the unfamiliar backdrop behind us.

"He said they're in Arizona," Andrea answers.

"Arizona! What the hell are they doing there?"

I look at Connor, whose expression has gone utterly lifeless. My shoulders bounce with quiet laughter.

"Clearly I'm not needed for this conversation so are we done here?" Connor interjects dryly.

"Connor Vining, you stop that," his mom chides. The man next to me charms her with a boyish smile that could send every woman in its vicinity into ovulation.

I set my sunglasses on my head. "How's the beach life treating you guys?"

"Can't complain. We're headed to Carova next week with some friends," Patrick says as an incredulous grin takes over his face. "I can't believe that's you, Gretch. You're all grown up."

I only knew Patrick and Andrea Vining for those few years Connor and Drew played football together in high school, but week after week of sitting in the stands together brings a sense of famil-iarity that's easy to settle back in to.

I rest my chin on my hands in a dainty pose. "It's me."

Connor catches my gaze off camera. He winks and a wave of butterflies soars through my stomach.

"What are you doing now, sweetheart?" Andrea asks and I fix my attention back on the screen. Connor throws his head back in exasperation. I reach for his phone, more than happy to give the Vinings my entire life story, but he pulls away.

"Nope," he says. "I'm not letting them trap you."

My head cocks and I lunge for the phone again, successful this time. "Why don't *you* make yourself useful, old man, and go get me a margarita while I talk to your parents."

His dad explodes with laughter. "You heard the woman, son. Skedaddle yourself on over to that bar and get the lady a drink. Leave us to it."

I lean back in my seat, phone in hand. Connor sighs as he gets to his feet. On his way to the bar, he throws a towel over my face which I swiftly peel off and hurl at his back as he walks away.

I turn back to the Vinings. "Now, where were we?"

For the next few minutes, I fill them in on everything Gretchen: college in New York, my degree and my job prospects back in the city.

"Tell us how you and Connor ended up in Arizona together," Andrea says, circling back to her earlier question.

"Well, it actually is a long story," I say as Connor returns with fresh drinks and takes his seat beside me. "The shortened version is that Drew was supposed to come with me, but he had something come up at the last minute, so Connor came instead."

Connor tilts his head into the frame. "And that's the end of the story, Mom."

Andrea hums thoughtfully.

"Mom," Connor says, drawing out the word.

"Oh, wipe that scowl off your pretty little face," she quips.

I press a finger between his brows, smoothing out the crease. "Funny. I thought that scowl was just his face."

Patrick, Andrea and I team up in laughter. Connor's twinkly eyes promise shenanigans a moment before he rips the phone from my grip with one hand, his other disappearing into the pool bag. Before I realize what's happening, he announces, "Hey Mom, guess what Gretchen still has?"

An arrogant, son-of-a-bitch grin splits his face as he lifts my copy of *Little Women* into the frame. My head rears back, mouth agape. He meets my gaze off screen and I mouth the words *"you bastard."*

"What is that? Connor, honey, I can't see it."

His face softens. "Remember that weekend you drove with me into the city and I bought that book from Gene?"

Andrea inhales sharply and I ease back into the frame. "Who's Gene?" I ask.

Connor looks to me, searching my face like his parents aren't mere inches away to witness it. "He's that book collector I told you about."

Memories click into place. A sad sort of smile tilts one corner of my mouth. I see it in the heavy bob of his throat, the moment he realizes that his timing, however playful he intended it to be, wasn't ideal.

"Gretchen," Andrea's lively voice chimes into the void, "have you met Gene yet?"

I almost did…once.

I paste on a smile before answering, "No, I haven't."

"Oh, you must. Connor, you take her to see him when you get back. And be sure you thank him for letting us use his Carova house."

Connor's voice is thick and resigned as he says, "I always do, Mom."

After we disconnect the call a few minutes later, Connor tosses the phone aside. "Sorry about that." He shakes his head. "I overstepped with the book."

"It's okay," I assure him.

Before he or I can say more, his phone pings with a text. He snickers as he reads the message.

"Who is it?" I ask.

"It's my mom telling me I have some explaining to do."

His phone pings again. "And that one?"

Connor looks at the screen. He rubs his thumb and forefinger over his eyes and groans. "She said 'and for the record, we love her.'" A tired shrug pulls at his shoulders with an inconceivable weight that I feel in my bones.

"I love your parents. We used to sit together at your football games. Your mom would draw with me sometimes and your dad always had bubble gum for me in his pocket." I grin at the memory.

"They always wanted a daughter. I bet you felt like a breath of fresh air for them."

Our chairs still tucked flush together, I lean deeper into my seat and Connor does the same. I don't know why I rest my head on his shoulder, but I do. I don't know why his fingers trace shapes over my knuckles, but they do. Are we ever going to figure this—*us*—out?

You have to be willing to talk about it, Gretchen!

"Guys look at you, too, you know," he says.

"What?"

"Earlier you were talking about women noticing me and I'm saying that men see you, too."

I scoff. "Yeah, well, I don't tend to keep their interest for long."

His body tenses. "Why would you think that?"

"It's how it's always been. They expect me to be a certain way and eventually they realize I'm kind of boring and I'm quiet and..."

The motion of his fingers over my knuckles stops. "And what?"

I sit up and turn to face him. He shifts to meet me.

"And," I say, "I don't give up parts of myself very easily."

"Will you tell me?" he asks.

"There's not much to tell. You already know about the stuff that went down in high school." He nods stiffly. "And I um...I didn't really date at all freshman or sophomore year of college."

I couldn't force the memories of those two years away no matter how hard I tried. Freshman year was full of so much promise and hope and it was all wrapped up in Connor. Then year two hit like a freight train. Hopeless and lost, I had to figure out how to adapt to a life where I'd suddenly woken up and a limb was missing. All the confidence that had taken me so long to get back, gone.

"I dated a guy for a few months junior year and he was really nice. I liked him." I didn't love him, but I'd given up on that by that point. "But I always kept him at arm's length…physically. He never pressured me though." I clear my throat. "Eventually, I decided to rip the band-aid and just do it, but when the time came…I couldn't. He was really understanding about the whole thing.

"He drove me home, kissed me goodnight and I thought everything was okay, but…I don't know, he suddenly got really busy and couldn't make time to see me. It took a couple weeks, but eventually he stopped calling."

If the silence between us was a movie screen, you'd see snapshots of every text, every phone call, every video chat that propelled me through my days as a freshman on campus. Hundreds of miles from home, Connor became my anchor, my safe space. I never said the words out loud to anyone, but I fell in love with Connor Vining that year. Before I ever tasted his lips or knew how good it felt to be pressed up against him, I loved him. I was ready to give every piece of myself to him on that balcony. He held my entire heart and I trusted him with it, implicitly.

"Who else?" he grits out. The anger, the pain in his eyes—it hurts him to listen to this.

"Why do you want to know so badly?"

"Because I need to know, Gretch."

I tilt my head. "You plan to defend my honor, QB?" It's a sorry attempt to lighten the mood. Not surprisingly, Connor doesn't take the bait.

"Maybe," he seethes.

I huff. "Good luck with that because the guy last fall was a foreign exchange student from Scotland who weighed like 300 pounds. A legit modern-day Viking. He'd have a field day on your pretty face and I'd prefer to keep your face intact."

"Did he hurt you?"

"Not any more than the previous guy did."

"What happened?"

I release a heavy sigh. "He was looking for a semester fling and I wasn't that kind of girl."

"Keep talking. What else?"

"Good God, Connor. You wanna know? Fine." I drop my voice to a furious whisper. "He waited until our sixth date when he had his tongue down my throat and his hand down my pants to tell me that he didn't want to be serious *or* monogamous."

The tense lines of his face pull tight. He pushes both hands through his hair, cursing under his breath.

"Connor, you're getting upset over nothing. I'm not heartbroken over either of those guys. I'm fine." I rest a reassuring hand on his forearm.

"I need names," he demands.

I bark out a laugh. "Yeah, that's not gonna happen."

"Gretchen."

"Connor."

I meet his gaze, a challenge taking shape. Things do not need to get this serious. I shove him in the shoulder, widening my smile. "I swear, you're allowed to let this go."

"And if I don't want to?"

"Then I'll give you their names and you'll probably get in a few good punches, but they will too and you'll end up with *another* black eye."

I give him a teasing look from under hooded lashes. Our gazes lock, both of us remembering the shiner he sported that summer he and Drew visited before they moved to Chicago.

"I'm not scared of a black eye," he says.

"Oh, I know. You never told me how you got the one that summer, by the way."

He furrows his brows...a little too much. "Yeah, I did."

"No. You told me you got into a fight over 'dumb guy stuff.'" I emphasize with air quotes.

"And...that's it."

"And...that's not it," I mimic. "That was a lie. At the very least it wasn't the whole truth."

He averts his eyes and scrubs a hand down his face.

"Come on, old man. Time's a wastin'." I grin, lifting my brows with a shoulder shimmy to nudge him along.

"Don't, Gretch."

"I need names," I growl. He looks at me sidelong, daring me to press him. "Tell me who hurt you, Vining."

"No." The command sounds more like a warning. My nerves begin to tingle, but I bite back the urge to return his intensity.

I laugh nervously. "Hey now! I just told you two very embarrassing stories about myself. The least you could do is give me one sordid truth from your past to level the playing field. Come on, QB. Where's that chivalry you're so famous for?"

The distressed look on Connor's face unnerves me and my conviction wanes.

His throat bobs an obscene number of times. He may as well be swallowing his voice box down into his chest for all the words he's *not* saying.

"Connor," I plead, unsure if I even want to know whatever it is he's intentionally kept from me for the past six years.

"It was your brother," he blurts out.

The words hang in the air. I'm confused, but I don't immediately think much of them. "Okay, you guys are best friends, I'd have assumed you've gotten in a fight or two over the years."

He folds his arms across his chest.

Cautiously, I ask, "What did you fight about?"

"McDormand was talking shit and Drew was drunk. He threw a sloppy punch and my face got in the way."

He won't look at me and it's the worst kind of tell.

"What was he saying?"

He finally turns, meeting my stare. "Why the hell does it matter?"

"Because it's written all over your face!"

"He was talking about you!" he spews. His eyes squeeze shut in the wake of the words he already wishes he could take back.

Bewildered, I reply, "I don't understand. Why was McDormand talking about me?"

Connor's next words tumble out of him like a relentless barrage of pellets from a BB gun. Close range precise hits that hurt like hell. "Because he saw you at the pool, thought you were hot and decided to poke the bear also known as your brother. Drew went ape shit on him, punched me in the process and loudly declared to all of us that his sister was off-limits."

My face drops.

Dots connect.

Rage, like a tsunami, consumes me.

Chapter Twenty-Eight

START AT THE BEGINNING

GRETCHEN

CONNOR REACHES for me but I'm already on my feet. I grab the pool bag and begin tossing everything inside.

"He was doing what any big brother would have done, Gretch. You were only sixteen."

I drop the sunscreen into the canvas tote with a *thunk*, take in a deep breath and whirl on him. My furious eyes are a poor cover for the hurt. This wound that's been cut wide open, now bleeds in earnest.

"I wasn't sixteen on that balcony, Connor. But it was Drew that made you leave me there, wasn't it?" I don't wait to hear the answer because it's plain as day. I hurl the bag over my shoulder and storm off.

He's on my heels a beat later. "Oh, so we're finally gonna talk about this now?"

I stomp all the way to the elevator, Connor a step behind. Neither of us keen on making a scene in front of a bunch of strangers, I resist the urge to kick him in the balls and he keeps his distance so his balls are safe.

And Drew. Big brother or not, he doesn't get a say in my relationships. It's one thing to step in when I was sixteen, but it's another to meddle in my life when I'm an adult capable of making my own decisions.

Finally, I'm furious with Connor. For not being honest with me from the beginning. For allowing my brother to make decisions that were not his to make. For walking away from me. For cutting himself out of my life without my permission.

The elevator doors close, a racing director at the ready announcing, ready, set, go.

Connor charges ahead. "We're going to talk about this, Gretchen."

Indignant, I pivot to face him. "Did you ever tell Drew about that year?"

"Did you?" he replies, arms thrown out wide.

Silence speaks a thousand words, all of mine a bitter rebuke.

I didn't. Full stop, I didn't tell my brother that I spent a year talking to his best friend. That he'd become my best friend, too. That I'd fallen in love with him.

"You were my entire world," I finally say. "And, goddammit, I hate how pathetic that makes me sound. I went into Drew's wedding weekend so excited to see you. And things felt perfect and then suddenly they weren't and then you kissed me and then you ghosted me for three years. And now I find out that it was all because of Drew!"

"It's more complicated than that."

"It doesn't seem all that complicated. I was there!" I shout.

"I was there, too! I remember every goddamn second. I've spent three years reliving it, torturing myself over everything I did wrong, everything I should have done diff—"

"'A million things', trust me I remember." I laugh mirthlessly. "You regret it, whatever, but you can drop the self-serving martyr act because I'm the one! I'm the one who was crying myself to sleep while you moved on to someone else."

"That's not how it wa—" His words cleave at the sound of the elevator chime. Our attention shifts as the doors open to an elderly couple waiting to board. Connor holds the doors open and I step off first, smiling at the couple as I pass them and make for the hall.

When we get to our door, I dig blindly through the pool bag for the room key. Connor moves in, key card in hand, and unlocks the door. Infuriated—and petty, apparently—I roll my eyes and stomp into the room.

I drop the bag on the ground and toss my sunglasses on the entry table. The door clicks shut behind me and I spin on my heels to face him.

"You were saying?" he prods, dropping his glasses and keycard on the table next to my things.

"You are not a martyr."

"I'm not a martyr. I know that, but for all the things I've done wrong, it *is* more complicated than you know."

I school my expression into neutrality. His subsequent silence sends my blood from a simmer to a full boil. "I'm sorry, are you keeping me in the dark on these complications because you think I'm still some sixteen-year-old kid who needs her big brother and his best friend to make decisions for her or are you *trying* to patronize me? News flash: I'm a big girl now."

He drags a palm over the stress lines on his forehead.

"No! You don't get to act like this is putting you out. I've spent three years thinking that kiss was you taking pity on me, or maybe I did something wrong to make you not want me, to make you cut ties without telling me, and now I find out that I've been kept in the dark for, what, six years? More than that? No. You owe me an explanation. So please, enlighten me on these complications you speak of."

I cross my arms in defiance. When his shoulders sink along with his eyes, I know what's coming.

Tears threaten at the edges of my vision. I repress the fear that tells me to run, to avoid difficult conversations and I brace myself for the truth I've waited three years to hear.

The first tear falls. "Start at the beginning."

Connor

This whole time I've been telling myself I was waiting for *her* to be ready. That as soon as she was ready to hear what I have to say, I would be prepared. But her eyes are crinkled at the edges in pain. Tears slide down her cheeks. And my confession only stands to make it worse.

The truth is, I've avoided this conversation as much as she has. My reasons are different from hers, but it's avoidance no matter how you slice it. The thrill of being near her, the high of being able to touch her—all of it has been a bittersweet distraction from the ugly truth that I owe her.

There's so much I need to explain, to help her understand. Even more to apologize for.

I start at the beginning. I tell her everything, never letting myself look away because every tear that slides down those cheeks is a reminder that *I* did this. This is what I deserve.

My punishment.

My penance.

Chapter Twenty-Nine

THE REHEARSAL DINNER

CONNOR

three years ago

> GRETCHEN
>
> Someone tell my brother that weddings are supposed to be fun.
>
> And by someone, I mean you!

I SMILE like a fool as I settle into the driver's seat. Before I put the car in gear, I shoot off a reply.

> ME
>
> No can do. He's making me wear a suit and tie tonight and a tuxedo tomorrow. No fun to be had here.
>
> What's he worked up about now?

This wedding is definitely Reagan's dog and pony show. Translation: Drew is hyper-focused on making sure none of us—his family and friends—do anything to mess it up.

GRETCHEN

He just barreled into my room and threw a
toddler tantrum over me not being ready
yet. Lol.

Apparently walking to the restaurant
ACROSS THE STREET could take more than
thirty seconds. *insert eye roll emoji*

ME

You could just use the emoji you know?

GRETCHEN

Connor. We've talked about this.

It's funnier this way.

Nerves of anticipation coil in knots in my belly. Every text and phone call and FaceTime chat has led to this weekend and all I can think about is that I'll finally get to see her—to pull her into my arms and hug her.

That summer she turned sixteen—three years ago—flipped my world on a dime. For obvious reasons, I kept my distance after her brother and I moved to Chicago. Gretchen and I had almost zero contact other than when she and her parents would visit Drew occasionally on the weekends. I'd see them in passing, but I mostly tried to make myself scarce to give the Fishers the space they needed for family time.

Everything changed when Gretchen turned eighteen and her parents lifted their social media ban. One little notification in my inbox and I didn't think twice before accepting her follow request. The moment I opened her page and saw the first picture—cap and gown, goofy grin spread wide across her face, holding up a peace sign, head cocked to one shoulder—I think I was done for right then and there.

She messaged me. I messaged back. Eventually we exchanged phone numbers, which led to texting. Texting Gretchen became an all day, every day, best parts of my day occurrence. By Christmas we were FaceTiming almost every night.

While our conversations have been friendly and only slightly verging on flirtatious, I haven't been interested in anyone else. Not since the day that follow request notification popped up. Not for the past twelve months, two weeks and three days.

I'm several years older than her and that's never going to change. But the more time Gretchen and I spend getting to know each other, the less time I spend thinking about her brother and his warning three years ago.

Drew and I are still best friends, but seasons of life change. He moved in with Reagan a couple months before I ever reconnected with his sister and I've been living alone ever since. Between he and Reagan navigating their last year of law school and planning their wedding, Drew and I's social meetups have become significantly less frequent.

His bachelor party last month was as close to our shared playboy days as I can remember. We barhopped through Chicago with a few buddies. Several of them picked up some ladies along the way, everyone playing wingman for someone else. Except me. I did my best man duty, making sure Drew stayed out of trouble and didn't get *too* wasted. He tried to get me to flirt back with one such cute bartender who came on very strong when she swiped my phone and put in her contact information without my consent. Little did he know, I planned to FaceTime his little sister as soon as I got home.

I want to see Gretchen face to face, find out if she feels for me what I'm feeling for her. My hopes are up—sky high. Every last one of them, up as high as I can throw them, helium balloons floating up and away.

If she's willing to give *us* a try, I don't care if I have to hop on a plane every weekend to see her. I'll do it. I'll come clean to Drew and make him a new promise: a promise to never hurt her.

THE DIMLY LIT restaurant hosting the rehearsal dinner boasts three long tables. Adorned with a runner of candles and flower arrangements, each table seats at least twenty-five people down its length.

Nearly everyone has arrived, except for the guests of honor and their families. A group of my old frat brothers and myself catch up by the bar as we wait for Drew and Reagan to make their big entrance. All my thoughts are about seeing Gretchen walk through that door, though. My hands shake with nerves. I clutch a glass of Woodford Reserve in one hand and stuff the other in my pocket to steady them.

At last, the front door swings open and the place erupts in cheers when the bride and groom step inside. Quickly swarmed by guests, I can't make out the family that follows behind them.

A couple minutes later, the happy couple breaks from the crowd. Drew hoofs it straight toward me and the other groomsmen at the bar. "I need a drink."

"Take it easy tonight, babe," Reagan says with a sweet finger to Drew's chest.

I reach past my glowering best friend to plant a kiss on his fiancée's cheek. "You look lovely tonight, Reagan."

"Thank you, Connor."

Drew secures a beer for himself and a glass of white wine for Reagan before she gets pulled into a circle with her bridesmaids. I'm still scanning the room for Gretchen, but the low lighting and tight clusters of people scattered everywhere leave me coming up empty. The hand in my pocket fidgets with my keys, nervous energy still buzzing.

Our friend, Mav, chimes in. "Fashionably late to your own rehearsal dinner, Fisher?"

Drew scoffs. "Apparently, only a very specific pair of diamond earrings were acceptable to wear tonight." His tone is exhausted but has no real disdain behind it because the guy can't stop sneaking lovesick looks at his bride across the room.

"I hope you also told them *you* were the one who failed to bring the *correct* earrings to the hotel as you were instructed," the female voice comes from over Drew's shoulder. I'd recognize that voice in my sleep. She's the precious gem a metal detector beeps madly for —the closer she is, the faster my heart pounds in my chest.

Drew steps aside and Gretchen comes into view. Clad in a shimmering burgundy dress that dusts the floor, she's an utter vision. Her signature fancy braid draped over one shoulder, strands hung loosely around her face drawing all of her beauty into focus, is even more captivating in person. Eyes the color of rich, dark chocolate, framed by dark lashes. Tanned skin. Light freckles dotting the top of her nose. Lips stained in a deep red to match her dress.

"Minor details," Drew mumbles into his pint glass.

"Ok, so really this is all *your* fault." I frown at Drew, who gives me an unamused look and stomps off to mingle with other guests.

The guys, Gretchen and I watch Drew's back for a few seconds before we all turn toward each other. Our eyes find each other, a collective whole-body sigh escaping both of us—the kind you *feel*.

"Hey, Fish." My smile is so big I should be embarrassed, but the smile she gives back fills the entire room and I can't bring myself to care.

I'm done waiting. I pull her in for a hug, arms thrown around her waist. Her arms around my neck, I squeeze her tight. A lavender vanilla scent invades my lungs as I breathe her in. My words are a breath against her ear when I say, "You look beautiful."

She steps back and runs a hand down my lapel. "You fix up nice yourself."

"Who do we have here?" Mav says, reminding me we aren't alone.

I paste a neutral expression on my face and turn to the grooms-men. While I grab my drink from the bar, I make introductions. "Guys, this is Drew's sister, Gretchen. Gretch, these are the grooms-men. Aaron, Maverick, Dylan and Trent."

Most of the guys offer a kind head bob or *"nice to meet you."* But Mav—*fucking Mav*—steps right into her space, man on a mission.

"This can't be the brace-faced girl from that picture Drew kept in his room at the frat house."

I'm ready to intervene, when Gretchen replies, "Ahhh yes, nice to know my brother really values my self-confidence by keeping wretched pictures of me on display well past their expiration date."

She turns to me with a shrug, completely unaffected by Mav's advances. Mav, unfortunately, doesn't get the memo.

"My friends call me Mav." He extends his hand and Gretchen politely accepts it. "Can I get you a drink?"

"No, thank you."

I chuckle into my highball glass as I survey the room. Drew stands at the other end of the bar, death glare aimed right at Mav.

"Oh come on, we're celebrating your brother tonight," Mav insists, blissfully unaware of a certain friend with the homicidal eyes. He ignores her request and orders a glass of champagne.

I give Gretchen a wink and grasp Mav by the shoulder. "Dude, she doesn't want a drink." Then, I turn to the bartender and add, "Can I get a Diet Coke, please?"

A dinner bell rings, calling for everyone to find their seats.

Confession: I may have swapped a couple of place cards behind the wedding planner's back earlier.

In my defense, the swap put me next to Gretchen. I'm not sorry. I'm counting on the fact this gathering is large enough that nobody will notice what I've done.

Gretchen takes the seat next to mine, an *I see what you did* glinting in her eye. "You think you're so smooth."

I set the Diet Coke next to her plate and reply, "I'd say I'm very smooth."

With guests settled at their tables, salads are served, the hum of dozens of small conversations form the cacophony of sound that fills the dining room.

Gretchen and I share a bemused look as we eye the plates set in front of us. Fully intact leaves of romaine lettuce lie garnished with a singular giant shaving of parmesan. Caesar dressing adorns the plate in some sort of broad-stroked drizzle effect.

"Note to self," she says, "serve human food at my wedding."

"Heard that. This weekend is too fancy for me."

She backhands me on the bicep. "Oh my God, right? I swear, when I get married I just wanna get engaged and pull together an impromptu wedding like the next day. I don't want all this fuss. Just family and good food, you know? We can grill burgers and hot dogs for all I care."

An image pops unbidden into my mind: us, our families, my

parents' beach house, Dad on the grill, Mom's potato salad. The thought propels my heart into a steady *thump, thump, thump* that says…

*thump…*it's her.*

*thump…*she's the one.*

*thump…*don't let her go.*

"Sounds way better than eating a salad by hand," I say, biting into the salad sandwich I've concocted by stacking the romaine leaves, parmesan wedged between them. I really thought I'd nailed this plan.

I did not.

Caesar dressing drenches my fingertips, running down the side of my hand. I drop the lettuce to the plate, cautiously eyeing the guests around us. I lick my fingers clean like a kid who's dipped his fingers in a honey pot, not the twenty-five-year-old man wearing a four-hundred-dollar suit that I am. Gretchen's shoulders bounce with quiet laughter, her napkin held to her mouth as a shield.

I nudge my knee against hers. "It felt like such a good idea."

"I sometimes have the feeling I can do crystal meth," she says. My napkin covers my mouth now, hiding my own laugh. "But then I think…"

"Mmmm…better not," we finish in unison, mimicking Fat Amy's intonation to a *t.*

Our entrees arrive several minutes later. If I didn't need both my hands to eat, I might have the courage to reach under the table and hold hers. As it stands, her knee against mine remains a steady point of contact that neither of us retreat from.

"When do you head back to New York?" I ask.

"I have to leave on Monday to give myself enough time to get settled back into my apartment before classes start. Oh, that reminds me. I really want to go to that book collector's shop you told me about before I head back to Bloomington on Sunday after-noon. Can you send me the address?"

I smile. Gene has been a family friend since before my brothers and I were born. He's the one who helped me pick out Gretchen's gift for her tenth birthday. I've told her about his little shop in

Chicago multiple times over the past year and there's nothing I'd love more than to see her beam with joy at the gems she's sure to find as she roams the narrow aisles.

"How about I go with you?" I ask.

Gretchen meets my gaze.

"Sunday," I continue, "after the send-off brunch, we can go together. Sound good?"

She offers a shy nod, bottom lip tucked between her teeth. *God,* I want to kiss her.

"Great." My eyes dip to her mouth. "It's a date then."

Her gaze pulls away, but that little grin remains as she works her knife through the meat on her plate. Quietly, she says, "It's a date," before sweeping a bite of chicken off the end of her fork. Yeah, I'm crazy about this sinfully sweet, shy, stunning girl.

I slice into the steak on my plate. "Is anyone going with you to help you get moved back into your apartment?" I'm ready to offer up myself for the task.

"My dad's coming."

I try not to let the disappointment show on my face.

"I'll be back at Thanksgiving though," she adds.

"Is that right?"

"Mmhmm. Mom and Dad are going on a cruise, so I'll be spending the break with Drew and Reagan." Our eyes meet again, identical smirks in place. "Where do you plan to spend Thanksgiving?"

I cut into my steak again. "Well, I have a few offers I'm considering. I don't want to commit too soon, gotta keep my options open."

"Obviously."

"But Thanksgiving at Drew's is definitely the front-runner." It's the only option. He already invited me and I've already accepted.

She smiles from behind her Diet Coke. "Maybe I'll see you there."

I smile from behind my water. "Maybe you will."

The open flirtation, the body language, making plans to see each other, knees pressed together—all of it compels me to make my intentions clear. I chance a quick glance around to make sure no brothers are murderously glaring my direction before I lean into her ear. "Will you save a dance for me tomorrow, Gretch?"

She backs away and I don't miss the blush spreading over her cheeks before she turns serious. "I don't know," she says, "You might have to get in line behind the many other suitors who'll be vying to fill my dance card." The tinge of sarcasm in her voice strikes a nerve. She honestly doesn't know how beautiful she is. I know for certain that every unattached guy (Mav being suspect number one) and probably some of the attached ones, will be looking for an opportunity to shoot their shot with her.

It's not the best segue, but something in me wants to claim her as mine before the chaos of tomorrow hits. We'd need to keep it quiet to avoid any drama with Drew before I have the opportunity to talk to him, but I don't want to wait to tell her how I feel.

With one final swig of water to settle my nerves, I shift my body to face her better. She turns to match me and our little conversation bubble becomes a cocoon. We lean in closer. Under the table, I extend my pinky finger toward hers. Her pinky reaches back, tiny hooks linked together in a silent promise. The smallest, most inno-cent point of contact, yet it feels like the beginning of…something. Not something. Everything. *Something* implies you don't know how things will work out. But *everything* feels like a question you already know the answer to.

"Gretch, do you think we could—"

Clinking glass pierces the air and all heads turn toward the sound. Paul Fisher rises from his seat. "I'd like to make a toast."

Parents, grandparents and a few close friends take turns toasting the happy couple for the next forty-five minutes. When Paul and Kelly finally declare an end to the evening, I try to pull Gretchen aside among the fray of dispersing guests to finish our conversation, but Kelly gets to her first.

Gretchen's mom leads her one direction as Drew grabs my arm and pulls me in the other. "Dude, I need to talk to you." His curt tone puts me on edge. Maybe I wasn't careful enough and he saw something he wasn't meant to see from the other end of the table.

Drew tucks us into a dark corner and says, "I need you to keep the guys away from Gretch."

"What are you talking about?"

"Oh come on, you know. All the guys coming in tomorrow. And Mav? He just asked me if Gretch was single."

The nervous tremor returns. I drag my hand around the back of my neck to hide it when all I really want to do is loosen this tie that suddenly feels like a noose.

I keep my voice casual despite everything inside me screaming otherwise when I say, "Don't you think you might be going a bit overboard? She's not a kid anymore."

"Like hell she is," he seethes. "She may be legally an adult, but name one guy coming tomorrow who's looking for anything more than a one-night-stand?"

Me.

As far as Drew knows, he's not wrong. But he of all people should understand that guys like us *can* change when the right girl comes along. Reagan was that person for him. Gretchen is mine.

"So you think Reagan's brothers never should have given *you* a chance?" I spew, but my hackles rise by the second.

He guffaws through a surly laugh. "Okay, so you're saying I should let Maverick *Mr. Right Tonight* Jones make a pass at my sister?"

God, that old nickname makes my skin crawl. I'd put Mav six feet under before I let him lay a hand on her.

"And by the way," he continues, "me with Reagan's brothers is totally different. They didn't know me before her. But Mav and all these other guys we went to school with…" He shakes his head in disgust. "I've seen too much, man."

I clench my jaw, the lump of regret lodged in my throat cutting off my ability to speak.

He's seen too much.

He's seen too much of *me*.

He's seen too much of me *before her*.

"Promise me you'll keep the guys away from her," he commands, tone final.

Defenseless and exposed, I agree—another promise made. He

claps me on the shoulder on his way out, leaving me to stand in the carnage of all my sky-high hopes that have just plummetted to the ground.

When I step inside my apartment, the emptiness is all-consuming. She's never been here, yet it feels like she moved out—like pieces of her that used to be here are now missing. But you can't miss something that was never yours to begin with. Even if I could convince Drew that I'm ready to change—that I've already changed —he would never test that theory on his little sister.

Every stolen glance, passing touch, whispered promise between us tonight—I have to take them all back. If there's one thing tonight has taught me, besides my best friend's lack of faith in his friends, it's that I can't just up and quit Gretchen. That girl is woven into the fabric of who I am—who I want to be. The only way I can look out for her *and* let go of the fool's hope that she could be mine is to put distance between us.

Distance and distraction. Only one idea comes to mind as to how to go about this and it makes me sick to even consider it. But what choice do I have?

Even as I type out the text, I tell myself *this is wrong, don't do it.* The response is nearly instant and it sickens me, but what's done is done. Gretchen will hate me, but I guarantee it won't be as much as I hate myself.

The only thing left to do is text Drew.

ME

Can you squeeze an extra seat in at the reception? I'm bringing a date, after all.

Just when I think the pain couldn't get any worse, my phone pings with Drew's reply.

DREW

Why am I not surprised?

Chapter Thirty

THE WEDDING: PART 1

GRETCHEN
three years ago

I'VE GONE and fallen in love with my best friend.

What began as a girl with a crush in need of a friend, turned into so much more. I found not only a best friend, but *my person.*

I don't know if he loves me back. But seeing him last night, the touches, the flirting, the date we planned for tomorrow—it feels like we're on the same page.

Secrets have never been difficult for me. This introverted girl of few words has relished in having Connor Vining all to herself for the past year. But I'm also not ignorant to reality—whatever this thing is between us can't stay a secret forever. While Drew's wedding isn't the time or place to hard launch the idea, we'll have to put it out into the open sooner rather than later.

But for at least one more day, until we get the chance to talk about what the future holds with him in Chicago and me in New York, I plan to enjoy our little secret for a bit longer.

The door to the hotel suite opens. Reagan and her bridesmaids file in, getting-ready bags and formal gowns in tow.

I'm not technically a bridesmaid—Reagan has plenty of those—but I have been helping with some wedding-related tasks from afar as needed when she and my brother's schedules got crazy with law school and studying for the BAR exam. Today, while the bridal party was downstairs doing a quick run through of the ceremony, I prepped the ladies' getting-ready suite.

"Oh my gosh, this all looks so great! Thank you, Gretchen!" Reagan exclaims as she peruses the assortment of snacks, mini-sandwiches and fruit I've laid out for everyone.

The girls hang up their gowns on the rolling rack in the living room while Reagan goes rummaging through her overnight bag.

"Has anyone seen my phone?" she asks.

A quick scan of the living area reveals nothing. "I haven't seen it."

Reagan looks under all the girls' purses littering the entry table. "I need to text the planner and tell her to add a seat at the head table."

"I think she's up in the ballroom. I can go up there and tell her."

"That would be amazing! Thank you so much."

I smile and grab my purse. "No problem. Just tell me where you need them to go."

"I guess Connor's bringing a date now," she says.

My head snaps toward her, but she doesn't notice as she's still on the hunt for her phone.

My thoughts go in two different directions. One says I wholly trust Connor—maybe the extra seat at the head table is for me. The other says I don't think he'd make such a bold move at Drew's wedding without talking to me first.

Dread sweeps in. My palms begin to sweat, eyes burning. "Okay," I strangle out. *Do not cry.* "Do you know her name? I can have one of Sharon's staff make her an escort card."

Reagan rolls her eyes. "No. It's some girl he met at Drew's bachelor party last month."

My heart pounds frantically one moment and barely registers a pulse the next. *Do. Not. Cry.*

I spoke to Connor that night. He told me he wanted to hear my voice before going to sleep. I told him that's the kind of line someone who's had a little too much to drink would say. He said he was stone cold sober. I blushed, even though he couldn't see it. He never mentioned anything about meeting someone.

Tears well. I sweep past Reagan on the way to the door as she adds, "I don't care that the girl gets an escort card. Just ask Sharon to add a seat next to him and leave it at that."

I'm already halfway out the door when I say, "Got it." The first sob comes before I even reach the elevator.

It's exhausting going hours with your tear ducts constantly at max capacity. Four hours in, I've developed a system where I escape to the bathroom every twenty minutes, let a few tears fall to relieve the pressure, clean myself up and return to wherever I'm supposed to be.

I haven't seen or spoken to Connor since dinner ended last night. Of all the ways I imagined today would go, none of the possibilities included me, in full hair and makeup and a floor-length formal gown, heaving over a toilet.

I've labored over every detail of last night, the past year, and can't, for the life of me, figure out how I misread everything so immensely.

Now, all of ours and Reagan's immediate family is gathered in the hotel lobby turned ceremony space awaiting the wedding party's arrival.

Right on schedule, the crew of tuxedo-clad guys and girls in shimmering purple gowns barrel through the lobby doors, my brother and his bride-to-be on their heels. The photographer at the helm immediately starts barking out orders.

Our family is up first as we're called to the front for pictures with the bride and groom. All the groomsmen are seated off to the side, but I don't let myself look at them. I can't. If I look at him and he's looking at me, I'll burst into tears.

When our side of the family is finished, I beeline for my seat on the front row. Eyes ahead, deep breaths in and out.

A warm body in a tuxedo slides into the seat beside me. My eyes pinch shut at the proximity. The bathroom is thirty paces off to the left, I remind myself.

"Let me be the first to tell you how hot you look in that dress." It's not Connor.

I turn toward the vaguely familiar voice. Tall, dark-haired, and broad-chested, it's the man I met last night. "Mav, right?"

His chest puffs with pride. "Hey, baby Fisher remembered my name." I wince, but quickly level it. He means to be endearing, but I hate those words.

I manage a soft smile. "Mav isn't really a name you forget."

Before he can say anything else, a voice from behind us interrupts him. "Mav! Get your ass back here."

There he is.

When I make for the bathroom a second later, I don't look back at him.

After my well-oiled routine of cry a little, repress a lot, check the makeup, I return to the ceremony space. The wedding party has left, likely instructed by the planner to head back upstairs until showtime.

In my periphery, I notice that guests are beginning to arrive. The ushers have yet to begin seating anyone, so I relish these final moments of silence. On the perimeter of the room, I lean against a pillar and release an unsteady breath. What I wouldn't give for this day to be over already.

My respite is cut short when I scan the room again. The man mirroring my position on the pillar across the room locks his eyes on mine.

If I didn't know any better, I'd say he looks as afflicted as I feel.

If I didn't know any better, I'd say *I* look as afflicted as I feel.

I don't move and, for long seconds, neither does he. Until he does. He pushes off the pillar, closing the distance between us in quick strides while I brace myself for another round of heartbreak.

"Connor!" a perky, female voice calls from the end of the aisle.

He stops dead on his feet. His face flashes with something like irritation as his throat bobs. Slowly, he turns toward the woman prancing down the aisle and every nerve ending in my body bristles.

She zips into my line of sight, throwing her arms around Connor's neck. Donning a hot pink micro-mini dress more suitable for a night of clubbing than a black-tie wedding and a pair of sky high five-inch heels, she's still a solid five inches shorter than him.

Her profile comes into view as she turns and that's when I see it. Bold makeup. Bright pink lips. Waves of platinum blonde hair—box dye number PL1. And there, on her right shoulder blade, is a hibiscus flower tattoo. The same tattoo she spent months begging me to get with her because we were *best friends*.

Thank God I didn't permanently mar my skin with that wholly insignificant, meaningless tropical bloom for it to end up as nothing more than a reminder of her betrayal.

"Gretchen! I knew I'd see you here." Her voice drawing closer snaps me out of my thoughts.

Shoulders squared and tear ducts in check, I meet her gaze.

"Alexis," I say flatly before unabashedly pinning Connor with a stare, his face stricken with confusion. I look back to my former best friend. "It's my brother's wedding, it'd be a shock if I wasn't here."

She knew exactly what she was doing by coming here. Alexis Adams may play dumb for attention, but she's not stupid. She plots. She schemes. She conspires. And she doesn't do anything by accident.

Be it desperation to not look weak or the need to compete with my friend-turned-enemy for dominance, I cross my arms, pop out one hip and let my thigh-high slit have its shining moment. What she did hurt me, but I've refused to let it break me.

Connor steps forward on cautious feet. "You guys know each other?"

"Duh!" She throws a look to Connor and then back at me, those familiar green eyes out for blood. "We graduated together."

The sour look on Connor's face is my cue to exit because I'm not in the mood to explain my history with Alexis Adams. I never used her name and I may have glossed over the specifics, but he already knows the bird's eye view of what happened in my last semester of high school because I told him. I *confided* in him.

"You said you were twenty-one," Connor says and I hold back my nasty retort. Alexis lying about her age is not the least bit surprising.

With that, I excuse myself and march toward my mom who's greeting guests at the entrance.

Mom notices my approach. "Did I see Alexis Adams pass through here?"

I take in a deep, leveling breath. I am unaffected. If only my heart and my face could get the message. "Yeah, Connor brought her. I guess they met somewhere in town a while back."

Mom's lips fall into a grim line. "You never did tell me what happened between you two, but for what it's worth, I never much cared for the girl."

Before I can stop it, a tear falls. People press in all around and I drop my chin to my chest to hide the emotion rushing to the surface. Mom hauls me into her chest. I cry for reasons she doesn't understand, but she holds me anyway.

Stepping back, I swipe under my eyes. "Dammit. I need to fix my mascara."

She digs through her clutch and offers me her room key. "Ceremony starts in twenty minutes. Go upstairs, cry, breathe, do whatever you need to do. I'll be right here when you get back."

I COULDN'T TELL you what song was playing when Drew and Reagan were pronounced man and wife.

I couldn't tell you what Connor said in his best man speech or what I ate for dinner or what flavor the cake was.

I've plastered on so many fake smiles, I couldn't begin to count them.

What I can tell you is how many times I've left Mom's side: zero.

How many times my traitorous eyes drifted to the head table where Alexis' hands were all over Connor in one obscene way or another: seventeen.

How many votive candles are on this table: six.

I can say with confidence that a three-hundred guest wedding reception makes it easy to hide, but it doesn't make it any easier to breathe.

It's not all terrible—there are glimpses of fun, like polaroids capturing moments in time. Drew and I dancing wildly to Walk on the Moon's "Shut Up and Dance" like we did when we were kids. Dad spinning me on the dance floor to "My Girl" right after the cake was cut. Taking a turn in the photo booth with my grandparents.

I'm in a mad dash to my mom on my way back from the bathroom, when Mav steps into my path. "Hey, Mav. You having fun?" My smile is forced but he doesn't notice for how loud I have to speak to be heard over the music.

He leans in close, nearly shouting, "Obviously, my little Drew got married! What I would love, though, is if you would dance with me."

He pulls back, rueful grin on display, as the song changes to something slow and soft. I arch a brow. "Did you plan that?"

I see the appeal in the boyish smile that spreads over his face—Mav isn't bad to look at. He's loud, boisterous, a total goofball, and so not my type, but I recognize that irresistible charm thing he has going for him.

He smirks. "I really wish I could take credit for that, but no." He holds out a hand. "What do you say?"

My eyes bounce from his hand to his face. I see no harm in dancing with the guy, but it's fun to make him squirm a bit.

Before I can accept his invitation, another hand swoops in and grabs mine. "She's not dancing with you, Mav," Connor declares as he lugs me toward the dance floor. Mav's laughter fades into the distance behind me.

Connor brings us to the edge of the dance floor and tucks me in close with a broad hand wrapped around my waist, braced on the bare skin of my back. Our clasped hands elevated between us, I bring my other hand to rest on his shoulder.

"That was kind of rude," I say as we begin to shift from side to side.

"You're not dancing with him and I need to talk to you."

I meet his stare. "Where's your date, Connor?"

"In the bathroom."

I release a tight breath through my nose. "Fine. You've trapped me, so talk."

He looks around for a beat before his eyes land back on me. "First of all, you look beautiful tonight and I've wanted to tell you since I saw you this afternoon."

"Thank you." I want to return the compliment because he's practically edible in his tuxedo…and because I love him. But I can't voice any of that.

There's a painful silence before he says, "I never should have asked her to come."

"It's not just—"

"I never should have asked anybody else," he amends. "It was a mistake and I'm sorry."

I want to ask why he did it because I don't believe for a second that he sat next to me at dinner last night, said the things he said, touched me the way he did, with plans of being here tonight with somebody else.

"Will you tell me what happened between you guys?" he asks. My eyes scan vacantly over his shoulder. "Please? I need to know. Is she the one you told me about? The one that hurt you?"

My heart wants so badly to melt into him and, for a moment, my body does just that. The hand on my back shifts, caressing, as I lean in, a plea for me to not pull away. But I'm not his date tonight. I shake my head, squaring my shoulders to put more distance between our chests.

"She, um…she was my best friend. Or I thought she was. A few months before graduation I found out she hooked up with a guy I'd been seeing. Come to find out, it wasn't the first time she'd done something like that behind my back."

I shrug as if that suffices for all the tears I shed over the rumors, the gossip.

"After it all went down, I also found out that everybody in our friend group knew the whole time." My gaze finds his, his expression full of compassion and *I'm listening*—it's the only reason I'm able to keep talking. "I thought those people were my friends, but they didn't even care enough about me to tell me what was going on. I don't know, it made me feel really stupid because I…I let her in, you know?" I scrunch my nose to push back the emotion stinging my eyes.

"You're not stupid and I know how hard it is to let somebody in." He squeezes my hand a little tighter. "I'm sorry she did that to you."

We sway in silence for a moment, my forehead desperate to fall against his chest as the song comes into focus—"About You" by The 1975. I wonder if I'll ever be able to forget him, to move on from him. All this time and he was never mine at all. And I already miss him.

I'm not sure I want to know anymore why he brought her here tonight. The answer will break me, I'm sure of it. It's obvious I've completely misread…everything.

"You know, I won't interfere, if you, um…" My God, I can't make myself say the words. "Grudges aren't healthy anyway, right?"

His hand tenses over my lower spine. "What are you trying to say, Gretch?"

"I'm saying I'll set aside my feelings about her," *and you*, "if you really like her."

I'll pretend the last year never happened.

Our eyes lock for a split second, his wide and searching, mine tired—so, so tired.

"Gretch, I—"

"Can I cut in?" Alexis' voice interrupts like the blunt end of a gavel—no clean break, just relentless pounding until whatever tether was there before is successfully crushed into oblivion. The moment is over.

We are over.

I step out of his arms and walk away.

I don't look back as I swipe my clutch from my seat and a champagne flute off a passing butler tray. Without slowing my stride, I down the champagne in one gulp, drop the empty glass on a nearby table and flee the scene.

The ballroom doors click shut behind me and the music simmers to a dull thud pulsing through the wall. I release a breath from so deep in my lungs it feels like I've been holding it for a lifetime. Or, at least for the past twelve months, two weeks and four days.

Chapter Thirty-One

THE WEDDING: PART 2

CONNOR

three years ago

THE MOMENT ALEXIS SHOWED UP, I knew I'd made a huge mistake.

When I turned and saw her at the back of that aisle dressed in something you could barely classify as a dress, I wanted to walk right up to her, apologize for my mistake and tell her to leave. But in a matter of seconds, her arms were around my neck, then Gretchen was there and I couldn't keep up with what was happening. Before I knew it, the wedding planner was whisking me upstairs to join the wedding party and I didn't know where Gretchen had gone.

And now, there she goes again, purse in hand, crashing through the ballroom doors like I'll never see her again. I want to chase after her, tell her she has it all wrong.

Alexis laughs, a harsh reminder that I've put myself between a rock and hard place. "That girl's still got it so bad for you?" She toys her fingers in the hair at the back of my neck. I bristle at the contact.

"What are you talking about?"

"Oh my God, you didn't know? Gretchen was, like, totally obsessed with you in high school."

"That's not true."

"Connor, are you kidding me? That summer after you and Drew visited, she could not stop talking about how hot you were. It was adorable but also kind of pathetic."

Her mouth crooks into a smarmy grin, a look that says she's won. Only, I didn't even know there was a competition to begin with.

I look down at her, my frustration evident. "Did you know who I was that night at the bar?" She rears her head back in offense. "Did you?"

"Of course I did. But you recognized me, too."

"Why on earth would I know who you were?"

"Because we'd already met!" she says incredulously.

"What are you talking about?"

She scoffs. "That summer you and Drew visited. I met you at the coffee shop and I was at Gretchen's house that day we were all hanging out by the pool." She pauses, eyes hopeful for remembrance to dawn on my face, but it never comes. "Whatever, it's fine. It was a long time ago."

I remember both of those days and I remember other girls being there, but I couldn't tell you what any of them looked like. Gretchen was all I could see.

"Well, I don't remember you." The words land with a harsher sting than I intend them to. "I'm sorry. That didn't come out right. If you knew who I was, why didn't you say that? Why did you lie about how old you are?"

"My boss was standing right next to me and I'd had to lie about my age to get the job. I thought you recognized me and were just playing some flirty game, pretending we didn't know each other."

I actually laugh. Out loud, because the notion is so ridiculous. "That's not how I flirt, Alexis. And I don't like liars."

Surprisingly, she looks remorseful.

"You're right. I'm sorry," she says softly. "Do you think we could start over?"

A better man would accept her apology. But I'm not the better man in this scenario. All I can think about is whether or not Gretchen is coming back.

As it turns out, lovesick morons stuck pining for the one girl they can't have make really terrible decisions.

I unclasp Alexis' hands from around my neck and step away. "I need a drink."

Gretchen

The nighttime Chicago skyline beyond the window sparkles with city lights reflecting off the tall buildings. Traffic weaves through the streets below sending streaks of neon red and gold painting the pavement.

The ballroom doors open and close around the corner. Stilettos clack on the marble floor, the sound drawing closer. I don't have to turn to know it's her.

"Can I help you with something, Alexis?" I ask.

Opposite me, shoulder propped against the oversized window frame, she says, "Just wanted to see if you were still out here pouting."

I shake my head and push off the wall to leave. "Have a good night."

"Go ahead. Walk away again, scared and wounded like the world is so unfair to you."

I stop, sucking in a breath as I turn. "Excuse me?"

"You haven't changed at all, have you, Gretch?" She cocks her head, words spewing like venom. "You see all these things you want, but you're too scared to reach out and take them. You just sit back and cry and blame others for the things you don't have."

"That's what you've told yourself?" The space between us narrows as I move closer. "You think I regret not having sex with a bunch of juvenile boys in high school? My only regret is believing you when you said I was your best friend."

Her eyes roll to the heavens. "It's just sex, I don't know why you're so uptight about it. And that was high school. Aren't we beyond that by now?"

"It was *last* year!" I take in my surroundings and step forward. Toe to toe, I lower my voice. "You wanna have sex with every guy that looks your way, I couldn't care less. I actually envied your confidence, Alexis. I never judged you. But *you* judged *me*. You pitted us against each other and, *shocker*, the girl who spread her legs first won." I throw out my arms.

"And here we are again." My lips twist as I fight back the burn in my throat, the ache in my chest. The mental image of her arms around Connor's neck plays on a continuous loop, insult piled onto injury over and over and over. "I'm beginning to wonder if you've ever pursued a guy that I wasn't interested in first."

She flips her hair over her shoulder and laughs, arms crossed in contempt. "Jealousy doesn't suit you, you know. If Connor wanted you as his date, he would have asked you."

There it is—the God's honest, ugly truth my heart can't bear. And damn the universe for letting *this girl* be the one who spells it out for me. He doesn't want me. He chose her.

I know exactly the kind of person Alexis is—mean, vindictive, conniving and selfish. But if hurt people hurt people, then I can also acknowledge that her punches hold very little weight. She may be out for blood, but her only weapons are dull blades, painful on impact but only capable of breaking skin if I push back hard enough.

"And insecurity doesn't suit you." I pause. Her face falls a fraction before she captures it and yanks it back into neutrality. "That's right, I see through the facade. You're not confident at all. No, this is insecurity masquerading as confidence."

I'm not interested in revenge. More than anything, I want to put her behind me. Up until about four hours ago, I thought I'd done that.

"I feel sorry for you, Alexis. I'm sorry for whatever happened to you that made you such a terrible friend to others."

She opens her mouth to reply, but the pointed finger I pin in her chest stops her short. "Let me make one thing perfectly clear. You know how much Connor means to me." *God, does she know.* "But he's made his choice. You win." Tears sting the back of my eyes. *Do. Not. Cry.* "I forgive you for everything. All of it. But if you hurt him? *That* I will never forgive."

Gazes locked, there's a taut silence until, "Everything okay out here?" Connor comes into view, his question a battle-axe that cleaves the air.

Alexis and I turn to face him. He steps closer, eyes on a pendulum swinging between the girl he chose and the girl who wanted so badly for it to be her.

I step back, face flat, heart a vast, empty abyss. "Everything's fine."

Connor looks at me and then he turns to *her.* "I think we should go."

The man I'm in love with leads another woman to the elevator with a hand on the small of her back. I suck in a ragged breath that teeters on the edge of a sob as I spin on my heel and run.

The door on the far wall opens to a wraparound balcony. Once outside, my lungs heave in an ocean's worth of oxygen. Without the incessant pulse of the music pounding from the other side of the stone wall, I'm not sure my heart would remember to beat on its own.

Connor

I press the button for the lobby as Alexis asks, "What floor is your room on?"

"I don't have a room," I answer.

She steps into me, pressing me to the back of the elevator. "Good. We'll go back to your place then."

Hands that feel all wrong coast up my chest. I grab her wrists and ease her back. "No. I'm getting you a cab and sending you home. I'm sorry, but this isn't working out."

Her face drops.

I scrape a hand over the back of my neck. "Look, this is my

fault. It was a mistake to invite you here tonight and I truly am sorry."

Her gaze zeros in on me like a sniper taking aim. I can't tell if she's about to cry or punch me in the face. "How much did you hear?"

"Enough," I say.

"So, you're gonna take her word over mine?"

"Depends. What's your word, Alexis?" I lean against the wall, hands sliding into my pockets. Her word means nothing, tonight alone has made that clear, but I am curious to see how she tries to spin this.

She tilts her head to one side. "That Gretchen is weak," she starts. "That she only has herself to blame for every guy that thought they wanted her and chose me instead. You want to pick her over me? Be my guest. Good luck trying to get lucky with that one."

I laugh without an ounce of humor. "You see, that's where you're wrong." The elevator dings as it reaches the lobby and I push off the wall. "Any guy that girl gives the time of day should consider himself the luckiest guy in the world."

Alexis stomps past me and I follow her all the way out the door. I don't stop until she's in a cab, brake lights flashing as she drives away.

I turn to face the hotel, eyes panning up the many floors that climb endlessly into the night sky. Gretchen's up there somewhere. Hurt. Disappointed. *Mistaken.*

She needs to understand I'm not interested in Alexis—it's the bare minimum of what I have to explain to fix this. But it doesn't address what got me in this mess in the first place—that I want my best friend's little sister. That I never stop thinking about her. That I think I'm in love with her.

I weave through the lobby toward the elevator as Drew's words from last night and three years ago echo through my mind. Only, they weren't just words—they were warnings.

For a moment, I let myself imagine what could happen if I say *to hell with Drew* and go after everything I want with Gretchen. He could cut me out. He could cut her out too. Maybe with time he could make peace with it. But what if he can't? Gretchen and Alexis were best friends and one person's betrayal irrevocably mangled that relationship. Drew could see what I've done—the feelings, the secrets kept, the year worth of texts and phone calls—and think it the same thing. A betrayal.

The air inside the elevator is stale, suffocating. I undo my bow tie and release a few buttons on my shirt. Even as the doors open to the ballroom floor, I still don't know what I'm supposed to do.

Gretchen is my friend as much as Drew is. How do I navigate this without losing one of them? Or worse, both.

Back inside the ballroom, the music thrums, feeding off the packed dance floor. I scan the dimly lit space for the girl with the midnight hair, matching black dress and heart of gold that makes my knees go weak, but I can't find her anywhere. I step back outside the ballroom to the place I last saw her and spot an exterior door on the far wall.

Through the doors, I come to a terrace. And there, off to my right, at the far corner of the balcony, stands Gretchen. Back to me, that black dress sweeps low, down to the soft skin at the lowest part of her spine. Back fully exposed, her hair hangs in long waves, wisps blowing in the wind. The satin molds to every curve from shoulder to upper thigh before flowing loosely to the ground, fabric fluttering in the breeze.

She turns as she hears my steps, eyes flashing with surprise. "You came back."

"I sent Alexis home."

"Oh," she whispers.

"I'm sorry, but I was eavesdropping on your conversation earlier. And I need you to understand something." I close half the distance between us. "I don't like Alexis. I don't want Alexis. I never should have asked her to come here and I would never choose her over you."

She averts her gaze. "But you did choose her. Last night I thought that—" She sucks in a breath. Her hand tightens around the stone railing with a white knuckled grip. "Why did you ask her to come?"

"Because I'm an idiot and I'm sorry," I plead.

"You never told me you met someone."

"I didn't. She was just a bartender at one of the bars from your brother's bachelor party."

"But you got her number."

"She put it in my phone. I didn't ask for it."

Confusion splits her face. "But you *did* ask her to be your date."

A rush of air escapes my lungs and I shrug. She turns to look out over the city.

The more I say, the less I can explain. They're not the answers she deserves, but any more would pull her brother into the middle and I can't do that to him on his wedding day. Drew's far from perfect and maybe he's gone overboard on the over-protective big brother act, but his intentions are good.

I offer her the only thing I can. "I'm so sorry, Gretch."

Her tired eyelids drift shut. "I forgive you."

"You shouldn't." She opens her eyes, meeting mine. "You shouldn't because I don't deserve your forgiveness. I don't deserve you."

Her brows crease as she cocks her head. "Then you don't know how good you are."

The mistakes of the past twenty-four hours alone prove that's false. Not to mention the mountain of terrible choices I made through college up to a year ago, some I didn't even remember the next morning.

"But you don't even know the worst parts of me," my voice breaks, rough and ragged.

"I don't need to know the details to know the truth. The last year has to count for something."

"What makes you so sure I haven't done anything stupid over the past year?"

She shrugs. "A feeling." A heavy breath expands her chest. "Unless I misread that, too?"

"No," I rasp. "I haven't done anything...stupid."

She nods down at her hand fidgeting over the railing. "Me neither."

Two muted confessions that speak ear-splitting volumes. I'd hoped as much, but I never dared ask if she'd been seeing someone else because it was no place of mine to stop her.

I have no plan here, yet I close the gap between us anyway. All I know is that I need to be closer. Every tear she's shed today, I want to be close enough to swim in them. Close enough to count the freckles atop her nose. Close enough to feel the air sweeping in and out of her lungs.

"What now?" Her voice cuts over the dull throb of dance music vibrating the wall. Question and hunger blaze in her eyes.

The thread that's been holding my self-restraint snaps and I throw an arm around her waist, my palm pressed into the skin of her back as I coax her around the dark corner of the terrace. Her back against the wall, I push in close, my lips in a pleading hover above hers.

She fists the open collar of my shirt and I sweep a few loose strands of hair behind her ear. I brush my thumb over her bottom lip, making her breath hitch.

"Why didn't you bring a date tonight, Gretch?" The question but a wisp of air floating from my mouth to land on hers. I already know the answer, but I'm a selfish man who wants to hear the words pour from her lips.

"Because you weren't supposed to have a date either."

My mouth claims hers. I take everything I've craved since she walked into that rehearsal dinner last night. She meets my intensity on contact. Our tongues sweep and sway and tangle in an unbridled frenzy.

My body flush up against her, my hands explore, roaming frantically down every curve and back up again.

I cup her breasts in my palms. The soft flesh swells above the bodice of her dress as I push them together and up. I rip my lips away from her mouth and slide my tongue over the peaks and valleys of her cleavage from one far side to the other in one languid stroke. My thumb grazes her nipple through the fabric of her gown.

She whimpers and I fuse our mouths back together to swallow that sound, to hold it inside and never let it go.

Our heads turn and swivel, mouths, tongues and teeth clashing. My hands move all over her while she keeps us flush against each other with every give and take of her own body to stay connected to mine.

We pull back, foreheads coming together, chests heaving as we suck air into our lungs.

I trace a leisurely path with my palm from her face, down her neck, collarbone, and back over her chest again. My hand on her waist, I pinch the soft flesh of her ear between my teeth. She takes in a rapid breath, tugging me even closer. I reach around to cup her backside and give it a rough squeeze.

"Your ass in this dress, Gretch. It's been driving me crazy all night."

I buck my hips forward and she moans. My smile caresses the hot skin of her neck.

I reach lower, finding the bare skin of her thigh through the slit of her dress. She hikes her leg up to my waist, granting permission. My hand glides up her smooth tanned skin—nothing but bare flesh all the way up.

Palm on her ass, my breath heavy on her jaw, I say, "God, you're sexy as hell."

Her exposed leg high around my waist, she's nothing but naked skin up to the apex of her thigh. Two layers of cotton stand between my hard-on and the bare space between her legs. She shifts and I do the same, our bodies chasing that friction. We moan in unison, mouths rushing back together.

I rock into her and she writhes to meet my every move.

Her hands coast up, down and all over me. Pushing into the neck of my shirt, weaving underneath my suit jacket. Every touch traces an exquisitely torturous path over my body—sparks, electricity, a raging inferno at every point of contact between us.

God, the amount of times I imagined being able to touch her like this, to kiss her, to feel her body against mine—it's so much better.

In a world with no sordid pasts, no big brothers, no broken

promises, there wouldn't be anyone else—it would be Gretchen and only Gretchen. Forever.

But that's not reality.

Gretchen flattens a palm against my chest before slowly lowering it over my torso. She grazes past my belt until she's gripping me through my pants. A groan rushes out of me—it's everything my body wants. My senses overload as awareness rushes in all around me.

Drew. Wedding reception. Promises made. Promises broken.

I peel my lips from hers and drop my head to the crook of her neck. After a few ragged breaths, I push myself off the wall, stepping out of her reach.

Heaven help me, I'm too much of a coward to even look at her. I've done it again. I've messed everything up.

"I'm...I'm sorry." I run a hand through my hair. "That was a mistake."

"What?" she rushes out, lungs panting.

"I can't do this. I'm sorry."

If I allow myself a moment to second guess it, I will. A jagged-edged boulder of regret lodges in my throat as I turn and walk away. With every step, my heart thumps to the rhythm of the music pulsing through the wall. Every beat screams for me to go back to her.

*thump...*it's her.*

*thump...*she's the one.*

*thump...*don't let her go.*

I don't go back.

I return to the reception in time to carry out my best man duties for the garter toss. What kind of best friend would I be if I didn't participate?

The best man who takes advantage of the groom's sister on the other side of this very wall, that's who.

I don't see Gretchen for the rest of the night.

When I return to the hotel the next morning for the send-off brunch, it's only to see her. I know I messed everything up, but I promised I'd take her to Mullins Book Collectors today. Though I don't have a great track record in the promises department, I'm hell bent on keeping this one. It's the least I can do for what I put her through yesterday.

Only, she's not there.

Her parents tell me she ducked out of the reception early last night because she felt sick. And this morning, before the sun came up, she told them she planned to get an early start and begin the drive back to school today instead of tomorrow.

The person that's come to mean the most to me in this world is in a car driving a thousand miles in the opposite direction and it's all my fault.

I start to text her, but my fingers won't move. Shame and guilt consume me whole. I played whiplash with her sensitive heart. I stirred up ghosts from her past. I played right into the caricature of how Drew sees me.

My best friend was right—guys like me don't get chances with girls like her. And they sure as hell don't get second chances.

Chapter Thirty-Two

I'LL KEEP TALKING

CONNOR

THE AIR in the hotel room settles heavy and tense as Gretchen waits for me to begin.

I lower my voice and start softly. "That summer Drew and I visited, things were...different. You were so unexpected and so pretty and it threw me. You'd meant so much to me before I left and then I was back after four years, feeling all these new things, but I couldn't act on them because you were sixteen."

"So, you proceeded to ignore me for a month."

I throw out my arms. "It was all I knew to do. Every time you were around, I wanted to be closer and I-I...couldn't."

She slaps away a tear. "You couldn't even be my friend?" The whispered words—the pain there—have my arms straining at my sides, aching to hold her. "If I hadn't run into you by the pool that night, you would have left the next morning without a word."

I take in a long breath, chin dropped to my chest. "I had already promised Drew that he could trust me not to cross that line with you."

Her eyes flare before narrowing. Expressions of confusion, frustration and anger sweep over her face as she mentally recounts that whole visit, looking for the pieces she missed.

"As it turns out," I continue, "I didn't do a good enough job of ignoring you because Drew sensed something."

Mouth pulled into a tight line, anger tenses her jaw.

"It's not his fault, Gretch. You were sixteen, he's your brother and he was only looking out for you."

"What did you tell him?" she grits through clenched teeth, voice unsteady.

"I told him he had nothing to worry about. That you were just a kid and that I cared about you the way he does. I promised him I'd look out for you."

She wants to run—I see it in the tears welled in her eyes, her hands and feet that she can't keep still. But I won't let her run from this. She deserves to know everything.

"And that's how you see me, isn't it? Just a kid," she says.

"Not now, of course not! But then...I...What the hell was I supposed to say? He caught me staring out the kitchen window at *you!* In your green two-piece, braid hanging over your shoulder, running your hand through the floppy hair of some asshole kid who was one cannonball away from getting my fist in his face."

Her gaze bores into me, steady as steel. Every warring emotion comes to a halt as she remembers.

I remember it all; every detail.

"So, yeah, I told him it was nothing. I told him he could trust me. He asked me to promise." I shrug. "And I promised."

"And the black eye?"

"It's like I said: the punch wasn't intended for me, but the message was that you were off-limits."

Animosity creeps into her features again—the same thing that appears every time I mention her brother.

"Gretchen, please understand that Drew was only trying to prot—"

"He was only trying to protect me!" she shouts. "Yeah, you've made that as abundantly clear as the fact that I was sixteen. I get it."

Her outburst gives way to a softer plea. "But I wasn't sixteen when we talked for a year." Softer now. "And I wasn't sixteen at Drew's rehearsal dinner." Barely a whisper. "I wasn't sixteen when you kissed me."

Her hurt scars my own wounded heart anew. I drag a hand through my hair then down my face. The damage I've done, the pain I've caused—*dammit*, I'm a sick bastard for making her carry this for three years.

"Connor!" she demands and all I can do is brace myself for what comes next. "Is he the reason you invited *her?*"

"Yes," I choke out. Her body deflates. Agony settles in my bones and I refuse to try and escape the pain because I deserve it.

"Explain, please."

I remember how close we were then, how I grossly mishandled that whole weekend and the months that followed—it all amounts to a series of the worst things I've ever done. Even though I want to, I can't stop here.

So, I keep talking. "From that first message you sent me at the beginning of that year, I was yours. I know that sounds ridiculous and I can't explain it, but it's true. Every message, every text, every phone call, every video chat…Gretchen, I lived for the next time I would get to talk to you. I'd moved into my own place by then and, I don't know, maybe it was the distance from Drew that gave me a false sense of confidence that you could be mine someday."

She presses the heels of her palms into her eyes.

"My plan going into Drew's wedding weekend was to talk to you about the possibility of *us.*"

Every tear that cascades down her cheeks is a single shred of my heart being ripped away—death by a thousand cuts. God help me, I'm crying, too, and I don't even try to stop it.

"When you walked into that rehearsal dinner, I knew it would always be you and nobody else.

"I wanted to take you on that date. I wanted to drive you back to school to help you move in. I wanted to hop on a plane to New York every other weekend to see you. And I thought—" My voice cracks.

"I thought if we both were sure of each other then we would talk to Drew together."

At last, she meets my eyes, cheeks streaked with tears to match my own. "I would have said yes. To all of it," she breathes.

I know. That's why it was so hard to walk away.

"Tell me what happened. And don't sugar coat it to make Drew look good. Tell me the truth."

While there's a small part of me that struggles to say anything bad about her brother, I can't deny the woman standing in front of me.

"Drew didn't want Mav or any of our old college crew making passes at you, so he pulled me aside after dinner and asked me to keep them away." Every muscle in her body goes taut. "And I told him that I thought he was going overboard, but—"

"Let me get this straight," she interrupts, indignation brewing. "It was just assumed that I couldn't handle myself with a bunch of twenty-five-year-old man-children?"

"He didn't mean it like—"

"Stop defending him!"

"I'm not defending him," I shout back. "I'm telling you how it was. He knew what kind of guys they were. Hell, I was one of them, Gretchen!" I move a step closer now. "The guy who looks for the one-night-stand instead of long term commitment. The guy who wakes up the next morning and can't remember the name of the woman lying next to him."

Shaking her head, she cries, "I never cared about your past, Connor! That's not who you are!"

"With you! With *you* I wasn't that person! For that year, I only saw *you*. I only talked to *you*. I only thought about *you*. But Drew didn't know that."

"Why does Drew's opinion matter more than mine?"

I stop, chest swelling with a heavy breath.

All I've ever tried to do is be a good friend. To not betray Drew's trust. To not come between him and his sister. But has all of that been at the expense of Gretchen's agency in the matter?

"What he says goes because I'm just the little sister, right? Who cares what *I* want or if I get crushed in the process as long as Drew's the hero saving me from the big bad frat boy." She huffs out a disgusted breath. "You know what, you don't need to tell me the rest, I know enough."

I move in closer. "Stop, no," I say. Her hand comes up and I skitter to a halt.

"No! You stop, Connor. Whether or not we were together was a decision for you and I to make. Not Drew. You let him decide and you didn't even consult me! Then you went and invited *her* and apparently that's all Drew's fault, too."

"I let Drew get in my head and I shouldn't have," I say hoarsely. "I fucked up. I thought that—" I shake my head to try and rid myself of the shame. "I thought if I could distance myself from you that would hurt you less in the end. *God*, it sounds so shitty when I hear myself say it out loud."

"And Drew's why you left me on that balcony?"

"Walking away from you was the worst decision of my life, Gretch." I take a chance and step closer. This time she doesn't stop me. "I can't even count the number of mistakes I made that weekend and since, but kissing you was not one of them."

Her eyes soften—she wants so badly to believe me. But the tense arms crossed over her front like a shield tell a different story—she's terrified I'll hurt her again.

"If that's true, why didn't you call? Why did you start seeing someone else?"

Instinct takes over as I reach for her, but she leans away. "Please, don't. Just answer the question."

I work my jaw a few times. "I must have picked up the phone to call a thousand times. I know it's not an excuse, but I was so ashamed. You were in every thought of every minute of every day. I couldn't even escape you when I slept because you were in my dreams, too." I pause, calling forth the memories of the darkest time of my life. "I think I was depressed. The more I tried to drown my sorrows in alcohol, the worse it got until I didn't even recognize myself. I honestly thought that even if I got a second chance, there was no way I could ever be good enough for you." I swat a tear away. "When Drew told me you decided not to come home for Thanksgiving, I knew. You told him it was because it was too expensive to travel, but I knew it was because of me. I turned into the worst version of myself after that. I never told Drew why I was such a mess, but he saw the mess, Gretch."

The tears fall relentlessly. Hers. Mine. Ours.

"I don't regret you. I could never. Everything I felt for you then didn't just disappear. Distance, alcohol, ignorance, other women…it doesn't matter what I tried. None of them were *you*. And I'm a selfish bastard who walked into a restaurant two months ago, convinced that I could handle seeing you again. That three years was enough time to move on. But it wasn't. Not even close.

"Because I'll never move on. It will always be you."

Always. Forever. I know down to the deepest part of my soul that it's Gretchen for me or nobody at all.

"I'm sorry I hurt you. I'm sorry I walked away. I'm sorry I never called. I'm sorry I let Drew decide for you, for us." I pause to give her space to talk, but her words don't come. After a few painfully silent moments that feel like hours, I add, "And I'll keep talking until you've figured out what you want to say."

I take another cautious step forward. Close enough to touch, to smell, to taste now—she doesn't step away. That ember of hope flickers to life in my chest.

In nothing but my swim trunks, the warmth of Gretchen's body so close to mine keeps the chill at bay. Still donning her cherry red two-piece, glimpses of sun-kissed skin tease me in all the places her cover-up isn't doing its job.

"I'm sorry I shut you out that summer." My hand grazes over the clasped arms braced tight across her stomach. I tug gently and they fall loose at her sides. This girl doesn't have to hide—she's the safest she'll ever be with me and I'll do whatever it takes to prove it.

"I'm sorry I never told your brother about that year." With a feather-light touch, I slide my palm between the fabric panels of her cover-up, placing it on the sliver of exposed skin above her high-rise swim bottoms. I use my other hand to remove her hair clip before tossing it to the ground. Thick, onyx locks fall in waves down the length of her back.

"I'm sorry for the birthdays and holidays I've missed." I tuck a finger under her chin and lift her face to meet mine. Her eyes are pinched shut, moisture specking the corners. "And I'm sorry," I kiss the corner of her left eye, "that you felt like you had to do this whole process of finding your birth mom on your own." I kiss the corner of her right eye.

"Let me tell you two things I'm not sorry for," I continue.

Slowly, I drag a hand down the length of her arm, my thumb barely grazing the side of her breast on its way. Her breath hitches.

"I'm not sorry that I'm here instead of your brother." I plant a soft kiss into the crook of her neck. Then another on her collarbone where the smell of coconut sunscreen invades my senses. "And I'm still not sorry I kissed you."

Gretchen deserves to be respected enough to make her own choices, to speak up and for the people around her to listen. Rather than dwell on the years wasted on my ignorance, I take the stand I should have taken three years ago.

"I choose you, Gretchen." I take her hand and place it over my chest, my heart thundering rapidly against her palm. "Do you feel that? My heart chose you a long time ago, but my head got in the way and I'm sorry. But I hear you. I see you. I respect you." I bracket her jaw, thumb sweeping over her cheek. "And I choose you."

Her eyes open and mine are right there to hold them—I'll never leave her again and she knows it. Heat flares between us. She sweeps her tongue over her mouth a second before she lowers my face to hers, both of us sucking in an audible breath when our lips meet.

One hand in her hair, the other grips her waist as I yank her closer. We instantly find a feverish rhythm. Mouths chase, tongues prod and seek, heads turn and then angle deeper. A kiss that feels less like the reckless, lust-ridden haze of three years ago, this one claims—she's mine and I'm hers.

She pushes up on her toes, arms thrown around my neck, hands in my hair. With a flick of my fingers, I pull the loose tie of her cover-up and the fabric falls open. Even though our bodies are flush, so much skin exposed in our swimwear, she's not close enough.

I grab her by the thighs, hoisting her up. She anchors her legs around my waist as I spin us to the nearest wall. Pressing her against it to hold her in place, my hands begin to roam. It's all hunger and passion, years of yearning and pining propelling every touch. I grab a fistful of her hair and tilt her head as she clings to my shoulders, shifting her lower body in search of friction.

The faint remnants of tequila and margarita mix linger on her tongue, but mostly she tastes like forever—my forever.

I press the heel of my palm over her peaked nipple through the fabric of her swim top and she gasps. I smile against her lips and do it again on the other side.

Her head drops back to the wall. "Oh my God," she whimpers. I swoop in like an eagle clutching its prey, my teeth and tongue moving across every inch of her neck.

My hand finds the apex of her thigh. I hover my thumb above that little bundle of nerves tucked behind a layer of red spandex. With my chest pinning her to the wall, I move my lips over hers once more. I tug her bottom lip between my teeth as I begin to massage her over the fabric.

She moans against my mouth, legs trembling around my waist. I want to rip this swimsuit off and drop to my knees in front of her, worship her. But I don't want to rush this. I *can't* mess this up again.

"I've missed you so much," I whisper against her mouth before plunging my tongue back in.

Another sweep of my thumb and she jerks back, breathless. "More, please," she pleads.

With a grunt, I position a hand back under her thigh and push off the wall with the other, turning us toward the bedroom. Her cover-up comes off, tossed aside somewhere between the living room wall and the bedroom.

We collapse onto the mattress, limbs entwined. Her legs fall open as my body settles over hers. My own need for release propels my hips forward, one quick thrust between her thighs. She sucks in a breath, holds it and then releases it in stilted bursts that land hot on the skin of my shoulder. Even with the layers of clothes still between us, the heat and weight of our bodies plastered together, every inch of her skin somehow in contact with mine, her nails raking down my back, the sounds she makes—*God*, I could come just from this.

More than anything, though, I want to see her unravel beneath me.

I slow the roll of my hips and run a hand over her cheek. "I need to know this isn't one and done, Fish. I need this to be real. I need to know if you forgive me."

She takes my face in her hands. Her resolute eyes, soft and steady, grab me by the heart. "I forgive you, Connor."

My forehead falls against hers and I breathe a sigh of relief. I kiss the tip of her nose as my hips resume lazy circles down below. "Other than Mr. No Name Viking, have you ever let another man touch you?"

Her throat bobs as she shakes her head. The bulge in my shorts hits the perfect spot and she sucks in her lower lip.

A half-smirk lifts one corner of her mouth. "He has a name, you know," she says.

"Not to me, he doesn't." I grab her leg and hitch it up high around my waist. My hips circle back again. The pressure pushes deeper and she hums in pleasure.

"That's a different tune than what you were singing earlier, old man."

"Yeah." I kiss her. "But now I've got the girl."

She chuckles, eyes on me—she *sees* me. "You've always had the girl." The words land easy and warm like she hasn't only forgiven me, but that she's forgotten my transgressions entirely.

Her smile parts the clouds, sun crashing in until there's not a shadow in sight. Even if it's hard for me to believe those words, I know one thing for sure: I'm never letting her go.

Chapter Thirty-Three

A GENTLEMAN WOULD ASK FIRST

GRETCHEN

He's always had me.

Despite the hurt, I could never let him go. Not entirely, at least. I missed him too damn much. Certain people I've long since tossed into my rearview would say that makes me weak. Yet, I don't regret that thread of hope I've carried with me all this time, that hope that he would come back to me.

He hurt me and that pain was real, but I know he didn't do it intentionally. The choices he made then were rooted in his loyalty to my brother and loyalty to a friend is noble, even if it clouds your capacity to think clearly sometimes.

A world without forgiveness is a world full of bitter people with resentment in their hearts and I don't want any part in that.

I choose him because I trust him. Heart, soul, mind and body— I trust him with all of my pieces.

Only him.

Like a master musician, he plays my body like an instrument.

His hands, mouth, and the rock of his hips pluck and tune every taught string of pleasure coursing through me.

He links our hands above my head, an anchor that says *I've got you*. When he shifts his weight, his hips lift, the pressure between my thighs now gone. I crave for it to return.

"Connor, please don't stop," I pant.

"I need to do this right. I don't want to rush this. I wanna take you on a proper date. I want you to be my girlfriend. I should do those things first, but right now I just wanna make you come."

"A gentleman would ask first," I tease, lips against his ear. He pulls back, a challenge in his eyes. "Politely," I add.

He gives me a wry smile. "Gretchen Fisher," his mouth hovers above mine, "will you, pretty please," *kiss*, "with a cherry on top," *kiss*, "go on a date with me?" *kiss*.

I think I say yes, but his lips crash down on mine too hard and too fast to be sure. A blissful, erotic haze clouds my senses as his finger runs delicate circles around my nipples through my swim top.

"Gretch," he whispers, "will you," *lazy circle*, "be my," *flick*, "girlfriend?" *pinch*.

I arch into his touch, my voice aching when I cry, "Yes." The curve of his smile ghosts along my neck.

His hand glides down until it rests just above where my body lay burning with desire, swollen, aching for him. I'm on fire, my nerves buzzing, electrified by the feel of his hands and lips on my skin.

"Fish." His voice rumbles, the vibrations sending shivers across my skin. His hand lowers to cup me between my legs, but he doesn't apply any pressure. My toes curl. My feet scrape against the comforter, hips falling open in anticipation. "Do you want me to make you come?" Sudden and firm, the heel of his hand presses into me, exactly where I want it to.

I moan. "Please!"

He shifts, bringing his hand to the waistband of my swim bottoms. "Gretch, look at me." I blink my eyes open to find his right above mine, soft but ravenous. "Ask me what I'm thinking?"

Breathless, I oblige. "What are you thinking?"

"I'm thinking of all the ways I've imagined being with you, none of them compare to the real thing. I want it all. The sweet and slow and, *God*, I wanna break some damn headboards with you too." I swallow deeply. "All of it."

A warm hand lands on my cheek, no doubt having read the shock on my face. "I'm telling you that so you understand how badly I want you, but I'm not going to rush you—*us*—through anything."

I bob my head, relieved. He knows what I need and offers it without me having to ask for it. I kiss him softly. "You know I want all of that, too, right?"

He smiles against my lips. "We'll get there, Fish." He kisses me hard. Heat stirs in my core again as he tucks his hand inside my waistband. "I'm only gonna use my fingers, okay?"

I sigh my approval against his skin.

Flattened palm against my stomach, his hand slides all the way down to rest firmly between my legs. Slowly, his fingers rub and swirl until they're drenched. "*Holy shit*, you feel amazing" he mutters, lips hard against mine, as all the sensations hit me at once and I moan, breaths erratic and shaky.

His fingers continue to move below. Pressing, circling, and prodding, teasing my entrance. Lips brush over my nipple through my swim top as one finger pushes inside me. The flick of his tongue over the hardened peak and the foreign pressure of his finger has me clutching at the sheets.

"You're so good and so tight, baby," he groans, holding his finger in place as I adjust to the sensation. A few seconds later, I can't wait any longer. My hips writhe in protest and his finger begins to thrust steadily in answer.

My breaths come loud and heavy. Shamelessly, I drag my hand all over his back and muscled chest, through his hair, seeking purchase. I need to feel more of him, to climb inside of him.

His finger retreats to tease around my entrance as he pinches my nipple between his teeth. Then, he plunges two fingers inside. My body jolts, my mouth falling open on a silent gasp. I arch into him, telling him *please don't stop* and *I need more*.

"Oh my Go—" The words die in my throat as he curls his

fingers, reaching a blissful spot deep inside my core that brings me near my climax on a guttural gasp.

Then he's too many places at once. His fingers scissor on the inside while his thumb works me over on the outside. His tongue flicks my nipple through my swim top, hips thrusting into the flesh of my thigh. The feel of his hard length as it rubs against me, his deep groans and grunts he brands onto the skin of my chest and shoulders—my senses are out of control.

Every sensation he's masterfully wound so tight over the last several minutes spins into another dimension inside me and I come, *hard*. I cry out my pleasure, moaning, panting, grinding into his hand to ride out every last second of this ecstasy. He doesn't stop until my thighs clamp together, nerves throbbing and over-sensitive.

Body limp with pleasure, my eyes open a minute later. Connor looks at me, wonderstruck, and I feel beautifully exposed. Even though we're still fully covered by our swimwear, it's a look that leaves me raw and vulnerable in the most I-just-got-wrecked-into-blissful-oblivion kind of way.

He shifts his weight so he's balanced evenly, my legs cradling him between my thighs. I can still feel he's hard through his shorts, but he makes no move to do anything about it. Instead, he kisses me deep and slow like he's a man with nowhere else he'd rather be.

He pulls back. "You're perfect."

I hold his gaze and bite back a smile. "Now," I lift up to kiss him, "what are we gonna do about that situation in your shorts?"

"*We* aren't going to do anything. *I* am gonna take care of it in the shower. Dibs!" he declares before he plants a peck on my nose.

"What? Why?" I pout as I roll my hips in an attempt to change his mind.

He brings his knees under him and pushes to his forearms. "Ah ah ah, no ma'am."

I run my hands down his broad chest, over the valleys of his defined abs, until I arrive at the waistband of his swim trunks. Brow arched, I smirk, daring him to stop me.

"I swear to God, Fish, the second you touch me I will come in my shorts." His voice drops low, all grit and gravel when he adds, "The first time you make me come, I wanna be buried inside you."

Heat begins to stir again. It's intoxicating to know I have this effect on him.

Fine, he wins this round.

I let out a playful sigh, hands falling dramatically to the bed. "You're a buzzkill."

He kisses my forehead. "You're beautiful."

CONNOR EMERGES from the bathroom ten minutes later in nothing but a towel and I'm in the exact same position he'd left me in: on my back, flushed and sated, hair splayed across the mattress.

"Well, that didn't take long," I tease. He rounds the bed to stand behind my head. I have to crane my neck to look up at him.

He swoops down low and kisses me. "I told you it wouldn't take much."

Unfortunately for me, the towel doesn't miraculously fall to the ground as he tugs his boxers on. His narrowed gaze finds mine—he knows exactly what I'd been hoping to see.

"See? Buzzkill," I say.

I launch myself from the bed and scamper to the bathroom to remove my contacts. After turning on the shower, I gather my hair into a messy bun. When I step back into the bedroom to grab my glasses, Connor's at the ready, dressed in a pair of thin, black sweatpants and a well-loved Chicago Cubs t-shirt, holding my glasses out for me.

He watches me put them on and then takes my face in his hands. "Beautiful," he whispers. The next second he unceremoniously spins me around, slaps me on the behind, shoves me back into the bathroom to take a shower and announces he's ordering us room service for dinner.

An hour later we're leaning back in a lounge chair on the balcony, bellies and hearts full, pajamas on well before dark. My back against his chest, he cradles me between his legs, his arms wrapped around me. And that's where we stay for hours as we watch the sun sink slowly toward the horizon.

Conversation ebbs and flows, stretches of quiet filled with nothing but the mindless weaving of our interlocked fingers in, out and over.

"How are you feeling about tomorrow?" he asks.

I inhale a deep breath, considering. It's been over eight hours since I left the note on Cheyenne's door and there's still no word. Even to my surprise, I'm not worried. Like Connor pointed out earlier, I've done all I can and there's a peace that comes with that. Having him here helps, too.

"Would I sound crazy if I said I'm not worried?"

He smiles into my hair and curls an ankle over mine. "Not crazy."

Silence settles again before I ask if he thinks Drew and Reagan are okay. We speculate for a while about what could have happened as our memories search for any clues from the past few weeks that we might have missed. Did something happen to somebody in her family? Something with work? Is she pregnant? Sick?

We both text my brother, but don't immediately get a reply.

Phones set aside, we rest deeper into our embrace. The sky turns a soft magenta as the sun melts into the horizon, reflecting off the red earth all around. Tufts of purple clouds dot the tips of the mesas in the distance.

"Can I ask you a question?" Connor kisses my temple.

"Mmhmm."

He squeezes me tighter. "What if Drew doesn't accept this?" His voice is tense with worry. When I turn my face up to his, a set of troubled eyes move over me.

I flip myself over and straddle his waist. With my palms framing his face, I pull his full attention to me.

"Hey," I say, my lips softly kissing his. "I choose you and you choose me. The only decision Drew gets to make is whether or not to support us."

"What if he cuts us out? What if he cuts *you* out?" This is what he fears the most, what paralyzed him on that balcony three years ago—that he'll lose a best friend and I'll lose a brother.

My heart refuses to believe Drew would ever be that cruel. But Connor's tender, good soul needs validation. I hear his fears and I'll never dismiss them.

"*If* he did then that would be *his* choice, not the fault of anything we did." I set his forehead to mine. "As long as we make each other happy, we're allowed to choose that for ourselves."

Connor breathes against my neck. I don't let go until the tension in his shoulders eases and his body settles, relaxing against me.

"Whatever happens, we're in this together," I say.

"Together."

When the sun finally sets and the sky fades to black, we head inside.

I'm halfway across the bedroom when he calls my name from the living room. When I turn to face him, he holds up an envelope branded with the resort's logo. "This was on the floor in the entryway."

Someone must have slid it under the door while we were outside. He holds the sealed envelope out to me, but I don't reach for it. I can't seem to make my feet move. The small distance between us closes as he pads softly toward me.

"I'm right here with you." He grabs my hand, places the envelope in my palm and tilts my chin to meet his gaze. "Read it."

Deep breaths.

I turn it over in my hands. Connor's hand settles on my shoulder and I tear it open. The single piece of resort letterhead tucked inside contains a handwritten message—short and to the point. I read it silently to myself three times. My thoughts pinball back and forth in my head as I try to absorb the words.

"What does it say?" Connor asks.

I suck in a breath and read.

Ms. Fisher,

A woman by the name of Cheyenne Ortega contacted the

front desk this evening and requested we inform you that they're very excited to see you tomorrow. Per her request, here is her phone number, should you need to contact her.

I look up and Connor's warm smile greets me like he knew all along this is exactly what would happen. My eyes water. I think I'm smiling, but I'm mostly hyper-focused on the piece of paper in my hands, running my fingers along the edges to ensure it's real, that this isn't a dream.

Earlier, I said I wasn't worried. Still, my emotions get the best of me. I'm lost to a wave of quiet, anxious thoughts and a heart that squeezes in my chest. Connor takes the letter, sets it on the dresser, walks me to bed and peels back the covers.

He moves about the hotel room, flipping off the lights and making sure the door is locked, before he climbs in beside me. There's no great wall of pillows between us this time. We both shift to the center of the mattress until our bodies find each other, limbs intertwining, like it's something we've done a thousand times before.

Connor still wears his sweatpants and t-shirt. "You're wearing a concerning amount of clothes for a man who says his body is a furnace."

"I didn't want to tempt you with too much skin and hard muscle."

"Says the man who groped *me* in his sleep last night."

He laughs as he rolls to his back. I follow suit, resting my head in the crook of his shoulder. My body uses his like a human body pillow, arm across his chest and leg hiked over his hip.

"Maybe I should put on more clothes so you're not tempted again," I tease.

He hauls me in tighter to his side. "Hell, no. You're perfect."

Several minutes tick by and I'm nearly lulled to sleep, nerves settled, by the steady rise and fall of his chest under my palm. His fingers lazily tunnel through my hair and the world's nearly gone dark, when he whispers, "Are you asleep?"

"Mmmm."

"Is that a yes?"

I snort. "What is it?"

"I just wanted to say thank you."

I tilt my face up to his. "For what?"

"For letting me be the one who gets to share this weekend with you."

"You know I didn't invite you, right?"

"*Touche*," he says. "But you didn't send me packing so I'm calling it a win."

I grin, my index finger sketching soft circles over his chest. "I did always want it to be you, though. I mean, I didn't know if it would ever happen, but whenever I imagined the possibility, it was always with you."

His body stills beneath me and he weaves his fingers with mine. "You did?"

I nod. "You remember my tenth birthday when I asked you if you thought my birth parents thought about me?" He squeezes my hand and I take in a deep breath. "I'd never voiced anything about my birth parents to anyone before, but I did with you that day. I didn't plan it, but you were there and you were always so nice to me and the gift, I just…"

He squeezes my hand again. "You just what?"

"I always felt safe with you. Not that I didn't feel safe with my family, but I don't know…it felt different with you, I guess." I shake my head. "Sorry, I know that doesn't make sense."

"No," he interjects, voice low and hoarse. "I get it."

Something about the way he says it tells me he really does get it.

After a few quiet seconds, he asks, awe and expectancy lacing his words, "So, I was your first choice then?"

I smile into the skin along his collarbone. "Always have been."

The breath that seeps out from deep in his chest carries years of longing and hope on its release and I squeeze my body closer to his in solidarity. *We made it.*

He kisses me softly on the forehead, lips idling there. "Tomorrow's gonna be a good day," he whispers.

And for the first time in a long time, I fall asleep actually believing it.

Chapter Thirty-Four

MY SOUL CHOSE HERS

CONNOR

Gretchen's hair, rich with the scent of vanilla and lavender, coaxes me awake. The sun slices through the small gap in the curtains drawn over the sliding balcony door.

Blinking, I do a quick assessment and confirm I still have pants on, but my shirt is...not on my body. More concerning, though, is how I'm playing the role of big spoon from the opposite side of the bed from where I began. I throw a lazy-eyed glance over her shoulder. *My* side of the bed sits vastly empty—one of life's greatest mysteries.

I run my fingertips up and down her arm. She stirs and flips to face me. Head burrowed in my chest, she tucks her hands under her chin.

She nudges her leg between mine. "How'd you end up over here?" she says sleepily.

I throw my top leg over her hip. "Sshhhh. I find it's best to not ask those types of questions, Fish."

Her breathy chuckle whispers over my bare chest. She's here in my arms, everything out in the open between us—the fact that I'm in love with her, notwithstanding. It feels too soon to say those words just yet.

If I wasn't already gone for her three years ago, the events of the last eighteen hours have solidified it.

I'd never fully realized how much I craved a partner that fit in with my family until she yanked my phone out of my hand and fell in step with my parents like they were long lost besties. The subsequent texts from Mom and Dad—of which I only showed the first couple to Gretchen—were a pure love fest proclaiming how much they love her, how beautiful she is and how they can't wait to see her again. Not knowing for sure if they still talk to Kelly and Paul Fisher, I erred on the side of caution and texted them while Gretchen was in the shower last night to tell them this was very new and to please not say anything to anybody before we are able to tell her family.

Maybe I'm crazy to think so far ahead, but I know she's it for me. I've known it for longer than I care to admit. Picturing a happily ever after feels like a level of permanency I'd never allowed myself to indulge in before now.

"I see you ditched the shirt," she mutters into my neck.

"Sshhhh," I coo, stroking her hair, "let's not try to figure out when or how that happened."

She plants a soft peck on my collarbone as I kiss the crown of her head, our entangled bodies and mindless kisses so natural and uncomplicated. This is home, I think.

She is home.

"What time is it?"

"Don't know," I yawn.

She props herself up, squinting over my shoulder. "Damn, I need my glasses."

With zero grace or consideration for my vital organs, she climbs over me until my hips are braced between her legs. She sweeps her hand across the nightstand and finally locates her glasses and slides them on.

"7:45," she says and then looks down at me. "What are you smiling at?"

"You." The girl with the sexy librarian glasses and her body draped over mine like a stage-five clinger baby koala.

"Mmmm, does my boyfriend have a glasses kink?"

"I have a you kink." I squeeze her ass and roll us onto our sides.

She giggles and I move in to kiss her, but she jerks back. "Ew, I need to brush my teeth first." I pout. "Romance is not dead one day in, old man."

I roll again so I'm on top of her, my hands pinning her arms by her head. "Oh, I'm gonna romance the hell out of you."

She lifts her chin defiantly. "Not with morning breath, you're not."

"Challenge accepted."

My lips come to a hover above hers but she keeps them locked down, refusing to budge. I shift tactics by scattering soft kisses along her ear, down her neck and shoulders, her body can't help but respond.

"This is manipulation," she says, as my lips flick over her firm nipples through her tank top.

"You ready to kiss me yet?"

"Never," she says, breathless.

Her body squirms as need begins to consume her. My lips continue over her collarbone and chest as my hands explore—waist then hips then thighs then exactly where she wants me. She grips the pillows, back arching up off the mattress.

She never does give me that morning kiss—she's stubborn like that—but she unravels beneath me anyway.

A COUPLE OF HOURS LATER, I'm getting caught up on work emails while Gretchen gets ready when my phone lights up with an incoming call from Drew. He's been impossible to get a hold of these last few days, his text replies coming in hours after the fact and with no insight as to what's going on.

I rush to answer. "Hey, man."

"Hey," he sighs.

"Gretchen's gonna be sad she missed you. I think she's still in the shower. Do you want me to have her call you back?"

"No, no," he rushes out. "I just wanted to check in. She doing okay?"

"Yeah, she's alright. Are you okay?"

It's only been three days since Drew called me in a panic, asking for a favor, but it feels like a lifetime ago.

"Yes, no, maybe. I don't know, man. I'm sorry, I—I'm not sure I know which way is up right now."

Silence falls. "You wanna talk about it? Gretch is really worried, you know."

"I know, but…with her birthday tomorrow and the trip and whatever it's about, I just don't want to add another thing to her plate."

Gretchen's face when she read Cheyenne's message last night, flashes forefront in my mind. Her news is ultimately good, even if it does carry shock value. But judging by the sound of my best friend's voice, it's obvious his news isn't as good.

"You could tell me then?"

Reagan calls for him in the background. "Be there in a sec, babe!" he replies before leveling his voice back to me. "Listen, I gotta go. Can you promise me Gretchen's okay? She's not in trouble, is she?"

"I promise, she's okay."

"Is there anything more you can tell me?"

I take in a deep breath, burdened by the weight of what an honest answer would be. *I'm in love with your sister. I'm taking her to meet her birth mom today.*

"Honestly, man, she'd prefer to be the one to tell you."

"Yeah, okay," he says. "Thank you for being there for her." The sound of his nails scraping along his face fills the pause that follows. "For me."

A boulder lodges in my throat and I struggle to fight against the emotion bubbling to the surface. "Yeah, man. Of course."

When we hang up, I shut down my laptop and bring the hand clutching my phone in a tight fist to my forehead.

Echoes of promises made and broken aren't so easily silenced when all I've allowed myself to think for the past six years is that I'm a terrible friend, I'm not good enough, and I don't deserve forgiveness. Hope exists now that I've chosen Gretchen once and for all, but it's new, still just an ember down deep inside, buried beneath the weight of the guilt I've carried for so long.

The bedroom door opens and I turn to find Gretchen there, a goddamn vision dressed in a pair of olive green, high-waisted khaki shorts with a thick belt made from the same fabric cinching her waist and a tucked in white shirt that's molded to her form like a bodysuit. Hair still damp, no makeup—she's perfect.

Taking in my expression, hers falters. "What's the matter?"

I drop my phone to the table with a *thud* and move to stand in front of her in three strides. Her face in my hands, I bring my lips to hers. I breathe her in, breathing life to that ember tucked away inside.

I have her. She's worth it. Everything will work out.

She clasps our hands together on her cheeks and brings them to rest between our chests, a soft, sweet reassurance that she instantly knew I needed. Her tongue sweeps out and I quickly grant her access. Our mouths glide softly around each other, but she keeps our hands locked tight, heart to heart—an anchor tethered to its vessel.

When we break the kiss, I rest my forehead against hers. "I talked to your brother." She looks up at me. "He called while you were in the shower."

"And?"

"And he asked about you, wanted to know what was going on, but I told him you'd probably want to be the one to tell him."

She nods, albeit nervously.

"He wouldn't tell me anything, Gretch. But whatever's going on with him is not good."

She rasps out an affirmation of what we'd both already assumed by now. "It scares me, too, but"—her eyes dart between mine—"there's more, isn't there?"

I run my thumb over our clasped hands. "He thanked me for being here for you *and* for him and…" I trail off, shrugging my shoulders. "Can I be honest?"

"Of course."

"I meant everything I said last night. I choose you. But I'm gonna need you to be patient with me when it comes to your brother. I heard what you said about it being his choice how he responds to this. And I get it. But he and I have a lot of history and I've spent years convinced that he would never forgive me if he ever found out about how I felt about you. That choosing you meant losing him…meant you potentially losing him."

I take in a deep breath, my lungs craving air. Gretchen's sympathetic gaze shows no sign of judgment.

"My head is a chaotic wasteland at the moment. I'm in this for the long haul because you're it for me, but those fears are still there and it's just…it's really hard to shut them off."

She pushes to her toes and kisses me again. "I wanna show you something."

I follow her into the bedroom and take a seat on the bench at the foot of the bed as Gretchen runs to the closet for something. When she settles in beside me, she props one leg underneath her, turning to face me. I take the old copy of *Little Women* she holds out for me. The same one I caught her reading on the hike and that I bought for her twelve years ago.

I gently run my hands over the cover, memories of her tenth birthday rushing in. "I saw this two days ago." I arch a playful brow and she rolls her eyes.

"I know, but you didn't see what was inside." The softest smile pulls at her mouth. "Look at the bookmark."

I open to the page marked by a thick piece of card stock that's not a bookmark at all. A three by five envelope with Gretchen's name scrawled across the center in my familiar handwriting lays between the pages. Tucked inside is the goldfish birthday card.

Gretchen's words stop me before I get the chance to open it. "I know keeping the card all these years is a little pathetic, but I—"

"I don't think that." I look at her, my stern expression the only cover for the heart somersaulting in my chest.

She smiles softly. "Five years old is my earliest memory of understanding I was adopted. My parents never kept it from me before that, but it's like I didn't fully grasp what it meant until then. Ever since, birthdays have been…bittersweet for me. But, my tenth birthday, when you gave me this, I felt seen in a way I never had before.

"I know it was twelve years ago, but it's still the most thoughtful gift anyone has ever given me."

Gretchen's hand comes to rest softly on top of mine.

"I've collected about a dozen editions of this book, but I only ever read this one. And it's not because it's my favorite story. It's because it makes me think of you. Eventually I found myself picking it up just so I could feel close to you."

I turn my hand over and weave our fingers together.

She runs her bottom lip between her teeth. "In the card you said I was your favorite and you called me *Fish*." She gives me a half-shrug, a shy smile playing at her lips. "I guess it was the first time you felt like more than my brother's friend, like maybe you were my friend, too."

I flip the card over in my hand, opening and closing it along the well-worn crease in its center, recalling the details of that day twelve years ago.

"Everything about that day has led me here. The gift, the card, the things I shared with you…it's why all the times I imagined this day, it was always with you.

"And I know it sounds dumb because I was only ten and it wasn't like I was reading all of this into it at the time, but when I think about it now? I don't know, it feels like it was the start of *us*, even if we didn't know it then."

Maybe love is that simple. It can arrive unsuspectingly into your life when you're just a kid. A love that starts out as something innocent and pure, but over time blooms into more. By the time you realize what's happened, you're so far gone you don't even know how or when it began. All you know is you love this person—*your* person—and you can't remember a time when you didn't.

I think, maybe, my soul chose hers long before my heart or my head ever could.

"Did I lose you?" She turns my face with her hand so my glossy eyes find hers.

"I'm here, baby," I rasp.

"I can be patient when it comes to Drew. But I need you to do me a favor."

Her deep brown eyes suck me into their hypnotic trance. I'll do anything for her and I hope she knows that.

"When all that history you share with my brother has you worried about losing him, I need you to remember that we," she takes our clasped hands, tapping them against my chest and then her own, "you and me...we have a history too."

I kiss her fast because I'm afraid of what I'll say if I don't. I'm bound to tell her I love her less than a day after asking her to be my girlfriend.

"I can do that," I say when we pull back. "And for the record, you're still my favorite."

"Yeah, yeah, you're obsessed with me. Old news. Now, respectfully, can you stop making this day about you and help me pick out which shoes to wear?" She plants a loud smack on my cheek as she hops to her feet and prances to the closet.

"Now who's the buzzkill," I holler after her.

She pops her head out, a look of pure mock outrage on her face. "Hey, that's my line."

I could do this forever.

Chapter Thirty-Five

ONE HAPPY THING

GRETCHEN

THE DRIVE back to Flagstaff is a stark contrast to yesterday—I only had to ask Connor to make one bathroom stop. I'm still awash with nerves, but not those of anxiety and uncertainty. It's eagerness, excitement and anticipation that thump a steady rhythm in my veins.

Connor parks on the far side of Cheyenne's driveway, the house blocking the front door from view. With his hand firmly in my death grip, he unbuckles, turns off the car and shifts to face me. "Ready?"

The air rushes out of my lungs as silence falls. I don't move.

"We're a few minutes early." He turns the car back on. "Maybe we just sit here for a bit."

His thumb continuously strokes my hand atop my leg that nervously bounces beneath it. He sits with me, never pushing me to move faster, never showing a morsel of impatience. Many nervous minutes later, I'm finally ready. "I think I should go by myself at first."

"Okay."

"I don't want to blindside her. We didn't tell her anybody else was coming."

He squeezes my hand. "It's okay, Fish. I'm here however you need me to be."

I breathe through the pins and needles in my chest and pull the visor down to use the mirror. "How do I look?" I use my pinky finger to wipe away a dot of rogue mascara in the corner of my eye and turn to face him.

He smiles softly. "Beautiful."

I get one leg out of the car before I turn back, kissing him hard and quick. "Thank you for being here."

With a fast, featherlight kiss to the tip of my nose, he answers, "Thank you for being mine," before I climb out of the car.

When I finally reach the front door, a fresh dose of nerves shudder through me, but I vow to rip the band-aid despite them. With one deep breath, I steel my resolve and ring the bell.

I hear activity behind the door almost immediately and the door swings open a few seconds later.

An adopted kid imagines this moment a million times in their lifetime in probably a million different scenarios. I've tried to envision what it would be like to see her for the first time and I never doubted that I would cry—because, well...hello, it's me—but I thought we'd at least exchange some words first.

How do I explain why the tears well the moment she looks at me?

Although the resemblance is definitely there, I'm not the spitting image of her. Her hair, dark like mine, is streaked with silver and sits several inches shorter than my own. Her eyes are almond-shaped like mine, but they're not brown. They're a deep, hazel-green.

At first glance, I'd guess she's three or four inches shorter than me, a detail made even more severe by the wedge heel of my sandals.

"Gretchen?" Her whispered voice slices through the emotion written across both our expressions.

Words course through my head a mile a minute but I find no

voice. I manage a nod at the same time the first tear falls and I quickly swat it away.

Her gaze roams over my face, cataloguing every feature. "Oh my goodn—" Her voice catches. "Can I hug you?"

I nod again, because it's still all I'm capable of, as I step into her embrace. It's warm and steadfast the way a mother's hug should be.

Through a shaky breath, constricted by her own tears, she says, "I don't want to scare you, but I have a rule with my kids that I'm never the first one to let go. You can decide when this ends. Okay?"

I dip my chin against her shoulder, whispering, "Okay."

She keeps her promise. And when I release and step back, both of us paw at our wet cheeks.

"Do you want to come inside?"

"Yeah." I look between her and the driveway. "If it's okay with you, I brought my boyfriend with me. Can I grab him real quick?"

"Of course, of course."

I jog around the corner and gesture for Connor to join me. As he approaches, I reach for his hand. My tear-streaked cheeks are obvious, but, "Come on," is all I offer as I pull him behind me.

"Connor, this is Cheyenne. Cheyenne, this is my boyfriend, Connor." Handshakes are exchanged before she leads us inside.

Trailing a few steps behind Cheyenne, Connor wraps an arm over my shoulder and kisses my temple. I lean into him as we pass through the small entryway and enter the main living area. Cheyenne invites us to sit before disappearing to the kitchen for drinks.

We take a seat on a well-loved gray couch alongside a wood coffee table that is worn at the corners, bearing several scratches in the finish from many years of use. The bookshelves on either side of the fireplace boast dozens of framed pictures scattered amongst books and decorative items. I want to inspect each picture, take in every face, ask who they are. *Patience,* I remind myself. There's plenty of time for that.

"Miguel had a work meeting this morning that he couldn't reschedule, but he's on his way. He's so excited to meet you." She passes us each a glass of water and swiftly runs her trembling hands down the front of her dress, every emotion still right there at the surface. As she settles into the chair to my left, she glances at her watch. "I expect him back any minute." Her eyes land back on me and a soft smile graces her face.

"Is he y—"

I'm interrupted by the sound of a door opening down the hall followed by a loud voice, breathless like the person ran here, "I'm here! Sorry I'm late." The foreign lilt to his voice is noticeable, but his words are clear.

"We're in the living room," Cheyenne calls over her shoulder.

A few seconds later, the source of the male voice steps into view and my heart stops in my chest.

All this time, I've been wondering if I'd look like Cheyenne, when in reality the man across the room looks more like me than I do. Even Connor, mouth slack jawed beside me, mumbles a quiet, *"Oh my God."*

The tall, dark-haired, brown-eyed, middle-aged man with freckles dotting his nose and a bottom-lip that's fuller than the top, stares back at me. It all clicks into place—the accent, the last name, my Mexican ancestry—a fraction of a second before he says, "Oh, mija."

Daughter.

Is this...real? I shake my head slightly, jostling my jumbled thoughts, but that only makes it worse. "Are you...um..." Nothing else comes out as my eyes slingshot from Miguel to Cheyenne and back.

Connor squeezes my hand and asks, "I think Gretchen is trying to ask if you're her biological father?"

My vision blurs as Cheyenne and Miguel look questioningly at each other. She leans in and rests her hand on my arm. "You didn't know?"

"No," I choke out. "Only your name was on my birth certificate."

Cheyenne sighs, looking to Miguel with a sympathetic smile.

My mind spirals out of control along with my tears. My biological parents are both here and they're...together.

"So, you're my…" I sputter, unable to finish the sentence as emotion claws at the back of my throat.

"I am, mija."

I rise on wobbly legs and close the distance between us. He folds me into his arms, shoulders shaking as his own tears fall. A few beats later, the gentle graze of a feminine hand runs over my shoulders, a warm body hovering close to her husband and the daughter they gave up.

The weight of this moment—a child reunited with her parents after twenty-two years apart—fills the air around us and I tell myself to log every detail. The words, the faces, the room. I couldn't possibly process it all in real time.

When the three of us step back, our faces streaked in tears and disbelieving smiles, I turn to Connor. He stands a few steps away, his phone held up in video mode to capture the interaction. I don't know when he started recording, but I already know I'll treasure that video for the rest of my life.

I give Connor a grateful smile. When he winks in answer, a tear falls down his cheek.

Turning back to Cheyenne and Miguel, I notice a large portrait on the wall just beyond where we're standing—something I didn't catch before.

My eyes locked on the family posed in a group hug, I recall all the evidence from our visit yesterday. "Are those your kids?"

They follow my gaze. Cheyenne takes my hand a moment later and leads the way until the three of us stand in front of the over-sized print.

"Yes. These are your brothers and sisters," she says.

My hands come to my face, cheeks soaked with tears. The only thought my brain can muster is *this is impossible.*

"This is Miguel Junior. We call him MJ. He's twelve." Miguel points at the tween boy with thick, wavy black hair that already stands taller than his mom. Brown eyes like mine.

"This is Rosa. Sometimes we call her Rosie. She's ten." Long dark hair. Full, plump cheeks and a dusting of freckles on her nose. Brown eyes.

"This here is Tally, short for Tallulah, and she's seven." Green eyes, like her mom, but more freckles like her dad. Her gap-toothed smile lights up her whole face. The head of curly dark hair sets her apart from the rest of her siblings.

"And this is our four-year-old, Kai," Cheyenne says of the last little figure propped on his dad's shoulders, smiling down at his big brother. The only one not fully turned to the camera, it's hard to make out his features, but the obvious notes are there: dark skin, dark hair.

These tiny faces—the faces of my two brothers and two sisters. My full-blood siblings. I never want to look away.

Cheyenne and Miguel each rest a considerate hand on my shoulders, but all I can do is swat at the tears dropping faster than I can catch them. Every time I think I've got my emotions under control, it starts back up again.

I pinch my eyes shut and force out the question that's paralyzed me since I saw the sidewalk chalk on the driveway yesterday. "Do they know about me?"

"Yes, Gretchen, they do." Miguel's answer is immediate—calm and reassuring. I sag in relief as the breath I'd held hostage rushes out. My face squeezes in on itself again when new tears begin to fall. I'm seconds away from full body sobbing right here in this hallway.

"This is a lot. Let's sit back down so we can talk," Cheyenne prods as we return to the living room.

We all make use of the tissue box Cheyenne passes around as Miguel says, "We didn't want to overwhelm you with the kids here, so we have a neighbor down the street watching them. If and when you're ready, we'll go get them."

I nod in understanding, thankful that I wasn't overwhelmed with all of this when I knocked on the door.

Cheyenne asks about what led me to her. With Connor's hand running smooth strokes up and down my back, I launch into the story about the DNA kit and the detective that provided me with her name and address, but no other details.

When I circle back to the part about Miguel's name not being on my birth certificate, Cheyenne turns to him and places her hand atop his. The look that passes between them feels fraught with regret and bad memories.

"Miguel was not able to be there when I gave birth."

"I wanted to be there," he rushes to add.

"But there was a lot of tension between our families."

They both pause and Cheyenne looks to Miguel, a sorrowful smile on her face. Miguel squeezes her hand, an encouragement to continue.

"My parents were high-ranking in the Navajo Nation government while I was growing up," she starts and then hesitates before finally saying, "they were...strict. Tribal culture and preservation was ingrained into us from an early age. It was expected of us to keep our relationships within the tribe."

My brows furrow.

"This was not a Navajo standard," she clarifies. "This was the rule in my house and the small tight-knit community of full blood Navajos that my parents kept us sheltered within on the reservation. They disowned my oldest sister, Winona, when she eloped with her British boyfriend. The fact that they were both medical students studying at Harvard made no difference to them.

"Anyway," she focuses back, "I met Miguel on a day trip into Flagstaff with a friend's family. I was fourteen and he was fifteen." They exchange a smile. "We started sneaking around to meet up with each other. After several months together, I wound up pregnant just before my fifteenth birthday."

Fifteen and pregnant. One sister already disowned, I can't imagine the fear she must have felt in that situation. Fear of disappointing her parents. Fear of abandonment. I fight to keep my expression neutral as she goes on.

"When I finally got the courage to come clean to my parents, well, you can imagine how they reacted. They tried to get me to terminate, but I refused and it was too late anyway."

Connor squeezes my shoulder as the grimness of this revelation settles over the room. In an alternate scenario, I would have never been.

Miguel clears his throat and moves the conversation along. "My parents tried to arrange a meeting with her family to discuss options about what the future could look like, but they wouldn't talk to us."

"So, I called Winona," Cheyenne supplies. "She was across the country at school, but she became my rock. My parents pushed for the adoption and, given how young we were and the conflict with our families, we both knew it was the right decision. Besides that, they weren't really involved other than setting the adoption terms and pushing it through."

"When you say 'adoption terms', what does that mean?" Connor interjects.

"There are federal adoption laws in place designed to keep Native children within the tribe as much as possible. It's all an effort to preserve our culture. Under more normal circumstances, Gretchen, you would have most likely been adopted by a member of my extended family or another Native living on the reservation."

"But yours weren't normal circumstances?" I ask.

"No, they weren't. My dad planned to run for President of the Navajo Nation and having one disowned daughter married off to a British man and another pregnant by a Mexican boy at fifteen was too scandalous for his campaign, or so he said." The hurt in her eyes turns to righteous indignation. "My pregnancy was kept a secret. When I started to show, they transitioned me to homeschooling and a tribal doctor made house calls for all my prenatal care. I relied on Winona to keep Miguel and his family up to date on the pregnancy because my parents wouldn't let me leave the house."

My head swims. Tidal waves of thoughts and questions run every which way as I listen to their story—*my* story.

"You were due the last week of June. My sister and her husband came back to Arizona and got a temporary apartment in Phoenix for that summer. My parents refused to see her, but they allowed me to spend the last few weeks of my pregnancy living with her so that I could deliver at a small private birthing center in Phoenix that my parents had selected for its discretion."

Because my grandfather couldn't have an unplanned, half-blooded grandchild, my mother was forced to give birth in secret.

"I'm sorry, I know this is a lot to absorb," Miguel says, reading the distaste on my face.

"No, it's okay. Um…yeah, I'm trying to understand. Can you go back to the adoption terms you said your parents set?"

Cheyenne bobs her head. "Yes, sorry. In extreme circumstances, a judge can approve, at the request of the parents—or in my case, *my* parents, since I was a minor—to have a child placed with a family out of state. Since my parents rubbed shoulders with all the higher-ups in the tribal government, they pretty much got anything they asked for."

Cheyenne reaches for another tissue.

"So, neither of you got any say in where I ended up?"

"No. It's always been my understanding that at least one of your parents has some Navajo blood which I suspect is why my mom selected them. On paper it was a more respectable choice, even if you wouldn't be remaining on the reservation itself."

Mom. She's told me that she has a small amount of Native American blood and that, when they were pursuing adoption, they added their names into every adoption database they could qualify for across the country. This must have been what compelled Cheyenne's mom to select them.

"And you didn't know their names or where they lived?" I ask.

Cheyenne shakes her head. "It was a closed adoption, so names and distinguishing information were all kept confidential."

These are widely known facts about closed adoptions that I'd come to understand well in my own research. It's how I know my parents couldn't have possibly known any of this.

"You said you weren't at the birth?" I ask Miguel.

"No." He squeezes his wife's hand, a silent apology for not being there. "When Cheyenne moved down to Phoenix, my family and I went to see her as often as we could that summer. As much as I wanted to be there for her when she went into labor," he pauses to regain his composure as a lone tear slides down his cheek, "they were worried her mom might show up during the birth and well… we all agreed it was best to avoid that confrontation."

"Did she come?" Connor asks.

"Not for the birth, no," Cheyenne croaks out on a shaky breath. "It was just my sister in the room with me."

"Winona's husband, Arthur, stayed in the waiting room and called me a few times, though, to give me updates," Miguel adds.

A teenager giving birth with only her sister at her bedside, under the cover of night and non-disclosure agreements, in a town two hours away from home—I can't even fathom.

"My mom showed up a few hours later, you had already been taken away by someone with the adoption agency." Cheyenne wipes at her cheek. "I don't know, the next few days are a blur. With the hormones and trying to suppress my milk, there's not much I remember other than sleeping and crying a lot." With a resigned sigh, she continues. "My mom filled out the birth certificate paperwork and I would suspect she left out Miguel's name so that if it ever leaked nobody could go digging."

The secrecy. The cover-up. And the two kids, who weren't much more than babies themselves, at the center of the drama unfolding around them without the power to stop any of it. I don't know what kind of story I expected to hear about how I came into the world, but it definitely wasn't this.

"Let me show you one happy thing that happened that day," Cheyenne says, voice soft, smile warm.

She moves across the room and retrieves a small picture frame from one of the bookshelves.

I take it from her as she says, "I got to hold you."

No larger than a four by six, the image is grainy and slightly out of focus. It's taken from too great a distance to make out any nuanced details and the camera flash combined with the dim lighting in the delivery room has left a light flare in one corner of the image. Yet, I see a teenage Cheyenne, face turned away from the camera, gazing down at the newborn baby cradled in her arms.

Me.

"It was only for a few minutes, but you opened your eyes and looked at me and…" Her voice trails off as she begins to cry. I run my fingertips over the glass. "My God, I saw it clear as day even then, you look just like your father." She laughs, voice thick with emotion. "I don't think he believed me before today."

I look over at Miguel who stares back at me, glassy-eyed but content like he's come face to face with a miracle.

"This is the only picture you've ever had of me?"

You can't even see my face in this picture. I'm nothing but a tiny swaddled blob cradled against Cheyenne's chest.

Miguel—for more than two decades he's been told that his first daughter looked just like him, yet he never saw it for himself until now.

He flashes an affectionate grin and a wink at his wife. "Yeah, I had to take her word for it."

For the past twenty-two years they've had nothing but this single blurry photo to remember me by. This photo that they've preserved, framed and put on display in their home alongside countless other family photos.

"A few minutes after Winona snapped this picture, a woman showed up and took you away. I'm assuming your parents took you home sometime after that."

I know the story from here. "They said they picked me up from a hospital in Phoenix a couple days after I was born."

A heavy pause settles between us, both our gazes fixed on the photo in my lap.

"And you've had a good life?" Her question comes out quiet, a little broken, but eager—a mother desperate to know that her child ended up in a good home.

I turn to Connor who hasn't said much but remains strong and steady at my side. His face is a display of pure adoration and pride behind a lens of unshed tears. I squeeze his hand and the dip of his chin in reply says, *I've got you.*

"I've had a great life," I say.

Cheyenne's smile is relief and curiosity wrapped into one. "Will you show us pictures?"

Chapter Thirty-Six

THEY'VE BEEN WAITING FOR HER

CONNOR

GRETCHEN'S PHONE COMES OUT, as does mine, and we begin to mine our camera rolls and our social media accounts as well as her family's profiles to find photos to share with Cheyenne and Miguel.

One look at the handful of pre-teen and teenage Gretchen pictures we find on her mom's profile and it wouldn't take an expert to see the Ortega siblings' resemblance.

When we pulled up to this house yesterday and Gretchen spotted the tricycle and sidewalk chalk, she was nearly scared away altogether.

Imagine if she had missed out on *this*.

Teenage parents who managed to overcome all odds. Despite her parents' strict forbiddance to the contrary, when Cheyenne moved back to the reservation after Gretchen's birth, she remained in contact with Miguel via secret messages and phone calls until she graduated high school and made the decision to come to Flagstaff for college. Her parents cut her off entirely at that point. Miguel's family, however, took her in like one of their own. Four

264

years later, they were married. Two years after that, Miguel Junior was born and three more kids came along over the next several years.

Gretchen's four full-blood siblings. If she feels any sense of abandonment from not getting to grow up alongside them, she doesn't let it show. Cheyenne and Miguel made the right decision in choosing adoption.

And Gretchen was right; she's had a great life.

She tells Cheyenne and Miguel about her parents, Drew and Reagan, and life back in Illinois. I'm able to chime in with my own anecdotal stories of the years I spent growing up with them, too. We smile and laugh, reminiscing over our shared history. *Our history*. It may only be for the sake of catching her birth parents up to speed on everything they've missed, but it does something for me, too—it fills the cracks and hollow spaces where doubt and regret used to be and replaces them with hope and undiluted adoration.

"How long have you two been together?" Cheyenne asks as she swipes through a photo album on Gretchen's phone from Drew and Reagan's wedding.

I hesitate because *"since yesterday"* sounds not only ridiculous, but also like a lie.

"Officially," Gretchen starts, "not very long, but we've been inevitable for years."

She winks at me before swiping to another photo. Just a casual one-eyed blink, like her words didn't send my heart into a free fall behind my sternum.

"When do you guys head back to Chicago?" Miguel asks.

"We fly back day after tomorrow," Gretchen supplies.

Miguel and Cheyenne share a look, wide grins in place.

"Listen," Cheyenne says, "it's probably more than you bargained for, and there's no pressure, but we're having a family get-together tomorrow and we'd love for you to join us. It'll be mostly Miguel's family, but there's a lot of them." She chuckles and Miguel offers an impish shrug. "Winona and her husband will be here, too, and I know they'd love to meet you."

"Oh…um…" Gretchen fumbles over her words and turns to

me, the conflict in her eyes a tell for that brain of hers that's working overtime right now.

Tomorrow is her birthday. It's not that she doesn't want more time with her family, but rather, she doesn't know if they recognize the significance of the date.

It's a mother's intuition, perhaps, that has Cheyenne adding, "It's something we do every year, Gretchen," she looks to her husband briefly and then back to her first-born daughter, "on your birthday."

Gretchen blinks rapidly as I stroke her back with my open palm. Of course they remember.

"The whole family? You…every year…a-all of you?" The words tumble and fall over each other, her throat tight with restrained emotion.

"Yes. All of us. Every year," Miguel replies with a kind smile.

"I wish I could say that my family would be here, but…well, they haven't been in contact since I left the reservation. It's just me, my sister and her family now." Cheyenne's eyes lie full of sorrow. A daughter who made some mistakes, as teenagers do, went through the unimaginable and whose parents, instead of offering support, shunned and disowned her.

Thank God for Winona.

"But, if it's too much too soon, we completely understand," Cheyenne adds, honing in on Gretchen's blank expression.

I grab her hand, drawing her gaze to me. She wants to say yes, but she's overwhelmed. "Yeah?" I whisper quietly, only for her, and nudge her knee with mine.

She nods. The unshed tears glisten beneath her lashes before she turns back to Cheyenne and Miguel. "Yeah, okay."

AN HOUR, three photo albums, and countless tears later, Gretchen finally musters up the courage to meet her siblings.

Cheyenne and Miguel take the short walk down the street to pick up the kids while Gretchen and I wait at the house.

When the door clicks shut behind them, I allow her a few moments to breathe in her own space while I discreetly prop my phone on a nearby shelf. She hasn't asked me to document anything, but I know she'll want to remember every detail of this day.

Gretchen paces the living room, thumbnail between her teeth, as I approach her. "I can't believe this is happening," she whispers. The improbability of today's events shines bright all over her, as fresh now as it was two hours ago when she knocked on the door.

I haul her into my chest for a hug. "I'm so proud of you."

She steps back and promptly begins wiping under eyes and combing her fingers through her hair. Before she can ask, I say, "Beautiful."

Shadows drift across the front window and I plant a chaste kiss on her lips, tell her she's got this and press record on my phone. I duck around the corner to let them have this moment for themselves. I'm out of everyone else's view but I still have a line of sight to where Gretchen stands at the threshold of the living room. The front door swings open on a held breath that swells the air with anticipation.

What comes next happens so fast, yet feels like slow-motion all at the same time. The Ortegas stand behind their four children in the entryway, Gretchen a few strides in front of them. The pause between them like that big resolute breath you take when you stand on the cusp of something you know is about to change your entire world. Gretchen offers a shy wave and quiet "hello" as her brothers and sisters close in. I don't even think Gretchen expects it until it happens.

A four-year-old Kai clings to Gretchen's leg. Tally wraps her arms around Gretchen's waist and the two oldest, Rosa and MJ, close in around her shoulders. The five of them latched together in an embrace, limbs crisscrossing around each other's bodies, the sound of sniffles and whispered words piercing the otherwise pin-drop silence.

My chest tightens at the sight of something that shouldn't make sense but somehow…does. Four kids embracing their big sister, whom they've never met, as if she's been here all along.

Like they've been waiting for her.

Cheyenne, Miguel and myself can do nothing but watch it all unfold.

Once tears are wiped away and official introductions are made, Gretchen asks each of her siblings about themselves which leads to a tour of their bedrooms upstairs.

MJ is really into movies and filmmaking, but he also plays football, so I get a chance to connect with him over sports.

Rosa loves art and is learning to play the guitar. With some gentle encouragement from Gretchen and myself, we're able to convince her to play something for us with Miguel accompanying her on his classical guitar.

Tally is spunky and full of life with her head of curly hair that bounces behind her everywhere she goes. She loves tumbling and ballet and proudly shows us the video of her most recent dance recital performance.

Kai is the baby and mainly just wants to show his big sister his Bluey collection. Figurines, stuffed animals, playhouses, costumes: the kid's got it all.

Before everyone settles back into the living room, I offer to take some photos.

The emotion in the room is a tangible thing when everyone shimmies into position for their first full family photo. I look through my little camera screen and choke back my own tears at the sight of Gretchen sandwiched between her birth parents, her brothers and sisters crowded in around and in front. Everyone squeezes in tight as I count down and the smile that breaks across Gretchen's face lights up my entire soul.

She's strong. She's brave. And she's never looked more beautiful.

HUGS ARE DOLED out like cotton candy at the fair as Gretchen exchanges goodbyes with her family. Plans are made for our return tomorrow afternoon, more pictures are taken, and then everyone hugs some more as Miguel and I stand off to the side as spectators.

An hour ago, despite how incredible today has been, I sensed she was ready to be alone to process it all. Cheyenne had invited us to stay for dinner and, even though I know she must be hungry because we haven't eaten since breakfast, Gretchen deflected with an ambiguous "maybe". At the first opportunity, I whispered for only her ears that it was okay if she was ready to call it a day. She sagged her body against mine and that was all the confirmation I needed. Not wanting to interrupt the third round of 'Pretty Pretty Princess' Tally had roped all the girls into, Gretchen finished the game before I conjured up a work call I needed to get back to the hotel for.

Thus ensued this carousel of goodbyes in the entryway.

I notice Miguel's face, painted in a soft canvas of peace and contentment and disbelief. I step in closer, voice quiet, "You guys have changed her life, Miguel. She gets quiet when she's over-whelmed and probably won't say it herself, but this means more to her than you'll ever know. So, thank you."

He shakes his head almost imperceptibly, gaze locked on his first born, arms wrapped around her little brothers and sisters, while the mother of his children dons the brightest smile, snapping picture after picture on her phone. "I've had six best days of my life. The first was twenty-two years ago and I wasn't even there to witness it. She made us a family." He pauses, a deep breath filling his chest. His next words come out thick and laced with emotion as he turns his attention on me. "I've never not loved Cheyenne. Marrying her was the second best day of my life and I've never regretted it for a single moment. But we were just kids when we fell in love. Who's to say what would have come of us if we hadn't had Gretchen. What would distance, teen hormones and strict parents have done to two starry-eyed kids who *didn't* have this big thing tethering their souls together…forever." His glassy eyes land back on his family—on Gretchen. "*She* changed *our* lives."

With a final round of hugs, phone number exchanges, photos and video airdropped from my phone to Cheyenne's, and promises to see everyone again tomorrow, Gretchen and I finally walk out the door. We turn the corner onto the driveway as the front door clicks shut behind us. Gretchen lets out a heavy breath, all the tension she's held tight in her bones escaping with it.

When we're clear from view, I turn her to face me. She doesn't hesitate as she curls her arms around my neck and buries her face against the skin there. Her sobs come on strong and heavy. I throw my arms around her waist and lift her up, her legs linking around my hips.

I ease back onto the hood of the car, her body wrapped tight around mine, and I let her cry. This is what she's held in for the past four hours. Tears have fallen throughout the day but only enough to relieve the pressure.

"Shhh, let it out, baby."

"I'm sorry," she chokes out, the words muffled against my neck.

"There's no reason to be sorry. You've just run a marathon… you know, emotionally speaking." That makes her laugh.

We stay for a few minutes as her cries dissipate and her breaths even out.

"You know what I'm thinking?" I whisper into her hair.

She pulls back, eyeing me playfully, brow arched.

"Margaritas."

Chapter Thirty-Seven

YOU WANNA MAKE OUT NOW?

CONNOR

An hour and a half later, we settle in at the bar of a Mexican restaurant in downtown Sedona. The sun still a couple of hours from dipping behind the mesa rock formations, the panoramic red desert view has us content to stay a while.

I order two margaritas from the twenty-something female bartender before she turns to Gretchen and asks for her ID. She slides it across the bar and the bartender slides it back a second later, attention now fixed on me. I expect her to ask for my ID as well, but instead, she simply grins and walks off to begin preparing our drinks.

Gretchen, mouth agape, turns her head on a swivel, gaze locked on the bartender's retreating form. "Unbelievable."

"What?"

"That bartender and I are gonna have to throw down."

I stifle a smile. "Is that so?"

"She just checked you out right in front of me."

"Maybe she was checking to see if she needed to card me?"

She snorts. "You know for a former playboy, you're very daft when it comes to recognizing when a girl is into you."

"Is that so?"

"Is that all you say now?" Her eyes lock on me, wicked with amusement.

"Hey, you're the one that calls me old man." I arch a brow.

"And?"

"And maybe I look older than you."

"*Or* maybe she's single, you're hot, she's not quite sure who *I* am to you, and she wants you to notice that she noticed you and, *if* you noticed her, she wants to make sure she comes off all cool and laid back like '*See, I won't ID you. Wanna go back to your place?*'…you know, in case you're single, too."

"But I'm not single."

Her smile is feral and all mine.

Said bartender returns with our drinks and two menus. Gretchen's expression turns conspiratorial as she leans across the bar. "Excuse me, miss? Can I ask you a question?"

The poor woman hums her agreement, but I don't take my eyes off Gretchen's profile as I pivot in my stool to fully face her.

"Why did you card me but not my boyfriend?" Yeah, she's out for blood, but in a cute way. Her grin is all smug and adorably possessive. I can feel the bartender's gaze flick to me before it lands back on my girlfriend.

Before she can reply, Gretchen cups one hand around her mouth, stage whispering for everyone within a ten-foot radius to hear, "Is it because he's hot?"

This girl. One second she's in her head, overanalyzing, and the next she's brazen and self-assured, proudly claiming what's hers. She may as well have written *mine* in black marker across my forehead. I'd tattoo it there permanently if she asked me to. I've never been happier to let someone else own me entirely, heart and soul.

The bartender coughs, clearly uncomfortable by Gretchen's shamelessly forward line of questioning. I can only smile at my girl as I yank Gretchen's stool closer to rest between my knees.

A couple of awkward beats pass before I throw the bartender a lifeline and ask for some queso and guacamole. She ambles away to put in our order as Gretchen turns to me, taking a generous sip from her margarita. "Was I too harsh?" The arrogant tilt of her lips as she sets her glass on the counter says she's not the least bit sorry.

"My little savage." I grip her chin and pull her lips to mine for a quick kiss. "I only ever want to look at you, babe." I kiss her again. "Got it?"

"Cheesy line, but okay."

She pinches my cheek and tousles my hair before her expression neutralizes, swallowing down the humor from a moment ago.

"Thank you for knowing what I needed today."

Confident and not the least bit ashamed about it, I use her own words from two days ago. "What else would you expect from the person who knows you better than anyone else?"

She purses her lips. "Don't get cocky, old man."

"I wouldn't dream of it." I laugh, kissing her once more. "Today was a good day."

Her lips smile against mine. "The best."

Our appetizers arrive and Gretchen excuses herself to the bathroom. As she walks away, I catch a table of dudes looking her up and down, Gretchen totally oblivious to the fact that she's the most beautiful woman in every room. All tan skin, long legs, black hair draped effortlessly down the middle of her back and big eyes as sweet and rich as chocolate.

And now I'm wondering what we'd look like with matching forehead tattoos.

I CUT myself off the minute Gretchen ordered a second margarita. After the emotional day she had, she needed to let loose. The ever-present glass of water I refilled between each margarita was as much as I could do to keep her from drinking herself into regretting her choices this morning.

She peaked at slightly tipsy before I suggested we call it a night. But what I now know is that slightly tipsy Gretchen equals excessively handsy Gretchen. If I wasn't so obsessed with the woman, I'd say I was taken advantage of last night. After I was sufficiently groped in the elevator—no complaints from me—we weren't two steps inside our room when she started trying to undress me. I quickly grabbed her by the wrists, pressed them above her head against the wall, kissed her hard and told her she wasn't allowed to touch.

Naturally, she called me a buzzkill and I told her she'd never been more beautiful. Then, I slapped her on the ass and ordered her to get ready for bed.

God, I wanted her to touch me, though. I want everything with her, but not like that. Not when she's not fully sober and not before she knows how much I love her. I'll no doubt be lusting after her until the day I die, but I don't want our first time together to happen in a lust-riddled haze that we could wake up from tomorrow morning and wish had happened differently.

Gretchen played dirty when she put on one of my t-shirts to sleep in. Hanging down to her upper thigh, she wore only a pair of panties underneath. Side by side at the bathroom sink, she jutted out one hip as we brushed our teeth, our eyes unashamedly roaming over each other in the mirror. That messy bun and those glasses almost did me in, but I held my ground. For about thirty more seconds, that is, before she spit into the sink, rinsed her mouth, turned to me and said, "Well, if you won't let me touch you, the least you could do is touch me."

Tipsy Gretchen is also no-filter Gretchen.

I smiled at her through my suds-filled mouth, toothbrush perched out the side of my lips. A second later, I spit into the sink, tossed my toothbrush aside, grabbed her by the waist and hoisted her onto the counter to give her exactly what she wanted.

After she came on my fingers, I kissed her tenderly and sent her to bed. She was fast asleep by the time I finished my shower.

I climbed under the covers and wrapped my body around hers. And, miracle of all miracles, it's the exact same position we find ourselves in—*glory be,* I'm fully clothed—when the ring of her cell phone wakes us up.

Gretchen groans into my arm. I clear the hair away from her face, kissing her temple. "It's probably your parents calling to talk to the birthday girl."

She smiles lazily before reaching for the phone.

"Hey, Mom," she answers, still half-asleep as she pushes herself up against the headboard.

I use the next few minutes to brush my teeth, splash my face with water and collect Gretchen's gift from my suitcase while she talks to her parents.

"Drew's good. He's not here right now though." Gift tucked behind my back, I give her a curious look and she waves her hand to say she'll explain later. "I'll tell him you guys said hi."

I climb back into bed as she ends the call.

"I guess Drew never told them that he didn't end up coming. I don't know what to do other than pretend things are fine." She shrugs, worry carved between her brows over thoughts of her brother back home.

"Hey," I say.

She looks at me, features softening.

"Hi."

A grin lifts her cheeks as she collects her glasses from the bedside table and puts them on. "Hi."

"Happy Birthday, baby." I set the gift wrapped in tissue paper on her lap as her eyes flicker with surprise.

"Hang on." She moves the present back to my lap. "I need to brush my teeth first."

"Why?"

"Because I know I'm gonna want to make out with you after."

I give her a long once over as she settles against the doorjamb. One hand moves the toothbrush, elbow propped on the arm she has wrapped over her middle. Hip popped out, wearing my t-shirt and nothing else, she knows exactly how good she looks—like my sexiest fantasy and greatest accomplishment all rolled into one.

When she's done, she bounces back into the bed and sidles up next to me. Gift back in hand, she peels back the tissue paper, her expression leveling as she moves the last bit of wrapping aside.

I wait for her to respond, but her eyes remain fixed on the front cover, fingers tracing the title.

"I saw you eyeing it at the bookstore the other day."

"It's too much," she says, voice trembling.

"Fish, look at me."

She meets my gaze, emotion warring behind the features she tries so hard to keep locked down. "I know how much this cost, Connor, and it's too much."

What the early edition hardback of *Little Women* means to her is way more valuable than the money in my bank account. After everything she told me yesterday about the first copy I gave her all those years ago, the birthday card she's kept, the fact that she rereads it because it reminds her of me—it means even more now.

I take her hand. "You said that the day I gave you this book the first time felt like the start of *us*. You asked me then if I thought your birth parents thought about you."

A tear runs down her cheek and I catch it with my thumb.

"Look where we are now, Gretch. The same boy gifting the same book to the same girl. And I get to be the one to watch you celebrate your birthday with your birth family for the first time today." I tap my finger on the book she now clutches to her chest. "This? It could never be too much because it's not enough. I'll buy you a new copy every year if you'll let me, to remind you of where we started."

Without a word, she looks at the book and then reaches across me to set it on the nightstand. After she wipes her eyes behind the lenses of her glasses, she pushes them back up the bridge of her nose and moves to straddle me. The look on her face a mix of affection and some sort of resolve, like she's decided to do something, has me awaiting her next move.

My hands land on her bare thighs, her shirt having ridden up high enough for me to see the peek of white cotton panties underneath. I try not to think about all the layers of clothing that are lacking between us in this position.

She rests her forehead against mine, my face cradled in her palms. "I…um…" She hesitates, fingers fidgeting in the scruff along my jaw. Her resolve withers with each silent second that passes. "Thank you," she finally whispers. It's not what she was going to say, that much I know.

"You're welcome."

My palms run the length of her legs, up to her waist and back again. Her eyes remain closed as she tries to find her words. Or maybe the courage to say them at all.

"You wanna make out now?" I ask into the nervous silence because I just want to see her smile.

A grin tugs at her lips before she slowly lowers her lips to mine. Her arms wrap around my neck, forearms squeezing me into her chest. I brace my arms across her back, my palm splayed over her shoulder blades.

It would be so easy to take things further, to let my hands wander the miles of exposed skin she has draped around me. She could make the first move with a single rock of her hips. But neither of us do anything of the sort. It's simply two mouths in harmony with two hearts and an embrace so tight it's hard to breathe.

She may not have said the words, but I feel them in the arms she has wrapped around me, her mouth that moves unhurriedly against mine, like she never plans on letting me go. Like she's in no rush because she knows as well as I do that there's a forever ahead of us. A forever that's as true now as it was then.

I'm glad she didn't say them.

Because I want—*I need*—to be the one to say them first.

Chapter Thirty-Eight

I DON'T THINK I BROUGHT ENOUGH TEQUILA

GRETCHEN

DREW

Happy Birthday! Sorry I'm not there to celebrate with you.

ME

Thank you! Love you.

DREW

Love you more.

I TUCK my phone in the cup holder as we pull into my family's neighborhood. As soon as my hand is free, Connor wastes no time taking it in his again.

The words almost slipped this morning and when they got stuck in my throat, he saved me. I'm relieved I didn't say it. Not because I don't feel it, but because the fear of what he might not say back is paralyzing.

It's easy for things to feel perfect, for us to say and do all the right things, when we're a thousand miles from home in a picturesque vacation setting, far from meddling big brothers and everyday lives. Returning to Illinois could peel back the shiny outer layer of our relationship. Who knows what cracks we may come to find underneath.

Maybe that's my pessimistic, analytical side talking or maybe it's the truth. For now, though, things do feel perfect. It feels like I love him and he loves me and the possibility of us not working out in the end is something I try to push to the back of my mind.

As we make the last turn, nearly a dozen cars lining either side of the street come into view. Connor sees it, too. He squeezes my hand as he comes to a stop and puts the car in park.

"How are you feeling?" he asks.

"Nervous."

Miguel told me yesterday about his parents, three brothers, one sister, and their families. He told me about how they were all born and raised here in Flagstaff and nobody's ever left. Cheyenne mentioned that her sister, brother-in-law and their family would be coming in from Phoenix as well. I shouldn't be shocked by the number of vehicles parked out front.

The Fisher family is small. Drew and I only have one set of grandparents who are still alive. My dad is an only child and my mom has two siblings, but only one of them has children of their own and they live in Florida. I'm not accustomed to large family gatherings and I've never been comfortable being the center of attention.

All of these people, this fuss, feels like a spotlight I'm ill-equipped to handle. They may be my blood, but what if I'm nothing like them?

Connor jostles my hand. "Remember, we can leave whenever you're ready. We can turn around and head back to the hotel right now if you want. But I think you'll regret it if you don't at least try."

He's right.

I came all this way with expectations of meeting my birth mother at best. Despite how overwhelmed I am, I've found something even better: an entire family. A family that could never replace the one I have, but a family that's mine in a different way.

Cheyenne and Miguel confessed yesterday that they'd considered the DNA kit testing many times over the years. The fear that they'd pop up in my matches and interfere with whatever life-narrative my adoptive parents had built for me kept them wary of pulling the trigger. In the end, they simply hoped that, wherever I was, I was happy and healthy and that one day, maybe, I would find them.

"No, I'm ready. I want to meet them."

Mariachi music booms from the backyard as we near the side gate where Cheyenne told us to enter. I cling to Connor's hand like a lifeline, his free hand wrapped around a bottle of tequila Miguel asked us to pick up on the way.

"Sounds like the party's already started." Connor gives me a teasing grin that I try so hard to return.

We move down the side of the house and turn the corner. We both freeze, my feet dead weights beneath me, anchoring me to the spot.

I survey the sea of at least thirty strangers scattered across the yard, none of whom have noticed me yet. *They do this every year? All of them?*

Connor leans into my ear. "I don't think I brought enough tequila."

I bury my head in his chest and laugh, immensely grateful for the distraction.

"Sissy!" Kai's squeaky voice calls out as he breaks through a group of adults and barrels toward me, arms open wide, Bluey stuffed animal clutched in his fist. I crouch down in time for my little brother to throw his arms around my neck.

All the conversation stops, but the music remains. An upbeat rhythm of guitar strums and blasting trumpets fills the air as dozens of strangers turn to look at me. Necks swivel, bodies shift this way and that to see over the crowd, all eyes on me. With Kai in my arms, I stand back to my full height, Connor's steady hand on my back. Anxiety rushes in but settles just as quickly when everyone erupts in excitement a moment later.

Cheyenne emerges to the front, wrapping me in a hug as soon as my arms are free. "Happy birthday," she says as a crowd closes in around us. Like she said she would, she waits for me to let go first.

My biological mother leads me through the crowd and I try to absorb every introduction. Some young, some old, some with tear-streaked cheeks, some with faces plastered in permanent smiles. I know I'm missing names and relations with how quickly I'm meeting everyone. A familiar faced brother or sister occasionally breaks through the crowd to greet me.

Necks are hugged. Tears are shed. Pictures are taken.

I look back once to find Connor has been suckered into tossing a football around with Kai and MJ. His eyes find mine, a question in his gaze asking if I need him. My smile comes easy when I let him know that I'm okay.

I'm more than okay. My heart is full.

"Winona had a patient go into labor early this morning," Cheyenne snaps my attention back. "But she, Arthur and the boys are on their way."

"Hola, mija," Miguel calls from my left. He wraps me in a hug before quietly adding, "My family is a lot and I apologize in advance."

We share a laugh as Cheyenne waves over two new faces I haven't met yet. Their faces light up in vivid wonder as I step closer.

"Oh Dios, mio," the woman says, hands over her mouth. Accent thicker than Miguel's, her hair is cut short and runs black with thick streaks of gray scattered throughout.

"Mom. Dad. This is our daughter, Gretchen." Pride swells in Miguel's eyes.

The dark brown-skinned gentleman sweeps the pads of his fingers over his cheeks, then brushes them on his shorts when they come away damp with tears. His hair is mostly gray, but his thick mustache still remains black as night. Deep brown eyes flank a nose dotted with freckles, like his son and eldest granddaughter.

"Gretchen. This is Antonio and Rosa Ortega. Your grandparents."

Rosa shakes her head in disbelief at the same time she pulls me in for a hug. "It's nice to meet you," I say.

She takes my face in her hands. "Oh, mija. I'm so glad you found us. Happy birthday, sweet girl."

"Simplemente no puedo creerlo," Antonio says. "Cheyenne, you weren't kidding." We all chuckle knowing Cheyenne's decades long claim has finally been vindicated; I look just like my dad.

My grandfather hugs me next, whispering a "Happy Birthday" into my ear.

Soon, everyone swarms the buffet of homemade tamales, rice, and beans that Miguel's mother, sister, and sisters-in-law have made a tradition of preparing every year. Miguel's brothers are the self-appointed bartenders, serving up an assortment of different flavored margaritas and, not to be overlooked, a tequila shot for the birthday girl.

That gets Connor's attention.

Breaking away from the full-fledged football game now underway with MJ and a bunch of boy cousins whose names I don't recall, Connor rushes to my side amidst the birthday chants. I toss back my shot glass, his smile beaming wide when my face sours and I cough into my wrist.

"Does the *gringo* want a shot?" One of my uncles—Gustavo, maybe—looks to Connor with a conspiratorial grin.

Connor's eyes leap between the three men. With a playful challenge in his smirk, he answers, "Just one."

"Eh! *Gringo!*" my three uncles singsong in unison. A shot glass twice the size of mine appears on the table and they fill it to the brim.

Connor throws it back with little fanfare other than a shake of his head as he plops the empty glass back down. "Should I be offended that you call me '*gringo*'?"

Amusement shines in my uncles' expressions.

"Don't let them fool you," a female voice comes from behind us. One of my uncles' wives, I recall. "Half the Ortega brothers married a *gringa*." She smiles, moving around the table to pull Gustavo's face down for a kiss.

She wraps her arms around her husband's waist and turns to Connor. "You're a *gringo*, I'm a *gringa*."

Another uncle—Diego, I think—points to a fair-skinned woman sitting at a table behind us. "That one's my *gringa*."

The third uncle—Carlos, with the full sleeve tattoo—finally chimes in. "If Gretchen says you're her *gringo* then you're a part of the family."

Connor tugs me into his side. "Gretch, can I be your *gringo*?" He accentuates the word with a terrible attempt at a Mexican accent that makes us both laugh. I lift on my tiptoes to kiss him.

"Connor! Stop making out with your girlfriend and get back out here," MJ hollers from the yard where all the boys wait impatiently for his return.

"Duty calls." He runs off and then flips to a backward jog and says, "No more tequila, Fish. We both know what a lightweight you are." He tosses me a wink before turning back to the boys.

I'm smiling after him when a little hand tugs on the hem of my shirt. My youngest sister, Tally, looks up at me, as my other sister, Rosie, stands at her side.

"I like your braid," Tally says shyly, twirling one of her curls around her finger.

I run a hand down the length of the single fishtail braid that hangs over my left shoulder. "Thank you."

"Ask her, Tally," Rosie prods.

"You ask her."

"Ask me what?"

Rosie sighs. "We were wondering if you could braid our hair like yours."

That's how I end up surrounded by more than a half dozen of my female cousins and my two sisters, all in line for me to braid their hair. Their mothers, aunts and grandmother form a circle around me while all the guys, big and small, participate in the football game.

The girls take turns in the braiding seat while I field questions about my life and all that led me here.

I mention the name Gabriella Ruiz that showed up on my DNA matches last year as my third cousin—once removed. My grandmother says the name Ruiz is from her husband's side, but that his extended family spreads so far and wide over the southwestern states and across the border, she couldn't pinpoint who Gabriella is with much accuracy but was certain she landed somewhere in Antonio's distant family line.

"How did the detective get your original birth certificate without having to petition the court for it?" That question comes from Gustavo's wife.

Chin ducked to my chest, I keep my eyes on the hair woven through my fingers and force a heavy swallow down my throat.

This is a part of the story I haven't mentioned before…to anyone because there are still so many unanswered questions in the weeds of it all. The complexities of adoption paperwork, sealed records and the different states with their different laws can make anyone's head spin.

Adoption records are sealed in Arizona—I knew this before I hired the detective. An adoptee, even if they're a legal adult, must petition the court for a copy of their original birth certificate. Even then, the request will only be granted if specific stipulations are met. Without any imminent health concerns to justify a petition, what I found online persuaded me that my request would likely not be granted.

Without access to my original birth certificate, I knew the detective was a long shot. But, as I soon discovered, I wouldn't need my original birth certificate after all. The truth is, the document the detective secured wasn't my actual birth certificate, but rather a photocopy of the birth certificate form—the form that Cheyenne's mother filled out.

A photocopy of a photo, to be exact.

A photo that shouldn't have been taken to begin with. *But it was.*

A photo that shouldn't have been hidden away in a file for twenty-two years. *But it was.*

Somebody inside that birthing center was my guardian angel that day and it's not lost on me that I should count myself lucky and not ask too many questions. The detective's words reverberate like a gong in my memory. *"Questions could lead to answers and those answers could cost someone their career."*

Whether he was referring to his own career or that of someone who worked at the birthing center, I still don't know.

Recalling the detective's parting words, I stick to the big picture of the story so I don't get trapped in the minutiae. "I don't know all the specifics, but I think he was able to speak with someone who worked at the birthing center." I glance at Cheyenne who exchanges a questioning look with Grandma Rosa at her side. "I guess you filled out some intake paperwork when you arrived that got filed away there. Between my amended birth certificate with my adoptive parents' names on it and the alignment of my birth date and time on the birthing center's paperwork..." I let my thought remain open-ended, shrugging my shoulders in nonchalance like the connection is obvious because intake paperwork should be standard.

Grandma Rosa places a hand on Cheyenne's forearm and I sense some sort of realization in the action.

Cheyenne's brows knit together as she says, "That birthing center isn't in business anymore. I don't understand how—"

"We're here," a voice calls from the side gate, a welcome interruption. Everyone turns as a middle-aged Native American woman with long onyx hair approaches. A blond-haired, fair-skinned man at her side and two pre-teen boys a few steps behind.

Winona.

Everything I've learned about how Winona supported Cheyenne through her pregnancy, how she was the only person with her during the delivery, how she's the only member of Cheyenne's family who didn't disown her—these two sisters, they're the only family the other has.

Cheyenne and Winona swoop into a hug, soft words whispered between them that nobody else can hear. Heavy emotion permeates the way they cling to each other and the quiet sniffles muffled by their embrace.

"I'm Arthur." The tall man with the strong British accent steps into my line of sight.

This is the man that sat in the waiting room and updated Miguel and his family during Cheyenne's labor. I bypass a handshake and go in for a hug instead.

I meet his and Winona's two boys, David and Dakota, who are fifteen and thirteen, respectively. They're quick to run off and join the boys' football game, leaving Arthur and I alone.

"I'm so sorry we're late. Winona had a patient go into labor in the middle of the night." His eyes roam my face. "You really do look like Miguel."

I shake my head and laugh. My gaze drifts over to Winona and Cheyenne who are still deep in conversation, hands swiping tears away. Cheeks wet, Grandma Rosa joins in and pulls Winona down to kiss her cheek.

"I'm sure Winona is so tired. It's really nice of you to drive all the way up here," I say to Arthur, but my attention is transfixed on the three women several feet away.

"Are you kidding? We wouldn't miss this. It was one of Winona's midwives' patients so she only had to be onsite in case there were any complications. She keeps a bed in her office at the birthing center for those nights." I turn to meet his gaze. "She's rested enough. Baby is happy and healthy."

He gives me a smile that I'm quick to return, but my mind whirls. "She works at a birthing center? I thought doctors only delivered at hospitals."

"Most still do but it's not uncommon for doctors to operate independent birthing centers. She hated being inside a hospital all the time, but she didn't want to give up delivering babies, so she opened her own practice."

"That's cool." I hope I sound much more natural than I feel as I brace for my next question. "Cheyenne said you guys live in Phoenix?"

Arthur locks eyes with me, sly grin forming, so slight it might not be there at all. "That's right."

I open my mouth, prepared to ask him...something, although I'm not sure what the question would be. Before I can, he jerks back, eyes suspended in the air above my head as he throws his hands up to catch an incoming football.

"Uncle Arthur!" MJ shouts. "You in?"

"Depends. You boys still calling it football?" he quips, really laying that British accent on thick. "Or do I need to give you another history lesson on the origins of European football and how they predate your American caveman excuse of a sport by nearly two thousand years."

MJ and the boys collectively groan with the intermittent *"not again"* and *"is he for real?"*

"Let's start at the beginning, shall we?" Arthur prods, ball held hostage in his grip as a slew of boys flock toward him. Arthur's face splits with a broad smile as he sprints off, the boys on his heels. "It all began in ancient China, Greece and Rome," he hollers, voice jilting as he runs. The boys catch up to him, jumping as high as their little legs can carry them as they try to swat the football out of the hand held high above his head. Meanwhile, the youngest boys attempt to climb him like a tree. "Did you know the balls were made of rock and stuffed with hair?"

Laughter breaks out from onlookers as one of the boys pokes Arthur in the stomach and he keels over. Arthur topples to the ground, a mountain of boys piling on top of him. "Cavemen, I tell you. Cavemen!" he shouts.

"Gretchen." I turn at Cheyenne's voice and come face to face with Winona at her side. "This is my sister, Winona."

Our gazes meet and a bone deep recognition I can't explain sparks like a flint between us. Winona takes me in with awestruck eyes before she wraps me in a hug, whispering, "Happy birthday, Yanaha."

My mind searches for her meaning until she releases me. At a loss, I ask, "I'm sorry, what's Yanaha?"

Cheyenne smiles and looks to her sister who smiles right back. The two of them reach for each other's hand. "I think it's time you open your gift."

Chapter Thirty-Nine

TEN-YEAR-OLD ME HAD NO IDEA

GRETCHEN

THERE'S BARELY a chance to respond before Cheyenne calls everyone to gather on the patio and I'm ushered to a seat at the outdoor dining table. Miguel makes way for my siblings to sit across from me, grins spread wide on their face. A surprise I'm clearly not in on.

Nerves already settling in, I crane my neck to find Connor. He appears a few seconds later and drops into the seat next to me. "I'm right here." He kisses my temple as he squeezes my hand, steadying me.

Cheyenne emerges through the sliding patio door with a large gift-wrapped box that she sets in front of me before moving in beside Miguel who stands behind my brothers and sisters.

"I wasn't expecting gifts," I say hoarsely, searching for a smile to match everyone else's.

Cheyenne's fingers fidget nervously over her stomach and my heart clenches at how familiar the action feels. For a moment, I'm comforted by the fact that her nerves get the best of her the way mine do.

"Well, it's only one," she says. "But we've been working on it for a long time,"

Music silenced, nobody says a word as I tear away the wrapping and open the box beneath it. Inside sets a large photo album. It takes both of my hands to heft it out as Connor clears away the box underneath.

It's a scrapbook. A scrapbook bursting at the seams, so thick I'm shocked the binding is intact. The jagged, uneven edges are made up different colored pages of varied thickness and texture as though pages have been added over time.

The photo pocket on the front holds a three by five purple index card with the word *Yanaha* written in an artistic script, decorated with hearts and stars drawn on in colored marker.

My fingers run over the word Winona whispered into my ear. Not a word. A name.

"It means 'brave' in Navajo," Winona's voice comes from my left.

"It's the name I gave you when I held you," Cheyenne adds.

The calm press of Connor's palm runs over my back.

"It's what I wanted most for you. I didn't know where you'd end up or what you'd have to face. I just wanted you to be brave in the face of whatever life brought you."

Any and all words get stuck in my chest. Emotion courses through me too rapidly for me to speak.

Brave is the last word I would use to describe myself. I'm cautious and careful. The person who volunteers to stay on the ground and keep watch over your personal effects instead of jump out of the airplane. The girl who stays home to read instead of going to the party.

"She's the bravest person I know," Connor says, voice warm and sure.

Tears free-fall into my lap as I shake my head. "I'm not brave at all." My words land so quiet I think only Connor hears them.

"Gretch, you *are* brave. You've never changed who you are for other people. You've never given pieces of yourself away just because everyone else is doing it. You left small town Illinois and moved to New York City without knowing a single soul. You worked your way through college."

I swipe the tears running down my face, embarrassed at this whole display in front of so many people.

"And when people have let you down." He swallows and my eyes lift to his. "When they disappoint you. When they hurt you." He pauses, squeezing my hand. "You forgive them. Even when they don't deserve it. When others choose to stay angry and hold grudges, you forgive."

I turn back to the scrapbook. My fingers drift over the first name I was ever given: *Yanaha*.

"*You* got yourself here," Connor continues. "You stepped out and you did the big, scary thing. You went looking for something not knowing if you'd find it. But you did find it, Gretch. Perhaps it was about thirty people more than you planned on, but…"

Amidst the sound of sniffles, light laughter bubbles up in tiny bursts across the patio and I can't help but laugh, too. Because isn't that the truth and, also, thank God I'm not the only one crying.

Connor finishes, voice certain; "You *are* the bravest person I know."

"Whew, mija," Grandma Rosa cuts through the emotion as she makes a dramatic show of wiping her eyes dry. "If you don't marry that boy."

"Right?" Cheyenne and several of the aunts say in unison, all dabbing away tears in one way or another.

I snicker into my chest, thankful for the lighthearted turn of conversation. When I look at Connor, his whole face twinkles as if to say *you heard them*. I mouth a quick *"thank you"* before turning to the first page in the scrapbook.

The inside front cover is a copy of the framed picture I saw yesterday of Cheyenne holding me as a newborn. On the right is a piece of notebook paper taped to the scrapbook page where Cheyenne has written out my birth story.

It will take hours to absorb every page of a book this large. For now, I flip through them, taking in as much as I can.

Two pages worth of pictures of Cheyenne and Miguel as teenagers, her pregnant belly on full display. This must have been those last few weeks of her pregnancy when she lived in Phoenix with Winona.

Yearly letters from Cheyenne and Miguel, addressed to *Yanaha* on my birthday.

Pictures of them as young adults, attending college in Flagstaff together. Their love story documented in photos and hand-written captions.

Wedding pictures. I never could have imagined that while I was a seven-year-old girl, doing the things seven-year-old girls do, my biological parents were a handful of states away, making vows to love each other forever.

Photos and letters telling the stories of the pregnancies and births of each of my siblings.

I flip forward a few more pages and find another birthday letter from my parents, except this time it's accompanied by a child's drawing.

"As early as the kids could understand who you are, we started having them make something for you on your birthday," Miguel explains.

Tears pool in my eyes as I take in MJ's rainbow drawing, complete with a sun and some flowers. His five-year-old hand scribbling out the words *i lub u* on my fifteenth birthday.

I look up at MJ who grins shyly at me and I give him a wink before turning my attention back to the book.

More pages, more drawings, letters and pictures from my siblings on my birthday. Even letters from Antonio and Rosa some years.

But it's not just birthday entries that fill these pages.

Dance recitals. Football games. School pictures. Vacations. Christmases. All of it personalized with captions written in the margins to highlight memorable details, significant dates and times. Varied handwriting makes it clear that many hands went into creating and filling each page. A documentation of their entire lives, it's everything I've missed. Except I didn't miss anything at all, because they've held me with them through all of it. Every moment captured and recorded for the sake of this book that is, literally, twenty-two years in the making.

"I love it," I choke out through tears.

ONCE EVERYBODY HAS CRIED and hugged as much as is humanly possible, Gustavo declares the party has resumed as he cranks the music back up.

Thankful for the time and space to breathe, I close myself in the bathroom for a few minutes to freshen up.

On my way back outside, the sound of movement in the kitchen has me detouring in that direction. I turn the corner and find Winona handwashing dishes at the sink.

"Can I help?"

"I should say no since you're the birthday girl, but I won't turn down the company."

She inclines her head toward a drawer where I find clean dish towels. I grab one and sidle up next to her.

"Cheyenne has always been the social one of the two of us. It's probably why she fits so well with Miguel's family. I love being with family, but I crave the quiet, too."

I nod, my towel moving in slow circles against the porcelain of the serving dish. "Same."

"Yeah?" She turns to look at me.

"Yeah."

Her hands pause in the soapy water, gaze locked on mine. "*God*, it is so good to see you again."

She turns her attention back to the sink, but her words stick in my thoughts like sap on a tree.

Winona was there. She saw me. She had a camera. She took a picture of Cheyenne cradling me in her arms. Maybe it's not the only picture she took that day.

I clear the hesitation from my throat. "Arthur said you had a patient go into labor last night."

She hands me a baking dish. "Yeah. Labor went long or else we would have been here hours ago."

"He said you own your own birthing center." Her hands slow their pace under the surface of the water. "In Phoenix."

"I do," she says, quieter now.

Setting the dry baking dish aside, I take the mixing bowl she passes over. "Cheyenne said the birthing center where I was born isn't in business anymore."

"Yeah, it was a hospital run birthing center. The midwife who ran it retired about ten years ago and the hospital didn't care to keep it open. Building sat empty for almost a year."

I worry my lower lip between my teeth, laser-focused on the glass mixing bowl in my hands.

It's Winona who clears her throat this time. "Wouldn't you know, someone else came along and bought it. Turned it right back into a birthing center under a different name."

I set the bowl down gently on the granite countertop. Winona's hands now braced on the counter's edge, soapy suds drip into the water beneath them.

"And, um…" She releases the drain, a deep gurgle echoing into the pipes below as the water recedes. Her eyes won't meet mine as she reaches for another towel and dries her hands. "When did you open your practice?" I finish.

She swipes the streaks of tears from her cheeks that I couldn't see before and throws the towel to the side before yanking me against her chest. The quiet cry and the fraught clutch of her embrace says everything words can't.

"It was you."

"It was me."

When she steps back, we're both wiping at our faces. I have a million questions, but I don't want to force Winona into any sort of confession that could get her in trouble.

Not surprisingly, she senses my hesitancy and speaks up first. "I can imagine you have a lot of questions."

I laugh as I reach for the box of tissues on the counter behind me. "I do, but I know it's complex and I don't need to know anything you're not able to share with me. The detective said there was a lot at stake for the person who gave him the information that helped me find Cheyenne. So…just…thank you for what you did. None of this"—I look to the windows overlooking the army of family through the glass—"would have been possible without you."

My lungs take in the air they've craved for far too long. "Does Cheyenne know?"

"As of about thirty minutes ago, she does," she says, chuckling, as she finds her sister through the window wiping icing off Kai's face. Her gaze swells with affection.

"You know, there are decisions I make as a doctor and there are decisions I make as every other title I carry. Mom, wife, friend… sister."

She turns to face me, hip leaning against the counter.

"The way our parents handled the whole situation—it broke her. I was on the other side of the country while my little sister suffered here and there was nothing I could do about it. And when the woman from the adoption agency came and took you away, it was like that last shred of light inside of her burned out.

"When our mom showed up, she focused on managing the paper trail while I consoled Cheyenne. I finally got her to sleep and found Mom in the waiting area. She didn't say a word to me, not that that was anything new.

"It just sort of happened. One second she had her nose down filling out the birth certificate form and the next she got up to go to the bathroom and left it on the table. I was deep enough into my career to know I probably shouldn't do it, but young enough to claim ignorance.

"My sister was hurting and I had no idea where you were going to end up or if you would ever come looking for her. So, I grabbed my camera." She shrugs. "I printed it and held on to it for myself. It's not like I had some master plan to do something with it and I didn't tell Cheyenne because I didn't want to get her hopes up."

"And what about the birthing center?" I ask.

She playfully tightens her gaze, a smirk pulling at her mouth. "If you ask me why I chose to open my own practice, I'll tell you it's because I hated being inside a hospital all the time, but I love delivering babies."

I laugh at the nearly word-for-word—dare I say, *rehearsed*—explanation I received from her husband earlier.

"And if you ask me why I chose to buy that specific birthing center"—her chin drops, but her eyes stay locked on me—"I'll tell you it's because of its proximity to the hospital in case of labor complications."

"Got it," I answer with a soldier's salute.

"And if you ask me why I called that detective back when he came digging for information about a baby born at that address on June 30th, twenty-two years ago," she takes in a deep breath, "I'll tell you it's because I always return my messages." She embellishes with a smile and I smile back.

"Did he know you and Cheyenne were related?" I ask.

She shakes her head. "I left that part out. Maybe it was a smidge of self-preservation on my part but mostly I just didn't know what was going to come of it. I sent over the photo like it was something I'd found in an old file cabinet left behind by the previous owner."

"Were you worried he was going to report you?"

"Wouldn't matter if he did. Still could if he wanted to. I would have given him the photo anyway."

"Really?"

"Of course."

"Why would you risk your career like that?"

Her dark eyes linger on Cheyenne through the window. She releases a heavy, thoughtful breath before turning back to me. "Because my sister went through hell to bring you into this world, not just the pregnancy and birth, but in the years since, too. A part of her heart left with you when the agency took you from her arms. You weren't here for the first twenty-one birthdays, Yanaha. She's smiling today, but that's because you're here now. She deserved the chance to know you and if I were to lose my career over creating a path for that to happen, well…it's not even a fraction of the sacrifice she made for you."

"Thank you for what you did." The words are far from enough and I know I've already said them, but they're all I can manage.

The risk she's taken, the secret she's kept and the hope she's held on to for more than two decades, never knowing if it would amount to anything, leaves me dumbstruck. And thankful.

So thankful.

Winona takes my hand in hers. "Thank you for making my sister's heart whole again."

The sliding door opens and Cheyenne steps inside, finding us immediately at the kitchen sink. She rounds the kitchen counter. "I was wondering where you both were," she says. When she finally closes the distance, our three bodies forming a triangle, she looks between us. "I'm guessing you guys have talked."

Winona nods and Cheyenne turns to me. "It's wild, right? I had no idea."

"Well," Winona declares, "*I* have no idea what you two are talking about and that is my official answer for any and all future questions on the subject."

We share a laugh but as the humor fades, the energy shifts. The last time the three of us were together was twenty-two years ago. The only two people related to me that ever saw my face at that birthing center are the two women standing before me. One of them held me, while the other held her.

Call it a family bond or instinct, but we all move at the same time. Our arms intertwine as we draw each other close in a group embrace. It's sloppy and full of dripping tears and snot-filled sniffles, but it's the perfect full-circle moment that my ten-year-old ponderings couldn't have begun to imagine.

"Do you think my parents think about me on my birthday?" My gosh, ten-year-old me had no idea.

~

I STEP BACK OUTSIDE with Cheyenne and Winona following behind as I'm swarmed by a gaggle of girl cousins, all of them eager for me to finish their braids.

Connor sits at the far side of the patio with Miguel and his family who have tried to no avail to get him to consume more alcohol all afternoon. Instead, he's stuck with water since he took that shot two hours ago. We lock eyes as I settle back into, what the girls have named, the braiding chair. He notices my tear-streaked face and moves to get up but I wave my hand to assure him that I'm okay. His lips pull tight and I smile to ease his concern. He gives me a wink before Miguel asks him another question about his glory days of football. The roll of Arthur's eyes prompts an unexpected giggle.

Thirty minutes later, I'm down to the last braid.

"Where did you learn how to do this?" Rosie asks. I did her hair like mine with a single fishtail hanging around one shoulder.

"My mom taught me."

"Does she have long hair like you?" Tally asks, her high-pitched voice sweet as sugar. I flash a look to her curly head of hair that wasn't so easy to maneuver, but I managed a boho, organic looking french braid straight down her back.

"No, but I think that's why she learned to braid," I begin, flipping and scooping my fingers through my youngest cousin's shoulder-length brown hair. "My hair has always been longer and thicker than hers, so she had to learn how to style it. She learned and then she taught me."

"Why don't you call my mommy *your* mommy?" That's Kai, who has somehow found his way into Cheyenne's lap to join the braid party.

"Honey, that's not really a polite question," Cheyenne whispers, arms wrapped tight around him in a bear hug. "She has a mommy who raised her and she calls her Mommy."

Kai looks up at his mom, all innocence and curiosity. "Yeah, but you're her mommy, too."

She gives her son a kind smile before turning a nervous one on me. "You know you don't have to answer that, Gretchen. I would never ask or expect you to call me Mom."

I dip my chin, thankful for her understanding. I'm extraordinarily grateful to be here, to have met these incredible people and I'm proud to call them family, but I don't think I could ever use the terms Mom and Dad for anyone other than the parents who raised me.

Cheyenne sets my mind further at ease when she says, "I think your mom is the most amazing woman on the planet and I haven't even met her yet."

"I think she has *two* most amazing mommies," Kai says with both palms smooshing Cheyenne's cheeks together, making the circle of us laugh.

The sound of a cell phone ringing from across the patio pulls my gaze. Connor looks at his screen and then excuses himself, before he disappears around the side of the house to take the call.

I finish up the last braid as one of my aunts orders the girls to huddle in close to me, showing off their braids for a picture. After she's snapped a few on her phone, they all turn and pile on one big group hug, thanking me profusely. Who knew that a little bit of braiding would make their day? I think it made mine, too.

"Gretchen," Connor's voice comes close as he rushes to my side. His phone is clutched in his fist and my nerves skyrocket. "That was your brother."

My heart slows because the panic in his eyes, the urgency in his voice—whatever comes next can't be good.

"Reagan's in the hospital."

Chapter Forty

BOUGIE-ASS PESTO

CONNOR

GRETCHEN and I hastily say our goodbyes with promises to be in touch soon. As soon as I explained that Gretchen's sister-in-law had been rushed into emergency surgery back home, the Ortegas understood our need to get on the earliest flight possible.

The second we're in the car, Gretchen turns to me for more details and I relay everything Drew told me on the phone.

Reagan is pregnant. Or, she was.

It was ectopic.

Her fallopian tube ruptured this afternoon.

She was bleeding internally.

An ambulance rushed her to the hospital.

She's currently in surgery.

The doctor doubts they'll be able to repair the ruptured tube and will likely have to remove it entirely.

With the time difference, Drew hasn't been able to get in touch with his parents in Italy, but Reagan's family is with him now at the hospital.

Everything laid out, we spring into action. We spend the last leg of our drive back to Sedona on the phone with the airline. Fortunately, we're able to grab two seats together on a flight that leaves in three and a half hours, but we'll be cutting it close.

Back at the hotel, we toss everything in our bags with no regard for who it belongs to. There's barely a moment to breathe between checking out at the front desk, making the two-hour drive from Sedona to Phoenix, returning the rental car, rushing through security and running to the gate. We make it just as the final boarding group is called.

We both heave out a long breath, our efforts still labored from our marathon sprint through the terminal. I tuck Gretchen into my chest and she melts against me. "Everything's gonna be okay."

I send up a prayer, hoping against hope for my words to be true.

Once we're in our seats, we reach for our phones. I notice a missed text from Drew that came in while we were navigating the TSA line.

DREW

She's out of surgery. Had to remove her fallopian tube but she's okay.

ME

Thanks for the update. I'm glad she's okay. Gretchen and I just boarded.

Not landing 'til after midnight. I'll touch base with you in the morning.

Love you, man.

I hold out my phone for Gretchen to read the message. "Drew says Reagan made it out of surgery."

"Thank God." She cracks her neck from side to side before she tells her brother that she loves him in a text of her own.

After her phone signals with a *woosh* that her message has gone through, we switch to airplane mode and stash both our devices in the bags at our feet.

Gretchen is asleep on my shoulder before we take off.

WE DOZED on and off for the whole flight. During the few times we were both awake, I distracted her by talks of the day's events. She launched into the story of Winona's "intervention" at the birthing center and promptly swore me to secrecy. Now that I know the details, I understand why.

We're zombies trudging through O'Hare at one-thirty in the morning.

Since I had Ubered to the airport, I take Gretchen's keys and offer to drive us back to my place. Again, she's asleep before we're out of the parking lot. At least she can't put up a fight when I pay her parking fee. It's hardly a sacrifice since she refused to let me help pay for the hotel.

I'm also a lovesick fool who just wants to do things for her.

This relationship is new and I'm certain the obstacles will come now that we're home. Gretchen's confidence in how her brother will accept our relationship helps some, but I can't shake the reservations in my gut that it won't be that easy. It's been a heavy, emotional few days for her so I keep my continued concerns about Drew to myself as I try like hell to grab on to a sliver of that confidence she has.

There's also the matter of her relocation back to New York. Her interview for the Executive Assistant position at Saks is next week and, even though she hasn't talked about it much over the past several days, I know she's excited about it.

Truth is, I'm ready to do exactly what I had planned to do three years ago. I'll become a frequent flyer, show up at her doorstep every weekend if she'll let me. And when the time feels right, I'll move there.

In the past, I dreaded relationship milestones. I wanted to cling to my independence, keep my own space, delay commitment, hold back on saying those three coveted words because it all felt too hard, like I was forcing it.

But that was before *her*.

With her, it's easy. I don't want to rush anything, but I also already know, beyond a shadow of a doubt, that everything that scared me in relationships past, doesn't scare me with Gretchen.

As I turn into my building's parking garage, I blink back the romanticism because I know Arizona was the easy part. No family, no sneaking around, no work, no interruptions. But we're home now. Our lives will go on as they did before and we'll not only have to make time for each other, but we'll have to navigate life's challenges together, too.

The realist in me says to remain optimistic, but stay on guard.

Stay hopeful, but plan for the worst.

Never stop choosing her, but recognize certain people may not like my choice.

Never stop loving her, but accept what it might cost me.

I put the car in park and turn off the engine. She sighs as my hand brushes across her temple. A set of sleepy eyes look up at me. "We're here."

She smiles through a yawn as she contorts her body into an adorably awkward four-limb stretch. She pats my cheek and I grab her hand, placing a soft kiss on the inside of her wrist.

Yup. Easy.

Upstairs, after a quick tour of my apartment, I offer her the bathroom first. While she's occupied, I whip up some mozzarella pesto grilled cheese sandwiches because neither of us has eaten since lunch.

She meets me in the kitchen dressed in a white cotton pajama set. Messy bun propped on top of her head, makeup washed away and those glasses perched atop the bridge of her nose, she's beautiful. Breathtaking.

"Is that…" Her words trail off as she leans over the pan, inhaling a deep pull of the aroma. "Pesto and mozzarella?"

"Yeah, I was starving. Thought you might be hungry, too."

"Hmmm. Interesting."

I narrow my eyes. *Does she not remember?*

I switch off the burner and transfer the sandwiches to plates. We lean our hips against the kitchen counter and turn to face each other.

"Do you remember the first time you made me one of these?" she asks, sandwich held aloft between us. She takes a bite, brows lifting as she waits for me to answer.

A slow smile spreads across my face.

"It was that night that Drew—"

"—threw that house party," I finish for her. "Yeah, I remember."

A faint smile crooks the corner of her lips between bites. "Then you took me to—"

"I took you to see *Pitch Perfect* and bought you the most inferior M&Ms one could ask for," I interject again.

She clears the crumbs from her mouth with a swipe of her tongue. "What did a peanut butter M&M ever do to you?"

I laugh as I bop the tip her nose. Her nose scrunches at the contact, causing her glasses to shift. She casually slides them back into place with her finger as she takes another bite.

Maybe I do have a glasses kink.

"Yours tastes so much better than mine," she says, her gaze pinned longingly on the sandwich between her fingers. "Why is that?"

I toss my sandwich onto the plate and dust off my hands. "You been making my sandwiches, Fish?" My arms come around her waist.

"Um, obviously," she says, "They are the superior of grilled cheese sandwiches, after all."

She winks at me and something warm flickers in my chest as I remember saying those exact words to her all those years ago.

I run my hands down her spine, kiss her jaw and nip at her ear.

Sandwich balanced precariously between our chests, she cranes her neck to take another bite as I flick my tongue over her earlobe. "Do not distract me with your big man hands and fancy tongue, old man."

I grin against her ear. "You haven't even seen all the things my tongue can do."

"Mmmm," she hums with a tilt of her head, baring more of her neck to me. Another bite and she mumbles through a mouth full of food, "Is it the pesto?"

Body shaking laughter overtakes me and I bury my face in her neck. Her chuckle matches mine as I pull back to find her eyes. She holds the last bite of her sandwich up to my lips and I swipe it.

Without a word, I retrieve the ingredients I used from the fridge, placing them on the counter in front of her.

"You shred your own mozzarella?" Her lips curl as she stares down the ball of cheese like it personally offended her. Then, she scoops up the pesto jar. "And what kind of bougie-ass pesto is this?" She spots the bread. "Artisan sourdough?" she shrieks.

She surveys the ingredients as though she's a five-year-old who just caught her parents assembling a dollhouse at midnight on Christmas Eve. I run my finger over the crease in her brow. "You get what you pay for."

"No. You get what you can afford," she retorts, hiking a thumb at herself. "Groceries in New York are expensive. I can't believe I've been making them wrong this whole time." She picks up the remainder of my sandwich and takes a bite.

I take her face in my hands, expression deadly serious. Her jaw stops, food hanging in digestive limbo inside her mouth as her eyes flare wide. "Never again. I'll buy you the fancy pesto and artisan bread. I'll even shred your mozzarella." I press my forehead to hers. "Never again, baby. I swear it."

She slaps my chest, mumbling something under her breath about me being a cheeky smartass. I swipe the last bite out of her hands with a caveman's grunt and toss it into my mouth before putting the dishes in the sink and turning us toward the bedroom.

When I come out of the bathroom five minutes later, she's already asleep, tucked under the covers, head on the edge of my pillow.

After I crank the air conditioning down, I climb in next to her.

Glancing at the clock, I see her glasses on my nightstand, her phone plugged into my charger. I set my watch next to the tiny hoop earrings she must have taken off before she fell asleep. The sight of her things next to my things makes me smile because I want them there. This entire nightstand can be hers if she wants it.

Easy, easy, easy.

Tomorrow doesn't promise the same, but I'll take all that I can get for tonight.

Chapter Forty-One

YOU'RE NOT ALLOWED TO TOUCH ME EITHER

GRETCHEN

"What's with the sweatshirt? It's summer," Connor says as he locks the apartment door behind him.

"It's also negative million degrees in your apartment." I didn't check the thermostat this morning for the actual number, but if my frigid extremities were any indication, I'd say negative million is in the ballpark.

"It's set to sixty-five. Hardly winter-wear weather."

"Sixty-five?" I howl, pressing the down button as we approach the elevator.

"I told you my body was a furnace."

"And I'm telling *you* I have frostbite."

"You have me to keep you warm."

The doors open and I whirl back to face him after we step inside. "I'll die from hypothermia first. Have fun sleeping next to my corpse." He presses the button for the parking garage.

His belly laugh is deep and warm, the sound turning my lips up at the corners. "Ok, so a compromise then."

I eye him sidelong as the doors close. "I'm listening."

"Sixty-six."

I scoff. "How generous."

Gaze directly in front of me, I catch his smug grin in my periphery as the elevator begins its descent.

"Seventy." I turn toward him.

"Sixty-seven." He faces me.

"Sixty-nine when we sleep." He quirks a mischievous brow. "Get your head out of the gutter, old man. Seventy-two during the day." I step into him, playing to win.

His breath coasts along my ear as he whispers, "Sixty-eight all the time."

My skin shivers at his proximity, but I remain focused. "Sixty-eight when we sleep. Seventy-two during the day when you're not around. Seventy if you're home." I nip at his jaw. "Final offer."

"Hmmm. You drive a hard bargain." He plants a peck to the tip of my nose. "Deal."

Hand in hand, he smiles the whole way to the car and it's as endearing as it is arrogant.

"What are you so smiley about?"

He curves an arm over my shoulder. "I like thinking about you staying with me. It feels very…" He shrugs, searching for the word.

"Domestic?"

"Yeah." He opens the passenger door for me. "Is that weird?"

Others may say so. To the outside world, Connor and I are shiny, brand new. But I feel everything he does and I know it's because we have more than what meets the eye. A history that nobody else knows about. A connection that's been to hell and back behind the curtain.

I shake my head. "Is it weird that it's not weird?"

He searches my face, chin atop his forearms resting on the door-frame. "Nothing about imagining a life with you feels weird."

Flutters swarm in my chest and my heart soars, but I know serious relationships and commitment have been a sore spot for him in the past. I can't help but ask, "Does that scare you?"

He runs my braid between his fingers, eyes cast down on the

action. I step into his touch, the door a barrier between us, as I wait for his response.

"For the first time in my life, no." Our gazes meet. "Does it scare you?"

"No," I say, "but, you know, there are still things we need to figure out." His eyes drop back to the hand twirling my hair and he takes a deep breath. "Like, how I'm going back to New—"

"I know," he cuts me off, moving around the door to bring his lips to my forehead. "But not today."

Not today, but soon. I wrap my arms around his waist and my body warms by the second in his embrace. Or maybe it's this parking garage and the fact that we aren't inside his sub-zero apartment anymore.

"Why is it so *friggin'* hot?"

He laughs as he open-palms my face and pushes me into the passenger seat.

~

On the way to the hospital, Connor and I discuss plans for how to tell my family, not only about meeting my biological family, but also about us.

Thanks to the time delay, my parents' rebooked flight out of Italy doesn't leave for another few hours and with their lengthy flight schedule and subsequent jet lag, it'll be a couple days before we see them. Not to mention, Drew has been through a lot over the past several days.

Later this week, I figure, maybe after Reagan is cleared to go home, we can find a time to be together and I'll tell them about Arizona.

I suggested we plan something separate with Drew so that we can break the news to him together about us, but Connor insisted that he wanted to be the one to tell him. Knowing the guilt he's held on to all these years, I can respect his wishes and take a step back in that conversation.

After a quick coffee stop for a decent morning pick-me up for everyone, we're on the elevator up to Reagan's floor.

"We need to discuss ground rules," I say.

"Ground rules?"

"For when we're around people who don't know about us."

"Seems pretty cut and dry to me, but carry on," he retorts with a grin.

"No touching."

"There will be no putting of my hands upon you. Got it." He salutes like a good little soldier.

"Good. And no—"

"Technical question," he interrupts. "What if you're choking or otherwise in need of assistance? Is the Heimlich permissible?" I blink. "Chest compressions?" I blink twice. "Mouth to mouth?"

I close my eyes and then open them slowly. *God*, help me. "Life saving permissions are granted." He's trying so hard not to laugh. "Secondly, no looking at me like you want to take my clothes off."

He bobs his head. "Uh-huh, uh-huh. But what if I *do* want to take your clothes off?"

"Think it. Don't *look* like you're thinking it." I bite back a smile as the elevator doors open.

Stepping off, I look to the wall placard to point us in the right direction. Connor's at my back a heartbeat later, his warm body pressed in close, breath on my ear. "You know I can't wait to get those clothes off you, Fish."

I whip around and slap him across his bicep. He leans away from the contact, shielding the cardboard coffee carrier he holds in one hand.

"Hey!" he whisper-shouts as he grips his injured arm like he's taken enemy fire. "I was thinking it. And if I'm not allowed to touch you then you're not allowed to touch me either." His brows hit his hairline.

I laugh and begin toward Reagan's room. We walk silently down the corridor, the steady rhythm of our feet hitting the linoleum floor the only sound. When I dare a sidelong look at him, the man winks at me.

Goddammit.

"No winking," I say through gritted teeth, voice a whisper that I hope sounds more like a threat and less like the human ball of swoon that I am.

He flashes that smug grin of his. "Sorry, did you say something? Hey, Drew!"

I look up as my brother emerges from Reagan's room at the end of the hall.

"You brought coffee. Thank God! This hospital sludge is awful," he says.

Schooling my bemused expression from before, I jog the last few steps and throw my arms around my brother's neck as Connor heads inside.

Drew sags into me. "Hey, sis."

"I'm so sorry this happened." He gives me one last squeeze before he steps back.

"Thank you. We're doing alright. I'm sorry you had to cut the trip short."

I shake my head, waving off his apology. "Stop it. You're more important."

Drew follows me into the room. I find Reagan in the hospital bed, a tired smile on her even more tired face. I approach her cautiously, noting the IV line in her hand, the dark circles under her eyes, and the hospital blanket draped over her lower half.

Connor sets Reagan's coffee on the side table as I take a seat on the bed's edge. Before we say anything, we wrap our arms around each other, hers heavy, laden with grief. She's lost a baby and been through a major surgery that will forever affect her ability to conceive again.

I rub my hand up and down her back. "I'm so sorry."

She sniffs as she leans back and wipes her eyes. "Ugh, I'm so sick of crying."

"The doctor said that was normal, sweetheart. Your hormones are gonna be out of whack for a while," Drew chimes in from the foot of the bed.

I give Reagan's hand a reassuring squeeze before turning toward my brother. "Drew, if I'd known she was pregnant I never would have asked you to go with me."

"No, Gretch. *We* didn't even know until last week. Our first appointment with the doctor to make sure everything looked good was the morning we were supposed to leave." He runs his hands down his face. "We were gonna get the ultrasound, hear the heartbeat, get the all-clear and then I would head to the airport."

The room goes quiet. He doesn't have to say what came next because Connor and I already know.

Drew continues, nonetheless. "Anyway, it wasn't…it was…" He pauses, unable to say the word: ectopic.

Connor squeezes Drew's shoulder. "It's okay, man."

He shakes the emotion away, before looking at his wife. The adoration and affection in Drew's gaze in the face of such heartbreak makes me so proud to call him my brother.

"Yeah, so, the doctor gave her an injection that was supposed to help her body absorb the pregnancy over a few weeks. We were obviously pretty shaken up over the whole thing. You were already in the air by that time, Gretch. I couldn't reach you. That's when I called you." He looks to Connor.

"We had a follow-up appointment on Saturday. Her hCG levels had dropped, but not by much, so we were supposed to come back today to check her levels again and possibly get another injection. But, on Sunday—" His voice stilts. Tears gather behind his eyes as he comes to Reagan's other side and takes her hand in his.

"I had some bleeding on Sunday morning," Reagan continues for him. "But they told me that could be a normal side effect of the injection so I didn't think much of it. By the afternoon it was worse. I felt a little woozy and then I got this sudden, piercing pain in my stomach when I tried to get up from the couch. Next thing I remember is waking up at the hospital, being prepped for surgery."

"She passed out," my brother adds as he takes a seat. He wraps an arm around her, her head falling naturally to his shoulder. "I called 911, they loaded her in an ambulance. It was a whole ordeal. They knew right away that her fallopian tube had ruptured so they rushed her into surgery as soon as we got here."

I swipe away the tears I didn't even realize were falling until one lands on Reagan's hospital blanket. I look to Connor who stands with arms crossed over his chest. Face grave and clouded with sympathy.

"I'm so glad you're okay. Thank God the doctor saw you early and caught it."

Reagan's breath shudders, gaze fixed on where her husband squeezes their palms together. Drew's eyes transform, only a little, but the sadness is heavier now than it was a few moments ago and something about the shift gives me pause.

I tilt my head at him. He looks from me down to Reagan who gives an acquiescent nod.

"The doctor had us come in early because we've...been in a similar situation before. Not exactly like this, thank God, but it's not our first loss."

Reagan buries her face in my brother's shoulder, my own tears falling unabashedly now as Connor paces the room, hands clasped at the back of his neck.

"So, you've—" I stop myself, not sure what to say. "I'm sorry, I shouldn't ask, it's not my business."

"It's okay. We probably should start telling people. I've...um... had three miscarriages before this." Her shoulders slump, weighed down by shame and guilt.

"Sweetheart, don't." Drew lifts her chin. "You've done nothing wrong and there is *nothing* wrong with you." Her body shrinks on a quiet sob and he kisses her forehead. His lips move to her ear, whispering a quiet "I love you so much" only meant for her.

After Drew and Reagan's emotional tell-all, they insisted we drop the subject and move on to happier topics.

When the doctor came in to do a check-up, Connor and I ducked out to grab lunch. We arrived back to Reagan's room thirty minutes later with a spread of greasy burgers, fries, sodas and milkshakes.

"I wanna hear about the trip," my brother says once we're all settled in our respective seats with our food.

I look to Connor who gives me a *this is all you* shoulder shrug.

Pivoting back to Drew, I gulp down my mouth full of fries and answer, "It was fun. We hiked Devil's Bridge, shopped around Sedona." I avert my eyes. "Spent some time up in Flagstaff."

Drew's attention darts between Connor and me. "And?"

He's already intuited that the trip was more than just a birthday celebration. I know he wants answers and I did promise them to him, but this is not the time or place.

"And," I drag out the word, searching for something to add.

"Oh, we had a pool day," Connor interjects. "It was hot as balls, bro."

Drew's curious gaze lands back on me and I give him a look that I hope conveys that I hear him and promise to tell him everything soon. It seems to work because he stops pushing. "I'm glad you had a good time."

Drew's phone buzzes beside him, a welcome disruption, and he quickly reaches for it. "Mom and Dad are boarding their flight in Rome and want to know if we can meet for lunch day after tomorrow. You in?"

I nod as I lift my burger to my mouth.

"I can bring something back for you," Drew says to Reagan who, though she'll be discharged tomorrow, will need to take it easy for the next couple of weeks. "Is that okay?"

Her mood has lifted since we moved past the heavy start to our visit. While I'm sure grief will idle under the surface of all that *badassery* for a long time to come, if there's anyone I know who can face this and come out stronger on the other side, it's Reagan.

She agrees and Drew types back a quick reply. Fingers moving over his screen, he adds, "You're invited, too."

Connor looks up. He scans the room as though there's anyone else here that my brother could be referring to. "Me?"

"Yeah, now that Mom knows you went on the trip instead of me, she wants to hear about everything from both of you."

Connor's agreement is a foregone conclusion and I can't help but smile because that definitely sounds like my mother. I find his gaze amidst the sound of crinkling burger wrappers, slurping straws and jostling paper bags.

It's merely a flicker of a moment, but he pounces. Smirk on display, the guy winks at me.

With a quiet huff, I immediately stuff my trash into one of the paper bags, making to leave. In protest that nobody except Connor is attuned to, I grab his half-empty fry box, throw it in with the rest of the trash and pretend not to hear his grumblings over not being finished.

A phone pings behind me, followed by Reagan's voice. "My mom's on her way up. She brought me a change of clothes."

Perfect timing.

"We'll get out of your hair then," I offer as I collect all the remaining trash.

"Oh damn!" Drew shrieks. All heads in the room turn. "I wasn't even thinking. Gretch, where are you staying? Did you get a hotel?" He reaches for his wallet. "Here, take my credit card."

"What? Drew, stop. It's fine. I'm staying with Connor." Matter of fact. Nothing to be worried about. This is totally normal.

Drew hesitates and then looks at his best friend.

"It's fine, man. She can stay with me as long as she needs," Connor says. His voice sounds much more natural than mine.

"But you don't have a—"

"I'm sleeping on the couch, she has the bedroom. Everything's fine."

The lie doesn't go down as easy with me as it seems to for Connor, but I know it's unavoidable in this moment.

"Yeah, right," Drew acquiesces. "Thanks, man."

We pass Reagan's mom in the hallway on our way out and exchange quick hugs before going our separate ways. When Connor and I finally settle into the elevator and the doors close, we both let out a breath of relief.

Pinned on opposite sides, we're as far apart as two people can be in a space this small. I rake my teeth across my bottom lip as I recount the last exchange with my brother. It was all a lie.

Chewing on my thumbnail, I worry that single deception will make things worse when Connor finally tells him. My phone pings in my pocket. I grab it and swipe up to view the text.

> **CONNOR**
> Stop it.

My previous mental spiral fades into the rearview in an instant.

> **ME**
> Buzzkill

> **CONNOR**
> Beautiful

> **ME**
> Can I help you?

> **CONNOR**
> Needed to see you smile.

> **ME**
> Mission accomplished.
> Thank you.

> **CONNOR**
> There's something else.
> A question, actually.

> **ME**
> I'm a woman with answers.

I chance a glance his way, but his chin is dropped to his chest, eyes intent on his screen. At last, he lifts his gaze to me from under hooded lashes a beat before my phone pings.

> **CONNOR**
> How about that date?

Chapter Forty-Two

NEW BUCKET LIST ITEM UNLOCKED

GRETCHEN

At six on the dot, Connor knocks on his own front door.

Butterflies take flight in my stomach as I clasp my dangly turquoise earrings and prance toward the door like a giddy teenager.

He left for the gym a couple hours ago, announcing he would get ready there, while I got ready here. Since I'm still living out of my suitcase and desperately need to do laundry, I opted for a pair of light denim shorts with a frayed hemline paired with a short-sleeve, coral, linen shirt that I've left unbuttoned down to my navel, revealing the white tank underneath. A pair of brown leather sandals finish off the outfit and I've kept my hair down in long, loose curls.

I swing the door open as wide as the smile on my face.

Connor leans against the doorjamb, hands in the pockets of his gray shorts, his broad shoulders and trim waist filling out his black V-neck t-shirt in the best way. The scruff along his jaw and around his mouth, still untouched by a razor, screams at me to run my fingers through it.

His throat bobs as his baby blues give me a thorough inspection. "Well, look at you, Fish."

I curtsey playfully as he steps inside. "Ah, ah, ah. I don't invite guys inside my place on the first date."

He rubs his lips together, eyes twinkling. "Oh, so this is your place now?" I smile. "You ready for our first date?"

"I'd say it's about time. What big gestures do you have up your sleeve? I already don't see a bouquet of flowers." I roll my eyes. "But there's still time to redeem yourself, I suppose. Fireworks? Private viewing of a Broadway show? Bottle of Don Perignon?"

"No, nothing like that." He pinches my waist and I collapse into him as his arm hooks around my back. "Because you"—he bops my nose—"don't like big gestures."

I hum out a contented sigh as his mouth drifts closer. "Says who?"

"Says the guy who knows you better than anyone else," he whispers.

"You're really gonna milk that one, aren't you?"

"Just stating facts." His hand cups my jaw. "I'm not supposed to kiss you until the end of the night." He pulls me in tighter. "Will you let me kiss you before it even starts?" His husky whisper is but a breath tangling with mine as he runs his hand down the column of my neck. "A little one?" His hand moves until his fingers knot in my hair and my eyes flutter shut. "The smallest kiss, I promise."

"Connor?"

"Hmm."

"Shut up and kiss me."

Our lips meet. He hauls me into him and my back arches, but his body follows, never losing an inch of connection. I angle my head, our mouths open, tongues greedy and seeking.

I throw one arm around his neck while my other hand kneads into his chest where I can feel the feverish beat of his heart. When he brings his hand down to meet mine, intertwining our fingers, they squeeze tight with the restraint I'm unable to find at the moment. The hand at my back moves down the backside of my shorts, his fingers finding the skin of my leg right below the hem before he takes my ass by the handful and tugs me up and into him, impossibly, ruthlessly even more than I was before.

Our lips give chase, a vicious circle of clashing tongues and teeth that I never want to end. I want to glide my hand down to where I know he's hard for me, but his grip on my hand is solid, not letting me move an inch in that direction.

Simultaneously, we release for air, foreheads coming together.

"These shorts are gonna be a problem," he says with a final pinch.

I laugh, still breathless, as we peel our bodies apart.

"I didn't bring flowers."

"Clearly."

"Smartass. But I do come bearing gifts." He pulls a package of peanut butter M&Ms from his pocket and the burst of laughter that escapes me is instant. "I know the way to your heart, Fish, and it isn't flowers."

I take the package, clutching it to my chest like a prized possession. It's such a tiny, silly thing, but thoughtful all the same and I love him for it.

I love him.

"It's the best kept secret for deep dish pizza in the city. It'll be worth the wait."

Connor holds the door for me as we exit the tiny Italian restaurant. We're on the wait list and now we have an hour to kill.

"Is this the part where we debate Chicago versus New York pizza?"

He scoffs as he takes my hand and leads me down the sidewalk. "Oh, please. There is no comparison. Deep dish for life."

"Nah, you just haven't had the New York experience yet. I'll convert you." I nudge his shoulder as my comment settles over the moment. My interview is next week and the painful reality is that I'll be leaving my heart behind in Chicago. He said we'd talk about it later and I don't want this subject to sour our first date so I push past the intrusive thoughts and plaster on a smile.

He nudges me back with a wink, his signature smirk all warm and smug. "If anybody could convert me, it'd be you."

He plants a soft kiss on the back of my hand, bringing us to a stop.

"We're here."

Only half a block from the restaurant, I look up at the unmarked shop before us. The windows are foggy and mostly barricaded by shelves pushed up against them from the inside. There's no commerce-friendly glass entrance door. Instead, a solid wood door, painted dark blue and adorned with an ornate antique gold knob at its center beckons those passing by.

"Where's here?"

"It's a surprise."

He leads us closer and I finally notice the placard on the door face in dire need of a polish. The tiny inscription says,

Mullins Book Collectors
est. 1973

My heart clenches at the memory.

Stepping inside is like stepping into your grandparents living room.

Worn velvet couches and settees of all different colors and sizes fill the gaps between the mismatched shelves. The lack of natural light is made up for with the abundance of floor lamps and overhead lights controlled by the delicate chains that float mere inches above our heads. The aisles created by the strategic placement of shelves leaves room for not much more than a single person to pass through at a time.

The whole place smells of paper and binding. It's divine.

"Isn't it great?" Connor whispers into my ear, my expression awestruck as we tread lightly into the quiet space.

"This is beautiful." I look around, taking in the stillness. "Are they even open?"

"I'm here, I'm here," a gruff voice comes from the back and an elderly man, no younger than eighty, steps around the corner. Shoulders hunched, he wears a knit sweater-vest over a checkered collared shirt. A pair of black rimmed bifocals hang around his neck by a gold chain.

"Well, I'll be. Connor, is that you?" the man asks.

"It's me, Mr. Mullins. And this is my girlfriend, Gretchen."

I introduce myself as Connor continues, "Mr. Mullins runs a very tight ship. Only stocking classics and books th—"

"Books that I think should be classics," Mr. Mullins finishes.

"It's a book collector's dream." Connor smiles fondly at the kind man. "Where's your daughter? I thought she's supposed to be running this place for you now?"

Mr. Mullins waves his hand. "Oh, Victoria and her husband are at the Carova house with your parents for a couple of weeks. My grandson was just here though. I'm sorry you missed him. He's actually going to be taking the reins soon." A proud gleam fills his eye.

"Three generations. That's impressive," I say.

"I'm a blessed man."

"Connor, how's your family?"

"Good. I'm sure they're getting up to plenty of trouble with Victoria and Tom out at the beach house."

The conversation with Connor's parents on the phone last week comes to remembrance: Carova house, Gene.

Their conversation volleys back and forth, the family history and connection evident in every affectionate word, until Mr. Mullins turns his expectant smile on me. "So, what are we in the market for today, young lady?"

"Oh...um...I don't know."

Connor's warm hand settles on my back. "I think we're just going to browse today, Mr. Mullins."

"Boy, how many times do I have to tell you to call me Gene."

For the next half hour, Gene gives us the grand tour of his little shop.

Every single book is tucked inside its own dedicated clear plastic sleeve, but it does nothing to detract from the jaw-dropping collection.

Entire shelves dedicated to early edition copies of Charles Dickens and another shelf entirely for the works of Shakespeare. Stacks and rows of J.R. Tolkien and C.S. Lewis. A half dozen rolling carts filled to the brim with Jane Austen, the Bronte sisters and Virginia Woolfe. John Steinbeck here, F. Scott Fitzgerald there. The whole place an eclectic amalgamation of whimsy meeting nostalgia. Every nook and cranny reveals literary treasures dating as far back as first editions printed over two hundred years ago.

"So, what's the most valuable book you have?" I ask.

Gene leads us to a small shelf tucked in the corner by the front counter. On it rests a handful of books. "These are my most prized possessions." He pulls a small, dusty hardback off the shelf. "They belonged to my father."

"May I?" I take the book he holds out for me. "*The Book of Common Prayers.*"

"I also have my father's bible," Gene says, thoughtfully running his hand over the cover.

I point to a thin spine that looks rather contemporary by comparison to the others. "And that one?"

"*The Big Book,*" he answers.

I swallow the heavy lump in my throat when I see *Alcoholics Anonymous* in big, bold print on the front cover. A quick glance back to the shelf reveals another spine that reads, *The Trauma of War.*

Gene tracks my gaze. "My dad was a military man. Korea wasn't his first rodeo, but even he came back different. He had to fight hard for his recovery. PTSD turned into alcoholism and the alcohol triggered the trauma. He fought like hell to break the cycle and these books were a part of what helped him. It was decades of ups and downs, but the prayers, the AA mantras, the survival stories, the promise of an eternity in glory—these books saw him through all of it."

Moisture wells behind my eyes and I'm not even sure why. "Thank you for showing these to me. I can understand why they mean so much to you."

"A book is only as valuable as the heart that carries it. Even if I wanted to sell them, they wouldn't make me any money, but they're worth more to me than anything else in here."

His words resonate, echoing off something deep within me. I've never been able to articulate why I've held on to some of the books I've acquired over the years, but Gene made it all make sense so easily. It's more than sentimentality or the need to hold on to the memories a book might possess. It's the way a book, and the people or events you associate with it, somehow forms you—makes you who you are. The logical side of your brain tells you that this tangible object can't really have an effect on the person you become, but the feelings side can't quite separate the book from the person. It's all so beautifully intertwined.

"Do you have a book that your heart carries with it?" Gene's soft, kind voice rings into the dusty air between us. The affection in his smile says everybody has one. Including me.

"*Little Women*," I say, the squeeze of Connor's hand over mine the ever-present reminder that I'll never be able to separate the book from him, nor him from the person that I've become.

"Lovely," Gene whispers. He looks to the man at my side for a moment and I wonder if he remembers selling Connor that copy all those years ago.

Pointing us in the direction of the wall behind us, he leaves us to explore by ourselves. We round one of the free-standing shelves running the length of the shop and find a shelf of Louisa May Alcott. Like the natural pull of gravity, I immediately seek out whatever copies of *Little Women* he might have tucked away in this unsuspecting establishment. He only has three copies, but they are magnificent.

A first edition dated 1868. An early French edition. And a very rare copy in braille.

"Kind of puts that one I got in Arizona to shame, doesn't it?" Connor says sheepishly.

"No. That one *is* incredible. Any collector would kill for it. But these…" My words die in my throat as I delicately pull the French copy off the shelf, careful to remove it from the protective plastic in the meticulous way Gene taught us earlier.

"I know. I think he makes decent money off walk-ins, but most of his sales are to wealthy collectors all around the world. Think foreign leaders, celebrities, European royalty, you name it. He's got a whole shipping operation in the back."

"It's amazing," I say, unable to stop my eyes from roaming in every direction. I want to see everything Gene has in here.

Connor's phone buzzes in his pocket. "Come on. Our table's ready."

"OKAY, so, tell me everything you know about Gene Mullins," I say through a mouth full of steaming hot deep dish pepperoni pizza. Connor was right; of all the pizza I've had in Chicago, this is by far the best.

He laughs. "It's not all that exciting, I'm afraid."

"Not exciting? You are closet besties with an eighty-year-old man who deals books to the King of England."

"Eighty-one," he quips, before tipping back his beer.

"King of England, Connor."

"My mom met his daughter, Victoria, in college. She and my dad started double-dating with Victoria and Tom, and they became fast friends. Victoria's family became my mom's family."

He pauses to take a bite as I sip from my Diet Coke.

"Gene built a house on Carova and he's let my family stay there over the years. My parents have been visiting since before my brothers and I were born, though. It's how they fell in love with the area. They really wanted to build a house on Carova like Gene did, but it's way too expensive. That's why they settled in Avon about two hours south of there."

"What's so special about Carova?"

"Carova Beach. It's on the northernmost end of the Outer

Banks. It's this long stretch of beach, like fifteen miles or something, that's only accessible with a four-wheel drive vehicle. No paved roads, no streetlights. Not even a restaurant or gas station. But people have built these houses out there and it's this protected reserve for wild horses."

Excitement brims in my expression that he doesn't miss.

"It's like no place I've ever been, Gretch. At night it's so dark and so quiet, it's just stars for miles and the sound of waves crashing on the shore. You can be on the beach during the day, lying in the sun and, out of nowhere a family of wild horses will wander into the surf twenty feet away."

"Wait!" I declare as dots connect in my brain. "Like in *Nights in Rodanthe*?"

"The movie with Richard Gere and Diane Lane?"

I roll my eyes. *Typical.* "No. The *book* by Nicholas Sparks."

"That was made into a movie," he deadpans.

My face falls flat.

"Yes, like *Nights in Rodanthe*, Fish."

"The horses are real? They just run wild along the beach?"

"Well, I imagine there were some cinematic liberties taken with the dramatic music and all, but yes. Not in Rodanthe, though. That's too far south. The horses are all in Carova up north."

"But you've seen them?"

"Yes."

"Wow," I breathe. "New bucket list item unlocked."

"I'll remember that," he says, winking as he wraps his ankle around mine under the table.

After dinner, we stroll through the city, weaving back and forth through the main thoroughfares and quaint back streets until we end up on the Riverwalk.

The sun sets on the horizon, peeking through the slots of towering skyscrapers as the Navy Pier ferris wheel rotates slowly in the distance. I know this night will end soon because Connor goes back to work tomorrow. It'll be like every other night for the past several days when we get back to his apartment, full of kisses and... other things. Yet, he still manages to surprise me. Mid-stride, he pulls us to a stop and gently nudges my back against the railing. The sound of the river drifts beneath us as he takes my face in his hands and kisses me into oblivion.

"I'm sorry it took me so long." His lips glisten from our kiss, thumbs stroking my cheekbones.

"What do you mean?"

"Tonight. Tonight should have happened three years ago." He kisses me. "I'm sorry."

"Do me a favor." I clasp my hands behind his back.

"Anything."

"Stop apologizing."

On our way back to his place, we stop for ice cream, which I enhance by adding the peanut butter M&Ms I had stashed in my purse, despite his huffs of disapproval.

He said earlier that M&Ms were the way to my heart, and he wasn't wrong. But there's another way and I'm not sure he realizes it entirely yet.

Him.

Chapter Forty-Three

I GUESS WE'RE SUPPOSED TO EAT FAJITAS NOW

CONNOR

THE OFFICE IS a ghost town for the first two hours, but it's exactly what I needed to get caught up after four days out of the office. Now that my colleagues have begun to file in, the sound of ringing phones, friendly chatter and fingers pecking at keyboards creates a dull murmur outside my office door. I'm still sifting through my inbox when my boss' assistant informs me that Mr. Driskill wants to meet with me this afternoon.

The last time we spoke was nearly a week ago. He was open-minded to my attempts to smooth over any tension surrounding my breakup with his daughter. However, though he's a fair CEO, he's also a family man. No matter how you slice it, I'm not his favorite person right now and this impromptu meeting that I have no context for has me feeling even more unsettled.

Thankfully, elbow deep in back-to-back phone calls and overdue team meetings, I'm quickly distracted.

I've just come up for air close to lunch time when my phone pings.

GRETCHEN

I'd like to clarify the terms of our thermostat agreement.

ME

Proceed.

GRETCHEN

I'm currently sitting at a delightfully cozy 72. You should try it sometime. It's glorious.

Anyway...

Is the expectation for the apartment to be 70 degrees when you walk in the door, or can I crank it down when you get here?

ME

Hmmm...

GRETCHEN

Right?! The fine print gets murky.

ME

Cranking it down before would mean you could wear one of my hoodies. And I do love seeing you in my clothes.

GRETCHEN

Solid point. But, on the other hand, at 72 degrees you would walk in the door and immediately have to start disrobing.

That feels like a win-win.

ME

I don't know. I need some time to weigh the pros and cons.

GRETCHEN

That's fair.

If I don't hear anything, I'll just surprise you.

Come home hungry. I'm making dinner.

A soft tap on my door pulls my attention.

"Sorry, I don't want to interrupt. I know you're probably swamped," Lauren says from the doorway.

Memories of our conversation last week has me out of my seat and moving in for a hug that's neither forced nor awkward.

"I'm about to head out to lunch, but I wanted to check in and um…so…it's really hot outside."

My burst of laughter turns a few heads in the cubicle pool beyond my door. We're friends now and it's exactly as it should be between us. "We'll always have the weather."

Her face sobers. "I talked to Reagan yesterday. I can't believe it. I had no idea."

"I know. Me neither."

Silence stretches for long seconds before Lauren shifts topics. "How was the trip?"

"It was…" I trail off. The last time we talked, I assured her there was nothing between Gretchen and me.

I didn't have the highest hopes then that anything would happen between us. But things have changed and the last thing I want is for Lauren to find out and think I intentionally kept it from her or, worse, that I did anything behind her back.

"It was good. Actually, there's something I should probably tell you." I pause, inhaling deeply. "When we spoke on the phone last week I didn't dwell on the fact that I was there with Gretchen because there wasn't anything going on there"—her face turns dour—"and that was the truth. Nothing was happening between us, but—"

"But there is now," she finishes.

"The trip had nothing to do with her and me, I swear. She had some other stuff going on and Drew asked me to be there for her." My words catch as I hesitate to go on. But I know I have to be honest with her. "But she and I had some baggage from back before I met you and—"

"You were together before?"

I shake my head. "No. We almost were. We kissed once." I've never actually admitted that out loud to anyone before. "That dinner a couple months ago was the first time I'd seen her in almost three years."

She nods absently and looks away. "Sorry. I'm…processing."

"I should have told you about Gretchen, but to be honest, Drew doesn't even know and I've been really scared of him finding out. But that's no excuse and I'm sorry."

"Is she the reason you ended things with me?" I immediately open my mouth to respond, but she holds up a hand to stop me. "I'm not jealous or anything. I know that breaking up was the right thing for us. I promise, that's not why I'm asking."

"No, I get it." I scratch the back of my neck. "I didn't break up with you so that I could date Gretchen, but…I think seeing her again made me see us"—I motion a hand between us—"more clearly."

A crease forms between her brows and I wish I had the right words to make it disappear. "God, I'm getting this all wrong. I'm—"

"No," she interrupts. "We want each other to be happy, right?"

"That's all I want for you."

"That's what I want for you, too," she says. "And you are?"

I stick my hands in my pockets and cock my head. "I am. Are you?"

"I am."

No animosity. No grudges. Both of us content to move on, we share a smile before a coworker pops her head in. "Lauren, your lunch date is here?"

She thanks her and moves toward the door.

"Lauren?" She turns. "I hate to ask, but could you not mention anything to Drew or Reagan? With everything that's happening, I just…I'm trying to find the right time to tell him."

"Of course. What are friends for?"

She's halfway out the doorway when I call out again. "What's his name?" She whirls back with a questioning look. "Your new guy. What's his name?"

"Oh, it's Kyle."

"Tell Kyle I think he's a very lucky guy."

~

My meeting with my boss was my last appointment of the day. As it turns out, I was worried over nothing. On the contrary, he offered me a team lead position on a large political campaign project.

The whole trip home from the office is spent weighing the pros and cons of accepting it. Four months of late nights and weekends. But to have such a significant project on my resume could be a game-changer for whatever comes next for me.

I've never been a big *what's next* kind of guy—wasn't ever sure I'd become one either. But with Gretchen, if my *next* doesn't align with hers, I'm not interested.

When I step inside my apartment, my senses go on overload—the look, the sound, the smell, the feel of coming home to your person.

Music blares from the living room speakers while dinner sizzles in a pan in the kitchen. I softly close the door behind me, drop my things on the entryway table, and peek around the corner to find Gretchen, dressed in tiny shorts and one of my t-shirts hanging off one shoulder revealing a black lace bra strap underneath. A single braid wraps to one side and her legs are bare from her upper thigh all the way down to her toes. She hovers over the stovetop, working a spatula with one hand while the other shifts her glasses on the bridge of her nose.

There's no big karaoke performance or wild dance moves, but she's perfectly her in the way she hums the song under her breath, rocking back and forth on her feet. Effortlessly, she consumes my space, like it was hers to begin with. I can't make myself look away.

Still unaware of my presence, I sneak up behind her. I pinch both sides of her waist and she jumps with a yelp.

"Holy jeez! Connor!" She presses a palm to her chest. "You scared the crap out of me."

"Honey, I'm home," I laugh as I haul her toward me, her back to my front, and rest my chin on her shoulder. "What are you making?"

"Fajitas."

"They smell delicious." I kiss her exposed shoulder. "I see you chose my clothes after all."

Setting the spatula aside, she reaches for the stereo remote and turns the volume down. She spins in place and loops her arms around my neck. "I'm doing our laundry because I had no clothes left. I hope you don't mind." She flutters her lashes.

"You can have them all. They look better on you anyway." She steps out of my hold to grab plates from the cabinet. "What did you do today?"

"I used your emergency key to Drew's to go over there and clean up. Stocked their fridge with a few things. Mom and Dad visited them at the hospital this morning and now they're at their hotel sleeping off the jet lag." She collects two forks from a drawer before pushing it shut with her hip. "I FaceTimed with Cheyenne, Miguel and the kids."

"How weird is that for you to say out loud?" I ask as she sets the plates and forks down on the counter.

She presses her hands into her cheeks, eyes wide in disbelief, but there's an undeniable joy there. "Oh my gosh, it's so weird. I went through more of the scrapbook and we talked through some of it." Her expression turns thoughtful before she shakes her head. "It's just wild, is all."

I tug on her braid to draw her into my arms again. "I missed you today."

Her soft lips land gently on mine. "Missed you, too." Another kiss. "But only a little because I went back to see Gene today."

I bark out a laugh. "You did not?"

"I most definitely did," she declares, turning back to the stove. "He's like Willy Wonka, but with books and, you know, without the creepy tunnel boat ride." She pulls a jar of seasoning from the cabinet. "He let me help package up a few books to ship out and, you didn't hear it from me, but Julia Roberts' husband is about to receive a very coveted copy of *The Great Gatsby* as a gift."

"Sounds like you've got a decent fallback in the book industry if this fashion thing doesn't work out." I quirk a teasing brow.

"Nah. I love reading too much to make books my job."

"Really? I'd think that's why you might love it."

Shrugging, she answers, "I thought about it when I applied to NYU, but I worried it would suck the joy out of reading for me. Like, if I go behind the curtain, I might come out jaded. I'm happy to just be a lover of books.

"I love fashion in the opposite way. The weeds of the industry—following trends, shopping designers to stock a store—that's the part I enjoy. I get to love both this way, I guess." Gaze fixed somewhere over my shoulder, she contemplates her words. "I don't know if that makes sense."

"It does."

"Unless Gene ever wants to hire me, then I might reconsider."

"Be honest, Fish. How much did you pester him about the wild horses?"

Her brows knit together. "I don't know what you're talking about."

"You know exactly what I'm talking about." I poke her in the ribs and the spatula she was holding drops to the counter as she hikes up a knee to block my reach.

"Connor, stop!" She breaks into a fit of giggles. I don't stop as I continue to poke and prod with my fingers, coaxing her where I want her to go until she ends up back in my arms. The air settles on our satisfied sighs as our hearts and our bodies melt into the embrace. Ever so slightly, we begin to sway from side to side.

My person, barefoot and dancing with me in my kitchen—I recognize the moment for what it is. Something I've craved. Something I've never had with anyone else...before *her*.

Her exposed shoulder with that peek of black lace teases me. I pepper soft kisses there and then lift to meet her eyes.

The kiss begins slow and unhurried, soft hums of contentment echoed between us as we languidly explore each other's mouths, bodies swaying. My hand cradles the back of her head while hers fists the back of my shirt. Before I know it, we're pushing harder, breaths heavy between every pull of our lips as the kiss deepens and I press her back into the counter.

Without breaking the kiss, I turn off the stove with one hand, her body tensing in anticipation, while my other hand moves under the hem of her—*my*—shirt. I caress the bare skin of her stomach and her mouth opens wide, a plea for more. We fall into each other, head first.

I will never tire of kissing this woman. Euphoric and claiming, I'm completely addicted.

My palms run the bare skin of her lower back, up and down her spine. Underneath her shirt, I squeeze one breast in my hand and she rakes her nails across my shoulders, a soft moan pressed against my lips. I drag a hand up her thigh and she hikes her leg up to my waist.

Slowly, I work my thumb behind the fabric of her underwear from under the hem of her shorts. Her head falls back on a stilted breath when I sweep over her already soaked entrance.

"I wanna use my mouth." I plunge my head toward her chest as my hand underneath her shirt peels the lace bra down to cup her bare breast. I suck the hardened nipple through the fabric and she arches into me, her palm slamming down, fingers clenched around the edge of the counter. "Can I use my mouth?"

Her head lolls forward as I run my thumb between her legs again. She whimpers, vigorously nodding in approval.

I hoist her up by her thighs and turn us to the dining area. I drop her on the table and shove the chairs aside as she sweeps the salt and pepper shakers and napkin holder out of the way. Items clattering to the ground, we giggle as our lips find each other again. I yank her forward, drawing her to the edge of the table. My shirt hangs long on her, almost completely covering the tiny shorts underneath. When my hands move up to grasp her waistband, Gretchen leans back on her palms at the ready.

"Hips up," I command, my hooded eyes locked on hers.

I swipe her shorts and underwear over the curve of her ass and down her legs in one fell swoop, tossing them aside.

Her legs dangle off the edge of the table, the hem of my shirt resting at the apex of her thighs, still covering the area I plan to devour in a matter of seconds. Knowing that I'm the lucky bastard she let strip her from the waist down, makes me want to own her. To make it so good for her that she could never imagine this with anyone else.

Nerves flicker across Gretchen's features. I stand between her legs and take her face in my hands. Like my life depends on it, I kiss her fiercely, stealing the breath from her lungs.

"If you want me to stop, just tell me," I say against her mouth. "Now, lay down."

With her back flat on the table, I run my palms over her, beginning at her shoulders, then over her breasts and stomach until they land on her thighs, her body arching into my touch every inch of the way.

I drop to my knees, taking in the sight of her bare for the first time. Biting back my groan, I strain against my zipper, as I trail hot, wet kisses up the insides of her thighs.

"Connor, please."

My girl aches for my touch and I intend to give her everything she needs. "You ready for me?"

She hums and I drag a finger up her center, my shoulders pushing her hips wider.

Her moan bounces off the ceiling and I wrap my arms under her legs to anchor her. I move in slow—one long, lazy swipe of my tongue and her back bows off the table as shivers of pleasure ripple through her.

"Oh my God," she breathes.

Her breaths quake on her tongue and I'm a man starved. With every move of my mouth over her, she writhes into me. When her body rocks back, I yank her closer. When she presses into my mouth, I push into her harder.

I groan against her, the vibrations moving up and down her core, encouraging her, and she doesn't hesitate to take and take and take. "Take what you need, baby."

I sense it the second before her orgasm hits. One hand lands with a smack on the table as her other fists my hair. Her thighs quiver in my grasp, but I don't relent. Licking, sucking and flicking, my tongue works her over, her breaths coming in rapid pants. Her cries pitch higher, louder as she shouts my name, riding wave after wave of pleasure to its complete end.

Body slack on the table, her chest rises and falls in a heavy rhythm. I rise to my feet and meet her gaze. I pull her to a seated position and she launches herself at me, kissing me hard, paying no mind to the taste of herself coating my lips and tongue.

Her hands drop to the waist of my jeans. "Gretch, stop. You don't have to—"

"I want to touch you." She looks at me like if she doesn't touch me now, she might combust and, *dammit*, I want her to. But I need her to know that I don't expect anything in return for pleasuring her.

"Please? I need to know that I can make you feel good, Connor." I'm standing between her legs, my shirt barely covering the best thing I ever tasted in my life, and my zipper clings on for dear life. I want her hands on me so bad. "I *want* to."

I let out a low curse that sounds more like a groan. "I won't last long."

"I don't care," she rushes out as she yanks the button of my jeans and pulls down the zipper.

Her hand slides inside my boxer briefs and my forehead falls to hers as she wraps it around me. It's an awkward angle, but she works her hand up and down as I thrust into her fist in tandem. My breaths stutter, jaw clenching. One tiny whimper from her mouth and my hand is back between her legs where I find her eager and ready again.

I'm close, so I waste no time and plunge two fingers deep inside her. She cries out, her body fully surrendering to me once more. I match the rhythm of my fingers to my hips as I chase my orgasm, hers within reach right along with me.

"Ahh! I'm gonna come again!"

"I'm so close. Come with me."

Temples fused together, our breaths come hot and heavy on each other's skin. I curse, unintelligible, as sensations collide inside me—her fist and my hips driving me toward my release, the slick sounds of my fingers moving in and out, the taste of her still on my tongue.

"Gretch, that feels so good!" I say, voice like gravel now as I climb.

This woman owns me. Every look, every kiss, every touch, every piece of me belongs to her.

Our cries echo, loud enough to reach the hallway but it only spurs me on. I want faster, louder, harder. My fingers move roughly inside of her, our movements growing sloppy, as we close in on that climax together.

Gretchen's mouth falls open on a silent cry, breath halted in her throat. "That's it, come again for me."

Her voice breaks, wild and free as she lets go, my fingers plunging and swirling. I grunt through three more rough thrusts as her fist tightens around me and I follow her over the edge, my groan vibrating against her cheek. I buck my hips into her until the bitter end, pulsing as the euphoria sweeps me under.

We stay there, her hand wrapped around me, my fingers still inside her as we ride out the aftershocks. It has *never* been like this before and I wasn't even inside of her. I knew being with Gretchen would be different. Special. But this? How will we ever get anything done? She's all I want to do now…ever.

She bites her lip and pulls her hand free as I do the same. "I guess we're supposed to eat fajitas now, like we didn't just traumatize this table," she says as she adjusts her glasses.

I kiss her long and slow until our bodies sink into the cradle of each other, completely spent. "We can traumatize every surface of this apartment if you want to." I wink, planting a final kiss on the tip of her nose. "I have to go clean up. And put these boxers in the laundry."

I retreat to the bathroom to the sounds of her laughter. Gretchen Fisher just made me come in my pants.

"ARE YOU NERVOUS ABOUT TOMORROW?" My words land softly in the warm silence between us as I stroke the arm Gretchen has draped across my ribs.

After dinner, we cuddled on the couch to watch *Pitch Perfect*, singing along to every song and laughing way too hard at all of the most quotable one-liners.

Keeping to the silly terms of our thermostat agreement, before we climbed in bed, she cranked it down to sixty-eight degrees right before she threw on one of my hoodies, donned a pair of fuzzy socks—a look I'm unexpectedly feral for—and crawled under the covers. When I followed a few minutes later, she draped her body around me like a sloth on a branch in an effort to keep warm.

Five minutes and an *I told you so* later, shared body warmth worked its magic and Gretchen peeled the hoodie off, leaving her in a tank top and shorts, her feet still clad in fuzzy socks woven between my legs.

"A little," she replies. "It helps knowing you'll be there, though."

Then I'll be there, all the time, everywhere, for all the things, I want to say. She doesn't *need* me when she tells her parents and Drew about her family in Arizona. She's strong and brave all on her own. Even still, any chance I get to be the person by her side, you won't find me anywhere else. Not anymore.

"Don't forget the rules when we're in front of Mom, Dad and Drew, old man."

I assure her I'll be on my best behavior, but make a mental note to text Drew in the morning about meeting up for drinks next week. I've made excuses, kept secrets and locked my feelings away long enough. The right time to tell him would have been three years ago, but I can't rewrite the past no matter how much I wish I could.

It's time for me to tell my best friend that I'm hopelessly in love with his sister.

Chapter Forty-Four

I CAN EXPLAIN

GRETCHEN

THE RESTAURANT my parents chose is swarming with people. And because I underestimated the time it would take to walk here from Connor's place, I'm late.

A rush of air hits my back as I attempt to peek around the mass of people crowding the hostess station. A moment later, the front door closes behind me with a *thud*.

"Thank God. You're late, too."

I turn to Drew with a mischievous smile. "I think it's the hostess' fault."

Drew lifts up on his toes to spot the innocent perpetrator. "Let the mousey girl who looks overwhelmed and not a day over sixteen take the fall?" He arches a brow. "Cutthroat. I like it."

The throng of people inches forward, pulling Drew and I along. "How's Reagan?"

"As good as can be expected. And by good, I mean she kicked me out this morning because—and I'm paraphrasing—for the love of God if I don't stop hovering she's gonna smother me in my sleep.

And if I don't bring home mac and cheese and chocolate cake, I'll be sleeping on the couch tonight."

I chuckle. "I always knew I liked her."

"If I'm missing come morning, there was definitely foul play involved. She can't be trusted."

"Hmm, I don't know. Maybe she called me and I helped her hide your body?"

Drew's shoulders sag, fingers pinching the bridge of his nose as his body quakes in silent, pitiful laughter. "That's so morbid, Gretch. Why am I laughing?"

Drew's always been a fixer, which is noble, but it can also be suffocating. Even I can tell that he's emotionally and physically spent. Whether his laughter comes from a legitimately funny or maniacally exhausted place, he needs permission to laugh. Reagan may have lovingly kicked him out this morning, but I think Drew needed space, too.

We inch forward a few more steps, finally reaching the hostess who directs us to our parents' table around the corner along the back wall of the restaurant.

Drew motions for me to walk ahead of him. Chivalry? One would think, but no. When the familiar cringe-worthy buzzing sound lands against my ear—the product of my mutinous brother's thumb and index finger rubbing together in that way he learned when we were kids—the hair on my arms stands up, body twitching. I spin on a dime and pummel my fist into his bicep. "Ugh, you're infuriating."

He cackles and rakes a hand over my scalp before I'm able to turn back around. I glare at him over my shoulder as I smooth a hand over my hair. "You are such a loser!" I grit.

"Children," Dad interrupts our squabble. "Nice to see you haven't lost that pre-pubescent petty charm about you." His tone is affectionate if not a little chastising.

Mom and Dad stand to greet us and we all exchange hugs. It's been a month since I've seen them and not even New York City—or Flagstaff—is a decent substitute for spending time with them.

As we pile into the half-moon booth, I follow the natural flow and end up seated next to Mom, Dad next to her and Drew next to Dad, leaving the empty seat for Connor on my other side.

Speaking of my boyfriend, Mom asks, "Is Connor still able to make it?"

Count to three. You don't know his whereabouts because you are not his girl-friend. He did not text you five minutes ago saying he's on his way.

Thankfully, Drew answers before I'm able to slip up. "He's on his way."

Mom and Dad ask Drew for an update on Reagan. My brother's face falls before he levels it out, offering, "She's fine."

My parents visited Reagan yesterday before she was discharged from the hospital. I imagine they were brought up to speed on everything.

The waitress arrives to take our drink order, and nobody is more excited for the interruption than Drew. As the waitress leaves, Connor appears at the table with a slap on Drew's shoulder and a bright smile to my parents as he moves into the empty seat beside me.

Remember the rules.

I say it as much to myself as I try to telepathically communicate it to him.

"Sorry I'm late," Connor supplies. "Still playing catch up at work and I lost track of time."

Memories of this morning flash through my mind. Connor luring me awake with his face—and fingers—between my thighs, both of us completely lost in the feel of each other. He was thirty minutes late getting out the door.

Do not grab his hand.

"No worries, dear," Mom coos.

"How's the jet lag?" Connor asks.

"Today's better than yesterday, that's for sure," Dad says with a soft laugh as Mom puffs out her cheeks on an exhausted exhale. "We were both awake for three hours in the middle of the night, but managed to fall back asleep for a bit after the sun came up."

The waitress returns with our drinks and we dismiss her a moment later, requesting more time to look at the menu.

"So," Mom prods, "I want to hear about your trip. Connor, that was so nice of you to step in when Drew couldn't make it. Thank you for doing that."

Connor sips from his glass as he waves off the gratitude with his free hand. Like water dousing out a fire, Mom's next question lands like a hammer on an anvil. "I hope your girlfriend didn't mind."

His expression falters for a beat and Drew must notice because he answers first. "He and Lauren broke up, Mom."

The stone cold stare that passes between my brother and my boyfriend communicates a thousand thoughts that only I can translate.

Drew still thinks Connor made a mistake.

Connor's guilt over our secret is eating him away from the inside out.

Do not grab his hand.

"Oh, I'm sorry to hear that," Mom says. "She was a lovely girl."

Connor smiles politely, breaking my brother's stare. "Thank you, Kelly. Lauren *is* great, but it just wasn't going to work out."

His leg brushes mine under the table. It could be excused as incidental contact, but he doesn't back away and neither do I.

Drew shakes his head so imperceptibly anyone could miss it, before he says, "Anyway, the trip. Let's hear it."

I practiced this part. I rehearsed the words in the mirror this morning. Yet, when I look at my brother across the table, his expectant gaze bores into me and my throat goes dry.

"Gretch, are you okay?" Dad asks.

I ping-pong my gaze between Mom, Dad and Drew. A soft hand wraps around the knee I have crossed over my other leg and my eyes drift shut briefly at the reassuring contact. Connor's breaking the rules and I don't even care.

"There's actually something I need to tell you guys." I push against the nerves threatening to take hold of my words. "I didn't go to Arizona to celebrate graduation or my birthday."

Mom looks like she wants to quiz me, but she doesn't rush to speak. Looking at Dad, I see the gentle father he's always been. Endlessly patient, he's never one to push me.

Connor's hand slides around to my upper calf to run a knuckle up and down in smooth strokes. The lulling movement says *you got this* with every sweep of his fingers.

I steel my spine, fixing my eyes on Mom and Dad. Silverware clatters to the hardwood floor somewhere nearby and I register Drew shifting in my periphery, as I begin. "I went to Arizona because," I take in a deep breath, my anxious thoughts narrowing in on Connor's touch to anchor me, "I found my birth parents."

Stares.

Silence.

"What the fuck!" Drew's booming voice draws every head to turn. He rises to his feet from a crouched position beside the table, burning with anger as he slams a fistful of silverware on the table-top. Connor removes his hand from my leg and...I know.

Drew towers over him as Connor raises both of his hands and says, "Drew, calm down."

"Don't you dare tell me to calm down, Vining," Drew seethes.

"Honey, sit down and let Gretchen explain," Mom tries to inter-ject, but it goes in one ear and out the other. Drew's attention is laser-locked on the man beside me.

"I can explain," Connor says, voice resigned.

No, no, no. This is all wrong. I need to say something, but I'm stunned speechless, terrified of the brother standing in front of me who fumes with a level of restrained aggression I've never seen from him before.

"I trusted you to look out for her."

"Andrew, you're blowing this out of proportion and you're making a scene. Sit. Down." But Dad's reprimand falls on deaf ears.

"Outside. Now."

Connor's shoulders drop before he turns to me with regret in his eyes as he reads the panic in mine. He reaches for my hand. No use hiding the truth now.

"Don't fucking touch her! Outside."

Connor pulls his hand away and my vision narrows to a tunnel. The restaurant fades into obscurity along the blurred edges as the mumbled words and labored exhales from my parents tell me they know, too. They realize what Drew has discovered—what we've been hiding. But I can't seem to find focus on anything other than the man sitting to my right, broken, despondent and looking like he wishes for one big do-over.

Connor winces, jaw tight like it's the only thing stopping him from lashing out. With a pained look at my parents, he says, "I'm sorry," before he gets up and follows my brother to the front door.

I'm unmoving as I watch them walk away. Like a coward, I say nothing.

"Gretchen." Mom's calm voice and gentle hand on my arm are a soft *tap tap tap* on the soundproof box I find myself in. "Sweetie?"

I turn to look at her, unseeing, no words to be found.

The three of us shift our attention to the windows at the front of the restaurant in time to see Drew storm on to the sidewalk, Connor on his heels.

My brother flings his arms and lands an accusatory finger hard onto Connor's chest, heads pivoting throughout restaurant, everyone with a front row seat.

Connor's hands come up in surrender.

Their mouths are moving, my brother's faster and more animated than Connor's steady, more stoic expression and tight-lipped responses.

Drew says something.

Connor replies.

I'm out of my seat, racing for the door, the moment Drew's fist connects with Connor's jaw.

Chapter Forty-Five

WORDS TRUER THAN TRUE

CONNOR

"You prick! I trusted you!" Drew shouts down at me as I clamor back to my feet. My fists clench at my sides as I crank my jaw to relieve some of the ache.

I know I broke the rules, but Gretchen needed me and I won't apologize for it. The moment she'd been fretting over for months, the strength it took for her to finally say the words out loud—I was so damn proud of her. Then, like a bull in a china shop, Drew wrecked the entire thing, forever tainting what should have been a beautiful moment.

"Dude"—I put my hands back up in surrender—"calm down and let me explain."

"Like hell I'm gonna calm down."

"Drew! Stop!" Gretchen's panicked voice rises above the cluster of onlookers conveniently slowing their strides to watch the two grown ass men throw punches on the sidewalk. The restaurant door crashes into the brick wall behind it from the force of her exit.

Shoving strangers aside, she reaches the front of the small crowd and rushes toward me

"I'm fine, Fish," I lie and she knows it.

"You don't get to call her that anymore," Drew spews.

Gretchen whirls around and shoves him with two hard palms to his chest. "Back off, Drew. This is none of your business!"

Undeterred, Drew continues his rampage like he doesn't even see her. "I asked you to be there for her, not screw her!"

"Andrew!" Paul commands, voice cutting like a knife. "That's enough, son."

Drew laughs. "No, Dad. I'm not even close to finished."

"Fisher," I beg, "can we just talk?"

"Yeah, let's do that." He steps closer as Kelly hauls Gretchen back, out of Drew's path. "What's it been, two months? That woman gave you two and a half years and you can't even keep it in your pants for two months after you dump her?"

"I've already told you Lauren and I weren't right for each other." I fight every urge to shout, to engage him with the same aggression he's giving me.

"That's a load of bullshit! I was there pulling your pathetic, drunken ass off the floor, kicking girls out of your apartment. That girl was the best thing to ever happen to you and you went and fucked it up."

I pin Drew with a stare, eyes furious. Gretchen, her parents— they're hearing all of this. I want to reach for Gretchen's hand, to tell her parents that Drew's got it all wrong. But I can't.

"And I'll be damned," he continues, "if I let you pull my sister into your mess."

"Drew, let him explain. Please!" Gretchen's attempt to mediate goes unacknowledged. He doesn't look her way. He doesn't even pretend to hear her. This is between him and me.

"Maybe you're right, Connor. Maybe I've been wrong this whole time. Maybe it was never right with Lauren because you never actually changed. Maybe monogamy just doesn't suit you," he spits, lip curled in disgust.

"That is not true and you know it!" I retort, defensive now, my muscles stiff with anger.

"Do I? Where's the evidence?" He throws his arms out, neck swiveling left and right in dramatic mockery. Gretchen drops her face into her hands.

"Where was *your* evidence before Reagan?" It's a low blow, especially in front of his parents, but it's my only defense.

A flicker of surprise crosses his gaze before he lets out another humorless laugh. "I suppose this is the part where you tell me that it's different with Gretchen." Drew's brows shoot up. "That you didn't mean for it to happen?" His eyes narrow. "That I can trust you?"

Disappointment coats his derision, that afternoon in his kitchen six years ago where I made him that exact promise flashing *Exhibit A in the Case of Your Best Friend's Betrayal* in big bold letters across his face. A thread tethered to a similar scene three years ago where I not only reiterated that promise, but I had every opportunity to prove I wasn't *that guy* anymore…and I failed. The strand of our friendship now rests under the weight of Drew's judgment. Every lie, every secret, every half-truth in between, pulling—fifteen years of friendship slowly ripping at the seams.

"What do you want me to say? You're mad at me. Fine. Be mad. That wasn't how I wanted you to find out. That's on me, okay? I'm sorry."

"I was here with my wife, fighting our way through something I wouldn't wish on my worst enemy, trusting you to be there for my sister. And I did. I trusted that you were looking out for her."

"I was! I will always be there for her."

"No. You were taking care of yourself!" he sneers. "Put a pretty girl, a bottle of tequila and a free hotel room in front of Connor Vining and you'll jump at the opportunity."

Gretchen stomps toward him. "What the hell, Drew?" Gretchen shouts. "You don't know what you're talking about."

"Gretch, that guy"—he points an accusatory finger at me—"I don't care what romantic bullshit nonsense he used on you, I know him better than you do. At worst, you're another one-night stand that he'll forget about tomorrow. At best, you're a rebound that will land him back with Lauren once you move back to New York."

Is this the man he thinks I am? The man he thinks I *still* am? Lauren wasn't right for me, but I was faithful to her for our entire relationship, yet Drew thinks I'm still the kind of guy to have a one-night stand or treat his little sister as nothing more than a rebound. I haven't been that guy for years. But he won't give me a chance to explain.

Gretchen's pleas for Drew to stop ride the waves of her tears. Her posture sinks like all the fight in her has vanished. He doesn't relent as he sidesteps past her and comes chest to chest with me once more.

"Tell me why," he says as Gretchen returns to her parents, gesturing and whispering, begging for someone to listen.

It's no use, I want to tell her. *Don't waste your breath. He's never going to accept this.*

"Why what?" I shrug.

"Why her?"

I stare at him. Tears sting the back of my eyes and my throat grows tight, but my emotion has no effect on Drew. Totally expressionless, he's content to watch me drown while he stews in anger.

"Because you had her in a hotel room for five days and couldn't keep your dick in your pants?"

"Stop it," I seethe, jaw clenched. My heart pounds behind my sternum as I suppress the words that are right there. The words I need him to hear without me having to say them—not here, not now.

"Because you know she's moving back to New York, so you thought you could enjoy some no-strings sex?"

"I would never treat her like that," I plead. *Please! Not now.*

"Because she's a rebound?"

"Because I love her!"

Drew stills as Gretchen jerks her head my direction, worried eyes fixed on me. The rush of adrenaline from uttering the words out loud does nothing to distract me from the guilt that instantly consumes me for *this* being the moment she hears them.

I drop my head as the first tear falls, a tiny splatter darkening the concrete at my feet. "Because I'm in love with her," I breathe, words truer than true.

The sky is blue. Two plus two equals four. The earth is round. I'm in love with her.

For what seems like hours, everything goes blurry, sounds muffled. I see nothing. I hear nothing. Then, Gretchen is in front of me, hands on my cheeks, pulling my universe into focus. *God, I love her.*

"I'm sorry," I whisper. The pad of her thumb swipes a tear from my cheek as she opens her mouth to speak.

"The funny thing is," Drew interrupts, "you actually think I'm going to believe that."

Gretchen lets out a frustrated breath, expression murderous.

"It took you a year to say it the first time, and now you went and fell in love in a week? Please!" He rolls his eyes.

Gretchen spins and prowls up to her brother until she's right in his face. "That is enough!"

"Drew, honey," Kelly chimes in. "I think we need to table this and discuss it another time when you're not so upset."

"No, Mom! You and Dad deserve to know exactly who this guy is if he's gonna stand here and say he's 'in love' with your daughter." He adds a mocking tone that cuts especially deep. "Goes for you, too, Gretch." He fixes his attention back on me. "Does she even know the half of it?"

I could yell. I could defend myself. I could beg him not to say too much. I could plead with him to not use the lowest moments of my life to define who I am. But I can't bring myself to stop him.

"I'm gonna take that as a no. And, hey, I'll do you a solid because, you know, best friends and all, and I'll skip over the frat house years."

I could remind him that we lived in the same frat house, but I don't.

"Hell, how about we just focus on those last few months before you met Lauren."

He stares daggers at me—an unflinching challenge in his gaze that dares me to stop him. But I don't.

"I get back from my honeymoon and Casanova over here is all but AWOL. If he wasn't drunk dialing me from the bar on a Tuesday night needing my help to get home, he was ghosting me. Lunch plans, workouts, dinner parties, didn't matter."

Hands hung low on my hips, eyes glued to the sidewalk, the shame of those few months rises to the surface. Drew's begun with the better of the two halves and I'm certain he's about to expose the worst one.

Still, I don't stop him.

"There was one place I could almost always find him, though. His place, usually face down on his mattress, passed out, naked more often than not. Some days I'd get lucky and whatever girl he picked up at the bar the night before would already be gone. Oh, but there were plenty of days I wasn't so lucky. Isn't that right?"

I'm a statue—concrete, void of life, motionless. The impact of every blunt force hit of the sledgehammer barely registers in my senses. The real pain lies in being powerless to stop it as pieces of me crumble and shatter to the floor.

"No, on those days, I'd have to carry his ass to the shower, clean his sheets and force him to go to work. The worst days, though?" He pauses and I wonder if this hurts him even a shred as much as it hurts me. Does he even care? "The worst were the days I had to kick the girls out. What was it, three, sometimes four, women a week?"

I wince.

"Wasn't always one woman at a time either, was it?"

The tears are back and I paw at my face like a weak child. This is it. The absolute worst version of myself on display. All of the careless and reckless behavior I fell into after walking away from Gretchen on that balcony. It doesn't matter that she can connect the dots and know that this all happened after Drew's wedding—that I was grieving her—because no explanation about the *how* or the *why* makes it any less true.

Nobody understands what it's like to reach rock bottom where you don't want to feel anything anymore until you find yourself there. I was angry at myself, riddled with guilt and I missed Gretchen. I missed her so fucking much. I had everything I wanted and then I threw it all away—destroyed it. I was lost and I handled it all wrong.

Here I am, having done it all over again. I've ruined everything.

I don't have to look at Drew, Gretchen or their parents to imagine what I might find on their faces. Disgust. Disappointment. All the things I feel about myself when I remember that time of my life. A dark period I thought I had moved on from. I thought my friend recognized that, too.

Maybe we never truly escape our pasts. Gretchen's forgiveness or not, I don't know how we move forward after this. You can't un-hear these types of things. What if she's picturing all of it? No, I'll never recover from that.

I once thought past sins were simply stains that would fade with time, but I was wrong. They're permanent. Tattoos forever marring our skin, painting the picture by which the people we love the most judge our character.

Pressing the heels of my hands into my eyes, I drop to a nearby bench. Elbows on my knees, my head falls into my hands.

"Fuck this! I can't deal with this right now. Consider this my formal decline to your invitation to get drinks. Go ahead and pencil me in your calendar for the twenty-third of never."

With that, he whips around and storms off, Gretchen crying after him, "Drew! Wait! Don't do this!"

"Let him go, honey," Paul says. "He needs to cool off."

Feet shuffle on concrete, then Gretchen crouches down in front of me. The expression on her face confirms everything I already know and I look away to avoid the feeling. To delay what I now fear is inevitable.

"I think I should go after him…see if he'll talk to me."

It won't work. I nod.

"I'll come back to your place later."

You promise? I nod.

"Connor. Will you please look at me?"

I look up.

"I *will* come home later."

I'm scared you won't. I nod.

A second later, I'm forced to watch as Gretchen chases after her brother. Mr. and Mrs. Fisher say…something and pat me on the shoulder before they depart in the opposite direction.

Twenty feet might as well be twenty miles as my best friend's frame fades into the crowd in the distance, the love of my life running after him.

I can't help but think that, despite my best efforts to keep them, I've somehow managed to lose them both.

Chapter Forty-Six

DON'T SAY THINGS YOU DON'T MEAN

GRETCHEN

AFTER TRAILING Drew for twenty minutes through three very intentional wrong turns, I conceded his desire to be alone. Rest assured though; I'm no quitter. That's how I ended up here at his doorstep. He'll come home eventually and I'll make him talk to me if it's the last thing I do.

Yet, there's a ripple in my gut that says to go back to Connor.

He's in love with me.

I wanted to shout it right back, but Drew wouldn't let anyone else get a word in edgewise.

Connor never told me the details of those months after Drew's wedding and I never asked for them. He said he became the worst version of himself. He told me he drank too much and he mentioned other women. Someone else might hear those things and think less of him, label him as one giant red flag—that was certainly Drew's hope when he decided to air his best friend's dirty laundry on a busy sidewalk for all of Chicago to hear. But I don't see the man Connor used to be. I see the man inside—the man he's always been.

His past has never mattered to me. Connor has to know that by now. But the way he looked on that bench where I left him? Broken. Ashamed. Vulnerable. Haunted.

His past still *haunts* him. Maybe I shouldn't have come here at all.

Or maybe it's exactly why the blood red rage staining my vision has me knocking on my brother's door, ready to fight for the man I love.

When Reagan opens the door, her smile falters as she takes in my expression. "What's the matter?"

"I know my brother's not home yet, but can I stay until he gets here? I really need to talk to him."

"Of course." She swings the door open and I step inside. "Did something happen at lunch?"

I plop down on the couch and fall back against the cushions as she takes up her previous spot on the chaise end of the sectional marked by the fresh Reagan-sized indentation and a blanket that's been tossed aside.

"You could say that."

Reagan shifts in her seat, grimacing through the discomfort in her abdomen as she repositions herself.

"God, I'm so sorry! I shouldn't be here. I can talk to Drew later. I'll let you rest." I move to get up, but she stops me.

"Like hell you will. I'm tired of everyone tiptoeing around me. If you have drama to distract me from mine, I'm first in line to listen." She pauses, breathing deeply. "I don't want to talk about me or *this*"—she gestures over her body—"anymore. It hurts. It sucks. I'm mad. I'm sad. End of story. Let's move on."

I swallow hard. Message received.

"So, out with it," she adds with an amused gleam in her eyes that immediately puts me at ease.

At that, the words spill out of me. "Well, basically, I went and fell in love with Drew's best friend and before I could tell my family that I found my birth family in Arizona—which is complete with a mom, a dad, two brothers, two sisters and a partridge in a pear tree, by the way—Drew found out about the aforementioned love-falling, completely lost it on Connor—who somehow loves me, too, only I didn't know that until about thirty minutes ago—and now I'm here to murder my brother for being a giant asshole."

Reagan's eyes are saucers, mouth agape.

"Yeah, I know," I say.

"Wow. Okay. That's a lot. Um…wine? Yes, wine. We need wine." Reagan gestures toward the wine rack in the kitchen and I oblige.

"Wait, you, like, just had surgery. Should you be drinking?"

The saucers turn to slits, face dour.

"Right. Wine."

ONE BOTTLE of red and an hour later, I've regaled Reagan with the whole story.

"I always knew that micro-mini bitch he brought to our wedding was bad news," Reagan says as she tips back the last of her wine.

"You have no idea."

Reagan's gaze looks somewhere beyond me, tugging at a memory. "So, that Thanksgiving? Connor was the reason you didn't come?"

I nod.

"And when he showed up at your graduation dinner, it had seriously been three years?"

I nod again and a weighty awkwardness settles between us.

"I know Lauren is your friend," I begin cautiously. "For what it's worth, I really liked her and I know Connor feels terrible about how he handled that whole thing."

She shrugs, albeit noncommittally. "Yeah, Drew and I weren't sure what to think when we heard that he dumped her, but…I mean, she's happy now. Like, really happy."

"Connor said she met someone."

"Yeah," she sighs. "Sounds like it was all for the best."

Reagan twirls the stem of her wine glass between her fingers and I worry that the sullen look on her face might be because she thinks as little of Connor as Drew seems to. If everything my brother said was true, then she had to have seen some of it.

"Do you think Connor's a bad person?" I ask.

"What? No, I could never think that."

"It's just...the things Drew said about him..." I can't even say it. My brain is too weak and my heart too weary to litigate every accusation again.

"Those months after our wedding were rough. Your brother was so worried about him. He tried to get him to talk about it, but Connor just shut down. Sometimes it was radio silence for days at a time." She taps her nail on her glass. "I guess now we know what was really going on."

"*You* do, but Drew won't give him a chance to explain," I remind her. "Connor wanted to be the one to tell him everything about us, but today went so wrong. It was really bad, Reagan."

She studies me for a beat before looking away.

"Listen, I know there's this marital code that says you're only allowed to see the good in my brother and that husband bashing is generally frowned upon. And that's fine. But I need you to let me be angry." I drain the last of my second glass of wine.

"Nobody can tell you to not feel things. The only encouragement I can give you is to give Drew time. Connor's a good man. Nobody knows that more than Drew." She reaches for my hand. "He loves you, Gretchen. Whether or not he sees it now, in the end, your happiness will trump any grudge he thinks he's justified in holding."

I manage a half-smile, hoping against hope that she's right.

Reagan's phone vibrates on the coffee table. My brother's name lights up the home screen as I pass it to her.

"Hey, babe," Reagan says by way of greeting as I collect our wine glasses and head to the kitchen.

"Yeah, your sister's here. She wants to talk to you when you get home."

Reagan meets my eyes across the room, careful that her expression not give anything away.

"That's okay, more girl time for us then," she chirps. I try to return her enthusiasm with a smile, but I know it looks forced. He's avoiding me.

"Gretchen will be here when you get home." She pauses. "Huh? What was that? You're cutting out. Okayloveyoubye," she rushes out before disconnecting the call.

"He's avoiding me, isn't he?" I ask as I toss the empty wine bottle in the recycle bin.

"Yes, but he can't do it forever."

"I can't be in your hair all day, Reagan. Who knows when he's going to come home."

"Nonsense! You're staying here. We're ordering takeout, because I'm starving, and you're gonna tell me all about your birth family."

I drop back to the couch on a laugh. It fades just as quickly when memories resurface. *My parents.* I told them I found my birth parents and then Drew lost it and everything turned to chaos.

"Hey," Reagan says softly. "Where'd you go?"

"My parents probably have so many questions," I reply, tone worried.

"They'll understand. You'll get another chance to talk with them soon."

"Yeah, but I should text them."

My hands ghost over my body, eyes darting from the coffee table to the kitchen to the entryway. I shoot up from the couch, scanning every surface as I spin in place. "Dammit!" I slap a palm to my forehead. "I left my purse at the restaurant. My phone's in there."

"Ahhh, okay. Damage control. Don't panic." She raises her phone and swipes it to life. "We're gonna call the restaurant and make sure they have it. And then we're gonna tell Drew to swing by and grab it on his way home."

"Right. Okay."

Her fingers tap away on the screen. "And I'll text Connor and tell him you're here waiting on Drew?"

"Yeah, please. And my parents, too, if you don't mind."

"On it," Reagan says as she effortlessly flips her lawyer-mode switch and gets stuff done.

Hours pass.

Reagan asks, and I answer, all of her questions about my birth family. We order takeout, watch a romcom, binge the first half of the latest season of *Emily in Paris*, and I paint Reagan's toenails.

The sun has set, the view outside their balcony doors transforming to the night canvas of a city illuminated by streetlights. Reagan stifles a yawn and I'm about to wave my white flag and head back to Connor's, when Drew finally walks through the front door.

He waves my purse at me before setting it on the entry table.

"Thank you," I say.

Drew doesn't respond as he drops his keys and wallet on the same table and walks himself to the kitchen for a glass of water.

"I'm gonna head to bed," Reagan says.

Drew doesn't look at me as he sweeps past me to help Reagan to her feet. He tosses her blanket to the side and guides her to the bedroom with a soft hand on her lower back.

I give them their privacy for a few moments while I move for my phone tucked inside my purse, eager to text Connor.

The battery is dead. Because of course it is. *Dammit.*

I toss my purse and good-for-nothing phone to the far end of the couch as I sit back down, steeling myself for this conversation. The hours since he stormed off and my conversation with Reagan have somewhat tempered my rage, so maybe that's for the best.

Reagan and Drew share a few whispered words before the bedroom door closes and my brother slowly turns to face me.

"I don't wanna do this right now, Gretch."

I rub my lips together and cross my arms over my chest. "We have to talk about it, Drew."

He shakes his head, jaw clenched so I know the anger is still there, but more than anything he looks tired.

"Drew," I whisper, pleading.

He meets my gaze.

"You can't shut me out."

"I would never do that. You're my sister."

"You can't shut Connor out either."

The brother looking back at me isn't the warm, compassionate, ride or die guy I've always known. This man is cold, heartless. Detached. "I don't expect you to understand—"

"Understand what?" I cross the room until there's only a few feet between us. "Betrayal? Hurt? Loss? Bitterness? I understand all of those things."

"You don't get it!" he snaps. "I trusted him."

"You can still trust him, Drew. He's your best friend."

"Not anymore, he isn't."

The finality in his tone, the icy look in his eyes—I search, I scavenge every corner of his expression for any hint of uncertainty. But I find none.

"Don't say things like that," I finally say. I shake my head, willing him to take it back. "I know you're upset. It's been a crazy week...for everybody. Emotions are high and we're all on edge. Don't say things you don't mean."

He scoffs. "He did this to himself, Gretch."

"There is so much you don't know. What happened today was not how it was supposed to go. Please talk to him. He wants to explain everything."

"I know everything I need to know. He lied to my face. He went behind my back. He promised me I could trust him and it's now obvious that I can't. There's nothing else to say."

Tears fall down my cheeks. My brother's accusations land like bullets in my chest. All this time, Connor's fear that Drew would cut him out, I thought he was exaggerating. But he was right.

"And if I tell you I'm in love with him?"

He sucks in a grating breath through his nose, eyes closing like he needs to center himself before he loses it. *Good.* Let's fight.

"Gretchen." My name is a warning. "I'm not doing this right now."

"Well, I am!" My voice amps up as my previously tempered anger bubbles back to the surface.

"Frankly, I don't care what you want. I've been walking the city for ten hours, I'm exhausted and I just want to get in bed with my wife."

If a heart can slump, that's what mine does. Right there behind my sternum, it sags in despair. And I try—I try so hard to extend grace because I know that buried beneath his anger and distrust is a thick layer of grief that I can't begin to comprehend. It's clouding his ability to think clearly. "Fine, but I'm not leaving. I'll stay here and we can talk in the morning."

"I'm not letting you sleep on my couch."

I'm not proud of it, but the need to corner him into compliance is all consuming. "Then I'll go back to Connor's."

His face pales. With every silent second that passes, his defenses fall and I know I've won. "Fine. You sleep with Reagan and I'll take the couch."

"Ew, and sleep on your sex sheets? I'm good, thanks."

He rolls his eyes, grumbling his way to the hall closet. When he returns, he shoves a stack of sheets and blankets into my chest. "There, you get the couch. Happy now?"

"Not particularly." He turns toward his bedroom. "Oh, wait. Can I borrow a phone charger?"

He spends the next ten minutes, begrudgingly, digging through junk drawers in pursuit of a cable compatible with my phone and comes up empty. Before he can slam his bedroom door in my face, I make one more request. "Drew?" He sighs in exasperation, but turns to meet my gaze. "I need you to text Connor and let him know I'm staying here tonight."

He mumbles a curse under his breath. "I'm not texting him."

"Please," I beg, tone serious. "He's expecting me and I don't want him to worry." After several seconds, he still makes no move for his phone. "If you don't, he may show up here looking for me."

With a final murmur of disapproval, he pulls out his phone and types something on his screen before the whooshing sound of a sent message cuts the tension.

"There," he offers.

"Thank you." He doesn't respond as he starts to close his door. "I love you."

Half-shielded in the shadow of the door, he stills. "I love you more," he replies softly before shutting it with a final *click*.

Connor

I watched Gretchen walk away until the last morsel of her silhouette disappeared. When I returned to my office, stomach empty, I was so nauseated I couldn't think about food.

Text after text that I sent to Drew, begging for him to talk to me, went unanswered.

I texted Gretchen several times, too, but backed off when I got Reagan's message that she'd forgotten her phone at the restaurant. She said Drew would pick it up on his way home where Gretchen was waiting for him.

That was hours ago.

The cavernous pit in my stomach has kept me restless all night. I paced the living room like an anxious pet for far too many of those hours. My phone doesn't ring no matter how many times I check to confirmed it's powered on. Ultimately, I end up in bed, holding my breath so that I don't miss the sound of Gretchen walking through the front door.

Because she promised she'd come back.

When my phone pings, it lights up my pitch-black bedroom, I toss the ice pack I had pressed against my jaw and rush to grab it from the nightstand.

> DREW
>
> Gretchen is staying here tonight. I'll be by tomorrow to get her things.

She promised she'd come back.

Gretchen should have her phone by now and I need to hear her say it. Like a lamb led to the slaughter, I type out a message to her that feels like the beginning of the end.

ME

Are we okay?

I wait and I wait, but she never responds.

Chapter Forty-Seven

TALK LESS AND LISTEN MORE

GRETCHEN

Morning comes early, or late when you consider I never fell asleep to begin with. I could blame it on my brother's couch or glass balcony doors that let in too much light, but I know it's the mess of feelings swirling around in my stomach. They're all in there gliding and launching like performers in some sort of synchronized swim routine.

I miss Connor.

I hate that my phone is dead. I hate that I couldn't hack into Drew's computer to send Connor an email. Anything. I was desperate for anything.

I hate that he was alone last night. I hate that he needs me, wants me, loves me, and I'm stuck here trying to neutralize the fallout with my brother.

Is this what love does to a person? Makes you the Stretch Armstrong of middlemen, where your heart pulls you one way, but roots pull you another? Both sides gripping and tugging until you're forced to lean into the weaker side, all while praying that the stronger arm can hold out just a bit longer before it snaps.

My impulsive decision to chase after Drew was for the sake of salvaging our relationship. That's what I told myself, at least. That it was urgent and required my immediate attention. But maybe I was wrong. The longer I stay, the more I feel like I made a mistake in coming here.

Up with the sun, I start a pot of coffee and station myself at the dining table to wait for Drew. It's after seven when the bedroom door opens.

Reagan, dressed in black leggings, an oversized tee and tennis shoes, announces she's going for a walk. Drew's scowl says he hates the idea, to which she replies, "The doctor said it's good for me to move a little bit."

With that, she kisses him on the cheek, throws me a half-smile and walks out the door.

"I made coffee," I say.

"Thanks."

After pouring a cup, he settles into the seat across from me. Steam billows up from his mug as he drags a tired hand down his face.

"Didn't sleep?" I ask.

"Not really."

"Me neither."

"Sorry if the couch was uncomfortable."

"Couch was fine."

His gaze slams into me, so disorienting I have to look away. He's as ready to get this over with as I am.

I spin my mug between my palms. "What did Reagan tell you?"

He crosses his arms and leans back in his chair. "Nothing. She was already asleep when I got into bed last night. And this morning she told me to talk less and listen more." I snort, but the twitch in his cheekbone shows far less amusement. "So, here I am, Gretch. I'm listening."

I lean back, arms crossed over my chest like him. "If you're expecting me to tell you the drawn-out story of how everything happened with Connor, you're not gonna get it. If you want that, you're gonna have to talk to him."

He bristles but stays silent.

"What I can tell you is that Connor and I didn't happen out of thin air in Arizona. There have been things between us in the past that you don't know about." His jaw clenches. "It's not what you think."

"Whatever it was, he kept it from me," he accuses.

"You're right. But so did I. For that, you have to point equal blame at me."

"Why didn't you tell me?"

Before yesterday, I never worried about how he would react to the idea of Connor and me. And yet, I still never told him. Dropping my shoulders, I say, "Honestly, I don't know. At first, I liked the feeling of having a part of him that was just mine. Then, there was some hurt that came later and I just...I didn't know how to process it, so I avoided it."

"He hurt you?" Drew asks, tone cold.

I'm not ashamed of this part of our story, although I know it doesn't do Connor any favors. But I've forgiven him and Drew deserves to know at least that much. Strong eyes steady on his, I answer, "Yes. He did hurt me. But I've forgiven him."

He considers that for a moment. "Did he cheat on Lauren?"

My brows furrow. "What? No! Before my graduation dinner back in May, I hadn't seen or spoken to him since your wedding."

His head tilts, but my lips remain sealed. "Gretch, you can't dangle that in front of me and not expect me to ask questions."

I work my jaw, gaze locked on the cold coffee in front of me. I could tell him. I could tell him everything about what happened on that balcony and the fallout that came after. It'd probably be easier coming from me than it would from his best friend, but Connor doesn't want that. For whatever reason, he needs this conversation and I don't want to take it away from him.

"All you need to know is that I've been in love with him since I was eighteen. The rest of the story you'll have to get from him."

Wood screeches as Drew's chair scrapes across the tile floor. He stomps into the kitchen and spins back to me. "You can't coerce me into talking to him."

"Then do it for me!" I'm up now, matching his defensive posture, braced for more.

"This is what he does. Don't you get it? He's said all the right things, made you feel all lovey-dovey inside so you'd climb into his bed and, guess what, Gretch? He'll spit you out like every woman that came before you."

"We love each other!"

"You think that word means anything coming from him?" My head jolts back like I've just dodged a slap to the face. Disbelief is an electric current—it blazes through me. "He said he loved Lauren, too. Look how that worked out for her. All this proves is that he's exactly the same immature, keg-stand frat boy he was ten years ago."

"I think you mean to say immature, keg-stand frat boys that you *both* were."

Surprise sweeps his face at a claim that he knows he can't deny.

"I changed!" he shouts, slamming a palm to his chest.

"I know!" I snap back. "So did he."

Drew's answering laugh mocks, not an ounce of humor.

"Wow," I breathe out, eyes narrowed on my brother's patronizing face. "You know, if Connor had known that his best friend thought so little of him, I wonder if he'd have bothered being so loyal to you all these years." I shake my head in disappointment. "At every turn, he's been out there defending you, trying to do right by you, all so he wouldn't lose you as a friend and you don't even think twice before airing his lowest moments on a busy sidewalk to a bunch of strangers."

The brief look of chastisement that passes over his features is no match for the anger that he's white knuckling in his fist.

"You don't have to like it, Gretchen, but I did it so you could see who he really is. I did it to protect you."

"You don't get a say in my relationships. I'm an adult capable of making her own decisions!"

"You're my little sister!"

"Two things can be true at once, Drew!"

Only the sound of our ragged breaths fill the air as silence falls. He won't give an inch and there's a whole mile to go. A renewed dose of stubborn indignation washes over me.

"Let me be perfectly clear," I begin, all pretense vanishing. "I came here because you're my brother and I love you. And I'm trying really hard to be patient because I know you've had a shitty week and you probably feel like everything's piled on you at once. I get it. But I'm not here to ask for your permission." He stiffens. "It's *my* choice to make and I've made it. I choose him."

"And if I think it's the wrong choice?" he asks through gritted teeth, tone unforgiving.

I shrug. "Then you have to let me make it." His chin drops to his chest. He rotates in place and rakes a hand over his head and down his face. "You have a choice, too. You can choose to be supportive."

He whirls on me. "No, I can't. I can't sit back, knowing the game that he's playing. I can't let him use you like that to get you in bed!"

"We haven't even had sex!" The words tumble out of me before I can stop them. Drew's face turns a ghostly shade of white and I don't know if it's because his baby sister just used the word *sex* in a sentence or he's genuinely surprised by the statement. "And that is the absolute last thing you will ever hear me say on the subject because it is none of your business."

Finished with this conversation, I grab my purse, phone in hand, and march to the door, leaving my brother aghast and frozen in place in his kitchen. My nerves buzz like tiny gnats crawling on my skin, a combination of disappointment and outrage that I can't shed fast enough.

I turn back before I reach the door. "Did you even hear what I said yesterday?"

His brows drop. "What?"

"Yesterday, before you saw Connor's hand under the table and went ballistic."

Drew expression stumbles a dozen different directions in search of an answer he can't find.

"You asked about the trip and I answered. Did you even hear it?" I repeat, waiting for some sort of realization to dawn on his face.

He shakes his head, a weak concession that provides me no comfort.

"I found my birth parents."

His eyes go wide before they fall closed entirely, throat bobbing. The first true sign of regret I've seen from him and it hurts even worse than I expected it to.

"I found an entire family, Drew. It's a wild story, actually. When you're in a better headspace, I'd love to tell you about them."

I don't give him a chance to answer before I walk out the door. But I don't let the door shut all the way before hollering from the hallway, angry but the words still true, "I love you!"

It's barely eight in the morning when my feet hit the sidewalk outside Drew's building. Lovesick, dressed in yesterday's clothes and in dire need of a toothbrush, I run the three blocks to Connor's apartment hoping I catch him before he leaves for work.

It's not until I pass a storefront bearing a 'Closed for July 4th' sign that I realize it's a holiday. It hadn't even dawned on me. Good, he'll be home.

Except, when I burst through the front door, he's not there.

I call out his name again and again, like the apartment isn't less than nine-hundred square feet. I run between the three rooms, check behind every closed door and then check again. Nothing.

Rushing to the bedside table, I plug my phone into Connor's charger. Too anxious to stand there and wait for my phone to wake up, I jog to the bathroom in search of my toothbrush.

It's gone. All my toiletries that were on the counter, cleared away. Worry slices me anew as I whizz back through the apartment and find what I missed when I rushed inside. My suitcase, packed and at the ready by the front door.

Like hell will I let him give up that easy.

I toss my suitcase back on the bed and yank it open. Warmth washes over me at the care Connor used in packing it. Everything properly folded and in its place like a cathartically satisfying game of Tetris.

Still, it all has to go. I dig out everything I need: stuff for the bathroom, a fresh set of clothes, my glasses.

My phone buzzes on the nightstand and I leap across the bed to grab it.

Twenty-five notifications.

I bypass the texts, missed calls and voicemails from my parents —that conversation will come later.

Five missed calls from Connor. No voicemails. Like me, he knows we can't have this conversation over the phone.

But the text messages. A dozen of them, the first one just minutes after I left him on the sidewalk yesterday.

> **CONNOR**
>
> I'm so sorry.
>
> Did you catch up with Drew? Is everything okay? What can I do?
>
> Please. Tell me what to do!
>
> God! I messed up everything, didn't I?
>
> Gretchen...
>
> Seriously, Drew's not answering me and neither are you. I'm starting to worry.
>
> Reagan texted and said you don't have your phone. Sorry for the first six texts where I sound crazy. Please call me as soon as you get your phone back.
>
> Still no phone?

> I don't know what to do. I feel useless here
> by myself, Fish. Please text me back!

> Are we okay?

And the last two that came through less than forty-five minutes ago.

> CONNOR
> I couldn't sleep without you.

> The part where I said I was in love with you?
> I meant it. You deserved better than for it to
> come out like that. I'm sorry.

Connor

Barely a bruise remains on my jaw. One small mercy from the universe, I suppose.

I couldn't face Drew when he came for Gretchen's suitcase, much less watch her pack her things if she showed up with him.

She hasn't replied to any of my messages. Maybe she needs space, time to think. Maybe she wants to back off until things settle down. Maybe her brother—and her parents—convinced her to end this. Maybe it really is over.

I packed her bag before the sun came up, left it by the front door and bolted. I didn't go to the gym to work out, I just needed somewhere else to be.

Two more texts went unanswered this morning and it was as though the clock finally struck midnight: our time was up.

After the gym, I head into work completely unsure how I'll be able to get anything done today with everything that's on my mind.

It's not until I step off the elevator to an empty office that I realize it's a holiday. The thought literally hadn't crossed my mind once. Fitting, I think, as I stroll through the desolate space that matches the condition of my heart: stretched wide as far as the eye can see, but wholly empty. No pulse. No life coursing through it.

Since I can't go back to my apartment and I'm here anyway, I boot up my computer, toss my phone on the desk and drag my feet to the break room to make a pot of coffee.

Back at my desk, cup of mediocre coffee in hand, I'm typing in my computer password when my phone buzzes.

My heart lifts at the sight of Gretchen's name on my screen.

GRETCHEN

Come home!!!

Chapter Forty-Eight

I'VE LOVED YOU ANYWAY

GRETCHEN

THIS IS where I should have been the whole time. I know it now with perfect clarity. The progression of concern, to panic, to defeat in Connor's messages that led him to pack my suitcase makes it painfully obvious that he was here, struggling...alone.

I should have been here. With him.

Hurriedly, I brush my teeth and put on my glasses, because my eyes are on fire from wearing contacts all night. I throw on a fresh set of clothes—jean shorts and one of Connor's t-shirts because I need to feel him close. I also crank up the thermostat because it's the *mother-effing* tundra in here. Then, I'm pacing, thumbnail buried deep between my teeth.

Ten minutes later, Connor tumbles into the apartment in a rush. Dressed in dark jeans and a light blue collared shirt, he's disheveled, breathless. He looks at me like he's just spotted his oasis in the desert when, in reality, he's mine.

I close every inch between us and throw my arms around him.

He buries his face in my neck, arms wound so tight around my waist I can feel the beat of his racing heart in my own chest.

"I'm sorry," I whisper. "I shouldn't have gone. I should have been here with you."

"Did I lose you?" he croaks, voice tattered.

I yank my head back to look at him, his eyes glassy and blood-shot. Jaw cradled in my palms, I sweep a soft touch over where my brother punched him. "No." I kiss him, his fists clenching into the fabric of the shirt at my back. "You didn't lose me," I get out between the give and take of our lips.

Breathless, we pull back and I bring his forehead down to mine.

"But I messed up everything for you," he chokes out. His tears are so heartbreaking, I can't help but cry, too.

"You didn't. I'll talk to my parents later."

He swallows thickly. "Everything Drew said about—"

"Doesn't matter." I kiss him again.

"But it was all true…"

In a dark room, I could hold a blacklight up to Connor and find streaks and stains, lashes of shame, spanning every inch of him. This man—this *good* man—has borne the guilt of his mistakes in broad daylight for years.

But his past doesn't scare me. *He* doesn't scare me.

"Stop," I command. "What happened back then doesn't matter to me." I've told him this before, but he needs to hear it again. "You can't change your past, but that doesn't mean it gets to define you."

Embarrassment clouds his features as he looks away.

"Look at me, Connor." He meets my gaze. "I know who you are, who you've always been. You're a good man. Now, then, tomorrow—you are good down to your bones. It's what pulled me to you when I was a kid." A tear slides down my cheek. "It's why I fell in love with you at eighteen." Connor takes in a shuddering breath. "And it's why I haven't been able to stop loving you since."

He crushes his mouth against mine, but retreats a moment later. "Baby, *goddammit*, I was supposed to say it first."

I arch a brow. "Well, technically, you did."

Finally, he smiles and the joy that breaks across his face has me throwing myself at him. I jump up and wrap my legs around his waist. He catches me effortlessly, hands squeezing the skin where the hem of my shorts hits the backs of my thighs, and he kisses me again.

Without breaking the kiss, Connor spins us to one of the dining chairs. My legs dangle on either side of his hips as his hands rake over me—up and down my bare legs, gliding up my sides, peeking under the hem of my shirt to touch the skin of my stomach and lower back. At last, one of his hands finds mine and he weaves our fingers together.

He grabs a fistful of hair at my back with a gentle tug and my mouth opens for more of him. We taste, we savor, we devour.

When we've pulled back to catch our breath, I play with the hair at the back of his neck and ask, "Why'd you pack my suitcase?"

"I got your brother's message last night and I never heard from you." He shakes his head, dislodging a memory he'd rather forget. "I didn't wanna be here when he came for your stuff."

Suspicion prickles in my mind. "What did Drew's text say?"

"That you were staying the night there and that he'd be by today to get your things." My jaw drops. "I assumed that meant—"

I hurl myself forward, arms around his neck once more. "Oh my God…That's not…no…" The words get caught at the back of my throat.

I should have been here.

His face in my hands, I let the words spill out. "I swear, Connor, Drew brought my phone back from the restaurant but the battery was dead and he didn't have a charger because my phone's a million years old, but so is yours which is why we can share a charger, which is just another reason why I love you. But he refused to talk to me and I refused to leave until he did talk to me which meant I was sleeping on the couch and I asked him to text you to let you know I was staying the night there so you wouldn't worry. Then I tried to hack into his laptop while he slept so I could email you but I couldn't figure out his password."

He grins and I fumble on some more. "I literally ran here this morning and when you weren't here, I freaked out. I plugged in my phone, found my suitcase by the door and finally saw all your messages right before I texted you back."

A smile fills his whole face as we both begin to laugh and I slap his arm.

My hands land softly on his chest as the humor fades. "I'm sorry Drew said that to you." His mouth tics and then settles. "He's still mad."

He nods, arms tightening around my waist as he whispers, "I know."

"We need to give him time."

The fear of losing his best friend—that he might have already lost him—is a tangible thing on him. Almost like I could reach out and pluck it right off his shirt. If only it were as easy as flicking a piece of lint away.

"I should head back to my parents' house this weekend. I still need to talk to them."

He looks over my shoulder toward the bedroom where my previously impeccably packed suitcase now lays open in utter disarray on his bed. "In that case, you could have left your bag packed."

I shrug. "I had a point to make."

"You want me to come with you?"

"I think," I kiss him softly, "I need to do this on my own."

"I promise I'll be good." He jerks his hands away. "See? No hands."

A laugh bursts out of me.

"Too soon?" Connor jests before he links his arms at my back again, pulling me in for another swift kiss. "When do you leave for your interview?"

Time slows and I let my gaze fall to the gap of space between our bodies. "I fly out Monday." His fingers slide under my shirt. "If I make it to the second round, I'll have to stay through Thursday." His hands run up my sides. "And if I get the job, I should probably stay through next weekend to look for an apartment."

"You're gonna get it, Gretch," he breathes, words landing in a soft puff on my cheek.

Moving to New York means leaving Illinois. It means leaving

my family. It means leaving Connor. We could do the long-distance thing, but to what end? Until I've had my fill of Manhattan? Until we miss each other so much we have no choice but to end things?

"I don't have to take it." His hands freeze on my hips. "I could find something here."

"No," he commands, hands cradling my face to pull my eyes to his. "You're going."

"But what happens to us?"

"I love you too much to let you give this up."

I grab his forearms and hold his stare like a magnifying glass held up to the sun. Embers of fire blaze to life in his blue eyes right before he tilts my entire existence on its axis with his words.

"I don't know when I fell in love with you, Fish. I've tried and tried to figure it out, but I can't. I don't think you *can* fall in love with someone when they already have your heart. The love is just... there." His thumb sweeps across my cheek. "I think I've always loved you. It looked different when we were kids and it didn't mean the same then as it does now, but it was there. It's like one day I looked up and there you were—my favorite person. Somewhere along the way my heart became so tethered to yours I'm not sure it beats apart from you anymore.

"It's why, from the moment you messaged me four years ago, I lost interest in anybody else. It's why, when I saw you at Drew's rehearsal dinner, I knew you were it for me. It's why, when I saw you at that restaurant two months ago, I knew I would never get over you and to even attempt to love another woman would be unfair to them, because I could never possibly love anyone as deeply, as wholly, as I love you.

"I loved you long before I kissed you and every day since. All the days I wasn't supposed to, all the days I shouldn't have—I've loved you anyway."

I kiss him until I can't breathe, squeezing him so tight I want to fold myself into his skin.

"New York is where you want to be. I know it is. It's where you need to be."

I choke back the emotion rising in my chest, my breaths choppy and muffled against his shoulder.

"I'm not going to let you change your plans for me," he adds.

A sob breaks free before I can stop it.

"I would do anything for you, Gretch. Buy you every collector's copy of *Little Women* I can find." I smile through a very unattractive sniff against his neck that I'm sure he felt down to his toes. "Take you to see the wild horses." His hands run up my spine and my body melts under his touch. "Hold you when you cry." My breathing steadies. "Move to New York to be with you."

I jolt back. "Wait, what?"

"I wanna move to New York."

My brain cannot compute these words. "But why?"

He rolls his lips and I swear there's a concealed smile there. "Because I want to be where you are."

I scan his face. "Why?" I ask like a total ignoramus because words are hard right now.

A quizzical smirk hitches up one side of his mouth before he says with a question inflection that is all tease, "For all the reasons I just said?"

Look alive, Gretchen.

I shake my head in an attempt to reorganize my jumbled thoughts before dropping my face into my palms. "Right."

Gently, Connor lowers my hands and folds them in his. "I know it's a lot. You're allowed to ask me to stay if you think it's too fast. We can do long-distance until you're ready, but I need you to understand that I don't want to be apart from you. I can be a graphic designer anywhere, Gretch. Please," he kisses me, "let me do this for you. For us."

"But your whole life is here."

"No, it's not. It's wherever you are."

On a normal day, you could drop a camera into my brain and all you'd find is mushy, muddled, conflicting-thought soup—a slew of nouns, verbs, adjectives, and adverbs strewn together, none of which I can parse into a single eloquent thought.

But right now, my brain is clear, like a windowpane buffed to such perfection you can't discern inside from outside. Only one thought floats through my head, free and unencumbered, at odds with nothing. Because *Connor* is where my head and my heart have always aligned.

"You don't have to decide right now. If you need time to—"

"No," I say over him in a rush. "I mean, yes!" *Stop. Breathe.* I suck in a big gulp of air and order my brain to speak in coherent sentences. "What I mean is…I love you and I don't want to be apart from you either."

He smiles. "I love you, too."

"Are you sure, though?"

Connor cocks his head. "About loving you or moving to New York?"

"Moving."

He pinches the tip of my nose and gives it a wiggle, my glasses shifting with the action. "Easy yes."

Connor's gaze is molten as I fix the frames back into place.

"And loving me?" I preen.

Without hesitation, he says, "Easy yes."

The space between us grows hot with want. I stare at his lips for half a second before he swoops in to kiss me first. There's no easing into it, no gentle touches to test the waters—only open mouths and greedy hands shamelessly seeking and chasing.

His hands are up my shirt, tangled in my hair, then kneading my ass through my shorts. My palms sweep up and down his torso, feeling the hard contours of his muscles underneath. He nips my neck and I grip his biceps for dear life.

"I need more," I breathe out between hurried kisses, unbuttoning the top three buttons of his shirt so I can touch his bare chest.

His hand back under my shirt, I gasp when his thumb sweeps across my nipple over my bra.

"You want my mouth or my fingers, baby?"

Without pause—because it was always going to be him—I pull back and peel the shirt over my head and toss it to the ground. "I want you."

His pupils flare, eyes hooded as they roam over me only to halt on the black lace cups holding my modest breasts. His throat bobs before he meets my gaze. "Are you sure?"

Your first time is supposed to be wrought with nerves and self-doubt. Constant worries over if you're doing it right, if you're pretty enough, or if your partner will want to do it with you again when it's over. But I feel none of those things.

"Easy yes."

Chapter Forty-Nine

EXACTLY THE RIGHT PERSON

CONNOR

I can't count the number of images of Gretchen that live rent-free in my head.

Barefoot and full of joy, running across her backyard at sixteen.

Propped against her headboard, messy bun in place, bundled in an NYU sweatshirt on our first FaceTime call.

That balcony, her silhouette in profile, hair floating on the breeze, smooth skin of her back on full display.

Stunned and stunning, yellow dress and turquoise earrings, sitting across from me at the restaurant two months ago when I realized I would never get over her.

Her sun-kissed face staring back at me through my phone as I snapped our picture on Devil's Bridge.

Content and peaceful, wrapped in the arms of her birth family.

Two days ago in my kitchen, dressed in my clothes and those sexy-as-sin glasses, making fajitas.

Now, this one: Gretchen in nothing but a black lace bra from the waist up. Portions of her nipples exposed, the patchwork material leaves nothing to the imagination, transfixing me on the rise and fall of her chest.

Her smooth, tan skin prickles with goosebumps in the wake of my fingers as I glide softly across her collarbone, then down. The pad of my index finger grazes her nipple and she sucks in a breath, hands gripping my shoulders. Lower now, my eyes follow the path of my hands in rapt fascination as her legs tighten over my hips.

"Connor, please," she pleads, releasing the next button on my shirt.

Sweeping up from the chair, her feet hit the ground as we become a frenzy of tossed clothes and locked lips. She rids me of my shirt and moves to the waistband of my jeans. Our mouths recklessly seek, tongues clash, as we shuffle toward the bedroom. I push her shorts down her legs and she kicks them off the rest of the way. I do the same with my jeans and shoes before wrapping an arm around her waist and launching us to the middle of the bed together. Her opened suitcase crashes to the floor with a *thunk* behind us.

I settle between her legs, every place where her bare skin meets mine like a million tiny lightning strikes startling all my nerve endings awake. Her breast spills out as I pull the lace cup down and take her into my mouth. She moans, head falling back as I do the same on the other side.

Her whimpers, her gasps, her cries—I need more of them.

I snap her bra strap against her shoulder. "Off."

Lifting herself up, she reaches behind her back, works the clasp and throws the bra aside with the confidence of someone that's done this a thousand times before.

Except, she hasn't.

Propped on my knees, tucked between her open thighs, I take Gretchen in as she leans back on her palms, topless and unashamed. Damn if she isn't the most gorgeous thing I've ever seen. "You are so beautiful." Eyes prowling over her once more, I ask, "Are you nervous?"

There's no attempt to hide her body, no hesitation as she drags a hand down my bare chest, tucking one finger inside the waistband of my boxers. "I'm not nervous about you."

I press forward until she's flat on her back again. This time, when my hips find their home between her legs, I rock forward as our lips meet. One hand restraining hers firmly above her head, I run the other over the rest of her—kneading her breast, grabbing the back of her knee to draw her leg higher, every inch of her skin soft as silk beneath my fingers.

"God, you're perfect," I say, grabbing the underwear at her hips as my need to be inside of her grows by the second

"I got tested at my physical last month and I'm good."

Flustered, she says, "Oh, um…I've never been with—"

"I know," I cut her off, hand soft on her cheek. "Birth control?"

She shakes her head and I roll across the mattress toward the nightstand. On my feet next to the bed, I yank her by the legs to the edge and she squeals, beaming a smile that's pure illumination. I'm going to spend the rest of my goddamn life making her smile like that.

I peel her panties off and shuck them aside as she sits up and tugs me by the waist to stand between her legs. She takes me in her hand, running hungry kisses across my stomach as I rip the condom wrapper with my teeth.

She pushes my boxers down and my breaths come in shallow pants as her lips drift lower, closer. "Gretch, if you put your mouth on me, I'm not going to last."

Adorable eyes laced with arrogance look up at me before I nudge her to scoot back. I quickly roll the condom on, position myself against the headboard, and pull her to straddle me so she can set the pace.

I slide my finger through her center and her palm slaps against the headboard, a shallow burst of breath escaping her mouth on a whimper.

"Mmm, you're ready, aren't you?" I rasp.

I shift her hips and my lower half until we're in position. The faintest touch of my length teasing her entrance has her gasping out intoxicating sounds of pleasure—every tether of my restraint wholly focused on not thrusting to the hilt in one fell swoop.

With my hands branding her hips, she lowers herself on to me. My head falls back, jaw shut tight as I force my breaths to steady. She winces before drawing back. "Sshhh. It's okay. Take your time, baby."

Air stalls in her lungs as she does it again. Inch by heavenly inch, her tight heat clamps around me. She lowers, pauses, then lifts a millimeter before lowering again, each time finding a bit more as I inch deeper inside her. We groan in unison as we settle into that deep-seated position when I push another inch upwards.

"Oh my God," she breathes. My hands run up her back, one tangling in her hair while the other grips her shoulder. Her knees on the comforter spread wider, hips sinking lower as I pull her shoulders down to find even more.

She moans into my mouth and I covet every sound. Starved, I worship her breasts as she rocks her hips, grinding against me. I hiss. "Fu—you feel so good, Gretch. I love you so goddamn much."

We find a rhythm that makes my head spin, that tightening in my spine already building. I glance down to where our bodies are joined together, me buried so deep I can't tell where either of us begins.

I throw my head back, eyes blinking at the ceiling, and force out a controlled breath.

She halts her movements, concern splitting her features. "Is something wrong?"

"God, no! I'm just trying to keep this from ending before it even starts."

"Oh." She nervously adjusts her glasses on her nose.

I cup her jaw, bringing our foreheads together. "I need a minute." Her hips shift and I groan. "That feels so good, but please don't do it again."

She snickers and I spend long seconds—an eternity—eyes shut, taking in deep breaths when that sexy voice whispers, "Whatchu doin' there, old man?"

"Just imagining the most unsexy things I can think of."

"I see," she says as she runs her fingers through my hair.

"Staplers," I offer, head leaning into her touch.

She sucks my earlobe between her teeth.

"Spreadsheets."

She drags her lips across my jaw and I fight to steady my racing pulse.

"World hunger," I supply, voice raspy.

Her mouth moves over my cheek until it hovers above me in an unmet kiss. My will to live dies a slow, painful death as she sweeps her tongue over my parted lips.

"Port-a-potties," I croak.

Mouths meeting, she pauses as silent quakes of laughter slowly take over her body. Her shallow huffs of amusement join mine as she kisses me through it.

"I'm grasping at straws here, Fish."

"Mmmm," she croons, trying so hard to be serious. "And port-a-potties were the way to go?"

We both lose it.

My chest bounces with unrestrained laughter as Gretchen throws her head back, giggling wildly, and the sound does something to my heart. The image clicks into place—one I'll never forget. The woman of my dreams in my bed, naked, straddling my hips, me buried inside her to the hilt, and we're laughing. Both of us, laughing with complete abandon over something that definitely should have killed the moment. Yet, it's perfect.

This is perfect.

She brings her lips to mine as her chuckle fades, saying, "I love you."

I push all manners of public restrooms from my brain and kiss her. "I love you, too."

Like a wave sweeping me under, my senses become consumed by her.

I see her hips bracketing my thighs, body perfect and ready for me. The deep brown eyes tucked behind those hot-librarian glasses.

I feel her skin warming under my touch. Long hair, soft and smooth, that slides through my fingers.

Lavender and vanilla fill my lungs as I coast my lips over her neck and collarbone, breathing her in.

I press my thumb to that bundle of nerves between her legs and her voice moaning my name becomes my new favorite sound.

My mouth finds her breast again, tongue flicking over her nipple. No matter where I kiss her, every inch tastes like mine.

Mine. Because she came back and called me hers.

Mine. Because I'm the only man she's ever given herself to.

Mine. Because I plan to keep it that way.

Tentatively, she rolls her hips again and this time I don't stop her. My fingertips dig into the flesh of her thighs to guide her movements. Her slow, staccato breaths come in rhythm with each rock forward.

"Yeah, that's it," I say.

I thrust upward once to meet the sway of her hips. "Yes," she breathes, "more."

Her breast in one hand and the other molded around the curve of her ass, I take control as I move her back and forth, her body fully surrendered to my lead. Picking up the pace, I buck my hips again and her sharp cry pierces the room.

"Tell me this is okay. I need to know I'm not hurting you."

She shakes her head in a rush. "It's okay. It's so good. You feel so good. Please don't stop."

I thrust again and again, groaning and grunting into the hot, shaky breaths filling the space between us.

A mumbled curse escapes me. "Gretch, it's like you were made for me. Every goddamn inch of you is perfect. I swear to God it's never been this good." My hooded gaze finds hers, satisfaction gleaming, a moment before she spreads her knees wider and grinds down into me, hard.

She slaps a palm on the headboard, leveraging her weight, before she does it again. Her chest hovers above me and I suck her nipple between my teeth, kneading the flesh with my hand. She gasps and it's my undoing.

The sounds between us are feral: curses clouded by heavy

breaths, groans parsed with the sounds of skin slapping skin, *I love yous* sung to the rhythmic pulse of the bed frame hitting the wall.

Every bit of my need spurs Gretchen on and I hold nothing back. I tell her how good she feels. I kiss her until she yanks her mouth away for air, and when her cries get louder, I'm right there with her.

Her hair tumbles across her face, falling like a curtain around us. I delicately tuck the strands behind her ear then lean all my weight against the headboard and launch my hips up, harder than I've dared to try thus far.

"Oh God, yes! There!" she cries as she rocks forward to meet my pace, nails digging into my shoulder. Everything's faster, harder now, both of us chasing more.

Heat rushes through me. Like gasoline thrown onto a raging fire, shameless lust breathes new life into this love that's brought us here, leaving me hopelessly, recklessly at her mercy, fully committed to giving her everything—*anything*—she wants.

Our tempo grows frantic as I arch up into her and she matches me point for point, the weight of our bodies pressing into the headboard to maintain this rhythm. Wood rattles and the bed frame shakes as we close in.

Heavy breaths turn to shouts as she pushes in and down seeking more and I dig my heels into the mattress to give it to her, braced for my own release that is so damn close.

Her orgasm takes her and she shatters. Her fragmented moan splits into a million pieces as it fills every inch of this room, this whole apartment. She's a goddamn masterpiece. Stunning and shameless in how she rides out her climax to the very end. Body tense, thighs clenching, she cries out her agreement over and over and I crest right along with her, coming on a loud groan. She writhes, rolling her hips to milk every last drop until we reach the other side together, sated, breathless, and completely spent. Wrecked in the most incredible, life-altering way.

I take her face in my hands and lower her lips to mine. I kiss her with purpose and intensity because no words are good enough.

When I was a kid, well-meaning authority figures waxed poetic about sex being special when you love the other person. Then, I became a hormonal teenage boy and convinced myself that those people only wanted to make me miserable by telling me to wait. Soon enough, sex was just…sex. This thing that feels good in the moment, but can leave you feeling empty when it's over.

But this…

If I had known it could feel like *this* with the right person, I would have waited my entire life for it.

I would have waited *for her.*

"I love you so much," are the only words I manage. They're everything I want to say and not enough all at once.

"I love you, too, old man."

After I dispose of the condom and clean Gretchen up with a warm washcloth, we move to the shower. I don't say anything and neither does she, both of us content to stand and sway in each other's arms as the warm water rains down over us.

We don't talk about the fact that she just lost her virginity. Doing so would minimize what we did to nothing more than a milestone checked off a list, something that's shaped and remembered by the event itself with no regard for the *before and after* of it all.

That doesn't do us justice.

Making love to Gretchen wasn't a milestone. It wasn't a bucket-list item. It was the culmination of a thousand puzzle pieces falling into place, a galaxy of stars in perfect alignment, dislodging a trapped coin in a vending machine to finally hear the *plink* of metal drop into the chamber—all of it adding up to being exactly where you're supposed to be with exactly the right person.

An hour later we're in the kitchen. I'm making another batch of pesto mozzarella grilled cheese sandwiches as Gretchen looks on from her perch on the kitchen counter. Glasses on, her hair is braided over one shoulder. The sleeves of my college sweatshirt are tugged down past her fingertips, knees tucked into her chest, arms wrapped around them, as her fuzzy socked feet rest on the countertop.

I pull out my phone and snap a picture of her.

"Why'd you do that?" she asks.

Someday I want to show our kids that you've always been this beautiful.
"You look hot," is what I say instead.

~

WE SPENT the rest of yesterday tangled up in each other, making love as many times as Gretchen's sore body could handle. Only stopping to nap or eat, we were too consumed with one another to care about watching the fireworks.

Gretchen thrums her fingers on the dining table as she waits for her computer to boot up. I step up beside her and bend low for a kiss.

The selfish part of me wishes I was going with her to talk to her parents, but my brave girl knows her strength and wants to do it on her own, so I put my desire to hold her hand through it aside. Her family deserves this time to themselves to unpack and process everything she's about to tell them.

"Text me before you leave so I know you're on the road," I say with another soft kiss.

"Okay."

"I'll pick you up on Sunday?"

She nods against my lips before sweeping back in. When she angles her body toward me to deepen the kiss, I let her because I'm just that weak around her.

"Don't go to work," she whines with a pout. "Stay here with me."

If she didn't have a pre-interview video-call in ten minutes and I didn't have an important meeting with my boss first thing at the office, I'd stay in a second.

I bop her on the nose. "I have to go to work"—I flick my eyes to her computer screen—"and so do you."

She heaves a dramatic sigh. "Whatever. Fine. Buzzkill."

I swipe my phone and keys from the counter, grab her chin between my fingers, and plant a loud, smacking kiss on her lips. "Beautiful."

Chapter Fifty

SHE'S BEEN WAITING FOR YOU

CONNOR

I KNOW the serpentine curve of the Fishers driveway like the back of my hand. That little bump where the gravel ends and my tires meet the paved concrete as the house draws closer hits like a wave of high school nostalgia.

Tucked back about a hundred yards from the main road, this house always felt like my second home. I've eaten meals here. Me and my teammates used the sprawling front yard for pick-up football games. I've raided their fridge, swam in their pool and bummed their internet. I know where they keep the coffee mugs, the extra towels.

Yet, on this sunny Sunday afternoon, it all feels foreign. I'm not only their son's best friend when I walk through the door; I'm their daughter's boyfriend. The same boyfriend they witnessed having the riot act read to him only a few short days ago.

Gretchen and I have called and texted all weekend. She kept me in the loop about how the conversation went with her family. Drew even made the trip home yesterday to be a part of it. Despite the fact that he won't respond to my messages, he showed up for Gretchen and that's what matters most.

He just needs time.

Her family was, understandably, surprised by her news, but they listened to the whole story with an open mind. Tears were shed, happy and sad. Gretchen showed them the scrapbook along with all the pictures we took. And before Drew headed back to Chicago last night, they all face-timed with Cheyenne, Miguel and the kids.

As I approach the front door, I take in a deep breath.

Should I knock? I haven't knocked since I was fifteen. Things are different now, though. Right? I should knock. Yeah, knocking is good.

When Paul Fisher opens the door, he spears me with a confused look before stepping aside for me to come in. "Can't remember the last time you knocked, son."

I run a nervous hand through the hair under my ball cap. "Yeah, sorry. I wasn't sure if I should—"

"Is that Connor?" Kelly hollers from the kitchen.

"Yeah, it's me!"

She appears in the kitchen doorway, same curious eye as her husband. "Why'd you knock? I thought you were another Jehovah's Witness."

Nervous feet carry me to the kitchen on Paul's heels. Through the window ahead, I spot Gretchen out by the pool. Back to me, she sits on the edge, legs dangling in the water.

With another deep pull of air into my lungs, I turn to her parents. "How are you guys?"

Kelly looks to Paul who lets out a bewildered chortle. "It's been a crazy few days."

Nerves prickle my skin, and I stuff my hands into my pockets, eyes drawn to the expanse of kitchen floor between us. "Yeah, it has."

Now's the time to explain. I practiced what I would say the whole way here, but now I wish I'd prepared index cards or written bullet points on my hand or something.

I still haven't found the words when Paul asks, "So, you met them?" He must read confusion on my face because he clarifies a moment later. "Miguel and Cheyenne?"

"We spoke to them on the phone yesterday. They seem great," Kelly says, weary from the weight of her daughter's heavy news. Heavy but good, if her tired smile is any indication.

"Yeah"—I glance at Gretchen through the window and back to the Fishers—"I did. They're wonderful. All of them."

"Well," Paul sighs, "we're thankful you were there with her."

"Of course," I say.

Silence falls, the elephant in the room stepping out of the shadows. Eyes bounce around, shoes shuffle on the floor, Paul runs a hand down his wife's back and I shift on my feet.

Ready to press on, I clear the thickness from my throat. "Listen, I owe you both an apology for how things went down at the restaurant last week. I didn't want you to find out like that and I'm sorry."

Kelly smiles warmly while Paul bobs his head once in acceptance.

"And the things that Drew said…about me…I need you to know that I'm—"

"You said you love her." Mr. Fisher's stern voice cuts me off.

"Yes, sir. More than anything."

"And you want something real with her?" he adds, his expression softer than his tone, but I don't cower.

"I want everything with her."

I'm serious about his daughter and this is my opportunity to show him that. Paul studies me and I hold his gaze before he turns to his wife. Kelly smiles up at him and they both look back to me. "Then that's all we need to know." He nudges his head toward Gretchen through the window. "She's been waiting for you."

Whether he means today or the past three years or a lifetime, I can't be sure. I suppose it doesn't matter, because they're all true. But one thing I'm certain of is that she'll never wait for me again.

Outside, I plop down next to Gretchen and drop my legs in the water beside hers.

"You made it," she beams at me.

Flipping my hat around, I lean in and give her a chaste kiss.

"I'm here," I say as I pull back, chin dropped, and give her a wink. "You remember the last time we were here, Fish?"

"You mean that summer you ignored me until I forced you to talk? Yeah. You're welcome, by the way," she says, tone dry, eyes rolling.

"In my defense, no one warned me I'd be coming home from college to an underage smoke show. I was trying to make it to my first real job without a criminal record. So, *you*," I kiss her, "are welcome, milady."

"Well, look at us now," she declares loudly to nobody at all, arms splayed wide. "We're young—well, I'm still young, you're old—and in love."

I throw an arm around her shoulder and haul her closer as she pulls my lips to hers. I oblige, but only for a moment. "Keep it PG, Fish. Your parents are inside."

Chuckling, she jumps to her feet, splattering water on my shorts in the process. "Let's get back to your place, then."

"I HAVE something I want to run by you," I say, fingers twirling through Gretchen's hair as she lays sprawled out beside me in bed.

She grabs her glasses from the nightstand and turns her naked body toward me, blanket tucked under her chin. "Okay."

"My boss asked me to lead this big project at work. It's kind of a big deal and it would look really good on a resume. But I'd have to stay here through November."

Her face gives nothing away, but the leg she squeezes between my calves and the hand reaching for my waist tells me she needs to be close.

"And you want to do it?"

The only thing I want is to be with her, but this is a big opportunity that could open even bigger doors for me in New York. "I'm not sure *want* is the right word."

"You think you *should* do it, then?"

Hair coiled around my finger, I wrestle with my hesitation. "You know Lauren's dad is my boss?"

"Yeah," she says, not a bit of worry or concern at the mention of my ex-girlfriend.

"I've worked for him for seven years and he's been really good to me. I don't know, a part of me feels like it's the right thing to do before I give him my notice."

She cradles my cheek, thumb sweeping in slow strokes. "But…"

"But I don't want to be away from you that long. I don't need to do it to get a good job in New York." I pull her in for a kiss. "And I don't want you to think I'd be saying yes out of some misplaced loyalty to my ex-girlfriend's dad when *you* are the most important thing in the world to me."

Ever since Mr. Driskill extended the offer, I've been weighing the pros and cons, intentionally trying to tip the scales in both directions to determine the best course of action. What I've come up with is there's no right answer, but there's also not a wrong answer.

"Careful, QB, my over-thinking is rubbing off on you," she says with a smile.

I shift down the mattress and level my eyes with hers. "What do you think I should do?"

"I think," she kisses me softly, "I'm yours, whether you move to New York next week, or four months from now." *Another kiss.* "And I think I already fell in love with you once over a year's worth of phone calls and texts." *Another kiss.* "I have no doubt, it'll be enough to sustain us for a few months. And," *kiss,* "I trust you," *kiss,* "and I think you should do it."

I blink slowly as my hand settles on the dip of her waist. "Are you sure?"

"Your loyalty is not misplaced. It's honorable and I don't fault you for it. You and me? We'll be fine."

Rolling on top of her, I settle between her legs, kissing her fiercely. As much as I needed to hear those words, now I need to touch them, to feel them.

When I make love to her this time, we don't need words. Our bodies talk and sing in harmony all on their own. My heart in rhythm with hers as I rock into her, there's no rush to the finish line. Many lazy, savoring minutes later, I inhale the satisfied cries of her climax, with a single "I love you" whispered against her lips.

THE NEXT MORNING, I drop Gretchen off at the airport on my way to work.

I opted for full transparency when I got to the office and told Mr. Driskill I'm excited to accept the team lead position but that once the project is over I'll be moving to New York. Thankful that I've given him four months notice of my departure, we shake hands and it's done.

That night, instead of texting Drew again—because that's gotten me nowhere—I text Reagan.

ME

Can you at least confirm he's alive and breathing?

REAGAN

Roger that. Confirmed. He needs more time.

TUESDAY COMES and Gretchen calls me after her first-round interview to tell me it went well. Encouraged by the good feedback she received and the glowing review Monica, her old boss, had put in on her behalf, she decided she was finally ready to start apartment hunting, but only online because she didn't want to jinx it.

Naturally, I started doing my own research and forwarded at least a half-dozen listings to her. Many didn't include pictures, which I found odd, but New York is foreign to me so I looked past it.

GRETCHEN

Oh sweet boy. It's really cute of you to think I'm going anywhere near the shoebox apartments in my price range in New York.

> **ME**
> This one says it's a studio with a street view and a walk-in closet.

GRETCHEN
Does it say square footage?

> **ME**
> No.

GRETCHEN
That's because it IS a walk-in closet.

> **ME**
> Are you sure?

GRETCHEN
Welcome to New York living.

> **ME**
> Do tell, oh wise one, how you plan to work in New York and not live there.

GRETCHEN
Jersey baby! It's where all the youths are living.

Don't worry. I'll get you grandfathered in, old man.

WEDNESDAY MORNING, Gretchen gets word that she's been invited back for the second round of interviews on Thursday and we make plans to meet in New York on Friday afternoon.

One, because I'm a lost puppy without her and I'm not ashamed to admit I miss the hell out of her.

Two, so I can accompany her on Friday and Saturday on her *tour-des-apartments* before we both fly back to Chicago late Sunday afternoon.

By the time we tuck ourselves into bed over FaceTime, I've

booked my flight and we have a list of scheduled apartment viewings lined up.

"I think I need to see at least one of these shoebox apartments in New York for myself." I arch a brow and she giggles.

Gretchen's head rests on her hotel pillow, one hand tucked underneath. "I'll add one to the schedule, if you insist. Don't forget your magnifying glass."

THURSDAY ARRIVES and I'm buried in work all day. I arrive an hour early, stay through lunch and leave an hour and a half after everyone else to try and make up for the fact that I'll be out of the office again tomorrow.

Gretchen called as I was leaving the conference room and it was the brightest part of my day. She said the interview went really well and it's the first genuine excitement I've heard from her through the interview process, as though she's finally recognized what I've known all along. This job will be hers.

It's well after seven when I get home. With Gretchen out to dinner with Monica and out of touch for a while, I use the time to pack my carry-on before thinking about what to order for dinner.

As I dig through my drawer of take-out menus, there's a knock on my door. I'm not expecting anyone, but I move to answer it without much thought.

I swing the door open and blink twice, body frozen in place.
Drew.

Tense arms braced over his chest, he stands in my hallway, every muscle taut as though merely knocking was a battle. He pins me with a suspicious glare before he slides his hands into his pockets. "One drink."

Chapter Fifty-One

I'M SORRY

CONNOR

> Your brother showed up. We're going out for a drink.

THE BARTENDER SETS two beer bottles in front of us, beads of condensation slinking to the wooden bar top. The murmured sounds of the few patrons scattered throughout the establishment are barely enough to cover up the sound from the television behind the bar.

Drew hasn't spoken a word since we sat down. As unsettling as that is, I know this conversation has to begin with me.

"I'm sorry you found out like that."

He pushes the beer down his throat with a click of his tongue, but doesn't respond.

"I wanted to tell you myself, I swear. I was planning on—"

"Well, here I am, Vining," he interrupts. "So, start talking."

I give myself one breath and one swig of beer before I dive in.

"I'm in love with her, Drew. And it didn't happen overnight or on a four-day trip to Arizona. It happened a long time ago."

His lips twist, nostrils flared. "Start there," he says before he takes another pull from his bottle.

"That summer after we graduated college—"

"Dammit to hell," he mumbles, leveling me with a look.

"Everything I said to you in your kitchen was true. I didn't lie to you. I cared about her and promised to always look out for her."

"I saw it," he accuses. "I caught you looking at her and you promised me it was nothing."

"It *was* nothing, Drew. Nothing happened between us then." I scan my best friend's face and then the woodgrain of the bar.

"I warned you—*all* of you—back then that she was off-limits."

"I know. And I heard you. It's why I kept my distance after that."

Silence settles as we tip back our beers.

"Then what?" he asks.

"Then," I sigh, "Gretchen turned eighteen. Your parents lifted the social media ban and she sent me a DM on Instagram." I shrug. "We were friends. That's how it started, at least. We were talking…a lot, and somewhere along the way it started to feel like more. We talked for a year, Drew." I turn my head to meet his gaze. "I didn't see anybody else that whole time."

His expression is unflinching and entirely unreadable. "Why didn't you say anything?"

I shake my head in thought or…avoidance, maybe. "I don't have a good excuse. You were living with Reagan, in your last year of law school, planning your wedding, we weren't seeing each other as much and I…I wasn't certain she was even interested. I don't know, maybe I convinced myself there wasn't anything to tell." I take a drink. "I mean, I knew I was in love with her, but I didn't know how she felt.

"I was planning to talk to her at your wedding, see if she had any of those same feelings for me before I talked to you about it, but I—"

397

"She said you hurt her," Drew supplies, unmistakable protectiveness in his tone.

Guilt presses in, but then I remember Gretchen's face, her repeated affirmations of love and forgiveness. I can do this. I can confess this painful piece to him.

"At your rehearsal dinner you said some things to me," I say and remembrance immediately flashes across Drew's face, "and I'm not blaming you for my mistakes because that's on me. No matter what you thought of me, I had the opportunity to prove you wrong or prove you right and...I made the wrong choice."

"You invited that bartender." His voice lands lethal and quiet.

I close my eyes and that's confirmation enough. "Did *you* know she was Gretchen's friend from high school?"

Drew gives me a look of pure horror. "What the hell?"

"I didn't know either."

Drew listens in riveted interest—or disgust—as I parlay the details of Alexis' connection to Gretchen, the bad blood between them, how her former best friend used me to make Gretchen jealous, how I was unaware of all of this until it was too late and how terribly my actions hurt his sister.

"After I sent Alexis home, I went to find Gretchen to apologize and try to explain." I pause, running a hand down my face. "I kissed her."

Drew bristles, his hand fisted around his beer bottle so hard it could shatter.

"Then I stopped it," I continue. "Because I felt guilty. I hadn't talked to you yet and what you'd said the night before kept ringing in my head and I felt like no matter what choice I made, it was the wrong one." I take another swig. "I walked away. I loved her and I walked away from her and it's the biggest regret of my life."

My phone buzzes on the bar. Thankful for the interruption, I flip it over to see Gretchen's response to the text I sent her before Drew and I left my apartment.

GRETCHEN

No matter what happens, I love you.

I turn the phone back face down on the bar, not caring if Drew saw any of it over my shoulder. Part of me wants to wave it in his face and say *"see, we love each other."* But as far as he's concerned, I loved somebody else two months ago. Even though I've tried to explain that it wasn't the same, it does nothing to make the love I claim to have for his sister seem any different.

If he saw Gretchen's message on my screen, he doesn't mention it. Instead, he prods the conversation forward. "And after the wedding?"

The heart in my chest feels like it weighs a thousand pounds. "I lost myself. I wanted to make things right with her, but I was too ashamed. The guilt fed the shame and the shame fed the guilt and…you saw me, man. I know it was bad."

"Yeah, I saw you," he starts, and I turn to look at him, his eyes stern but softer than they were before. "But you never told me why."

"I know," I say, voice hoarse. "I messed everything up and lost Gretchen. I couldn't stand the thought of losing you, too.

"All those times you saved my ass, I know I disappointed you and I knew if I told you the truth there was a strong possibility you'd never talk to me again. My behavior was disgusting and I hated myself. It's why I agreed to go out with Lauren, which was an awful way of dealing with the situation, but I just wanted to do something that you wouldn't hate me for. I think I thought if I could stop disappointing you then maybe I'd feel better about myself."

Because that's what it all really boiled down to in the end—and what Gretchen helped me see—I valued my best friend's opinion of me more than Gretchen's. More than my own.

"I was too much of a coward to confront the truth of it all back then. I'm sorry."

I suck in a deep breath like it's the first bit of oxygen my lungs have received in days.

"When you invited us to Gretchen's graduation dinner, I honestly thought enough time had passed but…I was wrong. All the shame and guilt came right back the second I saw her. Realizing I wasn't over her just made it worse."

Drew downs the last half of his beer without coming up for air.

"I never meant to fall in love with your sister, but I did." I level my eyes at him, sincere and intentional. "I can't un-love the only girl that has ever made complete sense to me."

It's several brutally silent seconds before Drew finally looks away, dragging a hand over his jaw.

"She said you're going to New York tomorrow to help her find an apartment."

"I'm moving there, Drew." He swivels his attention back to me. "To be with her."

The old me would avoid Drew's scrutinizing gaze, but the new me stands my ground. It's only by the mercy of the bartender's interruption that we break our stare.

We both wave off another round before Drew clears his throat and says, "All that stuff outside the restaurant...I shouldn't have done that. I was upset and...dealing with a lot." He swallows and a flicker of grief flashes in his eyes. "I was caught off guard but that's no excuse for the things I said. I was out of line and I'm sorry."

I only nod in response because the emotion taking hold in my chest threatens to spill out in dramatic fashion if I do much more. It feels like we're close. So close.

He looks at me, gaze steady. "You know I love you, right?"

I smile softly at his words because I really needed to hear them. "Yeah, man. I love you, too."

"Maybe we could get a do-over," he adds, voice quiet. "Pretend it's the day before my wedding and you have something really important you wanna say to me."

I angle my body on the barstool to face him. One elbow braced on the bar, I place a hand over my mouth and assess the intentions behind his offer.

He just baited me with the opportunity to set things right and I don't intend to waste it. "Drew, there's something I need to talk to you about."

"Bro, I'm getting married tomorrow. Can it wait?"

I snicker before saying, "No. It's really important."

He turns to face me. "Ok, then. Shoot."

I take in a deep breath.

He mutters a curse under his breath, stifling an eye roll. "Such a drama queen, Vining. Get to the point already."

My chin falls to my chest and I fight a smile. When I look back up, my best friend pins me with a self-assured grin that says he's enjoying this way too much. "Fine," I concede. "I'm in love with your sister and I want to—"

"You bastard," he says flatly, completely deadpan.

I hit him with an exasperated glare and continue as though he said nothing at all. "I want to ask her out."

"She's too young for you," he says.

"She's an adult," I volley.

"You're a man-whore," he volleys back.

"Takes one to know one."

"I changed."

"So have I."

"She's my sister."

"She's the love of my life."

Eyes narrowed, he pins his arms over his chest. "And if I say no? If I say choosing her means you'll lose me as a friend?"

"If Reagan were my sister and I made you choose, what would you say?"

He makes an egregious buzzer sound like we're on an episode of Family Feud. "No cheating. I asked you first."

I point a critical finger at him, only half serious when I say, "Cheating or exposing a double standard?"

He squints again. I arch a brow. There's a playfulness to our banter, but the serious undertone remains.

"Ask me again," I say.

"Me or her, Vining?"

"I choose her."

"Good answer," he says before holding up two fingers to the bartender.

We sit in contented silence, gazes fixed on the television mounted behind the bar airing the latest Cubs game.

When our second round of drinks arrive, he brings the bottle to his lips, but stops at the last second. He sweeps one menacing sidelong glance my way as he says, "If you hurt her again, I'll kill you."

This time, when he asks for my word, it's a promise to never break Gretchen's heart, to always make her happy. I offer the blood brother oath, but he insists that a handshake will do.

Also, I'm to never, under any circumstances—come hell, high water or act of God—talk to him about our sex life.

Chapter Fifty-Two

FOREVER AND THEN SOME

GRETCHEN

"You need a building with a doorman," Drew demands.

"Doormen come with a price tag," I retort, phone to my ear. Not even a thousand miles distance can keep my brother from his meddling tendencies. I roll my pointed eyes at Connor who snickers at the one-sided conversation he's privy to. He pulls me against him and plants a kiss on my forehead.

"Small price to pay for your safety, Gretch," my brother adds.

"I'm safe, Drew."

"A young woman living alone in New York City is not safe." There's a scuffle over the line. "Ow, shit! Babe, that hurt."

Reagan coming in clutch, as always.

"Okay, first of all, I hope there's blood. Second of all, I told you I'll probably end up living in Jersey."

"Potato, puh-tah-to," he singsongs, brushing me off. "You also need to live close to public transit."

"Oh, so the subway *is* safe now," I reply, sarcasm thick.

"Lesser of two evils, Gretch. I'd rather you be on the subway or a bus instead of walking the streets alo—you know what, put your boyfriend on the phone!"

I snort and hand the phone to Connor. "The helicopter wants to talk to you."

Noting the buildings that flank either side of the Greenwich Village street, I scan the awnings for the number we're looking for. A necessary distraction from the fact that it's almost five and I still haven't heard about the job. The interview committee said they would get back with all the applicants before the end of the day.

The late-afternoon sun drops behind the multi-leveled structures, casting shadows on the sidewalks below, and the flurry of people on their commute home from their offices creates a hum of weekend-expectant energy buzzing through the streets.

Brick exteriors rise four—some five and six—stories high in this neighborhood, with metal terraces cascading up to the rooftops and fire escape ladders that connect them all one to the other.

Connor insisted I look at apartment options in Manhattan for comparison so I mapped out a few for us to tour today. There are some affordable options that I could make work here and the commute to Saks would be a breeze, but I already know I'll get so much more apartment for my money in Jersey.

He'll see the same value when we go there tomorrow. I know he will.

"I know," Connor says. What my brother has him agreeing to, I have no idea. "Yeah, I know…uh huh…okay." He flashes his signature smile at me, all charm and affection, that says in equal parts *can you believe this guy?* and *how can you not love him?* A smile that beams even brighter now that Drew has come to terms with our relationship.

I bring us to a halt outside our last stop of the day with a hand to Connor's forearm. "I hear ya," he says into the phone.

Done with this nonsense, I yank the phone from his hand and take matters into my own hands. "Ok, got it, all good here, time to cut the cord, loveyoubye."

The third-floor apartment is decent enough. When the landlord steps into the hall to take a phone call, Connor smoothly asks what I think. He huffs a laugh at my noncommittal shrug. Three Manhattan apartment tours in and I've given the same response every time.

Apartment hunting in New York is a game of weighing price against location against square footage against amenities against storage against commute. When you're on a tight budget, there's unlikely to be one place that checks all your boxes and apartments get swooped up in the blink of an eye. There's no "let me think about it and I'll get back to you." It's cutthroat and competitive and you have to be ready to say yes when you come across a place that works.

"Do you like this one?" I ask. "You'll have to look for your own place soon, too, you know."

He hums thoughtfully but doesn't answer.

After I politely pass on the apartment, Connor and I start the trek back to the hotel. Hand in hand on a bustling sidewalk in midtown, we're only a few blocks out when my phone rings.

Butterflies take flight in my stomach. I almost drop the phone as I yank it from my back pocket in a panic, but Connor steadies me. "You got this."

I could get lost in the pure confidence and love in his eyes. This man has always been my biggest cheerleader. No matter what news I get, I know he'll wrap me in a hug, kiss me senseless and tell me he's proud of me.

"Hello?" I say.

For the next sixty seconds, I listen to the woman on the other end of the line. I offer the occasional affirmative response, but my gaze holds on Connor.

He grins.

I bite my lip.

His eyebrows soar.

I smile.

He smiles bigger.

I nod.

He throws a fist in the air then dips down to meet my eye and mouths, *"I told you."*

~

THE NEXT MORNING, I show Connor the joys of the hallmark New Yorker breakfast: a lox and cream cheese bagel on the go. We split the monstrosity between us wrapped in brown paper, passing it back and forth on our way to the subway station.

With the hotel only a couple of blocks from Saks, this is the perfect opportunity for us to get a sense of the exact commute I'll have to make when I start work in a couple of weeks.

Executive Assistant to the buyer for the shoe department at Saks Fifth Avenue. *Wild.*

We take the ten-minute ride to the stop at 33rd where we get off and switch to the Jersey bound PATH train. When we arrive at the station in Hoboken twenty minutes later, it's another ten minutes by foot to the area where we've scheduled tours in three different apartment complexes.

"See. It isn't so bad," I say as we step onto the sidewalk in Hoboken.

"Forty minutes is not a short commute," he chuckles.

"Maybe so, but it is easy." That wicked side eye teases me. "Just wait until you see the apartments."

We tour the first two complexes and I could easily say yes to at least one of the units I see. It's risky to keep looking, but the last building is the one I'm most excited about. And if Connor's increasing interest is any indication, I think these accommodation options this side of the Hudson might win him over after all.

Here, there's space to breathe, windows with views of the Manhattan skyline, washers and dryers *inside* the apartment, and the city's only a train ride away. The best part? When the sun goes down and the skyscrapers across the river come to life with light reflecting off the water, New Jersey is quieter, calmer. I prefer to slow down and embrace the stillness at the end of my day and it feels like I can find that here.

After a quick lunch stop, we head to the final complex.

The first apartment is a bust; first floor unit and no view. But the second apartment is perfect.

Up on the fourth floor—accessible by elevator, thank God—it has a small terrace that overlooks the complex courtyard below and it's close enough to the river-facing end of the building that I have a partial view of the Manhattan skyline. It's a studio, but there's enough square footage to create a separate living and sleeping space. And the bathroom has a vanity style sink with counter space and storage.

"I think this one will go quickly. We contracted another lease for this exact unit on the opposite side this morning," the leasing manager says as I scan the crown moldings on the ten-foot ceilings and the hardwood floors that look brand-new.

I give Connor a hesitant smile and his mirrored expression tells me he knows what I'm about to say. "I'll take—"

"You said you had some one-bedroom units available?" Connor speaks over me, directly to the agent and I spin to glare at him, but he avoids my dagger-hurling eyeballs entirely.

"We do. A couple floors up we have a corner unit. It's beautiful. Would you like to see it?"

Quickly, I sputter, "No, I don't thi—" Connor covers my mouth with his hand. I flare my eyes at him but he ignores that, too.

"Yes, that'd be great. Thanks," Connor answers.

Hot on the agent's heels, I'm tempted to elbow Connor in the ribs, but I refrain. The one-bedroom units in this building would overextend me financially. I know I'll love this gargantuan, river-facing apartment with the unobstructed view and end up disappointed that I can't afford it.

Connor leans down as we step off the elevator to trail the agent down the hall. "Relax, Fish. We're just looking."

I tug him by the arm and whisper back, "These units are fifteen hundred dollars more per month, Connor. I can't afford it."

He winks and pins me with a smile that could melt metal. Next thing I know, he ushers me inside the most perfect apartment to ever exist.

As expected, it's spectacular.

All open concept, the kitchen has a small island with countertop seating that separates it from the living space. A small space off to the right is perfect for a small dining table. But it's the bedroom that has my jaw on the floor. It's not over-sized, but big enough for a king-sized bed, two nightstands on either side and maybe a dresser along the far wall.

Two closets. I repeat: two closets.

The bathroom, twice the size as the studio unit downstairs, has a second access door that opens to the living room.

And the view—*my God*. The sliding glass door off the kitchen leads to a balcony big enough for a small patio set. The sweeping Manhattan skyline looks more like the work of an artist on a panoramic canvas than something you could actually experience in real life.

"Wow," I breathe…to nobody, apparently, because when I turn, Connor's not there. Rather, he's back inside in what looks to be a serious conversation with the agent.

I step back inside as the agent says, "I'll give you two a minute." Then she's out the door into the hallway.

Connor's giddy expression, while full of all his usual endearing magnetism, lacks a single foothold in *my* reality. His stubborn ass knows exactly what I'm thinking which is why he hikes his eyebrows three times. I can't help but laugh and drop my face to my hands. "Connor!"

"Pretty great, right?"

"Of course it is." The view beyond the balcony beckons my attention yet again. "It's amazing, but I can't afford it."

His face turns serious as he pushes a hand inside his pocket. "I have a proposal for you to consider."

He holds out his other hand to urge me closer and I panic. "I swear to God, Connor, if this proposal involves a velvet box, I'll never forgive you."

"Propose? Psssh," he scoffs. "I barely know you, woman." An arrogant smirk curls his lips because we both know that's a lie—he knows me better than anyone else.

Crisis averted, though, on the velvet box. He's just a man with his hand in his pocket.

"I'd prefer to date a woman more than seventeen seconds before I ask her to marry me."

"Glad we're on the same page, old man."

"Good. Now, my proposal."

I raise a hand. "Unless you're about to tell me that I won the lottery, there's absolutely no way I can afford this apartment."

"I know you can't," he says, eyes soft on mine with a sparkle of anticipation that has my heart rate barreling. "But *we* could."

I blink once, twice, twelve times.

"Together, Fish, we can afford this apartment."

"You want to live together?"

He tucks a strand of hair behind my ear. "I do, but only if you want that, too."

"But we've only been dating for seventeen seconds."

He laughs. "Yes, and somehow I still know you better than you know yourself."

He steps closer. I should say something, but the analysis paralysis has me in its firm grip.

"Like right now, you're wondering if it's too fast."

Accurate.

"And to that, I'd say, I've loved you for so long that the idea of building a home with you feels more like *it's about damn time*."

He kisses me.

"You've also never lived on your own and you're wondering if that's something you should do first."

Accurate.

"And I'd tell you that I would never take that experience away from you if that's what you want. I'll get my own place across the hall, down-stairs, two blocks over, doesn't matter to me. But full disclosure, I spent four nights apart from you this week and hated every single one, so if we're not living together, you better be prepared for a lot of sleepovers."

I grin as his lips sweep mine in a chaste kiss.

"And," he continues, "you're scared about what would happen if we break up."

I hate that this intrusive thought exists at all. I can shout from the rooftops that I love him, that he's the only man I want, that I choose him for better or worse, but life isn't a fairytale. Even the best laid plans, laid out by the most well-intentioned people, can fail.

"In case I haven't been clear," he says, "all the big future plans that couples are supposed to make, I want all of that with you. It may be too soon to propose marriage, but I do plan to marry you one day. And have babies with you. And adopt babies with you. And all the in-between days, however mundane or exciting they may be, I only want them with you. Even the hardest days, Gretch." He clasps our hands and swings them loosely in the space between our hips. "But if that's not the future that you see for us, I'm gonna need you to tell me now."

Like a machete against tissue paper, my worries are thin and defenseless against the strength of my feelings for him.

I hate not falling asleep next to him.

I want to call him my husband someday.

I want a life with him, full to the brim with love, laughter and babies.

I ease forward a step, swallowing the last few inches between us. "So, you're thinking forever then?"

He smiles. "I want forever with you *now* like I wanted forever with you *then*. Forever and then some."

"People are gonna think we're moving too fast."

"I'm done caring what other people think. I only care what you think."

I squint and twist my lips to the side, the air of a woman in deep consideration. The corner of his mouth lifts as he kisses my knuckles, eyes pure smolder. Manipulation by flirtation. I'll allow it.

"We need to revisit the terms of our thermostat agreement." Stepping back, I clasp my hands behind me and paste on my best negotiation face.

Connor crosses his arms and widens his stance. "Proceed."

I fight a smile. "You're not gonna like it."

"Try me," he says with a mischievous wink.

"I want full control of the temperat—"

"Done."

Our smiles are embarrassingly goofy as I launch myself against his chest and throw my arms around his neck.

"Is that a yes?" he laughs.

The agent raps her knuckles on the front door on her way back inside. "Checking in. Did either of you have any questions?"

I plant a loud kiss on his lips before spinning on the agent. "We'll take it."

Chapter Fifty-Three

YOU STARTED IT

GRETCHEN

"'SINCE U BEEN GONE,'" Connor and I whisper-shout in unison across the table at Drew.

It's my last night in Illinois before my dad, Connor and I drive the small U-haul to New Jersey tomorrow. Drew and Reagan invited us out for a double-date to celebrate and, lucky for them, we walked right into a *Pitch Perfect* themed trivia night at the bar.

"You guys are freaking me out," my brother says as he jots our response on the team answer sheet.

"For a man who's seen the movie, it's shocking how little you know about it," I counter.

"Next question," the announcer says from the stage. "Finish this line: 'I'm gonna kill him. I'm gonna finish him...'"

Connor and I simultaneously cover the corners of our mouths, lean toward Drew and whisper, "Like a cheesecake."

He guffaws, but writes the answer down. *You're welcome.* "God-damn, you guys are made for each other."

"I know," Reagan croons. "It's nauseatingly cute."

"Or just nauseating," my brother says, a smile tucked behind that amused scowl.

Connor grabs me by the face and kisses me, all show and no real action. But if the goal is to nauseate his best friend, mission accomplished.

He's tried very hard to keep public displays of affection around my brother to a minimum—out of respect, he says. Maybe it was Drew witnessing firsthand how genuine our feelings are, or maybe it's the time and space Connor's given him to accept and process everything, but things between them are on the mend.

When we told my brother of our plans to move in together, for a moment, we thought he stopped breathing. The next day he called me to talk about it and I braced myself for an argument. Instead, he said, "I just want you to be happy, Gretch." Then, he spiraled into a diatribe about how it's better that I won't be living alone.

I couldn't take the big brother out of that man if I tried.

Case in point: "Get your fucking tongue out of my sister's throat, Vining."

I tear my lips from Connor's, clutching my pearls as I whirl toward Drew. "Andrew Augustus Fisher! Language, young sir."

If a time-stopping record scratch happened in real life, this is the moment.

Drew swivels his head, eyes wide and homicidal. Reagan presses a closed fist against her lips as her gaze bounces back and forth between me and her husband. Connor opens his mouth in the most frat-boy *oh shit* look I've ever seen.

"Did you just middle name me?" Drew asks, words low and slow.

"Dude," Connor laughs. "Your middle name is Augustus? Fifteen years of friendship, how did I not know this?"

"Maybe," Drew says, glowering at me, "it's because I don't like it."

"Sorry, man. That's rough."

Drew turns his prickly attitude on Connor, who is not the least bit sorry. Reagan is Switzerland on my right: give the woman some popcorn and a free pass to bow out of the conflict and she'll sit back and enjoy the show.

"It's a family name," my brother defends, like that makes it any cooler.

Connor tips his beer bottle. "It's also the name of the chubby mouse in Cinderella."

"Awww, Gus Gus," I coo.

Drew blinks.

Connor takes a long swig, another insult locked and loaded behind those eyes. "And the kid who falls in the chocolate river at Willy Wonka's chocolate factory."

I slap a hand over my mouth.

"Don't worry, bro." Connor claps Drew on the shoulder. "Your secret's safe with me."

Reagan finally cuts in. "We're gonna need another round."

We win trivia night thanks to Connor's and my clutch efforts in the tie-breaking lightning round.

After the middle-name debacle, Drew drowned his sorrows in one too many drinks. We didn't let him cross the line into full inebriation, but tipsy Drew is a fun time.

On our way home, the four of us stop outside Drew and Reagan's building first.

"Sisssster," my brother slurs as he pulls me in for a bear hug. "I'm gonna miss you."

"I'm gonna miss you too, brother."

We step back and I keep my hands at his waist to steady his swaying feet. "I'm sssorry I wasajerk before."

"I'm sorry I middle named you."

He grins. "No, you're not."

"You're right, I'm not."

"But, no," he pinches his brows like he's fighting a headache, "Msorry I was a jerk bout Connor. I actually think he's the besss…t. I love tha guy."

I flick my eyes to Connor over Drew's shoulder. The boyish grin on his face tells me he's heard every word.

"I love you, big brother."

"I love you more."

~

THREE DAYS LATER, on a sweltering New Jersey Sunday morning, Connor and I say goodbye to my dad who begins the long drive back to Illinois with the U-haul.

The storage trailer was about the smallest one you can reserve. I only needed enough space for a few boxes, clothes and the handful of furniture items from Connor's place that will take up permanent residence here. Things like his couch, coffee table, entertainment cabinet, living room television and dining room table, which we've developed a deep sentimental attachment to—for eating…food, obviously.

I'll spend these next few months while he's back in Chicago, turning this place into a home. *Our home.*

Tomorrow is my first day at work and Connor catches an early flight back to Chicago for his first day as the marketing and media team leader on the Governor of Illinois' re-election campaign.

We spend the day tying up loose ends. I put my clothes away while Connor unloads all the groceries we ordered. I unpack the bathroom while he puts away the split amount of his dishes and cookware he brought from his place—he left some behind in Chicago to survive on until he's here permanently.

"I feel bad you'll be living in a nearly empty apartment," I say as I flap out the fitted sheet over our new mattress that was delivered yesterday along with a new bed from a local furniture store.

Last night, we were so exhausted from the drive followed by dozens of trips up and down the elevator unloading the trailer, we threw an old blanket on top of the bare mattress and called it a night while my dad crashed on the couch.

Connor catches the fabric and secures the corners on the other side. "I don't. I'm gonna be at the office so much, I'll barely notice." He reaches for the flat sheet still in its packaging and tosses it at me.

Our only concrete plans to see each other in the coming months is when he makes the trip to Arizona over Labor Day weekend—

over a month away. Cheyenne and Mom have been in constant communication these past few weeks, making arrangements for our families to come together over the holiday. I'll fly out of New York and meet my parents in Flagstaff. Connor will fly out a day later for a quick twenty-four hour visit before he has to get back to Chicago.

Beyond that, we'll squeeze in visits when, and if, we can. But flight costs add up and I'm focused on paying off my credit card before the end of the year while he's got rent for his Chicago apartment and half of this one to worry about for the next four months. Money will be tight for both of us.

I am today years old when I learned that you can miss someone before they've even left.

He smooths out the flat sheet on his side of the bed. "I got all of my streaming accounts connected on the television, by the way."

"Thanks," I say, voice absent. The pillowcase package in my hands is locked down tighter than Fort Knox—I yank and tug to no avail.

Quiet footsteps come around the foot of the bed, but I don't look up. Unbidden tears cloud my vision and I try so hard to suppress the ache in my chest, to mask it with my futile efforts to open this stupid pillowcase. Overwhelmed and emotional, I toss everything to the ground in frustration. "Dammit!"

Connor's gentle arms ease me into his chest and I clutch his shirt in my fists. "I'm gonna miss you, too," he whispers.

Moments later, when he takes my face in his hands and kisses me, I taste the saltiness of shed tears—mostly mine, but some feel like his. We both know tomorrow isn't a goodbye, but it doesn't make it hurt any less.

The need to touch, to feel, to taste, takes over and as we tumble into bed atop the fresh linens, he begs me not to cry.

I sniffle. "You started it," I say as I peel his shirt off.

"I most certainly did not." He drags my shorts down my legs.

Sitting up, I push his shorts and boxers down his thighs. Voice breathless, I say, "This is all your fault."

"How do you figure?" he muses as he grabs the hem of my tank top and yanks it over my head.

"Six years ago"—he unclasps my bra—"your obsession with me started." He snickers. "Then you had to go and make me fall in love with you."

"You messaged me first, Fish." He shucks his shorts and boxers off the rest of the way, an arrogant tilt angling his head.

Desire pools between my thighs as he sweeps my panties down and off. "Yeah, because I missed you."

After rolling on a condom, he crawls up the bed until I'm caged beneath him, although he holds a space between our bodies that is not conducive to touching, feeling or tasting. "Is that all?"

"No." I reach for him but he grabs my wrist and pins it above my head. Smiling, I try with the other hand and he does the same.

His knees spread my thighs wide. "No?"

Now only inches above me, his hardest part hovers so close, yet so far from where I need to feel him. I bite my lip. "I thought you were hot," I confess.

"Hmmm. So, you could say that *your* obsession with *me* started six years ago." He lowers his hips just enough to tease me and I hum at the contact.

I squirm, rapidly moving into needy territory as I sputter, "It was mutual, old man."

"I'm not sorry," he breathes against my lips.

"Me neither."

He makes love to me, one hand clasped tightly to mine the whole time. Whispered promises of tomorrow and forever land on wet mouths and feverish skin and in tangles of hair. He tells me I'm beautiful, that he's the luckiest man in the world, that he'll miss me...so much.

He tells me he loves me.

I tell him I love him, too.

And when he commutes with me to work the next morning, rolling suitcase in tow, he stands outside Saks and wraps me in his arms one last time, promising me, "Four months is gonna fly by so fast."

With another kiss that he guarantees won't be our last, he hails a cab and heads to the airport.

Chapter Fifty-Four

I'M HOME, BABY

CONNOR

August

ME

What are you wearing?

GRETCHEN

Clothes.

I'm not sexting you from work.

ME

Clothes can be hot. Are they hot?

GRETCHEN

You should be doing work things right now.

ME

I'm wearing clothes, too. In case you were wondering…

GRETCHEN

I wasn't.

ME

Give me something, Fish. I miss the hell out of you!

GRETCHEN

insert pondering emoji

ME

Still not using actual emojis, I see.

GRETCHEN

I'm wearing a skirt.

ME

Mmmm, what's underneath that skirt?

GRETCHEN

You're gonna regret this.

ME

I'll be the judge of that.

GRETCHEN

Nothing.

ME

This was a mistake.

GRETCHEN

Enjoy the rest of your day, QB.

insert winky face emoji

I miss the hell out of you, too.

September

Twenty-four hours with Gretchen in Flagstaff was not enough.

The only alone time we had was one night at the hotel. With her room adjoined to her parents, I couldn't do the things I wanted to do to her. We could only do careful and quiet things, hands-covering-our-mouths things. Better than nothing, but it only left me needing more.

The afternoon spent at Cheyenne and Miguel's house wasn't much different than Gretchen's birthday celebration back in June. Everyone embraced Kelly, Paul, Drew and Reagan into the fold like one of their own. Kelly and Cheyenne hugged for the better part of four hours, two mothers exchanging and wiping each other's tears.

Gretchen never told her parents about Winona's role in everything, maintaining that it was her story to tell. When Winona pulled Kelly and Paul aside an hour into the party, I had an idea what was happening. One by one, Gretchen, Cheyenne, and Miguel joined the hushed conversation and I watched with bated breath to see how Kelly and Paul would respond to the knowledge of what Cheyenne's sister had done.

"What's going on?" Drew asked when he caught me staring. A gaggle of young boys ran circles around us as I held a football over my head, but I didn't take my eyes off the conversation across the yard.

My response fell silent as Kelly hauled Winona into a hug, rivers of tears streaming down their cheeks.

I simply shrugged and said, "Not sure."

That was three weeks ago. Gretchen and I have had twenty-four hours together in the past two months.

"Vining, if you're gonna be a sour patch baby at your own birthday party, just go home," Drew chides from across the high table.

I wouldn't call it a party. Drew and Reagan arranged for a night at the bar with a few mutual friends. My parents even flew in to spend the weekend with me.

"Baby boy, turn that frown upside down," Mom says with a smile and a kiss on my cheek.

Dad tilts his beer at his lips. "What is it, two more months?"

"A little less, yeah."

Gretchen wanted to fly in for my birthday, but I told her to not spend the money. Soon enough we'll have every day together, I had told her. I'm so wise and frugal. *Dumbass.*

"Ask him how many days?" Drew says, eyes aimed at a message he's typing on his phone.

"I'm not that bad," I defend, but I don't have much fight left.

"How many days, Vining?"

I sigh. "Fifty-one."

"There it is." Drew shoves his phone in his back pocket. "Can I give you your birthday gift now? Or are you too much of a little bitch to get excited about presents?"

I glare at him.

He swipes his beer from the table. "You're welcome for this, by the way."

"For what?" I ask.

My best friend's response is nothing but a smug grin and a tip of his bottle over my shoulder.

I spin on my barstool. The breath gets knocked right out of my lungs when I see her. Gretchen stalks across the bar, heart-stopping smile set entirely on me. I'm out of my seat in an instant, sweeping her into my arms in three strides.

"Happy Birthday," she whispers.

"How are you here?" I pull back to look at her, but my mouth is on hers before she can answer.

"Drew bought my plane ticket. I have to go back tomorrow night."

I shake my head in disbelief and turn to find Drew in the crowd. When our eyes meet, I mouth, *"thank you."*

Gretchen squeals in delight when she spots my parents. She drops into the seat beside them like she's got all the time in the world and for forty-five minutes, I am patience personified. A saint, if you will. I feed her. I keep her Diet Coke full. And I listen as she and my parents catch up as hard as the day is long.

The moment she takes the last bite of her burger, I toss a wad of bills on the table, politely ending this charade. "Mom, Dad, I love you, but we're leaving now." Dad chuckles while Mom looks scandalized. *God love her.* Gretchen ducks her head in quiet laughter. Me? I'm not the least bit embarrassed that my parents know exactly what Gretchen and I are about to be up to for the next twenty-four hours, if I have anything to say about it.

With a final wave to my friends, I grab Gretchen's suitcase from behind the bar, throw her over my shoulder and bolt for the door.

Out on the sidewalk, Gretchen swats my ass and laughs. "You're such a caveman."

"We have less than twenty-four hours, baby."

"We'll get there faster if you let me down."

I ease her to her feet, take her by the hand, and roll her suitcase behind me with my free hand as we begin the two-block jog to my apartment.

"I feel bad I didn't get you a present," she spits out through sharp breaths but never breaks her stride.

"Don't need one. You're here. That's all I want."

We slow to a walk as we approach my building. "Actually, I did get you one thing, but it's not much of anything."

"Oh yeah," I answer absently, but try to show interest—her being here is truly all I could ever want.

A couple minutes later, we stumble into my apartment, a passionate storm of hands and lips. "You ready for your present?" She smiles as I kick the door shut behind me.

The shy turn of her face has a glint of mischief that looks like trouble.

She prowls backward past my empty living room. "I went to the doctor last week." Strands of hair fall haphazardly around her shoulders as she peels her shirt over her head. "A regular check-up, no big deal." I suck in a breath as she removes her bra, nothing but a pair of skintight jeans adorning her body—I've missed her so much.

I stalk toward her with the same slow gait she's using to lure me toward the bedroom. "What'd you get me, Fish?"

With a wink, she pushes her jeans down her legs. "I got an IUD."

We don't leave the apartment until I drive her to the airport a day later.

October

GRETCHEN

Living alone sucks.

ME

Facts.

GRETCHEN

Are you dressing up for Halloween?

ME

I think I'd make a good Ebenezer Scrooge.

GRETCHEN

Ahh yes. Old, cranky, full of regret. This tracks.

ME

I thought so. What about you?

GRETCHEN

Willy Wonka. I think the kids will love it.

ME

Willy Wonka…but with books?

GRETCHEN

How'd you know? *insert kissy face emoji*

ME

Gene says hi, btw.

GRETCHEN

insert melting face emoji

Do you think the trick-or-treaters will like peanut butter M&Ms?

ME

Nobody likes peanut butter M&Ms.

GRETCHEN

Sigh I don't think this is going to work out.

ME

We've been doomed from the beginning.

GRETCHEN

We should probably break up.

ME

Probably so.

GRETCHEN

We had a good run.

ME

I wish you nothing but the best.

GRETCHEN

Don't You Forget About Me.

ME

How could I? It's been only moments Since U Been Gone.

GRETCHEN

I Saw The Sign years ago, sorry it took so long.

ME

You spun my head Right Round. I'm to blame too.

GRETCHEN

Our love was Titanium.

ME

No Diggity.

GRETCHEN

No Doubt.

I love you.

ME

I love you, too.

GRETCHEN

I miss the hell out of you.

ME

Me, too.

November

"That's the last of it." I close the trunk of my car, filled to max capacity with the last of my things. My apartment upstairs is empty, save for the bed frame and mattress.

I peel the key off my key chain and pass it to my best friend. "The guy buying the bed is coming by in the morning to pick it up."

"Got it. I'll be here," Drew says, tucking the key into his pocket.

"And I told the office you'd drop the keys off on Monday."

Drew bobs his head, neither of us too keen on eye contact at the moment. "And Gretch still doesn't know you're showing up three days early?"

I shake my head. "Nope. No clue."

As far as she knows, I have some work stuff to wrap up over the weekend and will make the drive to New Jersey on Monday. Unbeknownst to her, thanks to many early mornings and late nights, my team has reached the end of the Governor's campaign project. I'll need to video-conference in on Monday morning to give a final recap to my boss, but he approved my request to make yesterday my official last day in the office.

The work I've done on this project, along with the generous letter of recommendation from Mr. Driskill, was my golden ticket to secure a marketing management position at a sports magazine start-up in Manhattan. My years spent as a quarterback may have done me a few favors, too. It's a mid-sized operation, spear-headed by a few athletes turned executives around my age, all of them with wives and kids—really down to earth guys that I'm excited to work with.

I met with my new bosses on a video call this morning and we hashed out the details of the position. I'll report to the office for my first day the Monday after Thanksgiving.

After I hung up from that call, I super-sonic cleaned my apartment, cleared out my fridge, packed up my bathroom and closet, and patched up the walls to ensure I get my security deposit back.

When Gretchen texted this afternoon to check in, I played right into the plan as she knows it.

"You sure you're good to drive through the night?"

"I'm good."

We're both stalling. He shifts on his feet while I twirl the key ring around my finger. Drew and I have never been more than a few blocks apart in the entire fifteen years we've been friends.

"Well, you should probably get going," he finally says.

"Yeah."

We step in at the same time and pull each other into a cross-body hug.

"Take care of her," he says.

"Always."

I clap his back one last time, release him and move toward the driver's side door.

"Love you, man," Drew says.

I throw him a shit-eating grin over my shoulder. "Love you too, Gus Gus."

He spears me with a blank stare as I drop into the car and a middle finger in my rearview mirror as I drive away.

Bathroom breaks and energy drink replenishment are the only stops I make on the road. I drive all night, timing things so I pull into our complex's parking garage an hour after Gretchen has left for work.

Barely conscious, I power through the next couple of hours as I haul everything from my car up to the apartment. When I finally make the last trip, I drop the final box next to the pile I've amassed in the living room and take in the space.

I haven't been here since the weekend I moved Gretchen in at the end of July. She's added shelves on either side of the television, every inch of them filled with her books. A small entry table sets by the front door and a sofa table rests behind the couch. Everything enhanced with knick-knacks, decorative pieces and framed pictures.

The living room wall that was once bare is now a massive collage display of picture frames. Something I haven't seen before now. Pictures of her family. Pictures of Cheyenne, Miguel and her siblings. She's printed and framed pictures of my family, too. My parents, my brothers, their wives and my nieces—pictures that she, no doubt, procured from my mom.

There at the center, surrounded by images of all our favorite people, lies a picture of us. Placed atop a white matte encased inside a thick black frame is an oversized print of the selfie I took of us on Devil's Bridge. My chest grows tight as warmth blooms in my heart. Back when I didn't think I'd ever get another chance, when I just needed an excuse to touch her, to pretend for merely a moment that she was mine.

Now she is.

After I unpack a few of the most urgent boxes, I take a shower and crawl into bed for a nap. Later in the afternoon, I feel marginally less tired, so I unpack some more while I count down to 5:45 when Gretchen usually gets home.

Mom's weekly phone call comes at five on the dot.

Throwing on a hoodie, I step out into the crisp November air and take a seat on the small patio set on the terrace. The sun has set and the warm amber colors of dusk reflect off the Hudson as the Manhattan skyline slowly comes to life with its glittering lights smattered across skyscrapers from one end of the island to the other.

Gretchen was right; this view is worth the commute a thousand times over.

"Hey, Mom."

"Honey, did you make it?"

"Yeah, I'm here. Just waiting for Gretchen to get home."

"She's going to be so excited to see you." Since their talk in Arizona, Mom's voice softens to a balm at any mention of Gretchen. A contentment I wasn't sure I'd ever have settles over me knowing how much my family loves her.

"I hate that you two are going to be alone for Thanksgiving," Mom says.

Gretchen and I don't hate it at all, but I won't tell my parents that. After four months apart, we've been counting down the days to next week when we can hunker down in our new home. Nowhere to be, no interruptions, nobody to entertain. Just us.

"Yeah, but we're coming to see you at Christmas," I supply, easing her disappointment.

"Want me to send you Grandma's cranberry sauce recipe to make for your first Thanksgiving together? You know it's a Vining tradition."

I wince. "It's also family tradition to eat none of it until Dad gets out the can of Ocean Spray."

Mom bursts out a laugh. "You're not wrong about that. Can't beat those ridges, can you?"

"Honestly, my mouth's watering right now."

We talk for a while and my dad chimes in here and there, while I keep my eyes peeled in the direction of the transit station where Gretchen should appear at any minute.

Right on time, I spot her two blocks down the road. Six stories up and I could pick her out of a crowd of a thousand if I had to.

"Gotta go, Mom. She's almost home."

"Ok, honey. Give her my love."

I hang up and immediately dial Gretchen from my balcony perch. She digs into the pocket of her knee-length trench coat and answers on the second ring.

"Hi," she breathes. The sound of her voice and the sight of her so close after two months apart sends my pulse soaring.

"Hey, Fish."

She glances over her shoulder before shuffling in quick steps to cross the street. "Three more days," she squeals. "*God*, I can't wait. I miss you so much."

Her hair gets swept up in the autumn breeze and she gathers it in one hand, pulling the strands around her neck. "Me, too. How cold is it there?"

"Starting to get a little chilly."

"Same here," I say. Maybe thirty yards away now, she steps on to the sidewalk that leads to the front door of our building.

"Hey, Gretch?" Flutters stir in my chest.

"Yeah."

"Look up."

Her steps falter as she comes to a stop in the glow cast from a streetlight overhead. She hesitates for a second before she finally tilts her head back. Curious eyes scan the floors of our building, up and up until she spots me, forearms propped on the metal railing of our terrace.

A soft gasp comes through the line and I offer her a small wave. Without a word, she disconnects the call and breaks into a sprint, headed for the lobby below. One minute later, the front door bursts open. Tossing her purse aside, she barrels toward me in her four-inch heels, coat split open and flowing behind her. She crashes into me, arms thrown around my neck, and mine link around her waist. I squeeze her tight, her feet lifting off the ground.

Together, we sigh. Her form fits perfectly against mine and I know I'm holding my *only* and my *forever* in my arms.

"You're home," she says, the words like a beacon in the night, pointing me back to where it all began—and where it began is where it was always meant to end.

Her. With me. Us. Together.

"I'm home, baby."

Epilogue

MY EYES ON HER

GRETCHEN

three years later

"WE'VE OFFICIALLY SEEN them all, Gretch." Connor peers at me with bright eyes matching the clear, blue sky above us. "Was it everything you've dreamed it would be?"

"And more," I tease. "Now, when do we see the wild horses?"

He promised me a visit to Carova beach this trip. We've been out to see his family a handful of times over the years, but never for more than a few days at a time, making it hard to block out an entire day for the excursion to the northernmost tip of the island.

In the meantime, we've worked to check off all five of the Outer Banks lighthouses. Aboard the ferry on the way back to Hatteras from our day trip to Ocracoke, we can officially say that number five is in the books.

"Next week, Fish. I promise."

We're here for ten full days this visit. Patrick and Andrea proposed the idea several months ago to get all of their kids and their families on board. For the first time in several years, they have all three of their boys, their significant others and their grandchildren under one roof.

All the couples split off for alone time when Connor's parents volunteered to take all the grandkids up to Kitty Hawk today. Connor and I don't have any grandchildren skin in the game yet, but we embraced a day to ourselves, nonetheless.

The week after Labor Day, the tourist crowds have dissipated, leaving mostly just the locals. Beaches are quiet, morning runs to the coffee shop, slow and un-rushed. It's idyllic.

I rest my head on Connor's shoulder as Hatteras comes into view in the distance. "I could retire here someday."

He looks wistfully out over the water. "Yeah, me too."

"Mr. Chief Marketing Officer means we could probably retire early," I say with a finger to his ribs.

The sports magazine that Connor began working for three years ago, exploded almost overnight. They've been in a constant state of hiring and expansion. Six months ago, they offered him the position and he accepted without hesitation. The men he works for—along with their families—have become some of our dearest friends.

"I don't know," he says, all coy. "I think it might be Saks' newest Assistant Buyer that could make that happen."

He lies. Not about the Assistant Buyer part, that's true, but the part about my promotion putting us on the early retirement path. Not even close, but it's a step in the right direction up the corporate ladder. Plus, the new position puts me back alongside Monica who's become a best friend to me over the past few years.

Obviously, we're nowhere near retirement, but dreaming up our future is a fun game we like to play. And we've dreamed of it all: travel, marriage, a river-front penthouse in Jersey, three or four babies (adopted and biological), moving to a suburb if city-life doesn't feel right once kids are in the picture, and now, retiring to the beach.

Someday, we've always said.

On the drive back, we stop at a quiet beach to watch the sunset, neither of us in a rush to get back to a house full of beautifully rambunctious nieces and nephews.

There's not another soul to be found within shouting distance in either direction. The steady rhythm of waves crashing the shore is the only sound other than thump of Connor's heartbeat at my back as I lean against him. His arms wrapped loosely over my shoulders, our fingers twirl and play together.

"You know what my favorite thing is about you?" he asks.

"Hmmm," I say, gaze cast over the ocean. "I'm gonna say boobs."

He chortles, sweet and rough in my ear. "Those, too. But not what I was thinking."

"Do tell, then."

His chest rises and falls at my back. "Everything about you is… easy."

"You calling me easy, old man?"

"Okay, that didn't sound right." He sighs. "What I meant was, you're…effortless. Falling for you was easy. Loving you is even easier. Even when life is hard, loving you isn't."

He exhales a shaky breath and my heart thrums a little faster in my chest.

"I love that you're not showy or fancy. Without a stitch of makeup, I think you're the most beautiful woman I've ever seen. And I know you think it's a character flaw, but I love that you hate being the center of attention." I smile. "You don't care about all the celebratory fuss. You don't want big grand gestures or to be under the spotlight."

He kisses my temple and, if I know this man as well as he knows me, I don't have to turn around to know his eyes are glassy with tears. His right hand pulls away, but I cling to his left, pulse racing now.

"It's why I can give you this." He holds up a ring in front of me. No velvet box, no pomp and circumstance. "And I don't have to get down on one knee or paint the words across the sky to tell you everything you already know."

A tear falls down my cheek.

"That you're my favorite person. That you're my best friend." He leans in closer. "Don't tell your brother that part."

I laugh through a sob.

"That I love you," he continues. "That I want to spend the rest of my life with you." His voice thickens like the words come from the deepest part of him. "That I want to be your husband. And I want you to be my wife."

He tilts the ring between his fingers and I'm beside myself with how perfect it is. The modest princess cut stone on a simple platinum band shimmers in the early evening light—it's exactly what I would have chosen for myself.

Cheek pressed against mine, he slides the ring on my finger. His voice, barely a whisper, finally utters the words, "Will you marry me?"

I nod like a jittery fool and choke out a teary "Yes" as I flip over and collapse into him. We fall to the sand wrapped in each other's arms.

WHEN WE ARRIVE BACK to his parents' beach house sometime later, our faces a little worse from wear from all the crying—and kissing—Connor stops me before I reach the front door.

"I have another surprise," he says. Before I can ask a single question, he swings the door open and we hit a wall of cheers. Connor's family hoots and hollers as we step inside, shouting their congratulations. I scan the living room and my breath catches in my throat.

My family.

Mom and Dad. Drew and Reagan—and the twin boys growing healthy and strong in her belly, the result of the embryos they adopted earlier this year. Cheyenne, Miguel, MJ, Rosie, Tally and Kai. My entire family—they're all here. I can't stop the beautiful ache that seizes my heart.

My hands come to my face. "W-what? How? I don't understand." I turn to Connor who looks guilty as sin.

"I have a plan," he says.

The impatient eyes of the twenty people gathered across the room bear down as they wait for Connor to catch me up.

"You once told me that you didn't want a big wedding. Just family, an impromptu ceremony and some burgers on the grill."

Something soft and warm flickers to life inside me as our conversation at Drew's rehearsal dinner unfolds like a worn, well-loved piece of paper in my memory.

"I can't believe you remember that?"

He cocks his head, tucking a strand of hair behind my ear. "I remember it all."

Andrea's voice booms through the room, bored of my hushed conversation with her son. "We have a beach outside."

"I grill a mean burger," Patrick offers.

"Dibs on officiating." That's my brother.

"The girls and I took a cake-decorating class this summer. We'll make a cake." Everett's wife, Emily, adds as she tugs her two daughters close, her youngest boy asleep on his dad's shoulder beside them.

"Cheyenne and I can drive you inland tomorrow to shop for a dress," Mom supplies, reaching for my birth mom's hand at her side. The three of us share a smile over what was once not much more than a tiny flicker of hope I carried inside me that has turned into a reality none of us could have imagined—my adoptive mother and my biological mother becoming the best of friends.

Owen's wife, Grace, chimes in next, their two-year-old son propped on her hip. "I don't know anything about flowers, but how hard can it be. I'll make a bouquet."

"Rosie and I brought our guitars. We can do the music," Miguel says with Rosie grinning sheepishly beside him. She's thirteen now, but forever a daddy's girl.

MJ throws his hat in the ring, hand raised like an obedient student, a true paradox with his massive fifteen-year-old frame that towers over Miguel. "I brought my video camera."

One by one, every member of our respective families volunteers to take something on to help us pull off a beach wedding in three days.

When I think everyone's finished, Reagan declares, "And I'll make sure all these fools are doing what they're supposed to do."

"Oh, thank God," I say, clutching my chest. Really, though—five months pregnant or not, she'll keep this whole circus in line.

With a proud smile, she says, "I got you, babe."

∼

THE NEXT THREE days are a blur. Everybody committed to their self-assigned tasks, all Connor and I have to worry about is what we'll wear, our wedding bands, and a marriage license.

Saturday afternoon comes, sun high in the sky, air warm. We sit around a table with our families, eating burgers, hot dogs, potato salad, and chips. Me in my off-the-rack wedding dress made of simple white satin that grazes the floor and Connor in his khaki pants and white linen shirt, we share a piece of the perfectly imperfect two-tier cake made by Connor's—*our*—nieces.

At his insistence that we leave for our honeymoon—the plans of which he won't tell me—right after the sun goes down, we went unconventional with the order of festivities.

Thirty minutes before sunset, we toss our paper plates in the trash, and wipe cake frosting from each other's faces before we all head down the stairs on the back of the house that lead to the beach. Bare feet in the sand, I hike up my dress as Connor takes my free hand and we run toward the shore.

MJ finds a picturesque spot near the surf where he deems the light is best for his video camera. Reagan barks out a few orders and within minutes our respective families are split into two sides, an aisle taking shape down the middle. Miguel and Rosie pluck out a classical melody on their guitars as Connor takes his position at the front and gives me a thumbs up. With a small cluster of white roses and ranunculus in hand, I loop my arm through my dad's and let him lead me to the unadorned, makeshift altar of sand and surf.

People often say there's the family you're born into and the family you choose. But I think the purest mark of family are the people that choose you.

Twenty-five years ago, a man, a woman, and their six-year-old son flew across the country to bring me home because they'd already chosen me, sight unseen. Their home became my home. The home where they raised me and loved me as though it was their blood flowing through my veins.

The two teenagers who brought me into this world may not have had a say in where I ended up, but they've chosen me every day since by weaving me into the tapestry of the family they went on to build so that, if I ever found them, I would find a home with them too.

One family gave me life and the other helped me live it.

Sometimes the choices we make in love, come with great risk. Will they love me back? Will it work? Will the obstacles ahead break us? Will I ever be worthy of this person?

The man in front of me—the man vowing to love me for better or worse, until death do us part—he chose me in the face of all those questions. And this day, we start a new family. The family we've chosen in each other.

"By the powers vested in me by the world wide web, I now pronounce you husband and wife," Drew declares, a wicked gleam in his expression, all too proud to call himself an ordained minister. "You may now kiss the bride." He leans in. "No tongue, Vining. Nobody wants to see that."

I roll my eyes, grab a fistful of Connor's shirt and yank him closer. His hands cup my face and he wastes no time bringing his lips to mine with a smile.

Perhaps the kiss goes on for three or four seconds longer than a public kiss should, but that's how it always is with him. Touches linger, electricity constantly sizzles beneath the surface, mouths taste and explore in case we don't get another chance to do it again for a while.

Our wedding kiss is no different.

And there's definitely some tongue.

Connor

Pack for four nights. That was all I gave Gretchen to go by. The rest is a surprise.

After the ceremony and a bunch of sunset family pictures on the beach, Gretchen and I loaded up and turned my dad's Jeep pointed north.

As expected, the moment I bypass the bridge that would take us back to the mainland and continue northbound, my wife turns that knowing look on me.

My wife.

"Don't look at me like that, Fish," I warn.

She bats her lashes. "Like what?"

"Like that." I sweep a hand over her face, but I can't help but take all of her in. That white shimmery dress that looks like it was sewed on to her, the way it molds to her narrow hips, delicate shoulder straps so thin they're barely there. And I can't see it now, but the way it scoops low in the back, right above where I know the perfect little dimples rest above the curve of her backside, has me weak in the knees. Her hair is mussed and wind-blown, but it only makes her sexier. "It makes me want to pull this car over."

"But you won't," she says.

"I won't because I'm not taking my wife on our wedding night in the backseat of my dad's Jeep."

"Hmmm…or it's because you're trying to beat high tide."

Of course this secret couldn't keep.

I sigh. "That too."

Gretchen bounces giddily in her seat, a playful shimmy popping her shoulders.

"How'd it feel to call me your wife, husband?"

"Mmm, say that again." I come to a stop at a red light.

She leans across the console and whispers, "Husband."

I grab her chin and pull her closer. "Wife." Our lips meet and the collective sigh between us turns the kiss ravenous in an instant. I forget time and space as I tangle my hand in her hair. She moans, her hand finding my bare chest through the open collar of my shirt.

A horn blasts from behind us.

I mutter a curse and press my foot on the gas as we skitter apart.

It's been hours since sunset by the time we make it to the end of the paved road.

"Temper your expectations, baby. It's dark out. We probably won't see any horses until tomorrow," I say as we cross the cattle guard onto the long stretch of beach that will take us to our final destination.

When I reached out to Gene with my plans to take Gretchen to Carova for our honeymoon, I didn't even have to ask. He all but threw the keys at me and said his house was our house for as many days as we wanted it.

The tires finally hit the sand and I roll down the windows to give Gretchen the immersive experience—a thirty minute drive along a dark beach, waves crashing to the shore only a few feet beyond the passenger door. The tide has already begun its slow rise toward the dunes. We made it here just in time.

The Mullins' home sits on a beach front lot. As I turn inland, I accelerate over the dunes to gain traction under the jeep tires and the property comes into view as we crest the top of the sandy mound. The house is illuminated by the exterior lights I turned on when I made the secret trip up here yesterday to set the thermostat to Gretchen's seventy-two degrees and stock the fridge.

Once inside, I set our bags in the master bedroom while Gretchen runs straight for the sliding door at the back of the house that opens to the second-floor deck.

After I kick off my shoes, I follow her outside and across the private boardwalk leading to the open-air deck that sits atop the sand dunes.

Gene owns the two empty lots in either direction making this property one of the most secluded beach front homes in Carova.

No streetlights. No city noise. Nothing but the glow of the moon reflecting off the water and the sound of the waves as they swell in and out at the base of the beach stairs ten feet below. No neighbors within sight in any direction.

I wrap my arms around her and settle her back against my chest. "Pretty incredible, isn't it?"

She hums her approval, arms crossing over mine around her waist.

I plant a soft kiss on her shoulder as a scuffling sound comes from beyond the deck. We perk up, breaths held in our chests. Neither of us make a move, but we scan the darkness beyond the railing for any sign of the source. When another chuffing sound breaks over the sound of the water, Gretchen steps out of my arms and walks softly to the far corner of the deck to investigate. I make it two steps in her direction when we both spot them.

"Oh my God," she breathes.

A chestnut brown mare on the heels of her foal crests the top of the dune. Their lower halves mostly hidden by the dune grass, the two horses freeze amidst the waving fronds as if taking in the view.

The foal nudges his mom with his snout, a request to go down to the water. The mare replies with a chortle and a stomp of her hoof, prompting the foal to lay down—a tantrum or acquiescence to bedtime, who can be sure.

"Amazing." Gretchen's words, heavy with awe and affection, pull my gaze back to her.

My wife. Palms braced on the wooden railing, her dress falls over her body like a silken nightgown. Her exposed back glistens in the light of the moon shining down upon the scene like a spotlight over the water, the twinkling stars overhead limitless in number. Black hair barely distinguishable from the night sky floats on the breeze in tandem with the dune grass beyond.

This woman who captured my heart as a teenager has owned it outright for the past seven years. She *is* my heart. My whole heart beating outside my chest.

Her eyes on the wild horses, my eyes on her, the word comes as easy as it always has. "Beautiful."

THE END

Afterword

A PERSONAL ANECDOTE FROM THE AUTHOR

On a crisp autumn day in 1998, our house phone rang and my barely pubescent, fourteen-year-old self was not prepared for how our family was about to be changed forever. My dad answered, entirely unsuspecting of the person on the other end being anyone other than a telemarketer, friend or any number of people you'd expect to hear from on any given nondescript day.

However, *this* phone call had been nineteen years in the making.

The newborn baby boy he and his high school girlfriend had given up for adoption when they weren't much older than babies themselves had found him. He'd found *us*.

What ensued in the coming weeks was a roller coaster of emotional meet and greets as my newfound big brother made the rounds meeting his extended biological family.

I wish I could say that our first meeting was as wrought with affection and emotion as Gretchen's experience was, but it wasn't. My dad and his former high school girlfriend hadn't gone on to find their happily ever after and there was no scrapbook photo album to be found. Yet, it was beautiful in its own right—the foundation, as it were, for the relationship that has blossomed and flourished in the decades since.

I could wax poetic about how nobody knew that my older brother had never been more than a two-hour drive from us for the entirety of his life up to that point, or how effortlessly he fell right into step with our family. But what I remember being the most captivated by was the discovery that, unbeknownst to most of the family, my grandmother had spent the previous nineteen years privately grieving the absence of her eldest grandchild every year on his birthday. A day that she spent meditating on where he might be and what type of man he had become. And when she laid eyes on him for the first time, the literal spitting image of my dad, you could have heard a pin drop.

Adoption can be a difficult choice, a painful one even. But, oh what beauty there is to be found in surrendering your own desires at the altar of denying one's self and allowing someone else to step in and care for that child in the way you know you never could. The way you know they deserve.

At birth, my brother was adopted by two amazing people who were able to give him an incredible life. Even though my family missed the first nineteen years of that life, the privilege it is for us to know him now, to proudly call him *son, grandson, uncle* and *big brother*, is a blessing beyond comprehension and one we'll never take for granted.

Acknowledgments

Is it okay for me to say that I simply can't find the words for this part? Asking for a friend.

Real talk, though, where do I even begin?

First, I am blessed beyond measure, far exceeding anything I deserve. The gift that I've been given to dream up love stories and the dedication, stamina, and life-margin I've been granted to make it to this point where I can officially declare myself a published author—I don't take any of it lightly. God is my source. Without Him, I am nothing.

To my husband: Nobody annoys me more than you do. There's also nobody on this planet who can make me laugh as much as you can. Thank you for supporting this little dream of mine. You haven't always understood it, but you've never left my corner. I always joke that every MMC I've dreamed up is Pacey Witter coded. Truth be told, they're all a little *you* coded too. Thank you for waking up and choosing me every day for the past twenty-three years. Let's go for fifty more.

To my kids: You're way too young to read this. Quite frankly, I'd prefer you never read it. Regardless, I hope you find in Mom following her dreams, that you can follow yours, too. If I have one purpose on this planet, it's to be your mom. I love you endlessly, without condition.

To my big brother: Not to belabor what I wrote in the dedication, but I love you and am so thankful to have you in my life. I can't imagine a world where you didn't do the big, scary, brave thing all those years ago and dial that phone number. Our family got flipped upside down in the best way and I wouldn't trade you for anything.

To my alpha readers: The fact that you read the dumpster fire that was draft one—all 173,000 words of it—and managed to find the story underneath all the fluff makes you heroes in my eyes. Lisa, Hannah, Ruth, Leah, Staci, and Bri, you are the real MVPs. Your encouragement is the only reason there was ever a draft two. Thank you!

To my beta readers: Jenah, Ashley, Hailey, Grace, Courtney, Megan, Abbey, Ellie, and Amy, you ladies were equal parts hype and honesty and *Forever Then* is all the better for it.

To my social media guru: Lisa, simply put, you're a lifesaver! Would there even be a Rachae Stevens Instagram page without you? I'm not sure there would be. You've gone above and beyond for me in so many ways and I am forever grateful for you.

To my human jukebox: Hannah, there would be zero songs on the *Forever Then* playlist if it weren't for you. Thank you for knowing every version of every song ever written by every artist in the history of time so that I don't have to pretend to know who SZA is.

To my author besties: Hailey and my Diamond Dolls, our daily group chats, unhinged voice messages and shimmy GIFs give me life. I'm so glad I met each and every one of you. You've made this indie author journey a lot less scary and a whole lot more fun.

To my editor: You didn't cut all my em dashes, Gabby, and for that, I thank you. Thank you for catching my overuse of "narrowing eyes" and saying, *"hey, you should probably come up with an alternative."* I may never master proper comma placement or paragraph breaks, but that's why I have you.

To my cover designer: I had very little to go by when I started this process with you, Mel. I just knew I wanted Arizona and for it to be discreet—you did the rest. Thank you for tolerating all my back and forth on getting the fonts just right. I'm so happy with how it turned out.

To my blurb writer: I swear to God, writing the book is less daunting than trying to write a blurb. Jessie, thank you for what you do! You took this big scary thing of taking a four-hundred page book and condensing it down to a one-hundred-and-fifty word synopsis and made it seem like the simplest thing ever. Truly, nothing terrifies me more than this task and I'm so thankful I hired you to do it for me. You killed it!

To my Street Team: There are too many of you to list here, but just know how thankful I am that you took a chance on a little ol' indie author like me. Your likes, comments, shares, edits, and overall enthusiasm in getting the word out about my debut means the world to me. YOU mean the world to me!

To all the readers (past, present, and future): Writing is scary. Putting something out into the world that you poured years of blood, sweat and tears into knowing full well that some people might hate it is terrifying. Yet, the scariest thing of all is the possibility that nobody will want to read it. But *you* did and I will never not be utterly dumbstruck by the fact that, out of all the books in the world, you somehow chose to read mine. Thank you a million times over!

Reader's Guide

Content Warnings
- detailed discussions of a closed adoption across state lines
- alcohol consumption ranging from social drinking to tipsiness to drunkenness
- mild and brief physical aggression between two adult men
- ectopic pregnancy and miscarriage discussed in past and present tense (not involving a main character)
- open door spice between two consenting adults

Spice Reading Guide
Below is an outline of the pages within specific sections to skip if you wish to adapt the story to a less explicit reading experience.

Ch. 9 - steamy kiss (pages 61-62)

Ch. 31 - steamy kiss (page 223)

Ch. 32 - steamy kiss and then some (page 233)

Ch. 33 - open door spice (pages 236-237)

Ch. 43 - open door spice (pages 333-335)

Ch. 49 - open door spice (pages 380-385)

*These pages are approximate. Please consider that the content *may* stretch half a page in either direction.

About the Author

Rachae Stevens is an author of emotional romances with plenty of swoon. She's a midwest girlie, born and raised. Living with her husband, three kids, and overly energetic doodle, she fills her days as a stay-at-home mom with copious amounts of laundry, dishes, Diet Coke, imposter syndrome, and writing.

instagram.com/rachae.stevens.author

threads.net/@rachae.stevens.author

tiktok.com/rachae.stevens.author

www.ingramcontent.com/pod-product-compliance
Lightning Source LLC
Chambersburg PA
CBHW020004120726
47903CB00004B/1135